Copyright © 2022 by **Lavender Field**

Typewriter Pub, an imprint of Blvnp Incorporated
A Nevada Corporation
1887 Whitney Mesa DR #2002
Henderson, NV 89014
www.typewriterpub.com/info@typewriterpub.com

ISBN: 978-1-64434-213-8

DISCLAIMER

ENEMIES WITH BENEFITS

LAVENDER FIELDS

To Dan and Ann Kristin
for their unwavering support of this book and my work.

Trigger Warning:
The following story contains profanities and homosexual and homopohobic themes.
Reader discretion is advised.

CHAPTER ONE
Mistakes Are Made

Being drunk is fun.

Making out with someone whilst drunk is fun.

Being too drunk to remember who you were making out with whilst drunk is fun.

Basically, Colby Williams had a lot of fun at a party last night. Granted, he didn't remember anything that had happened there, but he was pretty sure that he'd had a great time. If the hickeys on his neck were anything to go by, he must've impressed a very lucky lady last night.

That wonderful feeling, however, was instantly ruined earlier this morning. Partly due to his hangover, but mostly due to the arrival of an anonymous text message.

Colby had never seen the number before, so he initially assumed it was spam. It was only out of curiosity that an image had been sent instead of a message that caused him to open it.

"Shit. Shit, shit, shit, shit," he whispered to himself in a locked stall in the boys' locker room. He was supposed to be out on the field for morning football practice by now, but the picture had stolen all of his attention. That couldn't be Colby in the picture, could it? No, no, no, it had to be photoshopped.

There was no way in hell that Colby would ever kiss *him*. Actually, he would never kiss a boy. At all. Never!

1

Not because he was homophobic or anything; he believed everyone was welcome to their own proclivities. But that kind of stuff just wasn't for Colby. However, if one was to hypothetically put him in a situation where he would have to have sex with another guy, then he would not sleep with *him* of all people. Most likely, he'd go for a nice twink or something—perhaps a twunk. Were twunks a thing? Could he get a twank? He'd have to brush up on his gay terminology later.

All of that was beside the point.

He stared down in horror at his phone. A random number had sent him a picture of two guys making out. Colby thought it must've been some type of gay porn spam that his friends had signed him up for as a joke, but something was uncomfortably familiar about it. Colby had looked at the photo and thought, *I have that exact same shirt.* In fact, he was certain he'd worn it to the party yesterday. The world is full of funny coincidences like that—only, there were too many funny coincidences in that picture. How funny that the guy in the picture was wearing the same stressed jeans that Colby had worn yesterday. What a coincidence that the guy in the picture also had the same shoes. How incredible that he had been sent a photo of a guy that looked exactly like him in every way possible. Hilarious!

However, under closer inspection, he realised it was indeed him in the photo—with none other than Ezra Dickinson.

It was difficult to discern exactly what was going on in the photo. The lighting and the surroundings around the two were dark, with the sole exception being a window that had colourful strobe lights shining through it. They were outside of the party, and an empty vodka bottle lay on the ground by Colby's feet. Ezra had one arm wrapped around Colby's waist and the other pinning Colby to the wall. Colby had his arms tightly wrapped around Ezra's neck and a hand buried in Ezra's platinum blonde hair.

Now, this looked bad. Why? Because if a random person were to look at this photo, they might think that Ezra and Colby were kissing. That person would be wrong, and they should feel very embarrassed for thinking such silly things.

Colby knew exactly what was going on here; it was very obvious from the closeness of their bodies and the intimacy of their touches. Such sensual interactions could only have one explanation: Clearly, they were huddling together for warmth. Everything made complete sense when he thought about it in that context. They were outside, and Colby had been intoxicated that night. He must've stumbled outside, and when he realised how cold it was, he grabbed the closest source of warmth—which unfortunately happened to be Ezra—and snuggled up to it. Penguins did that all the time, so why couldn't Colby? He'd often been called a birdbrain, so it made sense that he would think like a bird.

That answer made so much sense. *Problem solved!* Kind of. A little. Not very much.

Okay, it made no sense at all.

If the penguin answer wasn't correct, then what was going on in this photo?

Three major things bothered Colby: One, who the hell took it? Two, why the actual hell would Colby kiss *Ezra* of all people? Colby had hated Ezra with a passion for over a year now. He was just so full of himself because he was captain of the football team—meaning he was the ultimate pussy-magnet and was the greatest guy *ever*. Seriously, fuck that guy. Three, why the actual fucking hell did Colby look like the submissive one in this picture? He had never been with a guy before, but he was 99.9% sure—theoretically—he'd be the top. Right? He was assertive, dominant, and a true alpha male, and now Ezra was trying to take that away from him too. That fuelled Colby's anger more than anything else on his list.

Before any more Ezra-related thoughts could invade his mind, a voice rang out inside the locker room.

"Colby? You alright in there, man? You've been on the toilet for like ten minutes now. Coach is getting pissed, get out here

3

already," said Finley. Finley was Colby's best friend—making him the perfect person to ask the important question to.

Colby threw open the stall door, slamming it against the wall. "If I were in a gay relationship, I'd be the top! Right?" he screamed at Finley.

Finley just stared back at Colby, unfazed by his outburst but surprised by the question.

"Listen, man," Finley said, resting a gentle hand on Colby's shoulder. "You know I love you whether you're straight, gay, or a furry, but no. You would not be the top. You're a bottom boy," he said, delivering his words as if he was a doctor giving Colby some really bad news.

"What are you on about? I am *so* a top! I'm going to prove it to you! Never *ever* call me a bottom boy again! *You're* the bottom boy!" Colby retorted.

"Nope," said Finley. "You're the bottom. I bet you'd cry during sex."

"I would not!"

"I bet you'd ask for a hug or to hold their hand when he's about to put it in."

"I would not! I bet you . . . you . . . you would . . . I bet . . ." *Come on, Colby, think of a comeback. A really good one that will shut him up.*

Finley was about to retort when they were loudly interrupted.

"I bet you're both going to be real sorry if you don't get your scrawny asses out on the field. Now!"

The boys recoiled in shock as Coach Clain screamed at them from the locker room door. At a glance, Sally Clain was not a scary woman. She was about five foot two, was in her forties, sported a dirty blonde bob, and wore the school's blue tracksuit that was a little too big for her. But you would be a fool to underestimate this woman. After all, the shorter they are, the closer they are to hell.

She had the lungs of a banshee and was cruel in her punishments. She wasn't the original coach; her husband had been the coach before her, but he mysteriously quit a few months ago. Rumour had it that Coach Sally had broken his leg on purpose by dropping the one trophy the team had won under his management because he was "a terrible coach"—which was true—and so she could become the coach instead. She knew the game of football inside and out.

Technically, the rumours of her purposefully breaking her husband's leg were found to be untrue. Turns out the guy just really didn't like football as much as he thought he did, so he quit and handed the job over to his wife—who actually liked the game and knew the rules.

"Now, boys, stop having a domestic and GET OUT THERE!" she screamed.

Colby and Finley sprinted out of the toilets and onto the football field, and that's when Colby saw him: Mr Kiss-you-at-a-party-and-ruin-your-day himself.

Ezra was leading some pretty intense warm-up drills in the centre of the field. His fair hair was stuck to his sweaty forehead. His sun-kissed skin glowed in the morning light, and his muscles clearly rippled underneath his skintight white pants and red shirt. What a dick.

Colby scowled at him before Ezra even noticed him.

"This is late. Even for you, Colby," Ezra said with his deep and gruff voice. The rest of the team snickered.

"I'm going to punch his perfect little face," Colby muttered to Finley.

"Please don't. I don't need your parents accusing me of corrupting their precious baby boy again," Finley responded.

"Do they still hate you because we set off those fireworks when we were twelve? We're seventeen now. Why are they still mad?" asked Colby.

5

"You tell me, man. They're your parents." Finley shuddered at the thought of an angry Mrs Williams.

"Come on, guys! We've finished warm-ups, so just get your gear on." Ezra turned his head towards Colby. "Are you capable of doing that, Colby, or do you need some more time before you actually start doing anything?" he said, flaunting his annoyingly nice voice and charming smile. All that was a scam, for the blond boy was a demon under all the niceties.

Colby shoved past Ezra, sending him a glare that was equally returned.

"You think you're better than me, dickhead?" scoffed Colby.

"You haven't done anything to challenge that idea, Colby."

I'm going to kill him, Colby thought. *I'm going to kill him for that stupid kiss and hide his body where no one will find it.* That thought kept Colby smiling throughout the entirety of the training.

∗　　　∗　　　∗

Coach had kept Colby after practice was done and made him clear up all the kit and equipment the team had used. Finley got to go on time because technically he had shown up on time and Coach said she felt bad for him always having to put up with Colby's crap—which was totally unfair, as Colby was sure that Finley loved dealing with his crap.

Ezra had talked to the coach after practice as well—not because he was in trouble, but for some other reason instead. *Always the little golden boy,* Colby thought.

When Colby had finally finished clearing up, he headed for the showers, only to find Ezra already using one of them; the one that Colby always used. Colby's shower.

"Hey, dickhead!" Colby stormed. "Get out of *my* shower!"

Ezra just sighed and faced away from him. "Colby, there are plenty of other showers that you can use."

"Yeah, but that's the one I always use. Ask anyone."

"Well, no one else is here, so what are you going to do about it?" Ezra turned back around to Colby and held him down with a glare.

Colby tried to ignore the fact that Ezra was naked in the shower and barged into the cubicle that he was in. Ezra looked shocked that Colby had actually come in. *Got him!* Colby thought.

"You think you're all that? Bet you even think that you'd be the top and I'd be the bottom boy. Well, you're wrong!" Colby mocked, his voice laced with triumph.

"What are you talking abo—"

Ezra's sentence was cut off by Colby slamming his lips onto his. The kiss had taken Ezra by surprise as Colby managed to shove him against one of the walls of the shower. Both of them got drenched by the warm pouring water.

Ezra opened his mouth to object, but Colby shoved his tongue in before he even got the opportunity to speak. Colby didn't know why he did it or why he was enjoying it, but he knew one thing: whatever this was, he was winning, and he was the fucking top.

Colby figured Ezra must have picked up on that thought too as he turned the tables on Colby. He grabbed Colby's hands, flipped them round so now Colby was against the wall, and pinned his hands above his head.

Colby tried to stifle the moan that was rising in his throat. Ezra had gotten Colby in a firm grip, so all Colby could do was battle Ezra's tongue for dominance. Ezra had a slight height advantage over Colby. He was six foot two whilst Colby was nearly six foot one—a fact that really annoyed Colby. Ezra was also stronger than Colby, but only by a little bit. If Colby showed up to practice regularly like the goody-two-shoes in front of him, then he would be that strong too.

Colby's pants began to feel tighter and tighter as the kiss went on. He wasn't the only one either. Colby could feel Ezra inadvertently pressing his hard-on against Colby's thigh.

Colby took a sneaky peak down. *Oh my god, that is big.* The intimidation passed quickly as Colby thought of the perfect idea to establish his top energy again. He slipped one of his hands from Ezra's grip and began to stroke Ezra's cock.

It worked. Ezra stopped kissing Colby and let out a deep groan, the sound of Ezra's voice only tightening Colby's pants even more. It's not that Colby was finding Ezra attractive. No, no, no, no, no, that would be ridiculous. It was just nature taking over. Any man would get turned on by somebody moaning and writhing under their touch. Yeah, that was it.

Ezra began to bite and suck on Colby's neck and teased one of Colby's nipples with his hand. Colby was sure it would have no effect on him because he was a guy after all. That stuff only worked on girls—or so he thought. Ezra gently pinched and rolled Colby's nipple in between his fingers causing shocks of ecstasy to go straight to his dick. Colby became a panting mess under Ezra's skillful touches. He wanted to start touching his own cock, but that would be admitting to Ezra that he was enjoying this and that was a sign of defeat.

Colby began to stroke even faster, trying to prove a point. What that point was, even he wasn't sure anymore. Ezra's hand eventually left Colby's nipples and moved down to his pants. Colby would never admit it, but he had been hoping Ezra would start touching his dick too. It was aching under the tight fabric of his pants, begging for some much-needed attention.

Ezra pulled down his pants and removed Colby's hand from his cock, and he began stroking them together instead. Colby could've sworn he saw stars at that moment, the warmth radiating off. Ezra's cock sent shivers up his spine as both their dicks leaked all over each other. His head rolled back in pleasure.

He couldn't hold it back anymore. He began to moan. It was embarrassing, but he couldn't hold the moans down any longer. He thought he was going to explode if he did. ". . . ster . . . aster . . ." he whispered.

"What?" asked Ezra.

Heat rose in Colby's cheeks, but since he figured that he was already in this situation, he may as well enjoy it as much as possible. "Faster. Do it faster."

Ezra smirked at the request but did as he was asked. He began to stroke faster. Ezra leaned back in for a kiss and claimed Colby's mouth with his own. Colby tried to convince himself that he was doing all of this to assert his dominance, but then his orgasm struck.

He grasped Ezra's shoulders and pulled him close, his body tensing and his legs trembling as he came all over Ezra's bare chest. Ezra came soon after and then they were left there in silence, leaning against the shower wall with the water no longer running. Colby's head rested under Ezra's chin as they both stood there, panting.

"Why? Why did you do that?" Ezra began to ask in between breaths, but then Coach screamed in from the outside.

"You good-for-nothings better not still be in there! You're supposed to take a shower, not start a fucking flood!"

Colby suddenly realised the predicament he was in. He was wrapped up in Ezra's arms, soaking wet with his dick out.

"Hurry up, jackass," spat Colby. He shoved Ezra away and stormed out, a firm blush still rested on his cheeks. He dried himself off, changed his clothes, and left, repeatedly asking himself in his head, *What have I done?*

CHAPTER TWO
Operation Revenge

At this point, Colby had no idea what he was doing. He was sitting in English Literature, with Finley and his other friend Sophie rattling on about something intellectual. His brain was too clouded with thoughts of stupid Ezra.

"I hate Macbeth in this passage," said Finley.

"You know who I hate?" asked Colby.

"Ezra," Sophie and Finley said in unison.

"Yeah! How'd you guys know?"

"Who doesn't know? You talk about him all the time," said Sophie.

"No, I don't! I have better things to talk about than that—"

"Dickhead," said Sophie and Finley, once again in unison. Colby decided to just be quiet now. There was no way they were right. As if Colby would ever waste his breath on Ezra. Well, technically, he did just a minute ago, but that was different.

Finley and Sophie resumed their smart talk when they were sure Colby wasn't going to pipe up again.

"Why do you hate Macbeth?" asked Sophie as she took a bobble from her wrist and tied back her long auburn hair. The silver crucifix that she often wore around her neck swung out from the collar of her shirt as she tilted her head forward to do her hair. "He's just doing what Lady Macbeth is telling him to."

"Exactly," said Finley. "He's got no backbone. He just lets her command him to do whatever she wants and now he's gone and killed somebody."

"She manipulated him, so it's more her fault than his."

"Is not. He still killed the king. She didn't force him to take the knife and stab him."

"You're not being very sympathetic."

"These characters don't deserve my sympathy." And that was that. There was no more arguing with Finley. He'd stated his point and asserted his opinion. There wasn't a thing in the world that could change his mind about it.

Sophie didn't bother to argue her point again. Colby, too, didn't bother to try and change Finley's mind, even though he had his own thoughts on the matter. Finley made it clear he wasn't interested in Macbeth anymore as he began to fiddle with the gold rings he wore on his fingers. Some were plain bands and others were more decorative with small engravings or rhinestones. They contrasted beautifully against his dark brown skin.

Did Colby need to invest in some jewellery?

"Did Ezra actually do something to you today, Colby?" asked Sophie.

"Woah, woah, woah. What do you mean 'Did he actually do something?' He's always doing something!"

Ezra was an asshole to Colby. Okay, yeah, maybe he didn't always *actively* do something. Ezra wasn't going around giving Colby wedgies, putting his head down in toilets, or giving him purple nurples or Chinese burns, but somebody didn't have to get physical to still be a dick. Ezra was worse than a random bully who could physically abuse Colby and who everybody in the school knew was like that. No—Ezra was a secret asshole.

He would exclude Colby—and only Colby—from certain activities in the football club, which was definitely abusing his position as captain. He would invite the entire school round for a party, except Colby. He wouldn't pass to Colby when they were

11

playing football. He wouldn't say hi to Colby in the corridors. He wouldn't even make eye contact with Colby when they spoke to each other. He was an awful person, and the worst thing about it was that only Colby knew it. Everybody else loved him.

Ezra, the golden boy. Ezra, the future supermodel. Ezra, the most likely candidate for valedictorian.

Only Colby knew what Ezra was really like. Ezra put the "dick" in valedictorian. Screw that guy.

Finley stopped fiddling with his rings—did he get more of those since the last time Colby saw him?—and rested his head on the desk to look at Colby. "So, what did he do this time?"

Sophie's phone pinged.

"I'll tell you what he did!" said Colby. "It was just me and him in the locker room after football practice, and he was being an asshole as usual. So, when he was about to go into the shower, I ki—" *Shit.* How was he supposed to explain that he kissed Ezra, got into a shower with him, and gave him a handjob? It was to prove a point; no other reason.

"Ki?" asked Finley.

"Don't tell me you kicked him?" said Sophie. Her phone started ringing again.

Oh, that was a good one. "Yep. That's exactly what I did. When he was going to the shower, I gave him a good kick up the butt."

Finley laughed at Colby's changing of events, but Sophie looked less than impressed.

"I get that you still hate Ezra after the whole Joanna incident," she said, "but you can't go around actually attacking him. What if you get in trouble? How hard did you kick him?"

"Um, it was just a little tap?" Colby said, debating whether to just come clean at this point. He wasn't expecting to actually get questioned on his lie. In the imaginary situation, Colby kicked Ezra. It wasn't that complicated.

"You don't sound sure."

"I *am* sure."

"Are you?"

"Yes."

"Really?"

"I think so?"

Finley finally lifted his head from the table. "Oh, leave him alone, Sophie. He said it was only a little kick. End of story. Who cares?"

"I care," said Sophie. "I don't want Colby getting in trouble because he keeps harassing Ezra."

Ping. Ping. Ping. Ping. Sophie's phone wouldn't stop going off.

"I'm really sorry," she apologised. "I—" Her phone went off again and she looked rather teary. "I need to take this."

She walked out quicker than anyone could stop her. Colby's dad tried to ask her where she was going, but she apologised and headed out.

He walked over to Colby and Finley's table in a more formal and teacher-ish way than he ever would at home. His dark, streaked hair was slicked back from his face and he was wearing his pair of seventies-style reading glasses that he thought made him look cool. However, how cool could he really look when he was also wearing an English-Literature-pun tie that said, "Only the baddest witches could make a whole forest move"? It had a picture of a witch with sunglasses on, waving branches around. Was it a terrible pun? Was it a dad joke? Or was it some disgusting mix of the two?

"Is Sophie alright?" he asked.

"She's fine, Trevor," replied Finley.

"Now, Finley, you know you have to call me Mr Williams at school. Can't have the other students thinking I have a favourite student."

"Are you saying I'm *not* your favourite student?"

Colby's dad gave Finley a subtle whack on the head with the furled-up English papers he was holding. He had been the school's English teacher for about nine years now. He was the main reason Colby could write a perfect English Literary essay without thinking too hard about it—his father had drilled it into him.

"Seriously now, why did she look so upset?" he asked.

"She went to go answer her phone. It kept ringing," Colby explained.

"Who was calling her?"

"Dunno."

"Well, what were you talking about before she left?"

"We were talking about stupid Ezra Dickinson." Even his name was stupid. "Dickinson." How much did your ancestors have to hate you to pass on a name like that?

"What's wrong with Ezra? He is a fantastic student, very intelligent, and has amazing manners to boot. You should take a page out of his book, Colby."

"The fuck I will!" blurted Colby. The very idea of acting like that stuck-up blond prick made him feel physically ill.

"Language," said Mr Williams, whacking Colby with the rolled-up papers a little harder than he'd done with Finley. "Should I go talk to her, or will you?"

"I'll go. Don't worry." He turned to Finley. "You can stay here and think about what you've done."

Finley laughed. "Shut up."

Mr Williams allowed Colby to leave the classroom and walked off to help the other students.

Where would Sophie have gone? Maybe she would've gone outside or hidden in the girls' bathroom. He'd wander the halls for a bit and see if he could just come across her by luck rather than brain power.

The hallway was lined with blue lockers that were covered in scratches and dents. He tried reading some of the engravings people had carved into their lockers, but some people's handwriting

14

just looked like chicken scratch. There was the odd *name was here* or couples carving their initials together and putting love hearts around it. Naturally, there were also a bunch of dicks either carved in or drawn on. There was also one vagina drawn onto a locker. Colby was fine with that; he supported gender equality.

He passed Ezra's locker on the way. It was pristine—no bumps, no dents, and no dicks. The locker had been beaten up like the others before, but Colby had witnessed Ezra spending time getting rid of the dents and painting over scratches. The guy had way too much time on his hands if he could be bothered to fix the appearance of his locker.

Only assholes cared about the appearance of their lockers.

He hated Ezra for the Joanna incident. He really hated him. Everyone believed that he was some sort of saint that could do no wrong, but Colby had learned firsthand that that wasn't true. He was an inconsiderate asshole who never thought about other people's feelings.

So why did Colby do that with him in the showers this morning? Was it some sort of revenge? Revenge—that could be it. Make the heartbreaker the heartbroken? Ezra had never thought about Colby's feelings before. Maybe it was time he did the same.

His scheming was interrupted as he walked full force into someone else whilst rounding the corner. At first, he thought he'd slammed into a moving brick wall, but it turned out to be a walking pile of textbooks that all fell onto Colby in a cruel twist of fate. Fate wasn't yet done being a bitch though—one of the said textbooks found its way under Colby's foot, making him slip and fall on his ass.

He looked up to the person and grimaced. "You're not going to apologise for bumping into me, dickhead?"

Ezra just stared down at him with his perfect sky-blue eyes. All of a sudden, Colby had found a new hatred for the sky.

". . . sorry," he said, continuing to stare like he was under some sort of hypnosis. It was a strange thing to say, but Colby almost felt naked under his intense gaze. Eventually, Ezra broke out of it. "Hold up. *You're* the one who wasn't looking where you were going. You apologise to *me*."

"Fuck off." Colby tried to stand but ended up slipping on another textbook. Mathematics Expanded Edition, you just made yourself a new enemy.

"Do you need a hand?" Ezra stretched a hand out to help Colby up, but he just swatted it away like it was an irritating mosquito.

"I don't need help from you. I'm perfectly capable." He stood up and tried not to wince from the pain of his ass, never breaking eye contact with Ezra as he did. Ezra really did have nice eyes, if Colby was to look at them objectively. It caused him to remember this morning, embarrassingly enough. The guy really liked eye contact. Heat rose in his cheeks. He began to pick up the textbooks so Ezra couldn't see his face; he couldn't show weakness to the enemy.

"Oh . . . thanks . . ." Ezra said. His tone gave away how genuinely shocked he was that Colby was helping him.

"I can be nice when I want to be." *Kill him with kindness.*

"Is that what this morning was? Being nice?"

Colby dropped the textbooks again in surprise. How could he just bring it up so easily? Had he no shame? *Of course, he doesn't feel ashamed of it,* Colby thought. *He's a fuckboy. I bet he's used to doing things like that.*

"I don't know why you're complaining, but by the way you were moaning, it seemed like you were enjoying it," Colby snarked.

Ezra didn't reply. Colby glanced at him just to make sure he hadn't walked away and left Colby to clear up the books by himself. He was wearing an oversized black sweater with the collar of a white shirt poking out from the top and some pretty tight-fitting jeans. *How is he wearing those jeans with the size of his . . . how does he fit it in there?* He decided that being able to defy the laws of physics was another annoying thing Ezra could do. Ezra was just smiling to himself. Why was he smiling? Was he making fun of Colby and he just hadn't realised it yet?

As Colby stood up, he had an epiphany of sorts. *I can't change what I did this morning, so I may as well show him what Colby Williams is made of.*

Without giving Ezra a chance to retaliate, he pushed him against the lockers and kissed him aggressively. This time, Ezra wasn't stunned for that long and began to kiss him back. He tried to change the position so Colby was the one against the lockers, but Colby was ready this time. He held his ground and his dominance.

Colby could predict where this situation was going to go if this morning was anything to go by, and he really didn't need that right now. His feelings about it hadn't been arranged in a way he could deal with them yet. To Colby's prior belief, people who had a deep-seated hatred for someone else—as Colby did for Ezra—did not engage in promiscuous activities with the person they hated. He was pretty sure they didn't anyway.

Colby pulled away from the kiss. Time to stop before things got more complicated than necessary. Ezra's cheeks were flushed as he breathed heavily, his eyes clouded with lust.

What the hell? That's cute.

It was like there was a magnet pulling him into Ezra. He wanted to continue; make him more of a mess. For revenge reasons, obviously. But then, the bell rang. Everyone would come streaming out of the classrooms any minute now.

"See you later, dickswab," Colby said, walking away from Ezra. Two points for Colby, zero for Ezra. Although it wasn't much of a victory as he spent the rest of the time looking for Sophie thinking. A lot of thinking. To clarify, he was thinking about girls. Nice six-foot-two muscly girls with blonde hair and sky blue eyes. Cute girls who looked like that.

Eventually, he bumped into Sophie, who was exiting the girls' bathroom on the complete other side of the school. Her hair was a little messier than before, and her entire appearance was more disheveled.

"Soph!" he called. "Are you okay? I've been looking everywhere for you."

Sophie straightened out her corduroy skirt and came towards him. "Yeah, I'm good. Sorry for worrying you."

"Who kept trying to call you?"

Sophie fiddled with her crucifix necklace. She coiled the chain around her finger, tighter and tighter, until the skin around the chain turned white and the tip of her finger swelled and turned red. Colby reached forward and took her hands in his. With a delicacy reserved for her and her only, he unravelled the chain. Tiny circles had already imprinted onto her skin.

"What's wrong?" he asked carefully. "You feeling a bit stressed today?"

She nodded. "Sorry." She waved her phone in the air. "My parents won't get off my back about something and now they won't stop calling."

"Why do they keep calling?"

"Because I'm a huge screwup who can't be left alone for two minutes." She laughed at herself, then wiped her eyes with her sleeve.

"Don't be silly, Sophie. Silly Sophie. Hey, that's sibilance." That made her genuinely laugh. "You're not a screwup. Your parents are just a couple of control freaks. Who cares what they think?"

She didn't reply to that, but she held his hand as they walked back to the classroom together.

The entrance to the girls' bathroom slammed once more. Colby looked over and saw a girl with the most gorgeous ginger hair he'd ever seen. She turned for a second, then looked at Colby with those big green eyes of hers. She winked at him, and Colby held his breath for a moment.

"Do you still hate Ezra for the whole Joanna incident? You know it isn't entirely his fault," said Sophie, snapping his attention back to her. She whispered the last part of her sentence and braced for Colby's backlash.

"Isn't entirely his fault? Then whose fault is it? Is it my fault he slept with her whilst we were dating?" Thinking about the Joanna incident always made his heart ache and brought out feelings he'd rather keep buried.

"I'm just saying it's been at least a couple of weeks since it happened so maybe"—she paused before carefully saying—"maybe it's time to get over it?"

Get over it? How could he? Joanna had been his first real love, and he loved her very much. He still remembered doing anything for Joanna. He would sneak out of his house to meet her whenever she wanted. He would buy her whatever gifts she wanted. He would do anything to keep her happy, but then Ezra came along and ruined everything. If Ezra had just kept his dick in his pants, then he would still be with Joanna.

"Listen," Colby said, "I used to think Ezra was a pretty alright guy too. But when you see him flirting with your girlfriend, to then making out with her, to catching him sleeping with her, then trust me, you would change your mind about him too."

Sophie had never quite fully understood the situation with Ezra and Joanna, as Colby had never told anyone how much he was hurt by it; it was embarrassing to admit. Even now, his vision began to blur as tears pricked at his eyes.

"Why would you say something like that?" he added.

She gave his hand a small squeeze. "I just don't want you to be sad anymore. You've changed since school restarted. You're angry all the time, and you're always upset no matter what Ezra does. I can't imagine what it must be like to be cheated on, but I don't like seeing you so sad."

"What do you think I should do then?"

19

"I don't know," she admitted. "I've never been in a relationship, but I want you to be happy. I don't mean to sound cruel when I say you should get over it. I mean that maybe you should focus more on working through what you're feeling instead of being hyperfixated on Ezra. I'm sorry, I don't know what I'm saying."

"You've changed too, Soph."

She didn't answer.

"You didn't tell me you were going to summer camp this year. I kept trying to contact you, you know. I tried calling you every day until your parents finally told me that you were at camp out of state. I gave them letters that I'd written to you, did you ever receive them?"

"You wrote me letters?"

That was a no then. "Did you have fun at camp?"

She shook her head. "No, not really. I'm trying to avoid going again, but it was for the best that I went."

"How so?"

"It was a bit like an intervention. It's going to make me a better person from now on."

"I already thought you were a good person. You don't seem much happier than I am now."

The bell rang as they were walking. Had they been missing from class for that long? Whatever. Colby was not in the mood for Shakespeare anyway. They headed to the cafeteria and found Finley sitting alone.

"Took you guys long enough. I looked like a loser by myself," he complained. "You feeling better?"

Sophie nodded. "Much better, thank you."

"I'm going to go grab some food," said Colby.

"Hurry up. They're serving your favourite dessert today," Finley informed him.

"It's Nutella crepe day?" Colby sprinted to the lunch queue and shoved some younger kids out of his way. He didn't resist

20

dropping out of high school early to get to senior year and not flex it all over the younger years.

The crepes were a school favourite, so if he wasn't quick, they'd all be gone. He rushed through getting his main course, picking up whatever slop was quickest. When he got to the dessert bit, there was only one crepe left. As he quickly reached out for it, someone pulled him back, and a big muscly arm draped across his shoulders.

"Let go, Ezra!" Colby yelled.

Ezra glanced down at him and smirked. "Aww, that's so sweet of you to save me the last crepe."

"Who's saving you the last crepe? Because it sure as fuck wasn't me." Colby lunged forward for it, but Ezra pulled him back again and took it.

"Thanks so much, Colby. I always knew you really liked me." He winked at Colby and gave him a final condescending smile as he walked away.

What was the point of living anymore?

"I'm going to kill him. I'm going to kill him!" Colby fumed as he returned to the table.

"What happened, man? No more crepes left?" asked Finley.

"Oh no, no, no, no, no! There was one crepe left. Count it, one. I was about to get it when Ezra stole it from me!"

"Oof, that's rough. Ah, well, life goes on," Finley said. He'd never been one to give a fuck about anything.

"You were talking with Ezra?" asked Sophie.

"Yep. And he did nothing but prove to me what a dick he is."

"He's kind of obsessed with you," she muttered, playing with a loose strand of hair.

"It's fine because I'm going to get my revenge."

"Revenge?" Sophie sighed. "What are you on about now?"

"Don't ask him that. You'll only encourage him. You going to the football training camp this weekend?" asked Finley, the king of changing topics to what he wanted to talk about.

"I don't know. It's not really my thing," Colby admitted. He wasn't into residentials, camping, or even glamping. In fact, he hated them and always tended to avoid them if he could.

"I'm being forced to go by my parents, and I am not going to act like I actually like the rest of the team for an entire weekend just because I don't have you to talk to. You're coming. That's final. Plus, I told your dad about it, and he thinks it's a good idea for you to go." He paused and pulled out a crumpled-up letter from his bag, Colby's dad's signature scribbled along the bottom. "Apparently, we have to share rooms of four. So, we need two other guys to join us."

"I'll see you guys there too. The cheerleading camp is happening at the same place," said Sophie.

"I'll go, but only if you keep Ezra as far away from me as physically possible," Colby said.

"I'll try, man. But he *is* the captain, so you can't stay that far away from him," Finley replied, putting the paper back in his bag.

Being stuck with Ezra all weekend was going to suck. But in the meantime, Operation Revenge was a go.

CHAPTER THREE
You Make Me Sick

Every day of this week, Coach Clain had organised an early morning football practice in preparation for the weekend. Anyone not at the practices was off the team and would receive a month of early morning detentions. Was she allowed to give out detentions for that? No one knew, and no one was stupid enough to ask. Not even Colby.

Playing football and being forced to listen to stupid Ezra Dickinson yelling orders at him was not how Colby wanted to spend his morning.

After the whole team had played a match together, everyone went their own way and did whatever training they wanted. It had to be some sort of training though or else Coach would rip the slackers a new one.

At least, it was a nice morning. The sight of the sun rising over the bleachers was the only compensation for being there so early. The light poured over the high seats of the bleachers and trickled down, row by row, until the summer grass of the football field was flooded with the golden light. The light drenched every player from head to toe, their uniforms and helmets glowing.

Colby removed his helmet and chucked it to the floor beside him. The sun brought the heat, and he wanted to feel it on his face rather than melt with his helmet on.

Finley did the same. The sunlight ran down his wide nose bridge and full lips. His black eyes twinkled, but he didn't look very happy to be here. His dark hair fell loose around his shoulders, revealing the intricate cornrows that his sister had meticulously done for him last night. The morning sun brought out every twist and careful sectioning she had done. How did Colby know it was Finley's sister that had done his hair rather than Finley? Because the light bounced off of and illuminated the bright pink beads that had been braided into the ends of his hair.

"Did you do it?" Finley asked suddenly.

"Huh, did I do what?" asked Colby. The two began passing a ball between them. Maybe not the most effective way of training, but it counted.

"Yesterday. You said you were going to prove that you weren't a bottom. I'm just curious if you did it, man," said Finley with that teasing smile on his face.

It was a good question. Had he proven he wasn't a bottom? He'd definitely dominated the locker kiss. The shower was a bit of a draw. Technically, couldn't Colby only discover if he was a bottom by having sex with Ezra? It would be great for his revenge plan. *I'll fuck him, get him attached, and then leave like nothing ever happened.* But was he really okay with the idea of doing it? With a guy? With Ezra? It kinda seemed like he was whoring himself out for the guy he hated.

Colby shook his head. "No. I don't think I've proven it yet."

"Wait, what? I was just joking, man. Are you actually trying to prove it? Like, for real?"

Colby completely fumbled the throw to Finley as he realised he may have admitted something—something he didn't want anyone to know.

"Pfft. I was just joking too, bro. The look on your face right now. Hahaha! Priceless." Colby desperately tried to backtrack, but Finley clearly wasn't buying it, judging by the mischievous glint in his eye.

"It's cool if you are, like I'm not gonna judge. I'm just surprised, that's all. Also, you need to work on your lying abilities, 'cos your fake laugh is awful."

Finley then looked past Colby, and his taunting expression stopped. He looked scared. Colby wondered if there was a monster behind him, or even worse, Coach Clain. "Also, also, I think Ezra saw you fuck up that throw and is now coming over here."

"My fake laugh is great!" Colby insisted. "Wait. What did you just say?"

"He probably said something about training to become a competent team member."

That stupid deep voice. Just the sound of it pissed Colby off.

"I can throw just fine, Dickinson," he spat.

"Only using my last name? That's not very creative of you. Finley, go practise with Brent whilst I give Colby a reminder on how to throw."

"With Brent? For real? I'd love to! Oh, wait. No, I mean . . . don't take me away from Colby, but . . . you're the captain." Finley mouthed a quick "sorry" to Colby, who just flipped him off in return.

"Your stance is all wrong. Spread your legs a bit more."

Colby felt the heat of Ezra's hands through his leggings as he ran his hand down Colby's thighs, making him shiver. Probably because of a cold breeze or something, no other reason. "Now straighten your back more." A finger ran up his spine, pausing when it got to his nape. "And angle your upper body slightly." Both of Ezra's hands now gripped Colby's shoulders and gently twisted him. Colby could feel Ezra's breath on his neck.

He tried ignoring the closeness of Ezra's body to his own, but that was much easier said than done. Wasn't this closeness a bit unnecessary? Colby couldn't remember a time Ezra got this up

25

close and personal during training. Until recently, Ezra hadn't even spoken to Colby very much, either on the field or off.

"I know how to throw. Just because I don't do it like you do, doesn't mean I'm doing it wrong." It didn't come out nearly as intimidating as Colby was hoping—his voice was more hushed than threatening.

"I can throw the ball with my stance, but you can't seem to do it with yours, which only proves my point."

"You are *so* annoying. You think you're so perfect and everyone should be like you. You think you're better than everyone. That you can do whatever you want. Take whatever you want from people."

For a second, Ezra stepped back and let go of Colby's shoulders. A moment of silence passed, and all Colby did was grip the football until his knuckles turned white.

"Colby, I . . ." Ezra leaned in close to Colby's ear. Colby could feel the warmth of Ezra's breath, his hands now touching Colby's waist ever so gently.

"Stay behind for a bit and meet me in the locker room."

With that, he released Colby and walked off, leaving Colby more confused and more pissed off than he was before.

*   *   *

"Aren't you coming, man? I'm going to grab something from the vending machine before class starts," said Finley.

Colby stared into his locker, unsure of what to do. The locker was filled with dirty sports clothes, an empty deodorant can, and one rotting apple core. He should really clear it out. He held the door open, the coldness of the metal contrasting with the warmth of Ezra's hands from earlier.

Ezra had asked him to stay behind, but why should he? He hated the guy, plain and simple. Operation Revenge involved confusing Ezra's feelings, but Colby was certain of his own. Surely,

26

he wanted him for something important. Why else would he ask Colby to stay behind? What if Ezra was going to demand an explanation for what happened in the shower? Colby didn't have a viable explanation that wouldn't reveal Operation Revenge.

Nothing could stop him from leaving right now, grabbing a snack with Finley, then heading to lessons. It would probably annoy Ezra, which would only help Operation Revenge. So, he should just leave, right?

Heat rose to his cheeks as he tried to imagine—not why Ezra had asked him to stay behind—but what would they do if they were alone together again. It was all so stupid.

"Are you alright, man? Your face is all red. Do you need to go to the nurse's office?"

"Huh?"

Finley came closer and rested his hand against Colby's forehead. "You do feel pretty hot. Please tell me you didn't catch something from that party on Sunday. This is why I keep telling you not to drink from other people's cups. Germs and shit, man."

That must be it. He was just feeling a bit ill, and that's why he's getting hot and bothered over the idea of doing something with Ezra. Hot, not horny. Definitely not over *that* asshole anyway. Maybe Colby had got salmonella; he knew he shouldn't have eaten his mom's chicken dish.

"I think I might go to the nurse's office. I'm not feeling one hundred percent."

Finley put both of his hands on Colby's cheeks; they were nice and cool. "Whatever makes you feel better, my precious little princey-wincey."

"Are you acting like my mom right now? For your information, she doesn't call me that anymore. She calls me her 'darling prince charming.' "

"It's still a lame nickname."

"It's a great nickname. Don't be so jelly."

27

"I'm not jelly. You're still my little princey-wincey, that's all." Finley began to place big slobbery kisses on Colby's cheeks.

"Ew! Gross!"

As the two laughed, there was a sudden huge metallic sound.

Bang!

"Oh shit," Colby whispered, his cheeks now incredibly moist. His plan of escaping before Ezra came for him had just crumbled.

Ezra held his hand firmly against his locker door. Even his friend Brent, who was sitting on the bench next to him, looked surprised by his actions.

"You all good, bro?" asked Brent cautiously.

"Yep," Ezra said, smiling innocently at him.

"Okay, cool. Good play today, Fin," said Brent.

Colby was pretty sure they didn't talk often, but Finley would constantly gush about the guy.

"Oh, me? Yeah, yeah, I'm good. I'm cool, cool like a cucumber, you know? Aha aha aha."

For the first time in Colby's life, he had seen Finley look flustered. Like *seriously* flustered. Properly, seriously flustered. What had happened to the chill Finley, the nothing-bothers-me-ever Finley, the no-shits-are-given Finley?

Colby could only stare at him in shock before he said, "Your fake laugh is just as bad as mine."

Finley quickly wrapped his arm around Colby's shoulders and pulled him into a headlock. "Shut up, man," he whispered furiously.

"Are you blushing?" asked Colby. "Why?"

Finley squeezed him even tighter, and Colby was pretty sure he heard some of his bones grinding together. "I said shut the fuck up before I make you," he said through gritted teeth.

Colby glanced at Ezra, who looked just as confused, then at Brent. Brent was a good-looking guy—tall, dark, and handsome.

Huge emphasis on tall. The guy must've been drinking ten gallons of milk a day to be that tall. What was he? Six foot eight? Six foot nine? Something crazy like that. The girls in the school often had debates over who was hotter: Ezra or Brent. Colby could definitely see the charm in Brent. He had such a nice face, and his skin was the colour of cinnamon. How was a nice guy like him friends with Ezra? Opposites attract, Colby supposed.

Why would Finley get so flustered around Brent, though? He was genuinely confused.

"You two are pretty close," laughed Brent. Ezra looked pissed again.

"Yep, yep, yep. We've been friends for ages, so yeah, we're pretty close. Pretty close indeed. Right, man?"

There was an awkward silence as Colby didn't respond. He was still trying to wrap his head around Finley not only being flustered but also rambling. Since when did he ramble?

The conversation went dead and they all stood quietly in the locker room. "I was just about to take him to the nurse's office," said Finley, finally disturbing the silence. "So, we better go. Better skedaddle. Make our way down there. Downtown. Downtown in funky town . . . aha aha aha."

"That's not funny," said Colby.

"Shut up!" Finley hissed, punching him in the side.

"Nurse's office? Why?"

Ezra finally turned around from the locker to face Finley and Colby, a look of concern etched on his face. First, Finley was flustered, and now Ezra was concerned? Was the world about to end? Were pigs finally learning how to fly?

"He just feels pretty hot, so I thought maybe he was ill. I think he caught something at the party. Don't want him spreading germs around, you know. Aha aha aha."

"I change my mind. Your fake laugh is worse than mine." Colby said, earning him another solid smack from Finley.

29

"Don't you have lessons?" asked Brent. "I mean, I know you do. We're in the same chemistry class."

"Yeah, but it's okay. Gotta look out for your buddies," said Finley, punching Colby in the arm pretty hard.

"Ow! What did I do this time?"

"Shut up."

"I haven't got any lessons now, so I can take him," said Ezra.

"Sorted then," said Brent. "Shall we get going then, Fin? Don't want Mr Gomez to give us detention."

Finley's mouth hung open like a fish out of water. What was going on with him? It was terrifying.

"Yeah, let's go." He leaned close to Colby's ear. "Sorry, man. But take one for the team."

"I'm gonna break your kneecaps the next time I see you," whispered Colby.

Finley practically frolicked away with Brent and looked unfazed by Colby's threat. He must've thought Colby was joking, but he was being oh so serious.

"Let's go then," said Ezra. "Don't puke on me on the way there."

"I would never do that. My puke deserves so much better."

The walk to the nurse's office could be encapsulated in one word: awkward. It was super-duper awkward. Colby and Ezra just walked next to each other in an uncomfortable silence. Ezra didn't look too fazed by it, but Colby couldn't stop fiddling with the drawstring on his hoodie and cursing Finley in his head.

Just make conversation. Anything, he thought.

"What'd you think of the party on Sunday?" asked Colby. *Why would you ask that?*

"The party?" Ezra glanced at him, then looked ahead again. "I thought it was kind of boring at first, but I was having a really good time by the end of it." A small smile graced Ezra's lips.

Good time? What did that mean? Did he remember the kiss? Was the kiss the "good time"? Surely not, or else he would've mentioned it. His ego would never have allowed him not to taunt Colby with it. Did he mean he'd had a good time with someone else? Was Colby even the only person he had kissed at the party? Had he been with Joanna again? His thoughts kept spiralling with a thousand different possibilities of what the "good time" was. Every possibility that contained Ezra being with someone else pissed him off. *I bet he was. Typical fuckboy.*

"What did you think of it?" The question interrupted the runaway train that was Colby's thoughts.

"I don't really remember most of it. I'm a bit of a lightweight. I remember getting there, having my first drink, and then everything else is a blur."

"Oh." The smile fell away. "That's not very responsible of you."

"Alright, no need to lecture me, Mom."

"You don't remember anything at all?"

Was this the right time to bring up the photo? Probably not. "Like I said, nothing. You going deaf, dickhead?"

"I'm not deaf. I'm just amazed at your inability to hold your drink." Ezra's eyebrows knitted together, and he refused to look at Colby anymore. Whatever. Colby didn't want to get dirtied by the bastard's eyes anyway.

When they finally got to the nurse's office, Sophie was there by herself, not a nurse to be found. He had never liked the nurse's office. Sure, there was a comfy bed to sit on, but the rest of the office was covered in used coffee mugs and empty Ibuprofen packets. Plus, the most the nurse could actually do for him was give him an icepack and tell him to toughen up.

Before Sophie could notice them, Ezra pulled Colby out of sight.

"Are you sure you're not feeling well?" Ezra asked, his body uncomfortably close to Colby's again.

31

"Yeah, I've just been feeling a bit . . ." He paused, unsure of how to describe his condition. Operation Revenge was too early in development to let anything slip, no matter how nice Ezra was pretending to be. Ezra might have everyone else under his spell, but Colby saw right through his good-guy act. "Since when did you care anyway!"

"Just trying to be nice." He gave Colby a quick peck on the lips before leaving.

"Hi, Ezra!" said Sophie when he came into her view. "I didn't see you there."

"Hey, Sophie. Take care of Colby for me, will you?" Why was Ezra acting as if he cared? It was really getting on Colby's nerves at this point. Whatever. Colby would bring him down eventually.

"Yep, will do." She took Colby by the arm and led him inside. "You're a really nice guy, Ezra. Everyone says that about you."

"Thanks, Sophie. I'll see you two later."

Colby could only stare at Ezra as he walked away, the light coming in from the window dancing in his golden locks. He ran his finger along his lips, checking if Ezra had really kissed him. It had been so soft and so quick. He wasn't sure if it even happened.

CHAPTER FOUR
Proactive Interference

"What's the matter, Colby? Come on, take a seat. Don't push yourself," said Sophie.

It was good to see her. Sophie always had a way of making time slow down for a second, for the world seemed a little less big. The things that weighed heavily upon Colby's shoulders didn't seem so pressing when Sophie was around. Perhaps it was due to the fact that they had known each other when they were still in their diapers. In Colby's eyes, Sophie brought a reliable source of comfort with her.

"Why are you here?" he asked.

"The nurse is off sick today, so the school asked me to cover for her since I'm first-aid trained. It's not so bad. I'm getting extra credit for it."

"How much more extra credit do you need? You're in every club I can think of."

She fluffed up some pillows for him and brought over a small cup of water. "My dad says it's good to stay busy."

"Don't push yourself too much." He sat on the bed, letting his body relax for the first time today. The bed was covered in thick fluffy blankets. No one knew how often they were cleaned—some said they weren't—but right now he couldn't care less. "I feel so hot."

"You feel hot after spending time with Ezra? Okay." She giggled to herself as she perched on the edge of the bed. Gently, she rested the back of her hand on Colby's forehead.

"What do you mean? He's a dick."

"He brought you all the way here and you still think that? Maybe you should give him the benefit of the doubt on this one."

"What the fuck are you on? Since when did you get a crush on Ezra?"

"Crush!" Her cheeks were burning red. She kept twisting a strand of her hair around her finger. "I mean, it's not that I like him. Or maybe I do. I don't really know."

"Well, do you like him or not?" Please say not.

"I don't know. Genuinely, I don't know. It's confusing. We talk to each other sometimes, civilly and politely, not . . . romantically. Or at least, I didn't think it was romantic." She turned away from Colby. "My friends think I flirt with him."

"Which friends?"

"You know, Netra, Megan, Trisha . . . Joanna."

"Joanna! Does Joanna think you're flirting with him too? She'd know plenty about that, wouldn't she."

Sophie didn't reply.

"Do you like him?"

"My friends say I do. I don't know. I've never really had a crush on a guy before. I don't know what it's supposed to feel like. I'm sorry, Colby. I don't think I am flirting with him, but I also don't know how I feel about him."

It didn't make sense. It was against all that was holy and right in this world. Sophie was so nice and sweet and good, and Ezra was everything but. Ezra was so Ezra, and that wasn't a good thing. Just the idea of it made Colby's stomach knot.

He could picture it—the two of them walking down the hall together, holding hands. Sophie would be blushing like she had been earlier and Ezra would smile at her lovingly. They would go on cute dates, and Ezra would buy her gifts and bring her flowers on their anniversaries. They would have sex, and Ezra would become a gentle and passionate lover *for her*. He would love *her*. She would love him.

The pain was indescribable, but he could feel it everywhere in his body. His stomach felt warm and uncomfortable like a hundred rats were trapped within him, trying to escape his body by clawing up his throat. The room began to swim, and he thought he was going to be sick.

He hadn't felt this way since he had witnessed the Joanna incident.

"Have you told him how you feel yet?" he managed to ask.

"No, not yet. Do you remember the party from Sunday?"

"Parts of it."

"I think he likes someone else, and I think they were at the party together."

Good. She hadn't told him yet. So why didn't he feel good about it? If anything, he felt even worse than before. A million questions rammed him at once. Was this the "good time" Ezra had mentioned earlier? Who was "someone else"? How would Ezra react if Sophie asked him out? But the question that bothered him the most was, why did he even care so much? His stomach was doing a full-on acrobatics performance inside him at this point.

"What do you mean 'I think', don't you know what actually happened at the party?"

"Uh, no. I kinda heard about it from someone else."

"Who?"

"It doesn't really matter. They might be lying."

"Who?"

"Or they could've misheard it from someone else."

"Sophie, who?"

"I heard it from Joanna."

First, Ezra likes "someone else." Then, Sophie has a crush on Ezra. Now, Joanna has information on Ezra. The building pressure became too much, and Colby threw up.

35

*   *   *

After what happened in the nurse's office, Colby was forbidden from going to class for the rest of the day. His mom wasn't home to look after him since she was doing a shift at the local hotel she managed, so he had sat in his dad's office for most of the day, with nothing to entertain him but the spinny chair. All day just spin, spin, spin.

He threw up in his dad's office.

When Colby wasn't wrecking his dad's office and filling it with the putrid smell of vomit that his dad would probably never get rid of, he thought about everything Sophie had said. He couldn't say why it bothered him so much. It was probably just because he'd known Sophie since kindergarten and she deserved better than that douchebag. Yeah, that was it. The strange thing was he was actually debating whether to go talk to Joanna about what she knew. He hadn't talked to her since the incident.

Then there was the issue of Ezra. Could he really continue with Operation Revenge if Sophie liked him? He wanted to. He really wanted to. So he could get his revenge . . . obviously. But he would feel guilty about it now, knowing how she felt about him. Maybe he did need to let go of the past already. But not right now.

He decided to try and find Joanna. His dad had a packet of extra minty chewing gum stuffed away in his desk. Colby used and chewed the entire packet. He didn't want to imagine how embarrassing it would be to see his ex again after so long while he stank of puke. The lunch bell had just rang, so he had a good chance of finding her in the cafeteria.

The closer he got to the cafeteria, the more nervous he got. It had been so long since they had talked. He wasn't really sure what to say or how to act. They did not end their relationship on good terms. Not even close.

36

He'd tried desperately to get over her and that happened to involve cutting her out of his life. Unfortunately, he couldn't have done the same with Ezra since they were on the football team together, but Joanna's life never seemed to cross with Colby's. A part of him was glad of that. That's why it was so strange that he was the one forcing them back together again. And for what? For himself? For Sophie? For Ezra? He didn't really know.

At the far end of the dining hall sat Joanna. She looked as lovely as ever with her strawberry blonde hair and lightly freckled face. She sat at a round table with a few girls and guys. He recognised some of the guys from football, one of whom was Brent. Poor Brent stuck out like a sore thumb as he dwarfed everyone else at the table.

Wait, if Brent was there, then where was Ez—

"What are you staring at?" Speak of the devil and he shall appear. Colby's skeleton nearly jumped out of his skin. For such a big guy, Ezra could sneak up on people pretty easily. Being sneaky seemed to be a well-honed skill of Ezra's.

"Um, I need to talk to . . . someone." Like hell was Colby going to tell Ezra why he was here. "Not like it's any of your business, dick."

Ezra just grinned at him. "I heard you threw up all over the nurse's office and gave it a nice new paint job. Did the kiss I gave you make you all nervous? Too many butterflies in your tummy?"

"Fuck off. I did throw up, and it's because of how disgusting it was to be touched by you." That came out a little harsher than Colby had meant it to. Ezra's face became cold and unreadable. He didn't even make a snippy reply or anything. God, he was being so weird lately.

"Are you feeling better now?" He said it so quietly that Colby nearly didn't hear him.

"Huh? Oh, yeah. Thanks, thanks for taking care of me, I guess."

Ezra leaned closely towards Colby's face. Their faces were so close that their lips were nearly touching. He could feel the heat of his breath against his lips. Was he going to kiss him? Right now? In front of everyone? Colby didn't pull away or push against Ezra, he just closed his eyes and waited.

But nothing happened. Or at least he didn't feel anything happen. When he opened his eyes again, Ezra was standing further back, smirking again.

"You still owe me a meet-up, you know? Since you bailed on me this morning," said Ezra.

"I don't owe you anything!"

"Next time I ask, you better not flake, alright?" Before Colby could insult him, Ezra reminded him of why he was actually here. "Didn't you want to talk to someone?"

"Oh, yeah!"

Filled with fresh annoyance from talking to Ezra, he marched over to Joanna's table without preparing something to say first. Big mistake. He just stood there silently until he could string a sentence together in his head.

"Uhh . . . can I talk to you . . . in private . . . please . . . ?"

She looked just as shocked to see him as he had been to talk to her.

"Sure, Colbs. It's been a while."

"You wanted to talk to Joanna?"

Ezra was going to be the death of Colby if he kept sneaking up on him like that.

"Why?" He looked and sounded pissed. More than pissed.

Before Colby could think of an explanation, Joanna stood up and wrapped herself around Colby's arm. With a sly smirk on her face, she said to Ezra, "Whatever it is, it has nothing to do with you. Colby and I have a lot of history, you know? We're allowed to talk about it." That only seemed to piss Ezra off more. "Come on, Colbs. Let's go somewhere more *private.*"

Colby could only helplessly glance at Ezra and Joanna as she dragged him away. He wondered whether he'd accidentally started a fight. He'd only wanted to ask about the party, not reignite the tension between the three.

Joanna dragged Colby through the school. Her baby-smooth skin was cutting off the blood circulation to his hand, and it was the softest python grip he'd ever experienced. They eventually settled on talking in an empty science classroom. Although, the life-sized skeleton in the back of the room was creeping him out a little bit. Those cold empty eye sockets. It had no eyes, but it was definitely staring Colby down.

"It has legit been too long, Colbs. How have you been?"

"Huh? Oh yeah, pretty good. Still in high school and all that. I wanted to ask you about the party on Sunday."

She leaned back against the teacher's desk. The mom jeans she was wearing hugged her body in all the right places, and the white corset top she was wearing complimented her bright hair colour. She was the hottest girl Colby had ever seen. He still remembered being shocked when she agreed to go out with him. It was too good to be true.

She looked uneasy at his mentioning of the party.

"Sure. What do you want to know, Colbs?"

"Well, someone told me, that you told them, that Ezra likes someone who was at that party. I was wondering who it is." He couldn't stand the sound of his own voice right now. He felt like a drama queen making such a big deal out of this, but he wanted to know. He *needed* to know.

"Who told you I said that?"

"I can't say." Colby wasn't often involved in drama, but he knew that you never rat out the name of your source of information.

"So, you want me to tell you who Ezra likes, but you won't tell me who told you something I apparently said? No fucking deal."

39

"But I need to know."

"Why do you need to know?"

"I can't really tell you that either."

"So you want something for nothing. Well, I've got things I need to keep private too, you know? Like the identity of the girl that Ezra likes."

"It's a girl?"

She paused and then smiled innocently at Colby. "Of course, it is. Why? You didn't think it could be a boy, did you?" She giggled.

Colby began to get that sick feeling from earlier, but so much worse this time. "No, of course I didn't. Who is she then?"

"Not telling. If this is all you want, then I've still gotta finish my lunch." She waved and left him there with the plastic skeleton. The door squeaked as she pulled it open.

"Wait! Just one last thing. Why? Why did you cheat on me?"

"This isn't me trying to be mean, but you just became, I don't know, too clingy." They stood there in an awkward silence for a while. That seemed to sum up Colby's entire day: awkward silences.

"Well, catch you around, Colbs."

It hurt so much. He couldn't pinpoint where it hurt or what was hurting him, but it hurt. A lot.

CHAPTER FIVE
Gino's Italiano

The pain hadn't subsided by the end of the day. Well, it wasn't really a pain but an unrelenting ache.

Nothing that had been said to him by anyone after lunch really sank in. The lessons of the teachers and the gossip of the students might as well have not been said at all. He couldn't bring himself to talk to people either, only ever sitting in silence by himself. Not even Finley could get a crack out of him, and that guy was hilarious. Sophie had even baked him some cookies in Home Economics.

After his last lesson, he caught a glimpse of Ezra making his way through the hordes of kids trying to get out of school. His body froze. *Please don't let him see me, please don't let him see me.* For once, the universe was on Colby's side as Ezra left without even looking in his direction. Just seeing Ezra filled Colby with so many violent emotions—emotions he'd only ever felt once and had hoped he'd never have to feel again.

"Wanna grab a pizza?" Finley asked, finally breaking through Colby's daze.

"Huh? I don't know. I'm not feeling too great."

"I know you're not ill, man. Like I know you showed the nurse what you had for breakfast and all, but I've known you long enough to know when you're sick and when you're sad. So, stop being a little bitch, and let's go, man."

Colby smiled at him. "Okay, let's go. But you have to tell me what's up with you and Brent."

"There's nothing up."

"You were flustered."

"I don't get flustered, man."

"Well, you were. So you better tell me why."

"Fine, whatever. Let's go already. I'm starving."

Gino's Italiano was the best pizza place in town. Sure, the owner wasn't actually Italian or called Gino, but he was called Greg—which was close enough—and he'd been to Italy at least once. And sure, they only just passed the health and safety regulations, but for flavour this good, anyone could put up with the rat shit in the corner and the weirdly coloured sticky spots on the tables.

It was decorated quite stereotypically with the black and white tile floor contrasting with the red walls, covered with pictures of celebrities that didn't even know this place existed. Plastic flora and fauna hung from the ceiling along with fake grapes that had lost their purple colour and were coated in dust. Not exactly the classiest restaurant but beggars can't be choosers.

"So, man, what's happeni—" Finley began, but Colby wasn't quite ready to talk about himself yet.

"Nope! You first or else you won't tell me. I know how you work."

"Ugh! Jesus, fine. What do you wanna know?"

"What've you got with Brent? I know straight girls go wild for him, but what's up with you?"

"Colby." He paused, placing his hands on the table. A very bold move considering the gross stickiness. "What's the opposite of a straight girl?"

"The opposite of straight is gay, and the opposite of girl is boy, so a gay boy." He had to take a minute to figure it out, Colby certainly wasn't the sharpest tool in the box. The realisation did hit him eventually though. "Oh my god! Are you gay boy?"

42

"I am gay boy."

"Oh, cool," he said slowly. "So, what's up with Brent?" He wasn't even close to being the sharpest tool.

"Jesus Christ, man. I like him. I am gay boy with a crush on hot boy. You understand?"

"Oh. Ohhh. Bro, I've never seen you with a crush before. This is exciting. Have you asked him out yet?"

"As a matter of fact, I did." A look of pride was plastered on Finley's face. He reclined in his seat, putting his arms behind his head. Gross, now his hair would be sticky, his sister's work gone to waste. "He's coming here soon, so tell me about you before he gets here. I'll be too busy getting my game on to listen to your problems, so chop-chop."

"Oh shit. Well, I . . ." He didn't know where to begin. Did he start with what happened in the shower? That was way too sexual! Or maybe the corridor incident? That's more tame but hard to explain why he did it without explaining what happened in the shower. He began to contemplate whether he was secretly a slut. Or maybe tell him about Sophie's secret crush? But what if she wanted it to stay secret for now? Come on, he only had so much time.

Without saying another word, Colby whipped out his phone and found the photo of him making out with Ezra from the party on Sunday. He hesitated for only a second before giving it to Finley. Gross, he probably should've asked him to wash his hands first before touching his phone with the mystery stick on his hands.

Finley's eyes widened in shock. He tried to speak a few times, but all that came out were gargled and disjointed words. "What . . . but . . . I . . . what . . . but you . . . and him . . . hate . . . what . . . ?"

"It was sent to me from an unknown number on Monday."

"What . . . but . . . that's you and Ezra."

"Yeah."

"Making out."

"Yeah."

"And it looks like you like it."

"Yeah—wait, no! You can't say that for sure!"

"I think I can. Have you got a boner in this pic?" Finley began to zoom in on the picture. Faster than Colby had ever moved in his life, he snatched the phone back and buried it deep in his pocket.

"Wow, just wow. Okay, sorry, I'll focus now. Do you have any idea who sent it?"

"No, not a clue. I don't remember most of the party and I definitely don't remember doing this."

"Right, because you're the ultimate lightweight. Drunk Colby is a troublemaker, so it's not unbelievable that you would do this." That was a bit of a hyperbole. Drunk Colby wasn't *that* bad. Not that Colby had ever been sober enough to remember Drunk Colby, but he'd yet to be arrested, so it couldn't be that bad. "Don't look at me like that. You know it's true. It was a big party, so there was a large number of suspects. However, the fact that this hasn't been spread around the school like wildfire suggests that it's someone close to either you or Ezra."

"Wow, you sound like a detective right now."

"Thanks. I watched Detective Pikachu last night and picked up a few things. So, that rules out gossipers, drama starters, and people who don't know you guys that well. Do you know whether Ezra remembers anything or whether he got sent the pic?"

"Oh yeah, I walked up to him during football practice and said to him, *'Hey Ezra, do you remember that crazy make out sesh we had on Sunday, or are you getting blackmailed with a picture of it as well?'*"

"Chill with the sarcasm, man. Just trying to help. Maybe you're right though."

"Maybe I'm right about what?"

"About the picture being blackmail. Maybe someone didn't want you two to go on an enemies-to-lovers romance arc and fall madly in love, so took the picture to keep you away from him . . . and that person is me. Why did you kiss Ezra?"

44

"I don't know! I was drunk!"

"Being drunk isn't an excuse to do something so disgusting."

"You're gay. Why are you mad at me for doing a gay thing?"

"You doing gay things with Ezra makes me homophobic."

"But . . . you're gay."

"People can be more than one thing, Colby. Don't put me in a box." Finley slammed his hand down on the table. Did he not feel the stickiness? "My point is, I think whoever did this has some sort of reason to want to keep you and Ezra apart, and I smell romantic jealousy."

"I don't know, that sounds pretty crazy."

"People can be crazy"—he reached forward, gently caressing Colby's cheek—"*for love.*" He finished it with a seductive wink that made Colby laugh.

"Eww, save it for Brent." The mention of love reminded Colby of why he was feeling down in the first place. "I talked to Joanna again."

Finley's jaw dropped and his hand moved away from Colby. Maybe he should stop shocking Finley—it looked like one more revelation would give him a heart attack.

"Why? But why? What? I thought you were done with her after . . . you know, the incident."

Greg, a.k.a Gino Italiano, then came over and gave them both their pizzas and the drinks they'd ordered. Colby had gotten a large pepperoni pizza with a mango smoothie. Nothing could lighten Colby's mood more than this.

"Thanks." He took a sip of his smoothie. He could see from the corner of his eye that Finley wasn't touching his food yet, clearly waiting for Colby's answer. "It's hard to explain why I went to her. It's not that I still like her or anything, or at least I don't think I do. Sure she's still super-duper pretty, and her eyes still sparkle when she talks, and she's still got that cute little mole on her left cheek . . . sorry. Anyway, I talked to her about someone else. And I don't even know why I talked to her about them, because I don't even like them. I fucking hate them, but Sophie said she knew something about them, and—anyway, I asked her why she cheated on me. I've just always wanted to know, I guess. Like was it something I did or said that pushed her away from me, and it turns out it was. She said I was too clingy. Which is okay, I guess I must have been. I know I can be a little too much and sometimes a little dim, but I don't mean to bother anyone with . . . myself." His voice slowly began to trail off as the pain came back and not even a pizza could fix it. Ugh, he really hoped he wouldn't throw up in Gino's Italiano. He had a bit of a hunch that it might ruin the mood of Finley's date.

"What do you mean is it something *you did*? She cheated on you, man. Who cares if you're a bit clingy? That's not an excuse to cheat. Nothing is. The reason why she cheated on you has nothing to do with you, but everything to do with her inability to commit. Fuck her, man. Fuck what she says. Damn, that's pissed me off now. Who does she think she is?"

"Hey, don't say that about her."

"Why not? She's a shit person, especially to you. What's Sophie doing staying friends with her? She should know better. I know it sounds like I'm being harsh right now, but you deserve the truth, man. You're a great guy who did not deserve to be cheated on."

Tears began to blur Colby's vision. "Thanks," he managed to say without his voice cracking.

"So, who's this 'them' you kept mentioning? A new lady, perhaps? Or are we swinging the other way now?"

"Them? Oh well." He stared out the store window to avoid Finley's interrogative stare. "Them is—Ezra? What the fuck is he doing here?"

Finley turned around to look out the window as well. Sure enough, Ezra was getting out of a white Volkswagen whilst Brent was getting out the other side. Oh, that's what the fuck he was doing here. He supposed that was uncharacteristically kind of Ezra to drop Brent off at his date. Bit of a bro move. The strange thing was, they were both coming towards the pizzeria.

"Did you invite both of them?" asked Colby.

Finley shook his head, the beads in his hair clicked together as he did. "Nope, just Brent."

"Did you make it clear that this was supposed to be a date? For just the two of you?"

Finley snapped his gaze back to Colby. "What do you mean? Of course, I did. Sorta. Kind of. Maybe. Not really. Shit."

"Better luck next time, buddy." He gave Finley a firm slap on the back, out of the kindness in his heart.

"Ow!"

It may have also been revenge for Finley punching him repeatedly in the locker room earlier.

The bell above the door sang as the pair of boys walked in. Brent smiled warmly at Finley and Ezra just smirked when he noticed Colby was there too. Why did he smirk? Did the loser not know how to give a genuine smile?

"Hey, Fin!" said Brent happily. "I hope you don't mind that I brought Ezra with me. He was hungry too, so I said he could tag along."

"Uh, yeah. It's no problem. It's cool. It's fine." Oh, great. Flustered and rambling Finley was back.

Finley and Colby had been sitting across from each other at the back of the pizzeria which meant there was a fifty-fifty chance that he would end up sitting next to Ezra. After the day he had, he really didn't want to. Just seeing the literal embodiment of douche behaviour made him feel ill all over again. But Finley wanted to sit next to Brent and he knew that. That's all he had to remind himself. *It's for Finley, it's for Finley, my main man.*

He looked Ezra in the eyes and mustered up the best smile he could manage. It must have not been very convincing by the way

Finley grimaced at it, but it was the best Ezra was going to get. He gestured for Ezra to take the seat next to him. Then Ezra was the one smiling. The smile was a little too genuine for Colby's liking. However, he resisted the urge to punch Ezra in the face when he saw how delighted and nervous Finley looked when Brent sat next to him. He'd never seen this side of Finley before and it was surprisingly adorable.

Eventually, conversation started up mostly between Finley, Brent, and Ezra. Colby wasn't really in a chatty mood, so he stayed out of it. Plus he was rather sure that if he did speak, then it would probably be to insult Ezra and he was trying to keep the atmosphere light so Finley could flirt. He expected some recognition of his top-tier friendship from Finley after this was over. Occasionally, he would catch Ezra glancing over at him. *Look at me one more time and see what happens,* was his main thought about it.

He only really tuned back into the conversation when Brent said, "I know! Since there are already four of us, we should share a room at the football training camp!"

"I'm down for that," said Ezra.

Finley was about to say something until he looked over at Colby, waiting for his answer. He knew more than anyone about Colby's hatred for Ezra, but Colby could tell from his big puppy dog eyes that he wanted Colby to say yes. Would he be able to survive the entirety of camp not only listening to Ezra yell commands at him but sleeping in the same room as him too? It sounded like a nightmare.

Why did Finley have to look at him like that though?

"Sounds . . . good." Every syllable hurt to say, but for Finley, Colby had essentially agreed to put up with Ezra.

Finley's face lit up, "Yep! We're in!" The things Colby would do for his best friend.

Without even looking in Colby's direction or giving any indication of what he was doing, Ezra placed his hand on Colby's thigh. He could feel the heat rush to his cheeks as Ezra tightened his grip.

He already knew he was going to do something really dumb tonight.

CHAPTER SIX
Something with Benefits

The four boys had been sitting in the pizzeria for approximately ten minutes. During that time, Colby had been in agony. Ezra wouldn't release his thigh, no matter how much Colby would try and pry him off.

It was like Ezra was tormenting him. His thumb would rub circles on Colby's thigh, that was actually kind of nice. The problem was when Ezra's hand would start moving further up Colby's leg. At first, it only moved up a little bit, then some more, and then a little bit further. So close to his crown jewels yet so far. Not that it would be very appropriate behaviour for a restaurant, no matter how gross Gino's Italiano already was. The hand would mischievously wander until it would move back down to its original spot.

The cycle would repeat. His hand began to move higher up Colby's leg, then higher, then higher, and then higher again until Ezra was rubbing not-so-soothing circles on Colby's crotch.

Immediately, Colby grabbed Ezra's wrist and tried to get him off without signalling to Finley or Brent that something inappropriate might be happening under the table. Nothing he did could budge the sadistic boy next to him. Geez, he needed to start going to the gym again.

Why couldn't Ezra give him a nice massage? A little deep tissue massage, and maybe some scented oils or relaxing spa music.

Colby would abandon Operation Revenge immediately if Ezra apologised by becoming his personal masseuse.

What really pissed him off was Ezra's nonchalant attitude about it. He carried on with the conversation and didn't even look at Colby. He simply sat there with one hidden hand on Colby's thigh and the other holding a glass of coke.

He decided he couldn't just make this easy for Ezra to do this to him. As subtly as possible, he shuffled closer to Ezra and began to give him the same treatment. At first, it was small suggestive actions: accidental brushes and light touches. Slowly, the actions became more intense. Ezra would accidentally stutter or completely freeze whenever Colby touched him. Colby even dared to unzip Ezra's fly, the metallic sound drowned out by the general hum of the restaurant.

Ezra didn't move, and he didn't answer the question Brent had asked him. Colby poked one finger under the material of his jeans. Was he wearing Calvin Klein underwear? Rich bitch. He ran his finger up the way and pulled against the waistband.

Coke was spilling across the table. Droplets were spilling over the side. The cup lay on its side in the centre of the table. Finally, he had gotten his attention, but he'd also gotten the entire restaurant's attention as well. Ezra stopped his movements on Colby's thigh and stopped talking as well. He stared at Colby, mouth gaping and his right hand still held high as if it was still holding his coke. Whoops, Colby may have gotten a bit too much of his attention.

"Ezra, you okay?" asked Brent.

Colby cursed himself under his breath. He was just trying to get even with Ezra, not get everyone's attention on him. Finley stared holes in Colby.

That horrible stare. So dark, so intense. Stop, Finley. Please. Finley knew too much and yet he didn't even know what had happened.

"I feel sick again!" Colby announced a bit too loudly as other customers were whispering among themselves about the weird teenage boys sitting in the back. Lowering his voice, he continued, "I didn't want to disturb the conversation so I tried to . . . signal to Ezra that I wasn't feeling good."

"What kind of signals?" Finley narrowed his eyes. Scary.

"Uh, you know . . . normal ones." Colby was starting to sweat under that burning stare.

"Maybe you should go home," said Brent with genuine concern in his voice.

Finley mouthed the word "bullshit" at Colby. Damn Finley and his ability to read Colby like a goddamn book.

He tried to think of a way to get out of this situation and make it up to Finley at the same time. He remembered Ezra had his car outside and he was Brent's ride home.

"You're right, Brent. I should go home. Ezra, take me home!" The other three boys just stared at Colby in disbelief.

"You want me to take you home?" asked Ezra, his hand slowly moving to zip up his pants. "Okay, let's go." He took Colby's hand and stood to leave.

Brent made an action to leave as well until Colby waved him down. "No, no, no, you two stay here and enjoy yourselves. Don't let me stop you."

"Oh, but . . ."

Colby didn't have time to listen to Brent's protest as Ezra rushed him out of the pizzeria. Gino Italiano gave them a mean look until he saw that Finley and Brent were still at the table. Clearly, just making sure someone was going to pay the bill. The bell above the door rang as they left. Now, Brent was stranded with no other choice but to rely on Finley for a ride home. The romantic potential of a car ride with two people stuck together. Finley was going to be so grateful. Colby surprised himself with his own genius sometimes.

The car park was devoid of life. There was the odd car here and there, but there was no one outside. When they got to the car, Ezra pushed Colby up against the passenger door and kissed him. It was surprisingly gentle at first. He felt Ezra nibble on his bottom lip and then swiped his tongue along it. Colby wrapped his arms around Ezra's neck and opened his mouth a little to give him more access. The kiss became more heated and passionate. With every movement, Colby became more entranced in what they were doing. Ezra's hands slipped around Colby's back. They slipped under his shirt and caressed the skin under there. Oh, maybe he was going to get that massage after all—until he heard the familiar ringing of the bell. He shoved Ezra away and whipped his head around to the pizzeria's entrance. Luckily, it wasn't Finley or Brent as Colby had feared. It was just Gino Italiano taking out the trash. His heart was beating so hard against his chest that he was afraid his ribs would shatter trying to contain it. He wasn't sure whether it was beating so fast because of the kiss or because of the scare. He tried to tell himself it was because of the latter.

He turned around and saw Ezra standing back from him, farther back than Colby had meant to shove him. His eyebrows were knitted together and he was scowling. Why did Colby feel guilty? Only a little bit. There was no way he'd feel bad about anything he did to Ezra, but still, the feeling was uncomfortable.

"Get in the car. I'll take you home already."

The car ride to Colby's house would've been completely silent if it wasn't for the softly playing radio in the background. Headlights flurried by in seconds as the evening light faded away and let the night take over.

He couldn't stand the silence anymore, so he asked the question that Finley had suggested earlier. "So"—he felt as though the air thickened as he tried to make conversation, shoving his words back into his throat—"did you get sent any pictures after the party on Sunday?"

Ezra's eyes never left the road as he answered, "Yeah, a couple. Why?"

The radio began to play a gentle love song by an artist Colby had never heard of. "Oh, you know, just wondering. Did you get any pictures of the two of us?"

A quick glance from Ezra was the most attention he gave to Colby. "No, I didn't get any of the two of us. Did you?"

"No, I didn't," he replied a little too quickly. "I just thought that since we were both there you might have got one."

Ezra only hummed at him in response. "Are you into me?"

What? The question took Colby by complete surprise. How was he supposed to respond to that? He couldn't deny it after the stuff he'd done with him. Operation Revenge required Colby to put on a convincing act of being madly in love with Ezra, but he wasn't sure in what way Ezra meant.

He definitely didn't romantically like him. He was a guy. He was Ezra! Never in a thousand years would he like him, but on the other hand, "Physically, I guess I'm into you." Half the lie, half the guilt.

"Oh, okay . . . let's do things together then. Physically." He paused and smiled for the first time in the past fifteen minutes. "Not that you haven't been already."

"Why do you make it sound like it's just me? You keep kissing me and you're the one who kept touching me at the pizzeria! You're the horny pervert here."

"Now, now. Let's not forget you started all of this by not only making out with me in the shower but then getting me off as well, which was very surprising by the way. And yes, I touched your thigh at the pizza place but you tried to get into my pants in front of our friends. I think you might be the horny pervert here."

When he put it like that, the horny pervert really was Colby. His face became flushed as he realised he had started this. Part of him wanted to bring up the picture from the party—Ezra looked dominant in that—but now he wondered whether he had started that too. When he got home, Colby needed to have a deep thinking about who he was as a person. Was that all he was now? A horny pervert? Oh, how the mighty had fallen.

"What are you suggesting then?" Colby asked.

"Friends with benefits, obviously."

"We're not fucking friends, dickhead."

"Really? That's the part you have a problem with." He ran a hand through his golden hair. "Alright . . . sexual partners."

"Partners? We're not playing tennis together."

"Fuck buddies, then."

"Same problem as friends with benefits. I'm not your friend or your buddy."

"Jesus Christ. Do you want to have sex with me or not?"

He hadn't expected him to ask so bluntly. Did he want this? From his actions over the past couple of days, he figured he must. "Okay" was the best response he could muster.

"Okay then. You can come round mine Friday night."

"This Friday? Before the training camp?" That was soon. That was very, very soon. He needed more time to mentally prepare for this. Whatever *this* was going to be.

Colby was too deep in his thoughts to notice Ezra's car finally coming to a stop outside his house.

"See you Friday." He smiled innocently at Colby, as if not even a minute ago he said he wanted to fuck. *He's a demon,* Colby thought.

"Yeah." His face was void of emotion as he tried to process what he'd just agreed to. "See ya."

Ezra closed the distance between them and placed a soft kiss on Colby's lips.

"I'm looking forward to it, but get of out my car already."

The cold night air came into the car as soon as Colby opened the door. He closed the door behind him and watched as Ezra drove away, the sound of the car growing fainter as the crickets chirping only grew louder.

He walked inside his house and went straight up to his room. He was going to have sex with Ezra on Friday.

Why did he do this to himself?

CHAPTER SEVEN
Sleeping with the Enemy

The rest of the week went quickly—a bit too quickly for Colby's liking. It was already Friday.

At a few points during the week, he had snuck off with Ezra to make good on their friends-with-benefits agreement. Most of the time, they would just make out after football in the locker room after everyone else was gone. Colby kept trying to rationalise all these times by calling them preparation for Friday night.

But all that preparation did nothing to cool his nerves when Friday rolled around. He had agreed to go to Ezra's house at eight o'clock sharp. School ended at three, which gave him a solid five hours to prepare.

As soon as he got home, he ran upstairs to his room and began to have a mental breakdown.

Why did he agree to this? Would Ezra make fun of him if he came first? What did you wear to fuck? Did you wear anything? Should he go shopping and buy some sexy underwear or something? Did he need to buy condoms? Lube? Should he shave? What parts did he shave? Should he drink some mango juice before he went?

He was getting so frustrated with himself for acting like an innocent virgin. He wasn't a virgin. Joanna had made sure of that. He had had sex before, so how hard could it be to do it with a guy?

Where there's a hole, there's a goal. Guys had fewer holes than girls, which might make it easier. That's when the true question came to him: Who's hole was the goal? Was he going to be the top or the bottom?

Finley had called him a bottom, and he was gay. Gays knew these kinds of things. After a few more minutes of panicking about his ass, he realised the best thing to do before any big test was to revise for it. He grabbed his laptop, went on incognito mode, and typed in "gay porn" for the very first time.

He clicked the first video that came up. It started with a strange plot about a guy who had broken his toilet and it was overflowing, so he called a plumber, but he was a really crappy plumber because he just ended up fucking the guy instead of fixing the toilet. Anyway, after the cringey porn acting was done, Colby watched every movement like a hawk, but mostly how the bottom behaved. He had to be prepared.

He analysed the way their hands touched each other, the way their bodies pressed together, and the way their breathing became short pants only ever interrupted by lustful moans. So far, it was pretty simple stuff but then the plumber began to finger the guy's ass.

Did that feel nice? he wondered, never really considering it before. *Would I enjoy it?*

He continued to watch the video, but the more he watched, the more he began to imagine himself and Ezra in that position— without a broken toilet exploding in the background, of course. Without even noticing he was doing it, he slipped his hand past the waistline of his jeans. Stroking himself at first but it wasn't enough so he undid the buckle, dove into his underwear, and grasped himself firmly. His breathing became uneven as the porn actors continued in the background.

He wondered what Ezra sounded like. Whether he moaned or groaned or panted. Whether his cheeks became flushed or whether he remained cool and steady. Whether he would be rough and aggressive or gentle and sweet. Colby couldn't decide which one he liked the sound most.

He fell back onto his bed, his hand still keeping a continuous rhythm on his dick. He closed his eyes and pictured Ezra that day in the showers—the way the water outlined his toned body and how his hair kept falling in front of his eyes, and yet he maintained a lustful gaze on Colby the entire time.

That fantasy alone brought Colby so close to his climax.

"Darling, I've got your washing—OH MY GOD!"

Immediately, he shot up and made eye contact with his poor mother. He screamed and she screamed back, dropping the washing on the floor. Both of them began to flail in panic.

"It's not what it looks like, Mom!" cried Colby, slamming down his laptop and trying to zip his pants back up.

"I don't know what it looks like! I didn't see anything!" his mother hollered back, spinning around in a circle with her hands up like a T-Rex. She ran out of the room, slamming the door behind her.

*   *   *

A few hours later, he was being driven to Ezra's house by his poor, poor mother.

"Now, you know I don't mind you doing things like that. You're my darling prince charming, and sexual urges are completely natural." She leaned over and pinched his cheek. "But at least lock the door before you give it a whack. For me."

"I will definitely remember to do that from now on, don't you worry." How mortifying. Part of him didn't even want to go to Ezra's anymore. He just wanted to crawl into a hole and die, but he couldn't back out now. He'd done too much prep. He'd douched! He researched and did it, and it was horrifying. A necessary evil. To think he'd douched for a douche, what was he even doing at this point? He couldn't even look at his mother right now. He was too ashamed.

"So, Ezra Dickinson, huh? I thought you didn't like him."

"I don't," he replied instantly without much thought.

"Then why are you staying the night at his place? Oh my God, don't tell me you're . . ."

Colby's heart stopped. Did she see his computer screen? He wasn't gay or anything. He and Ezra were just messing around. Even if he was gay, he wouldn't be gay for Ezra of all people. The gay porn was for educational purposes. Educational!

All of a sudden, the car veered to the left, straight into a lay-by area. His mother turned off the engine, turned to her son, and grasped the sides of his face. Her bleached blonde hair flew wildly around her face. Colby had no choice but to look at her now—and she looked furious.

"Colby, be honest with me now. Is that boy"—she paused and inhaled sharply—"Is that boy peer pressuring you?"

"What?"

She spoke slower this time as if his hearing was the thing confusing him and not her words. "Is that boy peer pressuring you to do illegal substances? Be honest, my love. I'm not going to judge you. We've all done the devil's lettuce at some point. Lord knows I have, but I don't want some other boy making you do it."

"No, Mom. That's not what's happening here."

Colby's mom never tended to jump to conclusions. Instead, she jumped in a catapult and flung herself a thousand kilometres per hour at the most unlikely possibility. The fact that she'd done weed didn't surprise him in the least.

"Oh my God, is it worse than that? It's meth! He's making you do meth, isn't he? Right, that's it, I'm turning around and going home."

"No, Mom! He isn't making me do drugs! We're just having a sleepover alright. Drug-free."

60

"Why would you have a sleepover with him if you don't like him?" She let go of his face now and looked confused. Why was she acting like he was confused? She was the confused one!

Colby's cheeks heated up a little at the question. "I guess I don't completely hate him. We've grown a lot . . . closer recently. Plus, he's driving me to football camp tomorrow at the ass crack of dawn, so you don't have to."

"That is very nice of him. Okay, let's go." She pulled back into the road and carried on to Ezra's house as if she didn't just accuse him of pressuring Colby to do meth.

*   *   *

Colby must have stood in front of Ezra's front door for at least ten minutes. His mom had driven off a while ago, so there was no going back. He just had to knock and . . . get at it, he supposed.

He hadn't expected Ezra's house to be so big and grand. It was one Lamborghini away from being dubbed a mansion. The walls were large beige stones that contrasted with the white roof and door. There was a wooden canopy over the front door to cover a porch with a rocking swing on it and all the windows were surrounded by white varnished wood that had intricate shapes and designs carved into it. Maybe he shouldn't have been so surprised that perfect boy Ezra lived a perfect life in a perfect house. What a dick.

He knew he was only stalling for time by focusing on all the details of Ezra's house. This time he would knock. He raised his fist, held it there, then put it down again. Was he having second thoughts? He wasn't really sure. He just felt weird inside. His muscles were tense and his stomach was doing backflips.

Once he went inside, there really wasn't much going back to his usual relationship with Ezra. Making out with Ezra and giving him a handjob, he could wave that off as spur of the moment. But purposefully coming to his house to have sex with him, that wasn't as easily explained away.

Before Colby could ponder the question any longer, the door flew open on its own. Colby was greeted by Ezra scowling at him. How were Ezra and Colby both dressed casually and yet Colby still felt underdressed? Ezra's ensemble of a grey hoodie with cropped sleeves at the shoulders and baggy black sweatpants was somehow stylish and attractive. Now Colby definitely didn't feel sexy enough in his loose red hoodie, jeans, and his Thomas the Tank Engine sports bag.

"You have been standing there for fifteen minutes. Are you coming in or not?" spat Ezra. He leaned against the doorframe with his arms crossed.

Colby was finding it rather hard to concentrate on anything other than those black sweatpants right now. "You knew I was here?" he asked, not breaking eye contact with Ezra's crotch.

"I was watching you from the window, but now you're just pissing me off." He turned and went inside, forcing Colby's eyes to go from his crotch to his ass. "Are you coming in, or are you going to call Mommy to come and pick you up?"

That got Colby's attention back. "You know what, asshole. Maybe if you were a better host, I'd actually want to come in."

Ezra didn't respond. He just kept walking deeper into the house.

"Wait up!" Colby said. The house was much colder inside and made Colby grateful that he'd chosen to wear his comfy jumper. It was also much grander inside, with a massive staircase in the hall that curved its way up to the second floor. The floor was marbled and the walls were decorated with pieces of original art. To sum the place up in word one: pretentious. Perfect for Ezra.

Ezra led him to a sitting room that took Colby's breath away almost as much as Ezra's sweatpants had. For starters, it had a huge plasma screen TV mounted on the wall, and underneath it was a fireplace. Facing it was a burgundy sofa with teddy bear blankets on it. Across the far wall were endless shelves of DVDs and books. The lamps by the sofa were made from driftwood. Just like the outside of the house, it was perfect. Perfect, but it almost felt like no one really lived here. It was too organised, too perfect, like no one ever used it. The closer he got to the DVDs and books, the more he could see the dust resting on every single one of them.

"Do you live alone?" He found himself asking. Immediately he regretted the question. Just because Ezra had invited him round didn't mean they were close friends all of a sudden. This was basically just a booty call.

"No, my dad lives here too. Pizza or Chinese?"

"What?"

"For dinner. What, you thought I was going to let you starve? Pick a movie while you're at it."

Huh? Dinner? Movie? What was this? A date? "Um, I'll have a chicken chow mein then, please. And yeah, you would totally do something like let me starve. Don't try and act all nice to me. I see right through you."

That made Ezra smile. Did he think Colby was joking? Colby didn't joke, not when food was on the line. Ezra left the room for a while leaving Colby to pick what they were going to watch.

He debated putting on something to set the mood like Fifty Shades of Grey, but he got embarrassed just thinking about it, so he wasn't sure he'd survive the entire movie. Action movies—as much as Colby would enjoy them—weren't exactly the sexiest movies to watch, unless some people got off on watching muscular actors run around all sweaty in torn clothing . . . okay, Colby understood the appeal. He couldn't watch a kids' film. That would be wrong. On the lowest shelf was Halloween. A horror movie would give them a good excuse to get close together. Did Colby want to be close to him?

It was the best of a bad bunch. It was the reasoning he gave himself in the end. He heard Ezra's footsteps come up behind him.

"Have you picked something yet, or do you need help reading the big words?"

"Excuse you, dickhead, I have—" Colby turned to face him, but didn't realise how close Ezra had come to him. Their faces were only inches apart and Ezra was slowly closing that gap.

"You have what, Colby?" he said in a husky tone, coming closer and closer. Ezra placed his hands on the shelves next to either side of Colby's head, trapping him there. It was just like that stupid photo all over again, Colby realised.

Just when their lips were about to touch, Ezra moved to Colby's ear and whispered, "Halloween's a pretty crappy movie."

"You're a crappy movie," said Colby. His cheeks were as red as his hoodie and his eyes were downcast at the floor.

Once again, Ezra looked like he was leaning in for an actual kiss. Then, he snatched the DVD from Colby's hand and walked away.

"You, asshole!" Colby exclaimed. Stupid Ezra with his stupid smug face and his stupid sweatpants.

Ezra simply turned and looked innocently at him. "What? I didn't do anything. Were you expecting me to?"

Colby threw himself on the sofa, bouncing up as soon as he hit the soft cushions. He crossed his arms and legs in a huff and refused to look at Ezra as he put the DVD in. Ezra ignored him right back. That wasn't fair! Colby was ignoring him, not the other way around.

"I don't even want to let you in my pants anymore," said Colby. "You're too much of a dick and I've come to the realisation that I am completely out of your league."

"But you *did want* me in your pants?"

"That's not what I meant!"

Ezra put on the movie and sat on the opposite end of the sofa as Colby. They didn't touch, they didn't speak, and they didn't even look at each other.

The movie had been on for about twenty minutes, but Colby couldn't even focus on it. Why wasn't Ezra moving over? Every second, he was glancing over at Ezra, but he didn't get the same treatment back. Ezra was just lying there, not even sitting anymore. Apparently, his side of the sofa was also a recliner so he was just lounging there whilst Colby's rage festered. Michael Myers had just escaped from the mental hospital and was stalking some chick when Colby finally decided to take matters into his own hands.

"Ezra, look over there!" Colby pointed to a random spot behind the sofa.

The moron looked. It was the perfect distraction, a classic that would never grow old.

As quietly as Colby possibly could, he shuffled towards Ezra's side of the sofa. The sofa's padding crunched under him as he moved, but the girl screaming bloody murder on screen was enough to cover the sound. Was this film always so gruesome? Not that Colby was frightened or anything, but that was a lot of blood. So much blood. Everywhere.

"Colby, I can't see anything over there. Was it a spider or something?"

Colby didn't respond to any of Ezra's questions. He was too absorbed in watching the senseless violence on screen. It was awful to look at, and yet Colby couldn't tear his eyes away. All those horny teenagers getting brutally murdered for having sex before marriage. What if Michael Myers came after him tonight because he was planning on having premarital sex with Ezra? Was he going to die tonight?

"Colby? Are you okay? You look kinda pale."

A large hand placed itself on Colby's shoulder, its awful weight bearing down upon him. A killer's presence behind him, ready to strike.

Colby screamed. He screamed so loud that he terrified Ezra.

"What?" Ezra said. "What happened? What's wrong?"

Was it Ezra's hand that had touched his shoulder, and not some serial killer? Colby took deep breaths to calm himself. His heart, his poor heart felt ready to explode. It thundered in his chest and in his ears. How embarrassing. He came here to get laid, not laid to rest.

"Nothing's wrong. Just . . . um . . . enjoying the movie." A half-dressed teenage boy got slaughtered on screen for—once again—trying to have sex. Oh God, that could be him.

"Enjoying the movie? Colby . . ." Ezra reached out to place a hand on Colby's thigh. Colby flinched, ready to scream again. "Okay, no touching. You know what, this is a really crappy movie. I'm changing it to something else."

"No, you don't need to. It's fine. I love horror movies. All the blood, gore, and guts. Love it and . . . oh my god, is that his brain?" Colby slapped his hands over his eyes. Hopefully, when he would open his eyes again, the movie would be finished.

There was no sound—no screaming girls and boys and no weird sound effects made to sound like a knife swinging around, just the sound of Ezra moving around the room and the whirring of the DVD player.

"What are you doing?" Colby called with his eyes firmly shut.

"I'm not watching Halloween," replied Ezra. "I think it's too scary."

"Ha! You're such a pussy." There was no reply. "Ezra? Are you still there? Ezra, please say something?"

The space beside him dipped. "You ever watched Paddington?"

Colby peeked through his fingers at Ezra. "No. Is it another horror film? Not that I don't want to watch one or anything. Is it though? Not that I care. Is it?"

Ezra nodded. "Oh yeah, it's about this terrifying bear-alien hybrid that goes around London, sneaks its way into people's homes, and then eats them as they sleep."

"Shit. Shit. Shit. Shit. Shit," Colby repeatedly muttered under his breath.

"I'm kidding. I'm kidding. It's a family film. No horror, all fluff, okay?"

"Okay."

True to his word, the movie was soft and funny. Instead of his heart being about to burst from fright, it was about to burst from the wholesome fun on the screen. There was a bear that wore clothes and ate marmalade living in London, how cute was that? Although, Ezra and Colby still weren't touching.

What if Colby pretended to yawn, then put his arms around . . . ?

Ezra yawned, his arms stretching up in the air. Colby was about to tell him to shut the fuck up, but then a strange thing happened. Ezra's arm wrapped itself around Colby's shoulders and pulled him close.

Then an even stranger thing happened. When Colby looked up to ask what Ezra was doing, he found Ezra looked rather bashful. Ezra swiftly averted his gaze and shyly looked towards the DVD and CD wall as if he'd been doing it the entire time. Was he always this cute?

Colby turned himself on his side and rested his head on Ezra's shoulder. No wonder Ezra had bagsied the reclining part of the sofa, it was great. The movie was good, but the most entertaining thing of the night was teasing reactions out of Ezra. Any extra physical contact that Ezra received would cause him to twitch or blush or try and get more touchy-feely with Colby. It was nice. It was really nice.

Perhaps tonight wouldn't be so scary after all.

CHAPTER EIGHT
Gentle

Whatever Colby had thought a few hours ago about tonight not being that scary, no, he was wrong. Dead wrong.

There weren't any serial killers in scary masks running about the place, Colby had made sure of that. He'd meticulously watched as Ezra locked and bolted both the front and back door, closed all the windows, and checked inside Ezra's ridiculously oversized wardrobe. No need to fear killers tonight, only the crushing fear to perform.

Eleven o'clock eventually rolled around and Colby was sitting on Ezra's bed, even though he knew they weren't going to sleep anytime soon. He was still wearing his jumper and jeans, although he was debating whether he should take them off yet or wait for Ezra to do it.

He'd never felt this nervous before, not even when it was his first time. Technically, this was a first time, but not *the* first time, and he was internally rambling now. He could hear his heart racing in his ears and every muscle in his body was tense. He wasn't even naked yet and he already felt exposed. Every insecurity he had about his body suddenly seemed huge and ugly. He could almost picture the disgusted face Ezra would make when he saw Colby's body.

He just needed to chill and collect himself before Ezra finally came in. Colby had asked him for a cup of water to buy him some time to calm his tits.

He could hear the stairs creaking underneath Ezra's feet as he was coming back upstairs. *Shit!* He couldn't even bring himself to look at the door when it finally opened. He just stared out the window onto the moonlit street, listening to the rustling of Ezra's movements. The moonlight was the only thing lighting the room, casting all the furniture and even Ezra himself in an ethereal silver glow.

He felt the bed dip behind him, and a warm hand rested on his shoulder. Chills rushed up his spine and his jaw clenched.

"Colby," Ezra said in a hushed tone, "if you don't want to do this, it's fine."

Why did this asshole have to be so nice about it? Since when was this asshole even so nice?

"I do want to do it," Colby whispered. His hands turned into fists as he grabbed the royal blue bed sheets. "It's just . . . this is my first time with a guy is all. Too bad it had to be you."

He heard a faint chuckle escape Ezra's lips. "Yeah, that's too bad." Ezra leaned forward and began to place kisses down Colby's neck. Colby moaned a little when Ezra hit a spot right next to his throat. Colby could feel Ezra's smile on his skin as he whispered to him, "I promise I'll be gentle."

Those words put Colby's mind at ease, but his body was still tight and tense. Colby turned his head so he could capture Ezra's lips with his own. It started as small pecks until Ezra's tongue invaded its way into Colby's mouth. Colby was sure that once the pair of them got going, then Colby would take control, that he would want to. The part of him that wanted to prove a point, to get revenge became small and insignificant to the majority of Colby's mind that enjoyed the pleasure of being touched and held by Ezra. He didn't do any silly fight for dominance. If Ezra wanted to take the lead, then Colby would allow it for tonight.

Ezra lightly tugged at the hem of Colby's hoodie, a wordless way of asking for permission to take it off. Colby reached down and dropped it to the floor. The shirt that he was wearing underneath became entangled and came off with it. With a firm hand, Ezra pushed Colby to lie down on the bed, never once breaking the kiss with him.

For a while they lay on top of each other, kissing. Their erections pressed together through the cloth of their clothes. Ezra began to grind his erection into Colby's. Colby wrapped his arms around Ezra's neck in an attempt to bring their bodies even closer, but it wasn't enough for either of them.

His hands trembled as he reached down to take off Ezra's shirt. The fabric shivered from his own movements, and he tried to grip it tighter to steady his hands. It was strange, taking the shirt off of the guy he'd hated. Perhaps Ezra noticed his apprehension, so he took Colby's hands from his shirt and took them to his face. He kissed Colby's palms and for some reason the action caused Colby to tremble more, but not in the same way he was before. He felt the softness of Ezra's face and the faintest scratch of a stubble that was cut down recently. He was almost flattered that Ezra might've nervously prepared and groomed himself as much as Colby had.

Ezra took off his own shirt and it disappeared beyond the borders of the bed.

He took Colby's trembling hands again and placed them upon his now bare chest. Colby had wondered before he came, whether he would have any enjoyment in a guy's chest. He was quite the boob man and struggled to see what was the appeal of a man's body. It turned out through his scientific groping of Ezra's chest, that there was much to appreciate about the male form.

There was something so soft yet firm about his chest. It was mesmerising in the strangest way. It was so dissimilar to the smooth skin and fluffy padding of Joanna's breasts. Ezra was an athlete and appropriately built like one. Colby stroked those muscles, which were so hard from persistent training, and enjoyed the feeling. He was bewitched by them. He ran his tongue down the centre of Ezra's chest just to experience them in a different way. He could've admired the curves and dips of Ezra's chest for the rest of the night, although Ezra probably wouldn't find quite the same enjoyment in it as Colby did.

Ezra's hands slipped down to Colby's waistline, and he tugged at the front of his jeans. He took the belt buckle into his grasp and glanced up at Colby. Colby nodded his head in approval, making Ezra smile with anticipation.

Without wasting a second, he undid the buckle and threw it away with an almost theatrical flourish. He tore off Colby's jeans and then the boxer briefs he was wearing. Colby shivered as his aching erection was exposed to the cold temperature of Ezra's room. There was nothing left to hide Colby's naked form from Ezra's gaze. He was truly exposed to Ezra, wearing nothing but a crimson blush.

Ezra reached into the drawer of his bedside table and retrieved a bottle of lube. He poured some onto his fingers and spread Colby's legs apart. Colby was none too familiar with gay sex, but when it was him having his legs spread wide, the experience became so alien to him that he had no idea what to do next.

He gasped at the sudden intrusion. The feeling became even stranger as Ezra began to move his finger. It took a minute for Colby's body to adjust before Ezra added in a second and then a third. Colby was still unsure of what to make of it. The feeling was so unfamiliar to him, but it was pleasurable too in a way he didn't want to think too much about. Ezra toyed with Colby, and if Colby's loud moan and the arching of his back were any indicator, he was doing a good job of it.

"You're beautiful."

Colby was sure he had heard Ezra say that to him. He could've sworn on his own mother's life that he had whispered it to him, but when he looked at Ezra, his head was facing down and he was acting as if he hadn't said anything at all. Did Colby imagine it?

Ezra pulled out his fingers and positioned himself in between Colby's thighs. He slid on a condom and lubed his dick. Colby had tried to prepare himself for this exact moment, but now that it was happening, he was kinda scared. Would Ezra laugh if he told him that?

Ezra began to push himself in, and it hurt like a bitch. Colby was beginning to panic now. He felt tears pricking at his eyes. He was so embarrassed of himself as he felt one roll down his cheek. He had never cried during sex and he'd never cried in front of Ezra. Now the two had come together and it was so humiliating.

Ezra stopped what he was doing and stared at Colby in bewilderment before he leaned in and took his face in his hands. "What's wrong? If it hurts, I can go slower or we can just stop?" He wiped Colby's tears away.

Colby was taken back by the genuine concern in his voice. "No, don't stop just . . ." He didn't know how to express his feelings.

"Just?"

"Just . . ." They were nothing more than fuckbuddies, so Colby knew he had no right to ask for this but, "Could you just hold my hand while you do it." He regretted saying it. He was never going to live this down.

Ezra looked like a deer caught in headlights for a second or two, shocked Colby would actually ask him for something like that. He did more than what Colby asked for. He repositioned himself between his legs, wrapped one arm around his waist and the other held his hand. He also pressed his forehead against Colby's, gazing into each other's eyes.

"Better?" Ezra asked.

Colby nodded, too embarrassed to speak.

Slowly, he pushed his way inside Colby, and the pain from earlier intensified. More hot tears fell down his cheeks as he screwed his eyes shut. It wasn't that it was particularly painful anymore; he was simply nervous and fully exposed in front of the last person he thought he would be.

"You need to relax more, Colby. Your body's too tense." Any other time Colby would've punched him for such obvious advice, but he wasn't wrong.

Ezra kept pushing himself in, and Colby silently cursed his stupidly big dick. If Ezra had a micro penis like Colby always thought he did, then they needn't be so much shoving in. He couldn't understand why people found this pleasurable until Ezra started thrusting into him. Colby had never experienced such waves of sexual euphoria before. All he could do was try and meet Ezra's quickening thrusts and cry out his name. The cold temperature didn't bother him anymore, for he felt like his body was on fire. His body was burning with every thrust and every touch Ezra gave him. He wrapped his legs around Ezra's waist and clung to him.

All he could hear was Ezra's panting and groaning and the colliding of skin. He couldn't understand how it had gone from so painful to so pleasurable, or how his hips suddenly had a mind of their own as they bucked for Ezra.

He opened his teary eyes to look at Ezra's face. How was he still so handsome right now? Colby was sure he was a sweaty, blushing mess. Ezra's blond hair was wild and his eyes were focused on Colby, never looking at anything else, not even for a second. His mouth was open slightly as he panted and murmured "fuck" every now and then. Colby wanted to kiss him. He *really* wanted to kiss him.

Colby captured his lips in a passionate kiss before anything could be said between them. It was the most intimate kiss the pair had ever had, and it was enough for Colby to climax. He cried out in ecstasy and moaned Ezra's name as his vision turned white and a warm liquid shot across his stomach.

He heard Ezra groan loudly until he fell on top of him and they lay entangled with each other in a sweaty heap for a few minutes as they tried to catch their breaths. Ezra buried his head in the crook of Colby's neck and tenderly kissed it. Eventually, he rolled off of him but refused to let go of his hand. He chucked the filled condom in the bin.

Colby's legs were trembling. Maybe this wasn't the best thing to do before a training weekend, but it had felt too good to stop at any time. But how could he say no when Ezra looked him in the eye and asked "Again?"

*   *   *

He didn't remember falling asleep or going under the blanket of Ezra's bed, and yet there he was. He was also wrapped tightly in Ezra's arms in the position of the little spoon. That kinda pissed him off. Sure, he'd been the bottom last night, but that did not mean he was a good little submissive boy now. Not even a little bit.

He tried to roll away, but Ezra just tightened his grip on him.

"Ezra, you fat ass, let go of me!" He struggled and squirmed in Ezra's anaconda-like grip.

"Can't you just let me sleep for a bit longer? You're so loud." Ezra pulled Colby even closer so his face was buried in Colby's hair. "How are you feeling?"

Colby's face immediately heated up as he remembered how he cried last night. He was waiting for Ezra to make fun of him for it. "I feel fine," he snapped. "You know we still gotta go to the training camp."

"Crap." Ezra's limbs released Colby as he looked at the clock next to his bed. "We've got about half an hour till we need to leave, so get dressed and I'll make breakfast. You're welcome to use the shower by the way." He chucked on some grey sweatpants and left.

Colby stayed in bed for a few more minutes before he decided to move. However, he wasn't prepared for his legs to buckle from just one step. His body crumpled onto the floor, and it trembled at the impact.

Ezra rushed back into the room and kneeled at Colby's side. How many times was he going to embarrass himself in front of Ezra?

"Are you okay?" Ezra asked. He placed his hands on Colby's shoulders and brought him to a sitting position.

"I'm fine." Colby swatted his hands away like they were annoying mosquitos. "Or at least I would be if you hadn't wanted to go multiple rounds last night. My ass hurts! If I'm shit during training today you cannot yell at me one bit 'cos this is your fault."

Ezra just laughed at Colby's complaining. "Are you asking for special treatment from me now?"

"Nope. Why would I want special treatment from a horny bastard like you?"

"If I recall correctly, I wasn't the only one wanting more last night, or have you forgotten the way you were moaning last night? *'Oh, Ezra! Harder! Don't stop!'*"

"Shut up! Go make me breakfast already, asshole." With that, Colby got to his feet and stormed into the bathroom on pure willpower alone. He really shouldn't have done so many times last night, before training as well. He was going to die.

CHAPTER NINE
Too Good to be True

Colby and Ezra arrived as the sun began to rise over the horizon, which essentially meant it was too fucking early to be here. If Finley hadn't guilted him into coming, he would've been asleep in a big warm bed right now.

He'd managed to get another hour or so of sleep as Ezra had driven them the entire way. No work for Colby this morning, benefit of bottoming. It was very kind of Ezra, uncharacteristically kind of him. Colby was suspicious, and his suspicions came true when Ezra pulled into the side of the road ten minutes away from camp and slammed his lips onto Colby's.

Colby's mind was still half asleep, but his aching erection told him his body was wide awake. Colby undid his seatbelt and swung his body over the central parting so he was sitting on Ezra's lap. It was heated and rough compared to last night, but Colby didn't really mind. He began to grind his hips on Ezra's hard-on, getting some lustful groans from him in the process.

"Colby," he panted.

Not a second was wasted as Colby released both their dicks from their pants and began to pump them together. The heat radiating off of Ezra's dick only excited him more. It was pure carnal lust that swallowed them both. They didn't even care if somebody they knew drove by and saw them.

Colby could feel the pressure building in him. He tore away from the kiss—which was hard to do since Ezra's mouth kept chasing after him—and erupted into a panting, moaning mess. Ezra followed soon after. Resting his head on Ezra's shoulder, he had to take a few minutes to catch his breath.

By the time they'd both finished, the windows of the car were fogged up. Colby was tempted to run his hand down the window like in that scene in Titanic. Eventually, he moved back into his seat and they were arriving at camp.

*   *   *

The camp was as shit as Colby had expected it to be, maybe more so. He'd never been big on camping of any sort, so being stuck in a tiny room with two bunk beds and the only sort of privacy he could get was the thin curtain that he could pull around the bed was hellish to him, not forgetting the strange damp smell in the room and the way the mattresses looked like a bedbug's wet dream. But it didn't end there. There were three communal bathrooms that were freezing, coated in dust and spiderwebs, and the water that came out of the taps was brown. Then came the fact that he had to play football all fucking day.

He loved football. He really did, sometimes. However, he didn't love it this much.

As soon as they were spotted by Coach Clain, they were ordered to get changed into their kit and get on the field for warm-ups. Apparently, they were some of the first to arrive, which meant Finley wasn't here yet, causing Colby to be even more miserable than before.

Finley showed up an hour later with a goofy grin on his face that Colby was about to slap off.

"Where have you been, young man?" Colby screamed, getting the attention of the rest of the team. They only gave him a quick glance, being pretty used to Colby's loud nature.

"Woah, sorry, man." Finley raised his hands in defense. "I didn't expect you to be here so early, so I came late. How are you so early? Is your mom feeling alright 'cos this isn't like her at all? Seriously, man, is Jemma okay?"

"She's fine. Ezra gave me a ride here," he mumbled.

"I'm sorry, what? You? And Ezra? In the same car? Without killing each other? Nah, you're fucking with me, man."

Colby stayed quiet.

"Wait! Like for real? Wow, since when were you two best buds?"

"We're not best buds! He just offered me a ride, so I took it. Is there something wrong with that?"

"No, I'm just . . . surprised. You two have been weird with each other lately, but I thought it was because of your whole Operation Revenge shit."

"Oh yeah, that. I'm rethinking all that a little bit, but we're still not friends!"

"Whatever you say, man."

Finley teased him about it for the rest of the day. Any opportunity to call Ezra Colby's BFF, he would. He'd give Colby a nudge or a wink whenever Ezra would look over at him and make kissing noises when Ezra would subtly—not subtly—go out of his way to talk to Colby.

Colby had never truly considered murder till this day.

Football dragged on for what felt like years to Colby. His ass was beginning to really hurt. Why did he think coming here was a good idea? He kept trying to power through the pain, but it was not working. All he got for his trouble was a limp and another reason for Finley to poke fun at him. He just wanted the day to be over so bad.

They took a brief break for lunch, but the food was terrible. Hungry, tired, and sore turned out to be the worst combination. Finally, practice came to an end for the day, and

Colby went to their stupidly small room with the stupidly uncomfortable beds.

Every muscle in his body simultaneously gave up as he collapsed onto a bottom bunk. He had no energy to try and claim a top one. He didn't even have the energy to sort his bedding out. His face was just lying there on the filthy mattress with strange yellow stains on it. Okay, maybe he should sort out his bedding first, then lie down.

He heard the door open when he was about to start setting up his bed.

"How are you feeling?"

"How am I feeling since football, or how am I feeling since you rammed your dick up my ass multiple times?" He couldn't be bothered to get up and face Ezra, so he stayed lying down on the bed.

"Both, I suppose."

"I'm alright. This place just fucking sucks."

"Stand up for a sec."

He wasn't sure what possessed him to do what Ezra said. Any other time and it would've ended in bloodshed, but Colby was way too exhausted to put up any sort of fight. He allowed Ezra to pull him to his feet and watched as he set up his bed for him. Why was Ezra being so nice? It was getting scary.

Not scary enough to tell him to stop doing things that helped Colby. As soon as Ezra was finished putting on Colby's bed sheet, pillow cover, and blanket, Colby flopped down onto the bed again. It smelled like home probably because his dad had washed it with the same detergent they used for all of their other washing. He hadn't really noticed it was a nice smell until he was away from home . . . Colby might be a little homesick.

He heard Ezra's feet shuffle across the carpet towards his bed. The mattress sank near Colby's leg.

"I'm not really in the mood to do anything right now." Damn, he didn't think he'd miss home so much. He was used to a certain level of luxury—his dad making him edible meals, having a warm bed to sleep in, and his mom being . . . his mom. Ugh, he wanted to go home.

"That's good. Neither am I." And yet Ezra moved further onto the bed until he was spooning Colby from behind. He pulled the curtain around the bed to hide them away from any unwanted eyes. It was nice. The warmth that came from Ezra's body made up for the severe lack of heating in the room, and the curtain made it feel like they were in their own little world.

"Do friends with benefits usually cuddle?" asked Colby.

"Oh, are we finally friends now?" replied Ezra who had begun to absentmindedly run a hand through Colby's hair whilst massaging his lower back with the other. Colby knew this day was coming. He officially had his own personal masseuse. That was the goal of Operation Revenge, right? Probably. His sleep-deprived brain couldn't remember.

"You know what I mean. I don't think they're supposed to be as gentle as you are either," he whispered the last bit, a little embarrassed he'd said it at all.

"Do you not like that I'm gentle?"

"No, I like it. It's just—not what I was expecting, I guess. I was more anticipating the rough quick fuck in the boy's bathroom or something. No extra touching if it wasn't necessary. Down and dirty. Pretend you don't know each other when you pass by in public. That's what happened to my friend on the hockey team anyway."

Ezra laughed at Colby's wild ideas. "I'm not really the type to do that. Well, I'm not the type to really do friends with benefits either."

"What does that mean? I'm special, so I get no strings attached?"

"Colby, listen." Ezra sat up. "About this whole arrangement we've got going. I—"

81

Whatever Ezra was about to say was cut off by Finley and Brent barging into the room, laughing with each other.

"Colby? You in here, man?" Finley asked.

"Yep!" Colby responded back before Finley could pull the curtains back. "I'm tired, so I'm just gonna crash here for a bit."

"Don't push yourself if you're tired, man. You seen Ezra? Coach is looking for him. Says it's urgent."

"Um." Colby looked up at Ezra, who stared straight back down at him, smiling. "Nope, haven't seen him anywhere. I'll tell you if I do though." Ezra covered his mouth to hide his laughing. What a doofus.

Maybe it was how tired Colby was or how Ezra looked kinda handsome in the dim light, but he leant up for a kiss. It seemed to catch Ezra by surprise for a moment. Damn, maybe Colby was in the mood.

It was amazing until Finley interrupted the moment, "Colby, why you got a Thomas the Tank Engine bag?"

Colby had to break the kiss to answer. "My asshole of a cat pissed in my normal bag, so my mom had to go out and get me a new one and she chose that. I told her it was for kids but then she said that I'm always going to be her baby boy, so I should shut my yap and stop complaining." Just thinking of his mother's logic—or lack thereof—gave him a headache.

"Your mom sounds like quite the character." Laughed Brent.

"That's one of her more normal moments," Colby replied.

"Alright, we should probably keep looking for Ezra then," Brent said. "Give us a shout if you see him."

"Will do." The door slammed as they left the room.

If Brent and Ezra weren't there, then Colby would've maliciously made fun of Finley for laughing like a schoolgirl around Brent. Oh, he could imagine all the awkward flirting and clumsy moves Finley was trying to pull. He had to try and get it on camera at some point. He'd never let Finley live it down! In the nicest way possible.

"I should probably go," Ezra whispered. He said it so quietly as if he was afraid to break the peace he and Colby were under.

Colby just nodded in response before leaning in for one last kiss. He was secretly beginning to enjoy kissing Ezra, not that he'd ever tell him that. Didn't need to boost the guy's ego anymore.

Once Ezra had gone and the warmth of his body had brought left with him, Colby decided to sleep. The sooner this weekend was over, the better.

The next day was roughly the same. They were all up too early playing way too much football and getting really shit food during breaks. By lunch, Colby was starving, but the unidentifiable food they were given quickly suppressed his appetite. He wondered whether he could convince Ezra to leave camp early with him. They could go hang out somewhere or catch a movie, not in a date kind of way. Definitely not. They would hang out in a bro kind of way, definitely not a date. A bro-date—a brate. But if he wanted to go hang out in a bro way, why wasn't he asking Finley to ditch with him instead? Finley was way more likely to agree, but he wanted to spend more time with Ezra. Why Ezra?

That was enough thinking for today.

Finley and Sophie came and sat with him. Finley was gushing to them about Brent, so at least one of them was enjoying this camp from hell. Sophie looked quite cute in her little green cheerleading outfit, and her hair was tied up in the tightest ponytail Colby had ever seen. Her hair must've been made of steel to withstand how hard it was pulled back. It wasn't just Sophie though. That's how all the cheerleaders had their hair tied up with a big bow to top it off.

"I think I'm going to ask Ezra out," Sophie said. "If that's alright with you, Colby."

She was going to what? Why was she going to ask out Ezra? Sure, she'd mentioned something about liking him a couple of days ago, but now she was going to ask him out?

"Don't you think it's a little soon, Soph? I mean do you guys even talk that much?"

"I knew it would bother you."

What was that supposed to mean? Colby could feel himself getting worked up about it. It wasn't a big deal. He knew that. Something about the whole thing though was so . . . frustrating. "I'm not bothered by anything, especially anything to do with fucking Ezra. You wanna ask him out? Fine. Be my guest. But don't be surprised when he says no 'cos he's an asshole."

"Maybe to you, but I think he's really sweet. And yes, we have been talking more recently. He even offered to give me a lift to camp, but I had to turn him down because I was already going with Jessica. She's the one who's encouraging me to ask him out. She says we'd make the perfect couple."

That hurt more than Colby expected it to. Ezra had offered to drive Sophie first? Was he planning on having sex with her as well?

Sophie continued, "Listen, I don't want anything to ruin our friendship, Colby, but I think I really like him and some people have said"—she twirled her fingers through her ponytail and cast her eyes to the floor—"that he likes me too."

"He doesn't!" Colby said way too loudly. "I mean, I don't think he does. Come on, Soph. He'd shag anything with a heartbeat. You deserve better than that."

She gave him a strange, almost pitiful look.

"It doesn't bother me. It doesn't! Why would this bother me? You and Ezra could make a cute couple. Of course, you could. But just because you could doesn't mean you should. Right?"

"I'm sorry, Colby," said Sophie. "If it bothers you, just say the word and I'll—"

"It doesn't. Why does everyone seem to think it bothers me? I'm fine. You . . . you should ask him out. You two would be great together."

"Really? You think so?"

"Yep, yep, yep. You should do it." He felt hot and dizzy all of a sudden. A sharp ache in his stomach and a headache quickly came upon him. When would this stupid fucking camp be over? He wanted to go home. "I'm going to go take a leak. Be back soon."

His friends called out. He vaguely heard Sophie ask if he was alright, and Finley ask if he wanted Finley to come with him. He waved them both off.

He wanted to go home.

Ezra could take him home. Ezra would take anyone home.

Why did this bother him so much? Colby couldn't comprehend why he felt so bothered by everything. Had he become a big sensitive baby overnight?

They were just friends with benefits, so he shouldn't be so worked up about what Ezra did with others . . . but he was. He cared whether he dated Sophie. He cared whether Ezra had offered to drive other people to camp before him. He cared whether Ezra slept with other people. It pissed him off. He felt indirectly toyed with, and it wasn't the first time he'd felt this way because of Ezra.

He couldn't concentrate for the rest of the afternoon. Every time Ezra would even look at Colby, he'd get pissed off and annoyed and sad, but mostly pissed off. He managed to vent out some of his anger by tackling his teammates harder than necessary.

By the day's end, he still felt angry and what he saw after practice was just the cherry on the cake. He walked off the field to find Sophie pulling Ezra to the side, a rosy blush painting her cheeks and Ezra looking as handsome as ever. They looked so perfect together. The perfect couple. Barf.

He could go over there right now, separate them, say something—anything—to either of them. Say that he was uncomfortable with the idea of them dating. He didn't fully understand why. Maybe because of the Joanna incident. Maybe because Sophie was his oldest friend. Maybe because he and Ezra were . . . something.

Instead, he went back to the bedroom and tried to go to sleep. He could go home tomorrow, and that's all he wanted right now. However, a few moments later the door slammed open and awoke him when he was halfway to sleep.

In the doorway was a furious-looking Ezra. Before Colby could ask him who had shat in his cereal, Ezra asked him a question.

"Is this entire thing that we have, you getting revenge?"

CHAPTER TEN
Operation Backfired

"Is that all this was? Some ridiculous revenge plot?"

Colby had never seen Ezra look upset before. Thinking back, he'd never seen Ezra look fazed by anything. All the taunting and teasing Colby would throw at him, all the shit other boys who were envious of his perfection would talk about him, and none of the rumours jealous exes would spread about him got to him. But this? This. Colby had broken Ezra.

How did he know about Operation Revenge? Who would tell him? Only two people knew. Finley would never. No, not Finley, the ever-loyal, not Finley the guy who took "ride or die" much more seriously than anyone else. Colby had told Finley he was reconsidering the stupid idea. That left Sophie. Sophie wouldn't rat him out, would she? She'd always been the nice one of their trio, the girl next door, the goody-two-shoes, the girl who when you asked her for homework answers would send them to you, no questions asked.

However, Colby had seen her talking to Ezra earlier. When they were by the bleachers having a cutesy couple's moment. Disgusting. It could only be Sophie. Please don't let it be Sophie.

"Well, are you going to answer me, or are you too thick as shit to do that as well?" Ezra spat.

Colby couldn't stop when he threw himself out of his bed and faced off against Ezra. He didn't consider the repercussions of what he was going to say. It was instinct. All the resentment, all the festering hatred, and all the vile emotions that Colby had harboured with no true release. All of them came pouring out of his mouth before there was any time to think.

"Oh, *I'm* thick as shit? I'm not the idiot who thought any of this was real. What, you think that sex would make us best friends all of a sudden? How could I ever be friends with you? I haven't forgotten that you slept with my fucking girlfriend behind my back. You have everyone around you convinced you're some sort of a saint. Do you know how many times I had to hear from people 'Ezra wouldn't do that,' 'Ezra would never be a homewrecker,' and 'he just made a mistake.' Made a mistake my ass. You knew exactly what you were doing when you went round to her house and fucked her! Do you know how it felt to see you in bed with Joanna? When I came over to surprise her on her birthday and I found you two together. Did you apologise for it? Did you even try to fix anything between us? No. You just stared at me as if I had been the one to do something wrong. You couldn't even look me in the eye until a couple months ago. You know what's funny? For a second there, I forgot about everything you did. You really had me going there, got swept up with all your charm and sweet nothings. But that's all that this is, Ezra, nothing. So what do you want me to say, Ezra? That this was genuine. That I didn't do all of this to get back at you for Joanna. That I really fucking like you. That I love you? How could I ever after what you did?"

Colby was panting by the time he finished. He hadn't stopped for a breath. He just let it all out. He had been waiting for this moment for such a long time, to see Ezra crumble in his hands.

Where was it? Where was that promised satisfaction he would feel after fulfilling his plan and reducing Ezra to a blubbering mess? Where was that assurance he would feel to let him know that he hadn't sunk down to Ezra's level? That this was the right thing to do? That he wasn't a bad person?

Ezra just stared at him, his mouth hanging open, tears forming and threatening to spill from his eyes at the slightest movement.

"Is that how you feel about me?" Ezra's voice choked as he said that. The words didn't come easy to Ezra in his emotionally obliterated state. He kept looking up to stop the tears. His brows would furrow in anger only to twist into an expression of agony, and his mouth would open for a second only for nothing but a strangled breath to come out. Finally, he composed himself enough to be able to speak. "Joanna didn't love you. She never did."

"Take that back!" Colby bellowed.

"No!" He wiped his eyes on the back of his sleeve. "If you are still hung up over Joanna of all people, then I'm going to beat some sense into you right now. It wasn't just me she slept with. By the time I joined the team, oh, she was dating you alright, but she was sleeping with the entire team. You know Jordan Park? She fucked him in the back seat of his car at your seventeenth birthday party. Roland Marin? They fucked at a party that *you* were at. Jerry Winship? Janitor's closet. Joanna had you twisted around her little finger. I thought you were either stupid or blind not to see her infidelity, but it turns out you were in love. You were in love with her, and I couldn't understand it. She was the school slut and yet you always looked at her like she was a treasure. You dated her for three years. Three full fucking years I watched you give away to her. I didn't understand it at the time, and I still don't understand it now. I couldn't stand the fact that *she* was the one you looked at like that. She didn't appreciate you, she didn't care about you, and she didn't love you. So I slept with her because I thought that's what my weird feelings were about . . . but they weren't. When you caught us . . . and still looked at her like she'd done nothing wrong and still loved her . . . I couldn't take it anymore. I don't understand, Colby. Why? Why her?"

"What do you mean? Joanna wouldn't . . . you. You're lying." He didn't admit it at the time and he didn't want to admit it

89

now, but part of him knew what Joanna was up to. The signs were all there—the constant cancelling of plans, calling Colby clingy if he asked where she'd been, and the way certain guys snickered at him when he'd come into the changing room. But he loved her. Genuinely, she was his first love. He didn't realise it had always been unrequited. He didn't need Ezra to be the one to show him that. Why did it have to be Ezra?

At that moment, Finley and Brent chose the wrong moment to come into the room. Brent's lips were swollen, and his clothes were disheveled as if they were carelessly thrown on. Finley was the same. The beads in his hair clinked together as he turned to giggle like a lovestruck schoolgirl at Brent. They had obliviously come into the room—all lustful winks and smiles—until they saw Ezra crying and Colby trying not to.

"Tell him!" Ezra demanded, turning his attention to the pair.

"Tell him what? Colby, you okay, man?" Finley rushed to Colby's side and put a comforting arm around his shoulders. "What did you do?" Finley scowled at Ezra.

"I was telling him the truth," Ezra insisted.

"Ezra, what's going on?" Brent asked.

Ezra kept his eyes trained on Colby, saying nothing.

"Fin, it's not true, is it? He's lying," Colby asked Finley, his words laced with desperation.

"He's not." Finley cast his gaze to the floor.

"You knew?"

"I heard a few guys talking about her, but you two had already broken up. I wanted to tell you, I really did, but you were a complete wreck at the time. The only thing you clung onto at the time was that Ezra was the worst person in the world, and Joanna was an angel he took advantage of. I thought it would just hurt your feelings even more if I told you. I'm sorry."

Finley, Brent, Ezra, and every single fucking teammate. They all knew. They had been making fun of him this entire time. He was such an idiot.

With one last ounce of rage, Colby locked his eyes with Ezra's and said, "I fucking hate you."

Ezra turned and stormed out the room with Brent hot on his heels.

"Colby, I really am sorry. I just—"

"Please go. I-I don't want to talk right now."

Finley nodded silently and left the room, closing the door behind him. Colby shook as cries racked his body. He covered his mouth to soften the noise. He felt like such an idiot.

He'd been called an idiot his entire life. From when he was a kindergartener and *wasn't as academically gifted* as the other kids in his grade, to the family joke they had that Colby had *nothing between the ears*, to people at school dubbing him a *himbo*. What even was a himbo? He had no idea and no one would explain it to him.

All of that he could put up with, under the assumption he'd made that it was all a joke. This entire time, people were laughing at him, but not for the dumb shit he'd say or the stupid stuff he'd do. No, because he was a brainless moron who was being lied to by the girl he liked and all he would do was smile and nod. He was a simple idiot, not for the things he would do but for what he believed in. Everybody must have enjoyed the show, watching Colby make a fool out of himself at the mere mention of Joanna and Ezra. How they must have laughed when Colby would defend Joanna. Poor Colby. Poor simple stupid Colby, playing the part of the fool without even knowing it.

He picked up his phone and did what he always did when he didn't know how to handle a situation: he called his mom.

After a couple of minutes of giving a vague explanation of what had happened and after hearing Colby hold back a few tears and call himself an idiot multiple times, she agreed to pick him up.

The drive home was silent until his mom decided it wouldn't be.

"Do you want to tell me what happened?" she asked in a gentle tone that only a mother could do.

"You remember Joanna?"

"Old girlfriend? Nice boobs but ginger?"

He snorted at her description. "Yeah, that's the one. She was sleeping with the entire football team, probably others as well, and everybody knew but me."

"What, even Finley?"

"Yeah. He said he didn't tell me because he only found out after we'd broken up and he knew it'd only upset me more."

"That's understandable, dear. You already learnt she was cheating on you. No need to deepen the blow by saying how many. Oh, my baby."

"Can I stay home tomorrow? I don't really want to go back to school."

His mom sighed. "Colby. The last time I let you stay home—"

"It'd only be one day! Only until Tuesday."

"The last time I let you stay home," his mom started again, "you said you'd only stay off school for one day. Then that one day turned into multiple days, which turned into weeks, which turned into a solid two months of you refusing to go back to school. So, no, I'm putting my foot down on this. You're going to school tomorrow, and everything is going to work itself out."

"How do you know that?"

"I went to high school too, dear."

"Was it hard?"

"Let me think about that. Was it hard being in high school while pregnant with you and my parents kicking me out? Yes."

"Geez, didn't ask for your life story, Mom." Colby received a whack on his leg from his mom.

"How did you find out about Joanna?"

"Ezra told me."

"Maybe he was trying to do the right thing by telling you. Your dad only says good things about that boy, so maybe he didn't mean it maliciously."

He didn't have the heart to tell her that the only reason he knew about Joanna's cheating in the first place was because he'd caught her with Ezra.

"Maybe" was all he responded with.

CHAPTER ELEVEN
Square One

Colby had begged his mother to give him the day off from school. Just the thought of having to deal with shit from Sunday made him feel physically sick—but she insisted he rip the bandage off and face it. So, there he was, awkwardly standing by his locker, wondering who the hell he was going to sit with at lunch and what he was going to do if he saw Ezra.

"Hey, man," Finley said. His fingers were playing with his bag strap as he wore a timid smile on his face. "How are you feeling?"

Colby hated it here. He didn't want to be here anymore. He wanted to disappear to the opposite side of the world where nobody knew him and no one had a reason to laugh at him. "Not great."

"Listen, man. I know I fucked up by not telling you about all the other stuff Joanna had done, but I swear I didn't even know until I heard someone else whisper about it, and by then you two had already broken up. I know that's not an excuse, and I should've just told you, but . . . you hadn't come to school in over a month. All you did when I came to your house to see you was sit around in different places. I missed you so much, and I hated seeing you like that. I just wanted you to come back to school. So, when I heard Joanna had always been a cheater, I didn't tell you because I didn't want you to keep dwelling on her. I thought it was for the best. I'm so sorry, Colby." Finley sniffled as he finished his little speech, and he dabbed his eyes with his palms.

"Are you crying?" Colby asked, absolutely shocked.

"No." A tear ran down Finley's face. "Fuck off. I've just got hay fever. Stop staring at me!"

How could Colby stay mad at that? "Come on, bring it in."

"No, it's fine. I only wanted to apologise, not hug—"

Colby squeezed the living daylights out of Finley. He nearly suffocated the guy with all his love and affection and a really strong grip that Finley was not getting out of anytime soon, so he should really stop struggling.

"See, this is nice." Hugging Finley reminded Colby that there was a height gap between the two. Finley's chin barely reached Colby's shoulder.

Finley slapped Colby's back. "Okay. That's enough. Our bromance is mended. I get it."

"No, let's carry on for a little more."

"I don't think that's a good idea."

"You afraid you'll like it?"

"Don't make this gay, man. You know I already disapprove of your lifestyle."

"What if I gave you a little kiss on the ear." Colby followed through with his threat.

"Never do that again. That's gay."

"You're gay."

"No, you."

"If you're not gay, then tell me what you did with Brent at camp."

Finley cracked. A smile spread across his face from ear to ear. "Oh, you know, guy stuff. Straight guy stuff."

"Promise to tell me at some point."

Finley nodded. "So we're good?"

"Yeah, we are." Colby finally released Finley from his iron grip. "Plus what else was I going to do? Find someone else who puts up with my bullshit like you do? Impossible."

Finley just laughed at that and gave Colby a solid pat on the shoulder. "Now you don't have to answer this, completely your choice, but what happened, man? You and Ezra were getting on great and then all of a sudden, BOOM! You're arguing worse than I've ever seen you argue before like you were crying. I've seen Ezra piss you off, but I've never seen him make you cry before."

"He found out about Operation Revenge, and he confronted me about it. I think Sophie told him. I saw them talking by the bleachers on Sunday. But she wouldn't do that, would she?"

"I don't know, man. She's rocking some pretty major feels for Ezra according to her friends on the cheerleading team. She'd probably tell him anything if it got her a date with him. I don't think that she'd do it in a mean way. It was probably just a slip of the tongue. I thought you were slowly giving up on Operation Revenge anyway."

Colby leant his forehead against the cold locker. His brain was overheating with the number of times he'd gone over the argument. He barely got any sleep last night because all he did was think about Ezra and what he'd said. "I was, but I didn't tell him that. I don't know, I just got so angry and ended up saying a lot of stuff."

"Did you mean any of it?"

"I don't know . . . maybe. After the whole Joanna incident, I knew I was mad at him, but I didn't realise how much resentment I was still holding onto. But then we became friends and did . . . other stuff together. I did forget about getting revenge, but then he brought it up and started asking why, so I just exploded I guess."

"So now that you've calmed down, how do you feel about him?"

"I-I don't know. We both said some pretty mean shit to each other, so should we really be friends? Seems like we'd just kill each other or keep quietly hating each other. Then again, I did like spending time with him and I think I'll miss not being friends. On the other hand, now that we've got it all off our chests, are we okay to have a relationship with each other?"

"That's pretty deep, man. I think it's fine if you're still conflicted over stuff like that, gotta figure it out in your own time and that's okay. How do you feel about Joanna?"

"You know what?" Colby took his weight off the locker and stood tall and proud. "Fuck Joanna. I am over her. Colby Williams is over it and moving on!"

"Yeah! About time. You were way too good for her anyway." The pair high-fived.

The bell interrupted any more of their deep talk time, as Finley called it. Colby was glad he had a friend like Finley. The guy listened to his problems big and small, but never called him stupid for having them. They walked off to first period together.

"So"—Colby wiggled an eyebrow at Finley—"do I get details on what happened with you and Brent?"

"Oh my god, man. If I ever get him alone in a room, I'm going to pound his ass so hard into the mattress. Let me set the scene: football practice is over, everybody's hot and sweaty, Brent hears there's a creek nearby that you can swim in, I say sure, and Ezra dips, so it's just me and him." They had got to the door of their classroom. "Long story short, we skinny-dipped and then he kissed me. We fooled around for a bit, gotta good feel of his huge mommy milkers. I *was* going to take him back to the room to do a bit more, but you and Ezra were having a meltdown, and it kinda ruined the mood. But *he* kissed *me*. I've always been the one to kiss first. It was amazing having him make the first move."

"Yeah. Well, sorry for ruining the mood with my meltdown, but I get what you mean, I always kiss first too, like with Ezra—" *Oh shit.*

"I'm sorry . . . what? Did you just say . . . you kissed Ezra? Wait, do you mean you've kissed him outside of that picture you showed me? For how long? When? Why? How? Colby!"

Colby charged into the classroom and took his seat. A good way to ignore Finley and hoped he forgot about Colby's slip-up? No. They sat right next to each as they did in all the lessons they had together.

The entire lesson, he had Finley whispering things to him, like "You're not gonna act like you didn't just say that," "You have to tell me," and "I knew there was something weird going on between you two." After an hour of this, Colby agreed to tell him everything at some point. That seemed to appease Finley and it gave Colby enough time to think of a way to explain his complicated relationship to Finley.

Why did he get himself into these situations?

Lunchtime rolled around and somehow Colby had managed to not see Ezra the entire day. The problem now was asking Sophie whether she had been the one to let Operation Revenge slip.

He really didn't want to bring it up though. Sophie sat on the opposite end of the table to him, and she looked ecstatic. She was wearing her favourite pink dress that showed off her cleavage—Colby knew this from the number of times she'd mentioned how good it made her boobs look—and she was humming a happy little tune to herself.

He had to rip the bandage off like his mom said. "Hey, Soph. Can I ask you something?"

Sophie finally tuned back into the real world. "Sure, what's up?"

"I saw you talking to Ezra by the bleachers on Sunday and I—"

"Oh my goodness, are you angry? I didn't mean to upset you by talking to him. I've just been getting this vibe recently that he liked me and all my friends kept saying the same thing, so I

98

thought *why not?* and tried to shoot my shot. Please don't be mad. You say the word, and I'll never speak to him again," she rambled on as her cheeks were tinted with blush.

That comment did irk him though. He wasn't mad that she was talking to him in general. It was just that comment that she was trying to flirt with him that annoyed him. He didn't really get why, and he didn't want to dwell on it either. "I'm not mad at you for talking with him. I was just wondering if you talked about me with him."

"Huh? I mean, yeah, I guess you came up. He asked what your favourite food was, how close we were, how close you were to Finley, and what you thought of him. He got mad at that last one and walked off. I think he wants to be your friend. It was so sweet. He kept asking what kinds of things you liked, and whether you were into anyone at the moment. Maybe he's trying to set you up with a friend. Wouldn't it be so cute if the four of us could go on a double date?" She let out a small giggle.

"What exactly did you say I thought about him?"

"Well"—she paused, trying to remember her exact words—"I think I just said you didn't like him very much after the whole Joanna thing . . . then he asked how mad you were about that, and then I said . . . I think I said you were still mad and had made up this whole Operation Revenge thing, but then I said that probably just meant you'd prank him or something. I told him to always check that the salt shaker lids are on tight, I know that's your go-to move. Yeah, I think that was it. Why?"

"Ezra had a go at Colby because of the things you said," Finley deadpanned. Colby hadn't expected that from him. Normally, Finley was the chill one, but now he looked kinda pissed. "Come on, Soph. What were you thinking? You can't just go telling guys stuff because you like them. What happens in the group, stays in the group. No exceptions, even if you have got a little crush on them."

Sophie looked equally surprised by Finley's bluntness before what he'd said sunk in. "Oh my god, really?" She turned back to Colby. "I'm so sorry, I wasn't thinking. I just—I just wanted him to like me. And it sounded like he wanted you to like him. I'm sorry, Colby. Do you want me to go say to him that I misunderstood what Operation Revenge was or that I misheard you? I'll tell him I made the whole thing up." Sophie immediately stood up and began to walk off in search of Ezra.

"Wait, Sophie!" Colby called.

She turned back.

"It's fine. What's done is done now, and there's not much going back" was all Colby could reply with. He didn't want to talk about it anymore. He didn't want to constantly be bombarded with the image of Ezra and Sophie dating each other or Ezra hating him. He'd find a way to deal with it.

"Are you sure Ezra is into you, Soph?" asked Finley. He turned his gaze on Colby. "I hear he's already got someone he likes."

Heat rushed to Colby's face. He was going to kill Finley.

"Really? I haven't heard anything like that," said Sophie.

Colby zoned out of their conversation, letting the two gossip and bicker. He'd find a way to fix things with Ezra or he'd find a way to deal with the loss.

*   *   *

Why did they have to have football on Mondays? They just had an entire weekend dedicated to the sport. He was exhausted and didn't want to go. That and he wasn't ready to face Ezra. Ezra had said some awful things, but Colby had said awful stuff too. There was only one question from Sunday that Ezra had asked him that Colby still didn't have an answer for. *Is that how you feel about me?* Feelings were not Colby's strong suit and his feelings for Ezra were messy, to say the least.

The team was already warming up in the field by the time Finley and Colby joined them. Fashionably late as always. They all gathered around in a semi-circle to listen to Coach. Ezra wasn't there yet.

"Alright! Listen up, you little inbreds! Your games on the weekend were decent, but your teamwork was atrocious. I don't care whether some of you don't like it, but you are a TEAM! So start acting like it! We're going to be working on team building and trust today and—Dickinson, you're late."

Everybody turned to watch Ezra stroll up to the group. He looked just as perfect and stoic as usual. His golden hair glistened in the afternoon sun, but he was never late to practice. Ever. Coach Clain always used him as an example of what the rest of the team should be like. This was very unusual for the school's golden boy.

Ezra didn't even spare a glance at Colby as he apologised to Coach.

"Whatever. Don't let it happen again. We'll be doing another game today, same teams as Sunday."

Great, so Ezra and I are still on the same team. Ezra was the quarterback and Colby was a wide receiver.

To say Colby wasn't on the ball today was an understatement. Most of the time, Colby wasn't even near the ball. He couldn't focus, so a couple of times the ball would slip right past him. What made it worse? Ezra wasn't focusing either. Their team was losing badly, and it was even beginning to throw off the other players, so now they weren't performing well either. It was a mess.

Colby wasn't exactly sure what happened. He wasn't sure whether he had collided with Ezra, whether it was the other way round, or even if they hadn't bumped into each other at all and it was somebody else entirely. Either way, Colby was face up on the floor with a banging headache and was staring up at a fuming Ezra with a bloody nose.

"What the fuck is wrong with you?" Ezra fumed.

No way was Colby putting up with this shit right now. He pulled himself up to his feet. "Me? What's your damage, huh? You're the quarterback. Start doing your fucking job right."

Ezra stormed up to Colby and held him up by the collar of his jersey. "Or what? This game doesn't matter to you." He seethed, but then he lowered his voice to a harsh whisper, "Nothing matters to you."

"What's that supposed to mean?" But Colby never got an answer as a very short angry Coach came onto the field and began to blow her whistle until the sound was ringing in everybody's ears.

"Cut this shit out right now!" Coach screamed. For a tiny lady, she was filled with a ginormous amount of anger and aggression. "Practice is over. You two, my office. NOW!"

Ezra threw Colby back down to the ground and followed Coach off the field. Colby was so confused. What had happened? Ezra never treated him like this. Sure they fought yesterday, but he wasn't expecting this kind of treatment, it hurt.

Finley helped him back up. "Do you want me to wait for you, man?" he asked.

"Nah, don't worry about me. You go home. I don't know how long this'll take."

CHAPTER TWELVE
Rock and a Hard Place

The atmosphere was stiff as Colby and Ezra waited outside of Coach Clain's office.

Ezra still wouldn't look at Colby. His eyes never left the office door, as if he was trying to will Coach to hurry up so he could leave. His entire body was taut. A small muscle in his jaw kept twitching every time he tensed up, and his back was as straight as a pole.

Colby felt like he should say something—break the tension—but Ezra didn't look much in the mood to talk though. Hell, Ezra looked like he'd rather be anywhere else in the world right now.

Colby just needed to bite the bullet and say something, but he was pretty pissed off with Ezra's behaviour. What did he mean by *"nothing matters"* to Colby? That made him sound like some emotionless asshole, which he was not! Ezra was the one being an asshole right now with his unwarranted aggression towards Colby. Colby should still be mad at him for sleeping with Joanna. Just because he told Colby about all those other guys that did the same thing, didn't mean Ezra didn't do it.

He wanted to talk to Ezra though. He just didn't know what to say. He was torn between "*I'm* sorry about Sunday" and "Why haven't *you* apologised to *me* about Sunday?"

Eventually, he decided a simple "about Sunday" might be the best way to start, to gage Ezra's reaction to it. Maybe that'll prompt him to apologise to Colby.

Colby sat there for a couple of minutes trying to will the words out of his throat. The tension in the room kept forcing them back down. His heart was racing. There were two words that he needed to say, but he just couldn't do it.

Okay, three . . . two . . . one . . . "About Sunday." Colby's voice cracked as he said it. That was embarrassing.

Ezra didn't move a muscle. He didn't even acknowledge that he'd heard Colby. "I don't want to fucking talk about it," he snarled.

This asshole, Colby thought, grinding his teeth together. "You know what? I don't get why you're acting so pissy with me. You should be begging for my forgiveness after the horrible shit you said or would that be too much for your pride to handle."

That got Ezra's attention. He snapped his head towards Colby and glared at him with such fury that Colby had never seen on him. "I said some horrible shit? How dare you say that to me after what you did." Just as tears began to form in Ezra's eyes, he turned away from Colby. "When you first kissed me in the shower I . . . I thought you realised."

"Realised what?" Colby tried to coerce him to continue but to no avail.

Coach Clain came out of her office a few minutes later.

"What happened on the field today was unacceptable. I do not tolerate that kind of behaviour. You have embarrassed yourselves and disappointed me. Explain yourselves."

Neither boy said a word. Frankly, Colby thought Ezra was going to talk first. He was the captain and had never exhibited any of the behaviour he showed today. He had much more to explain than Colby. For Colby, not entirely knowing the rules of the game until he dumb lucked his way to victory was run of the mill. Only a month ago, Colby had got on the wrong bus to a football game and

104

ended up playing wide receiver for an all-women's football team. They were super nice, and Colby was still in contact with them. He even got invited to their games from time to time.

Coach should've been very used to Colby's shenanigans, but not Ezra. He was better than that.

"Well?" Coach prompted. "Nobody's got anything to say?"

Colby glanced at Ezra who was still staring straight at Coach's office door. Freaky. Did that mean it was Colby's turn to speak? Coach wasn't really looking at Colby. Was Ezra stupid? He was going to get in so much trouble if he didn't start talking. Colby was still angry at him. He still wanted an apology. He still wanted to keep being angry at Ezra because it was much easier than trying to figure out how he really felt, and—goddammit—he was going to hate himself for doing this.

"I'm sorry, Coach," said Colby. All of her attention turned to him. "It's completely my fault. I wasn't with it today, and I hit Ezra by mistake. I shouldn't have gotten angry with him afterwards. It was entirely my fault." Gross, being the bigger person left such a bitter taste upon the tongue.

"Thank you for your honesty, Colby," said Coach. "But I'm not blind. Ezra wasn't, as you say, with it either, and even then that was no excuse to resort to violence. Was it, Ezra?"

Ezra said nothing.

"As punishment, you both have detention after school. Every day of this week. Now get out of my sight." She waved her hand dismissively and went back into her office.

Colby glared at the door in disbelief. "She made us stay here for an hour . . . to tell us that?"

Ezra made no effort to reply as he picked up his bag and stalked out of the room. His walk was more sluggish than usual, his feet dragging across the floor with every lazy step.

"Hey! I'm not done talking to you yet," Colby called after him. He whipped his bag onto his back and made haste after Ezra. Why? He wasn't quite sure, but he felt like he needed to.

"What more is there left to say, Colby?" Ezra snapped. "Pretty sure you made your feelings about me crystal clear."

How was he supposed to respond to that? *Oh, sorry, Ezra. I did mean to get revenge on you for the Joanna incident, but the sex was so good, I completely forgot about it.* Colby was dumb, but he wasn't stupid, at least not stupid enough to say something like that. But sex, sex could work.

"So what?" Colby began. "You're just pussying out of our friends-with-benefits agreement. I wouldn't expect that from you." A taunting tone overtook his voice before he really processed whether it was a good idea to bring their agreement up like this.

Ezra stopped in the middle of the hallway they were walking down and turned to him. All the other students had cleared out an hour ago and had gone home, so it was just the two of them. Ezra stared at Colby like he was the most confusing thing he'd ever seen, which was fair enough. Colby was pretty confused now too, but he stood confident with what he'd just said.

"We are not friends, Colby. I thought you knew that." Ezra stared at Colby for a few moments longer. "Alright. Let's do it now."

"Now? Where? What if we get locked in the school?" Now Colby was really confused. Firstly, he hadn't expected his half-baked plan to work, and secondly, he didn't expect his plan to work so quickly.

"Yes, now. Boy's bathroom. We are not going to get locked in the school because the swim team and tennis team are here till seven, so they can't lock the school until then. Are you pussying out, Colby?" Ezra smirked though his eyes didn't quite match whatever solemn vibe he was trying to give off.

Colby wasn't sure how Ezra had managed to get the upper hand there, but he promised himself he wouldn't let it last. "I'm not a pussy."

He walked into the boy's bathroom and realised what a shithole it was. The stall doors were covered in graffiti and dick

106

drawings. The tiles on the wall were cracking, and the overall smell of the place was . . . unpleasant. Why was he doing this for Ezra?

He tried to imagine he was back in Ezra's lovely bedroom with the big warm bed, his naked body wrapped in the soft sheets. He tried to imagine Ezra was being ever so gentle with him. He imagined Ezra was sweetly smiling at him, and his tender caresses were covering Colby's body.

However, that wasn't the reality. The smell made sure to bring him back to the real world. Instead of a big soft bed, his body was pressed against a cold metal stall door, and his trousers were around his ankles. The worst thing was that instead of Ezra being gentle and careful with his body—worshipping him like some precious jewel—the few touches Ezra did give were rough and uncaring. Ezra didn't smile at him. He wasn't sure what Ezra's facial expressions were as Ezra had decided to turn Colby around so they no longer faced each other. There were no affectionate caresses or unnecessary touches, not even a single kiss; just sex.

He moaned when Ezra slid his cock between his thighs, but it didn't have the same feeling as the things they had done before. It still felt good, but something was missing, and Colby's heart ached as he longed for whatever had been lost between them to come back. Ezra didn't ask Colby if he was alright, like last time. He just grabbed Colby's hips in a harsh grip and moved him to suit his own needs.

They both tried to keep down any noises they were making. Occasionally, one of them would let a moan slip, but with the atmosphere between them and their current relationship—or lack thereof—it felt like their expressions of pleasure for each other were no longer welcome.

Despite all that, Colby still came, discarding it into some tissue paper. He bit his hand to suppress any noises. He wished he was facing Ezra. He wished he could embrace him as he came, bury his head in Ezra's neck, and be held by him. He wished to kiss Ezra. Even a small peck on the lips. Anything would do.

Ezra came soon after without a sound. For a moment, a very sweet little moment, Ezra leant forward and his head rested upon Colby's shoulder. Colby couldn't see what face he was making. All he could do was rest his head upon Ezra's and let him put all his weight on Colby for a moment.

He removed himself from Colby and zipped himself back up. Colby did the same, pulling up his trousers. He didn't need to humiliate himself more than he already had by staying where he was with his ass hanging out. Colby turned to Ezra and stared at him expectantly. *Just give me a kiss* was all Colby could think about.

Ezra opened his mouth and lifted his hand. He looked like he was about to say something, but he stopped. "See you tomorrow" was all Ezra said before leaving the stall, before leaving Colby.

"I hate this," Colby whispered to no one but himself.

That night, he called Finley and told him everything. He needed to tell somebody. It was eating him alive the way he was feeling. He couldn't keep it to himself anymore.

"Wow," Finley said once Colby had finished describing all of his encounters with Ezra over the past week. "Just wow. You and Ezra, man. Did not see that coming. So, let me get this straight real quick . . . you make out with Ezra and jack off with him in the communal shower. Gross, by the way, man. Other people have to use those things but whatever. Anyway, you do this to prove you're not a bottom, but plot twist, on Friday, you proved you are a bottom just like I said you were. Then, during the weekend, you were all lovey-dovey with each other, but then he found out about Operation Revenge, got mad, and stopped talking to you. Until today, when you insisted you two keep fucking, but now he isn't lovey or dovey to you anymore, and now you're upset. Not forgetting you still haven't figured out who sent you the picture of you and Ezra making out that started all this in the first place. Have I got all that?"

"Yeah, that's pretty much it. It's been a pretty busy week," Colby said. An invisible weight lifted off his shoulders. He finally had a confidant. "I don't know what to do, Fin. He's being a dick to me, and I kinda deserve it, but isn't he being too much of a dick? Like I'm not going to break things off with him because I like fucking him—"

"You mean being fucked by him." If Finley was here in person right now, he would've received a solid punch in the nose for his valid correction.

"Shut up. What do I do?" Colby pleaded.

"I'm not sure, man. Your relationship with him is complicated, and I don't mean to add more worry to it, but what's Sophie going to think when she finds out you've been sleeping with her crush?"

Colby had completely forgotten about Sophie's crush on Ezra. He remembered it when he was away from Ezra, but it's as if as soon as Colby saw Ezra, it's like all thoughts of anything else would fly out of his head. He was the worst. The worst of the worst.

"I didn't even think about that," Colby said. "She's going to hate me if she finds out."

"I don't think she will. She's only spoken to Ezra a couple of times if you ask me. Her crush is pretty one-sided at the moment. Plus, a lot of it is just her friends trying to play matchmaker. But ignoring her for the time being, why not just apologise or try and talk it out with him? Get back to the way you were before or tell him you didn't mean anything you said when you snapped at him."

"I can't because I did mean what I said. Well, not the part where I said that all the sex was based on revenge, but me hating him for the longest time and wanting to get back at him is true. I can't take it back because then I'd be taking back all those angry feelings again, and I don't want that. Plus, he seemed like he's been pissed at me for a while too. Something about the way I looked at Joanna annoyed him apparently."

"I suppose you're right, but at least now the feelings are out there. Now you gotta deal with them. Did that sound smart?" Finley's voice was suddenly cut off by a loud yell. "I gotta go, man. Dinner's ready, but call me anytime if you still want to talk. See you later."

"Thanks, Fin. Bye."

The feelings were out there, and now he just had to deal with them. Finley could sound pretty wise when he wanted to. The thought exhausted him though. He'd never been good with feelings, especially not his own.

CHAPTER THIRTEEN
Mystery Solved

"And then I accidentally dropped one of my textbooks, so Ezra picked it up for me, and then we were talking about the English Literature exam coming up. He looked super cute whilst he was doing it too. Anyway, he said we should study together! Netra thinks we could make one of the cutest couples she's ever seen. Megan thinks so too. My mom is speaking to me more than ever. She can't stop giving me boy advice," Sophie gushed.

All she seemed to talk about recently was Ezra this and Ezra that. Sophie made every small interaction she had with Ezra sound like the most romantic thing that had ever happened to her, and it was really beginning to get on Colby's nerves.

Why did she have to talk about him all the time? And in such a lovey-dovey way. Barf.

"That's a great idea!" Finley gasped. Before, he had been slouched in his chair with a bored expression on his face, but for some reason he had sprung back to life. "We should *all* study with Ezra!"

"What?" Colby and Sophie questioned at the same time.

"We all need to study, right? So let's do it together," Finley said. He looked very pleased with himself.

Sophie opened her mouth a few times to speak, but she just ended up looking like a fish out of water. "Wait, wait, wait," she finally said. "I'm not sure he meant everyone. I think he meant .

. . just the two of us. Or maybe he didn't. Oh my goodness, do you think I've misread this entire thing? No way, Tyler said he thought Ezra was definitely into me. So, he must've meant just me, right?"

Finley sat up in his seat and stared Sophie directly in the eyes. "Nah, I doubt it."

"What do you mean 'you doubt it'? That's what happened. He asked me *specifically*," spluttered Sophie.

"Oh yeah, he definitely asked you. But in a sense, didn't he ask all of us? What do you say, man? Up for some revision?"

Colby was about to reply to Finley when Sophie answered first.

"Why are you asking Colby? There is no way he'd want to do that. Colby has always been more comfortable keeping his distance away from Ezra. Plus, Ezra wants to revise English Literature. Colby is a literary prodigy, so he'll just get bored. He hates Ezra. He doesn't need to revise."

"Woah, hold up!" Colby finally said. "I-I don't hate Ezra." It was weird to say out loud after so long of telling anyone who would listen how much he despised the guy. Yesterday's events and especially his conversation with Finley had opened him up to the fact that he really didn't hate Ezra, at least not as much as he used to.

Sophie looked surprised at the revelation as well. "Since when?" she asked.

"I don't know," Colby started. "Since the party. Not last Sunday, but the one before. We've just been hanging out more, and you were actually right. He's . . . he's a pretty cool guy." It was a small thing to say, but it felt huge to Colby.

"Nothing happened between you two at that party though, did it? And, if anything did, you were probably just drunk and didn't mean it," Sophie exploded.

The trio sat in silence for a moment.

Colby was the first to interrupt the silence. "I didn't say anything did happen between us at the party. I just said we'd been hanging out since." *What was up with Sophie?* Colby wondered.

Sophie didn't have a response. She looked pretty embarrassed about her outburst and continued to sit quietly.

"Okay . . ." Finley drawled. "So it's decided then. We're all going to the study session with Ezra. Brent will probably be there, so I might not be putting all my thinking power into the right kind of head, if you get what I mean." Finley winked at Sophie who blushed profusely at the insinuation. The funniest thing was Finley's laugh. He laughed like a dirty old man who sits on the bus and makes fart noises to entertain himself and inconvenience others. That was the only way to describe Finley's laugh.

"Gross, bro." Colby punched him in the shoulder but laughed at the joke too. Even Sophie snickered as she placed her hands on her face to hide her blush.

A study date between Sophie and Ezra? It definitely wasn't a date because he and Ezra were . . . were . . . were what? He didn't have any say on what Ezra did romantically or anything he did with other people. That's what their friends-with-benefits agreement was. Some dark and twisted part of him wanted to tell Sophie just how close he and Ezra really were—especially behind closed doors—but that was plain wrong. She was excited about this, and Colby needed to support her.

"So, when is the study session?" Finley asked.

"He's got detention after school, so I'm going to join him in the library today," Sophie replied

"Perfect. Colby's got detention too, so he would've been there anyway," Finley said.

"What? Why? Did you take a nap in the teachers' lounge again? Just because your dad is a teacher here and can use it, doesn't mean you can."

"No, I did not. And, yes it does!"

"He got in a fight with Ezra during football practice," Finley mentioned casually.

"Really?" asked Sophie. "He didn't mention that to me just that he'd got a detention, and he just said to meet in the library. Did he hurt you, Colby?"

He shook his head. "No damage done." None physically anyway. "It's okay. We were both being assholes to each other, then took it too far. Water under the bridge now. No biggie." Technically, his relationship with Ezra could be classified as a biggie. It was a big pain in the ass for sure. Maybe having some quality time together in detention was going to be a good thing. Yeah, he could make this work.

They all agreed to be there after school.

Detention at their school was a bit of a lawless land. A student with detention had to sign into the library and stay there until their time was up. No one actually came to check if they were there. Sometimes a very pissed-off teacher would pop in to make sure the student they had sent there hadn't left, but that was about it. Students were advised to do homework during this time but with no supervision. Technically, they could do whatever they wanted.

Colby had never been so nervous before. His palms were sweaty and his heart was going a million miles an hour, all because of stupid Ezra.

Finley and Sophie were already in the library, but Colby needed a minute to gather himself. What was he supposed to say to a guy he had great sex with, then had a serious argument with, then had emotionless sex with in a bathroom stall?

He was torn between so many things. He wanted to get Ezra alone so they could talk. Colby had tried preparing the ultimate speech multiple times, but the words just weren't coming to him. So far, all he had was *forgive me so I can forgive you, dickhead*. Scratch that last part. He wanted to tell Ezra not to flirt with Sophie, but he had no right to do that. He also wanted to be intimate with Ezra again, but if it was going to be as cold as last time, then he'd rather not.

A big hand slapped him on the back. Colby looked to find Brent giving him a warm smile.

"Hey, Colby! You coming to the revision session too?" Brent always seemed so cheerful. Colby envied him for that. All of Brent's problems seemed to be solved with a can-do attitude and a smile. That's why he was so popular with people; his positivity was infectious. He was a big friendly giant.

Colby smiled back at him. "Yep! Although I didn't get much choice in the matter, got chucked in here with Ezra for the fight we had on the field." Colby's smile dropped a little at the memory.

Brent's smile dropped as well, to Colby's surprise. "Yeah. Listen, I've been meaning to talk with you about what happened at football camp." Brent's hand fell from Colby's back and awkwardly stroked the back of his own neck. "I just want to apologise, because of the Joanna thing. When you and Joanna were still dating, she started texting me. It was small things at first. You know, basic conversation, asking about how my day was and all that. Then it went a bit farther. She, um, started flirting with me and . . . I'm just going to be honest here, I flirted back. I did shut it down after a week when she started sending nudes and kept asking me to send some back, but it shouldn't have taken me so long to stop. I shouldn't have texted her at all. I can't even tell you how sorry I am. I can't even give a reason why I did it, other than I was so surprised that anyone was flirting with me that I struggled to let the attention go. I'm really sorry, I should've told you about this ages ago."

"Wait." That was a lot to unpack, but the thing that bothered him most: "You were surprised that someone was flirting with you? But, you're so hot."

Brent shook his head, and he fanned his face with his hands. "Oh, gosh, is it hot in here?"

"You're super hot. Mega hot. When Fin, Soph, and I play kiss, marry, kill with you as one of the options, you always get kissed, if not married. Never killed. Never."

Brent couldn't meet Colby's eyes. Colby started to purposely make eye contact with Brent so he could watch as he became flustered and would pretend to be interested in anything else in the room. He had never pegged Brent as the insecure type. He always seemed so confident around people. There wasn't a single person in the school that didn't consider Brent their friend. How had nobody flirted with him before? Colby would if Finley wasn't already on that.

"That's pretty cool." Brent shyly smiled. He was so cute, like a tiny puppy trapped in the body of a huge dog. Colby could top Brent, one hundred percent. "I'm having a party round mine this Saturday. You should come. I'll . . . I'll ask Finley as well." And with that, Brent practically scurried into the library, dragging Colby in behind him.

Ezra, Sophie, and Finley were sitting at a table near the back of the library. Sophie had moved her chair to be right beside Ezra's, but she couldn't seem to get much flirting done with Finley constantly challenging Ezra to thumb wrestles across the table. Colby wasn't sure why, but he was glad Finley was preventing any sparks from flying between Ezra and Sophie. Sophie was way too good for him and Ezra was okay too, he guessed. The thumb wrestle ended when Finley's face lit up at the sight of Brent coming in.

Brent sat in the chair next to Finley, leaving Colby either the seat next to Ezra or the one next to Brent. Sophie tried to subtly hint that Colby should sit next to Brent, but Colby pretended the hint was too subtle and ignored her.

"Hey," Colby greeted Ezra with a small smile as he sat down next to him.

The corners of Ezra's lips tugged up. "Hey."

They actually did end up doing revision in the end. Colby taught them the tricks to writing the perfect literary essay. His dad had taught him well. They went over the books and poems they needed to know for the exam and even managed to get a practice paper done. All in all, it was a job well done. Best of all, Sophie couldn't flirt with Ezra at all as Colby got to interrupt any flirting with literature talk. He was the anti-Cupid. Was it underhanded? Yes. Did he regret doing it? No. Did he feel bad about it? Yes. The guilt was starting to tear into him.

"We should do this again sometime," Brent said. "Let's make a group chat. I don't think I've got all of your numbers." Brent gave a cheeky glance at Finley, who was grinning like an idiot.

"I've got nearly everybody's numbers here," Colby said. "All I need is yours, Brent."

"And mine," interjected Sophie. "I got a new phone the other week, but I haven't given out my number yet."

Colby plugged Brent's number into his phone first, but something strange happened when he tried to do Sophie's. His phone seemed to think that he already had her number. Colby didn't remember Sophie giving it to him but according to his phone, there was already a text conversation with Sophie's new number.

He found the number in his contacts, double-checked it was hers, and changed the name to "Sophie <3." He scrolled through his text messages and found the conversation with that name on it. Sure enough, Sophie's new number had sent Colby one picture.

He opened the chat and froze. The picture of Ezra and Colby kissing at the party—the picture that had started all of this—was sent by Sophie.

CHAPTER FOURTEEN
Better As . . .

What. The. Fuck.

It was Sophie? Colby's Sophie? Sweet little Sophie that used to help Colby with his math homework when they were younger because he was too stupid to do it by himself? The Sophie that let Colby cry on her shoulder after he found out Joanna was cheating on him? The Sophie that would bring his school work round for him when he was staying off school for those two months and would feign innocence when Colby would ask why most of the answers were already filled out. That Sophie?

No way. She would never send that picture to Colby. It simply wasn't in her nature. She was a peaceful and nice person. Sending the photo of Colby and Ezra making out at the party was beneath her. She wouldn't do it. It had to be a mistake.

"Colby, you alright, man?" Finley asked.

Colby didn't respond. He couldn't find the words. He passed his phone over to Finley so he could see who sent the message. Everyone else at the table stared at the two curiously as Finley's jaw dropped. Finley kept glancing between the phone and Colby, obviously going through the same thought process as Colby.

"It must be a mistake," Colby said. But even he wasn't convinced by his words.

Finley shook his head.

"Are either of you two gonna tell us what you're looking at or is it a secret?" asked Sophie with a giggle.

Colby stared at her in disbelief. His Sophie wouldn't do that. She would never try to blackmail Colby with that photo, but maybe it wasn't blackmail? Maybe she was trying to warn Colby of what he had done at the party. Yeah. That made more sense. Sophie was just trying to give him a heads-up in case other people had found out, right?

"It's a secret between bros," Finley said. "Some things aren't meant for the delicate eyes of a lady."

Sophie looked disgusted by Finley's answer. God knows what she thought he meant.

Colby didn't know what to do now. Why would Sophie— his oldest friend—send him that photo anonymously? It made no sense.

"Are you okay?"

Colby awoke from his internal conflict at the sound of Ezra's genuine concern. There was nothing special about the way Ezra was looking at Colby. However, the simple gesture of Ezra being concerned about him after the fight they had, made Colby's heart swell. Colby wanted to kiss him. He was kiss deprived since Ezra refused to give them out anymore.

Colby smiled and replied a bit cheerier than he really felt. "Yeah, I'm good."

Ezra nodded and turned away, but Colby continued to watch him happily as Ezra resumed writing his notes.

"Shoot!" Brent exclaimed, looking at his wristwatch. "I need to get home." He was about to get up when he nervously glanced at Finley. "Do you . . . want to come round for dinner?"

Finley stopped his glaring and his face exploded into a wide smile. "I'd love to! Oh, wait, but—" He looked at Colby apologetically.

Colby grinned and mouthed *go* to him.

"I'll call you later."

119

The two left the library together.

Colby laughed to himself at seeing the height difference between them. It was like watching the Statue of Liberty go on a date with a garden gnome.

The remaining three—Ezra, Sophie, and Colby—sat around the table in unbearable silence. He wanted to go home. He felt like an idiot sitting there as Sophie tried to flirt with Ezra, but that was the exact reason why he couldn't leave.

Sophie would *accidentally* nudge Ezra's side or scoot closer to him to get his attention. Ezra, in turn, would smile at her and chuckle at the things she whispered to him. They would make a cute couple. It was all Colby could think about. He really should go home and leave them to it but he couldn't, because for every smile and chuckle Ezra gave to Sophie, he gave Colby a quick look from the corner of his eye and that was all Colby needed to stay.

It was an agonisingly long half an hour until Sophie was finally forced to admit defeat and go home for her scheduled bible study. She gave both the boys a hug before she left. Colby didn't deserve a hug. He'd spent the entire time cockblocking his best friend, who might or might not be blackmailing him. To feel guilty or not to feel guilty, that was the question.

And then, there were two. They only had twenty minutes left of detention together, so Colby had to work quickly.

"Do you like her?" Colby surprised himself by asking that first, but it was the question that weighed on him the most.

Ezra looked quizzically at Colby before answering, "She's a nice girl. Pretty too."

Colby huffed at that. Sophie was pretty, but Ezra didn't have to say it. Plus, she might not be as pretty on the inside, if the photo revelation was anything to go by . . . Was he becoming a mean person? Oh God, he didn't even recognise himself anymore.

He shook the thoughts from his head. He had a goal to achieve. With a deep breath, he tried to do something he really struggled with, expressing his emotions in a sensical and understandable way for others to comprehend.

"I-I don't like the way things are between us right now," Colby said.

Ezra turned towards him and gave Colby his full attention.

"Like, before we had our fight, I thought we were getting really close. I mean, physically, we got really close but emotionally as well, I guess." He really did hate having to articulate his emotions on the spot. He was hoping Ezra would jump in and take over, but he was just intently listening to Colby's every word. "I miss that, and I'm sorry about what I said."

"Did you mean the things you said during the fight?" Ezra asked. His poker face was impenetrable, so Colby had no idea what was bubbling beneath his calm demeanour.

"Some things. Everything did kind of start because I wanted to get back at you, but after a while, I completely forgot about that and ended up enjoying the time I spent with you." Embarrassment was the only thing Colby felt at that moment, but he pushed through. "What we had—it did mean a lot to me and I liked it . . . which is why I really hate the way we are now."

Ezra looked down at the neatly written notes he'd created during the study session, drumming his pencil against the pages. "Me too. I will always regret what I did with Joanna. I assure you, she is not the person I wanted to have my first time with."

No way did Colby lose his virginity before Ezra. Ezra was a fuckboy, a player, or at least Colby thought he was.

"I shouldn't have treated you the way I did after it happened either. I couldn't bear to see you looking at me with such disgust anymore," continued Ezra.

"Were you in love with Joanna?"

"God, no." He cleared his throat. "Excuse me, sorry, I didn't mean for that to sound so rude. But, I don't care about Joanna. I, especially, don't care for her. It wasn't about her really—it's hard to explain. It was pure circumstance that she happened to

121

be the girl you were dating at the time and I was having a rough time. She reached out pretending to care, and"—he threw his arms up in exasperation—"I don't know what you saw in her. What you still see in her."

"Come on. Joanna is a . . . serial cheater and compulsive manipulator. But she didn't have it easy growing up."

"What's wrong with her?"

"Let's just say, her mom had very sticky fingers and a real appreciation for the five-finger discount. Joanna didn't really have anything that belonged to her because what was hers was her mom's, and what was her mom's was probably someone else's."

"That's not an excuse for how she treated you."

"Why do you care how she treated me?"

Ezra looked back down at his notes as his face became tinted with pink. "I don't know. You could do better," Ezra whispered.

"So could you," Colby replied.

Ezra glanced back up at Colby, only for a second. He then swiftly turned away completely and his hand rubbed the back of his neck. Cute.

"With Joanna," Ezra began. "I am sorry about what I did. It's not much of an excuse, but I had a lot of . . . stuff going on back then that I was struggling to deal with and"—he paused and looked Colby dead in the eyes—"and some really difficult feelings that, at the time, I didn't know what to do with. I thought I was messed up and wanted to sleep with Joanna so then I did . . . and in a way that did make me understand my feelings better, but not in the way I had hoped."

Colby wanted Ezra to go on, but he stopped, clearly not wanting to talk about it anymore.

"So, are we good now?" Colby asked. "Back to same old, same old, dickhead?"

Ezra nodded.

Fantastic! This worked way better than Colby had expected. It didn't take long for Colby to get wrapped up in his joy and forget to establish with Ezra what kind of *same old* the two were going to have from that point onward. He didn't even think to ask what Ezra wanted, which was why he was so shocked that when he finally kissed Ezra, he was pushed away.

Well, he didn't push Colby away at first. Colby had moved in for a kiss without warning. As soon as their lips connected, Ezra kissed him back. There was no silly fight for dominance or competition between them. It was just a great kiss. Until Ezra became stiff and unresponsive under Colby's touch, and he was shoved away.

What? Colby was so confused. Why did they stop? They both agreed the fight was bad, but they were good now, so what was the holdup? The saying went "Kiss and make up." Colby wanted his kiss and he wanted it now.

"I can't," Ezra said. "I can't keep doing this."

Colby reached forward and took Ezra's hand into his own. Ezra's poker face had completely crumbled at that point. His eyes were brimming with tears, and he was blinking quickly to try and get rid of them. It was breaking Colby's heart to see him like this.

"That's okay," Colby said reassuringly. "We don't have to do anything right now."

"No. You don't get it. I'm not supposed to do things like that ever." Ezra's voice cracked as he tried to get through his sentences.

"What do you mean? We did things much worse than a kiss last week," Colby said. Last week they were getting each other off, having sex in Ezra's bedroom. Hell, just yesterday they fucked in a bathroom stall. So what was the problem now?

"I know. I know." Ezra paused. "My dad found out you came round on Friday . . . and I stupidly left the condoms in my bedside drawer . . . This has to stop, Colby." He patted Colby's hand and forced a smile. "Let's be friends. Just friends."

123

Colby was pretty sure his heart stopped when he said that. It both was and wasn't the outcome he was hoping for. He wanted to press the matter more, try and convince Ezra to give it a second chance, but Ezra had looked so upset.

"Okay," he agreed. "Just friends."

Colby decided to walk home from detention after his time was up. His dad was a teacher at the school and could've driven him home, but the man refused to stay after school longer than he had to. He said it was Colby's punishment to bear, not his.

During the walk back, he got a call from Finley.

"Hey, how's the dinner at Brent's going?" Colby asked.

"Really good. His family are super nice but they are all so tall, man. His parents are both well over six-foot. Pretty sure his dad is near seven-foot actually. You can totally see where he gets his height from. Even his sister is over six-foot and she's fifteen! Bro, I feel tiny in this household and I can't even be mad about it because they're all so nice. I'm hiding from the giants in their bathroom right now." Finley laughed at the other end of the phone, then he became Serious Finley. "Did you talk to Sophie?"

"No, I didn't get the chance. She has been acting weird lately, right? Like, it isn't just me?"

"Nah, it's not just you. I think it's all because of her new Ezra obsession. She really likes him, but sending that picture. I never would've guessed that was her, but love does funny things to people."

"For fuck's sake, Fin. You have one successful crush, and now you think you're a love guru." Colby laughed. "I talked to Ezra. We decided to be friends."

"Friends with benefits or just friends?"

"Just friends. He said something about his dad finding out I was at his house on Friday. Maybe it's for the best. I'm not even gay."

Finley let out a huge sigh. "Man, you've had sex with a guy. That's pretty gay."

"But I'm still attracted to girls." Which was true. Colby had considered being gay, but he still liked women, and he'd considered being straight, but he liked men, it was too confusing.

"This is going to blow your mind, man. There's this thing called bisexuality. It means you like girls and boys. Does that solve your problem?" Finley might not be a love guru, but he could be a sexuality one instead.

"Yeah, it does. Cool." He felt a bit better for having a word that explained his attraction. It seemed to fit quite well too.

"I gotta go now. Brent's mom has made pork chops. I already love her. We'll figure out a Sophie confrontation plan tomorrow. See ya."

"Bye."

The remainder of his walk home was filled with the single thought that he'd probably kissed Ezra for the last time today.

CHAPTER FIFTEEN
To Be Normal

Ezra's life could never really be described as easy.

For as long as he could remember, his parents were either arguing or threatening divorce. After fourteen years of a nonfunctional relationship, it was only three years ago that his parents finally got divorced. It was a suffocating mix of uncomfortable custody battles, manipulation from both his parents to lie about which one of them was the better caregiver to the judge, and lonely nights as his parents ran away to their lovers, leaving Ezra by himself. To summarise, it was awful.

Years upon years of this had made him silently hope for them to get a divorce already. He was foolish enough to believe that the divorce would settle everything. He had hoped it would end the arguments, the screaming, and the yelling if they ended their marriage and lived apart. Of course, that wasn't the case.

Even now his parents would scream at each other the moment they came into contact. Thankfully, his parents' interactions were few and far between.

When the dust had settled and the divorce had reached a conclusion, his father had won full custody of Ezra. It was an odd result because he was told by his mother's lawyer that usually, the mother won court cases such as this. After all, the female caregiver was always assumed to be better than the male counterpart—a misogynistic flaw in the justice system that benefitted women who wanted to keep their children, but Ezra's mother was not one of those women.

"He ruined my life." She had said it so easily. It wasn't planned in any speech written by her lawyer. It was a slip of the tongue that revealed to the entire court how she really felt. He hadn't meant to ruin her life, hadn't intended to ruin anybody's, and yet the list of his victims grew ever longer. Ezra would never forget the way his father had comforted him when his mother said that. It had been genuine comfort, no ulterior motives for doing it. He missed the father that had instinctually cared for him.

His life didn't get any easier when puberty hit, and he slowly came to the sickening realisation that he was attracted to boys and one boy at his school in particular. He'd done so many "Am I gay" quizzes. Each time he would try to get straight or heterosexual answers. But one day, it occurred to him that if he was doing "am I gay quizzes" at all, the answer was probably yes. Straight people didn't do the quizzes.

To say he dealt with his feelings well would be a lie. He tried his hardest to be straight, did all the stereotypical jock shit, flirted with girls without ever going further with them, and kept physical contact with guys very low. Not even the strongest gaydars could detect Ezra. His reputation was flawless and it could've stayed that way if he hadn't sabotaged himself.

For three whole years, Ezra heard the whispers of the infamous Joanna. She'd do anything with anyone, they'd say. Ezra never slut-shamed her as the others did. Everyone was entitled to their own proclivities and that was no business of his. He only had one reason to hate her: she was cheating on the boy he liked. It was unfathomable to Ezra that she would cheat on Colby. You don't win the lottery then still beg on the street for spare change. It didn't make sense. She had what he wanted. She had what he dreamed of, and she didn't even care. It kept him up at night. Why her? What was so special about her? Why did Colby look so happy to be with her? Why would she cheat on him? Why, why, why?

He wanted to know. He needed to know. So, he ruined everything. After a year of Joanna trying to pursue him and Ezra ignoring her, he finally agreed to meet her alone.

He could still remember the way she kept shoving her tongue down his throat and the way her acrylic nails scraped against his bare skin. She'd led him to her bedroom and they both undressed. Joanna had bit and sucked on his skin and let out cute little giggles that would've aroused any man that heard them—but not Ezra. Eventually, he willed himself to get hard at her lustful touches, but he did so with his eyes closed whilst picturing someone else. They slid under the sheets of Joanna's bed, and Ezra thought he was suffocating under them. It had been so hot under there. The weight of the blanket was damn near to crushing him, and the space around him grew ever smaller. At the same time, he had to save face and fuck Joanna.

It's not that it felt bad. She certainly knew what she was doing, but it felt wrong somehow. He kept his eyes closed the entire time picturing the boy he liked. What would he look like under Ezra? What sounds would he make? How would he feel? Ezra wanted to hear him cry out his name, for him to say—

"Ezra?" His heart had stopped at that moment, his body petrified. Even Joanna was shocked at the sight of Colby standing at her bedroom door. Ezra would never forget how heartbroken he'd looked. The very boy he'd been fantasising about had shown up, but instead of looking at him with lust, Colby glared at Ezra with such hate, and he would carry on to do so from then on.

It was for the best, Ezra decided. This way everybody thought Ezra was straight as rumours of him sleeping with Joanna spread like wildfire and Colby stayed far away from him, which helped Ezra rein in his feelings for him. Of course, that didn't work out either.

Colby suddenly kissed Ezra whilst he was in the locker room shower. It took Ezra by surprise, but he wasn't going to let the opportunity go to waste. That entire week that he spent kissing, touching, and then making love with Colby had been the best week of his life. Sure, Colby was still pretty hostile towards him at times, but Ezra didn't mind, whatever kept him close.

It only lasted a week.

In hindsight, Ezra should've seen it coming. After everything he'd done to Colby, why did he expect his feelings to be returned? It was just like the divorce, a childish fantasy that things would get better.

Ezra drove home by himself after the football training weekend more pissed than he'd ever been in his life. A revenge plot. That's all it had been, and Ezra had fallen hook, line, and sinker for it. He felt like an idiot and that point was proven when he got home to find his father waiting for him.

Ezra currently lived with his father, but the two didn't tend to interact very often. Same house, different worlds. That's why Ezra already knew he was in trouble when he saw his father sitting on Ezra's bed with an opened bottle of lube and a few condom wrappers next to him.

Crap. Panic swallowed his body before he could even begin to think of excuses.

"Ezra." His father's voice had always sounded cold to Ezra, like he was nothing but a pest in his father's eyes. "Do you have any way to explain yourself?"

Ezra hardened his face and tried his best to sound honest and confident. "I had a girl round on Friday."

His father glared at him, peering at him over the frame of his glasses. "Really? Because Miss Herson next door didn't mention seeing a girl come round on Friday, but she did mention a boy."

That nosey old bitch. She called herself the neighbourhood watchdog, but she just liked knowing everyone's business and then tattling on them.

"We've talked about this, Ezra. You know how I feel about this kind of behaviour." His father stared at Ezra expectantly.

"My behaviour isn't right," Ezra said, maintaining the agonising eye contact with his father.

"Exactly. I let it slide when it was just porn on your computer."

If you called being screamed at for two hours over the gay porn Ezra had forgotten to erase from his computer history "letting it slide."

"But to actually invite a boy round and do . . ." His father's face twisted with disgust. ". . . God only knows what with him. That's taking it too far, and you know damn well it is. Did you think for a second about how this would affect me? You think Miss Herson is going to keep the fact that my son is inviting boys to my house late at night to herself?"

"No," Ezra replied quietly.

"No!" his father repeated louder. He got up from Ezra's bed and came closer to him than he had in months.

Ezra had grown to be around the same height as his father, but at that moment, he felt like a tiny child under his father's angry gaze.

"Not only are you humiliating yourself, but you are also dragging my name through the mud with every misstep you take. It's a phase, Ezra. You'll get over it. Do yourself a favour, get a nice girlfriend, and be embarrassed that you ever acted this way. You are normal. Now start acting like it."

With that, his father left the house and probably went to whatever woman he was sleeping with.

"Normal," Ezra whispered to himself. What did that mean? He felt normal. He felt like himself when he was with Colby, but maybe it wasn't. Maybe that's why Colby didn't feel the same because their relationship wasn't normal. He wasn't sure whether he wanted to cry or punch something. Why couldn't he be normal?

He tried his hardest to be normal at school. Colby had apologised for what he said, but he was normal. He liked Joanna. Joanna was a girl and Colby was a guy, so it only made sense that

Colby had lingering feelings for her and not Ezra. Although, it pissed him off. Joanna wasn't loyal to Colby and certainly couldn't love him the way he deserved . . . but if that's what Colby wanted, then Ezra would have to grin and bear it.

Ezra tried to be normal by flirting with Sophie. She was nice and pretty and fun to be around. She did most of the flirting and seemed okay with it even if Ezra only smiled at her. He was acting normal.

How come Finley and Brent didn't have to be normal? They were openly together with the approval of their parents, a situation Ezra could only dream of. They kissed in public, which was kind of funny to watch with the height difference. They didn't have to act normal. They were themselves and didn't care what others thought.

Ezra had never told anyone about his confusing feelings, but now with Brent dating a guy, he felt it could be okay to finally confide in someone a little bit. It wasn't easy.

Ezra and Brent had been playing video games for about an hour before Ezra finally had the balls to bring up the subject of boys. Saying it like that, he felt like a schoolgirl. "So, you and Finley are together now?"

Brent smiled to himself and kept beating Ezra at the game they were playing. "I guess. We haven't put anything official on it yet, but it's just nice to be around him, you know?"

He didn't know. He had never known what it was like to be around a person and feel nothing but nice, to not have a thousand thoughts eating away at him about how he was doing something wrong. He envied Brent's ability to go with the flow and not care what others thought of him. Image was everything, as Ezra's father often said.

"You two are cute together."

"Thanks. What about you? Got any girls on the pull?"

How was Ezra supposed to respond to that? He knew he should come clean and admit he was . . .

No. No, he couldn't say it out loud. Then it would all become real and come back to bite him tenfold. Brent wouldn't judge him and he wouldn't tell anyone, but still, it was too much. He was a normal guy, not that he thought Brent wasn't normal. It was simply that he was lucky and got to be different and follow his desires.

"You know me. Every girl's got a chance." He was such an awful guy, lying to his best friend, lying to himself. He felt like shit.

"Well, you could go for Sophie. Finley said she's got a thing for you, and Josh said Joanna's been talking about you again."

Great. That's exactly what he needed—two girls he could never truly like, liking him. At least it would get his dad off his back. Ezra often found himself wondering whether Colby had been right, that he really was a selfish prick that only cared about himself and took from others. Here he was, fully prepared to date a girl to avoid the wrath of his father.

"Could even go for Colby, if you were into that." Brent laughed until he turned to see Ezra had stopped playing.

"What do you mean?" Ezra demanded.

Brent looked flustered now. He was unsure whether he'd said something to upset Ezra. "I'm only joking. You two seemed to get on so well last week, and Finley said Colby had finally gotten over Joanna. Sorry, it was silly."

Colby had gotten over her? It had finally happened? Then maybe, maybe there was a chance . . . no. No, he needed to give up this pointless chase already. There was no home for anything between himself and Colby. He needed to remember that this time.

"Ezra? Are you okay?"

"Fine," Ezra replied through clenched teeth. He shouldn't keep hoping.

CHAPTER SIXTEEN
Best Friends Forever?

Colby did everything in his power to be the best fucking friend Ezra Dickinson had ever had.

Ezra needed change for the vending machine? Boom! Colby was there with a messed-up dollar bill that couldn't be accepted. Ezra forgot to do his homework? Boom! Colby's already slid him Sophie's answers. Ezra was late to class? Boom! Colby's already made an excuse for him.

Colby was trying super hard to build something between himself and Ezra, but for some reason, Ezra was so skittish around him.

It was like Colby had some sort of infection because Ezra was avoiding him like the plague. The main thing Colby noticed was Ezra would never be alone with Colby.

The day after they'd decided to just be friends, they ended up in the library alone together after school since they still had detention. To say it was awkward would be putting it lightly. Colby talked about anything and everything, trying to get a response out of Ezra, but nothing was working. Colby talked about football, school, even going as far as to talk about Joanna, which he did *not* want to do, but desperate times call for desperate measures. Ezra would just hum or say "really" as a response. It was like he was a million miles away even though he was sitting right in front of

Colby, still as handsome as ever. But Colby didn't get annoyed over that anymore. Nope. He decided to enjoy the view instead.

"So, you going to Brent's party on Saturday?" Colby asked, hoping talking about a party would liven Ezra up a bit.

Ezra didn't look up from the chemistry textbook he'd been flicking through for the past five minutes. It wasn't very subtle that he was only looking at it to avoid looking at Colby. "Yeah" was all Ezra said in response.

"Cool, cool. You gonna drink at it?"

"Absolutely," Ezra murmured under his breath.

Did that mean Ezra was stressed about something or an alcoholic or a party animal? No way he could be stressed about Colby, right? After all, he'd been trying to make their friendship as non-stressful as possible. Nothing but smooth sailing for them.

Colby began to panic and fret over the possibility that he was the source of Ezra's stress. That would explain Ezra's blatant discomfort to be around Colby. Was it the kiss they had in the library? Did Colby annoy Ezra? Did Ezra not actually want to be friends and was now stressed because Colby had been too dense to notice that Ezra was kindly trying to tell him to piss off? There were too many possibilities for Colby to think about. He thought being friends with Ezra would be easier than what they were before, but now it seemed sex was simpler.

Colby decided to try and ask whether he was being a bother.

Ezra stared out the library window, his eyes glazed over in thought. Tentatively, Colby reached across the table separating them and placed a gentle hand on Ezra's arm. Without even asking, he got the answer to his question.

Ezra pulled away from Colby's touch as if it burned him. His eyes came alive but looked wild, and he frantically checked to see if anyone was watching.

"What are you doing?" Ezra demanded. The librarian shushed him from somewhere in the maze of books.

134

Colby was not expecting that kind of reaction, and it hurt slightly. "I was just trying to ask you a question?"

Ezra's hand was firmly clasped over where Colby had touched him. He seemed to be calming down a bit now, but he kept checking for something or someone. "Well, what do you want?"

"It doesn't matter now." It really didn't. That reaction was enough for Colby to get the hint that Ezra had no desire to be friends with him. Only a couple weeks ago, that answer wouldn't have bothered Colby at all as he had felt the same, but now . . .

"I think I'm going to head home," Ezra announced, already packing away his things.

"But there's still another hour left of detention. What if Coach Clain finds out you skived?" The very idea of Coach sent shivers down Colby's spine.

"It's fine." Ezra swiftly left the library, and he didn't come back. Not that day, the next day, or the day after that.

Colby spent every detention alone until Friday was over and thus so was his punishment. Honestly, he wasn't even sure if he wanted to go to Brent's party anymore. Clearly, Ezra didn't want to be around Colby, but Colby had promised Finley and Brent that he'd be there. Ah, well, he could drink his night away. Wouldn't take much, considering what a lightweight he was.

Finley came round to Colby's house the following evening to get ready, and he'd brought half his wardrobe with him.

"I want to wear something cool but sexy but not overly sexy. Something that says 'You can introduce me to your friends' and 'We can go have awesome sex' at the same time. You get what I mean, man?" asked Finley. He was holding up two different pairs of black jeans that Colby thought looked exactly the same, but Finley insisted there was a difference. Apparently, one pair of jeans made his butt look good, but the other pair made his dick look good.

Colby still wasn't used to No-Shits-Given Finley actually giving a shit about somebody. "Don't get mad at me, but I think you need to chill. He's only introducing you to like five new people that he's friends with out of school. It's not that deep." Colby didn't think too much about what he was going to wear. He'd chucked on some black jeans with a Hawaiian shirt and called it a day. Truth be told, he was going more for comfort than fashion. He planned on showing everybody he was at the party, then locking himself away in a bedroom—no Ezra, no Sophie, and no Joanna—and watching Love Island on his phone until it was over. That way, he'd fulfilled his promise to Finley and Brent by showing up to the party whilst not putting himself in awkward conversations with people. Problem solved.

"You're right, I *am* overthinking this, and as the gay one with a fashion sense here, I know for a fact I should go with this pair." He held up the pair of black jeans in his right hand that looked identical to the jeans he was holding in his left.

"Cool." Colby couldn't wait for the night to be over. The party hadn't even started yet, and he wanted to go home.

"You okay, man? You talked to Sophie yet?" Finley asked. He'd now moved on to examining all the different shirts he could wear.

"Ugh," Colby whined, "I'm so tired of having to talk to people. Why can't they just be straight-up and tell me how they feel? It's exhausting."

"Yeah, it is exhausting, but if you want a relationship with someone, platonically or romantically, you gotta talk to each other, man. Do you think Brent would prefer me in a red shirt or a white one?"

"Red, it suits you better." What do you know? Colby did have some fashion advice in him after all.

"You know, man, they say red is the color of lust." Finley sent a cheeky wink at Colby.

"Gross, don't you think about anything else when you're with Brent?"

"No, not really." Finley laughed at his own pervertedness.

Poor Brent, Colby thought. The poor guy's not going to be able to walk after Finley gets his hands on him. Well, Finley would have to bring a stepladder just to kiss Brent. But as soon as Brent bends down to Finley's height, his ass is grass and Finley is going to be the goat eating it.

Colby knew Brent was a popular guy. He was nice and kind to everyone, and yet the number of people already wasted at the party when Finley and Colby showed up fashionably late was ridiculous. The front lawn was scattered with empty beer cans and drunk teenagers dancing to the faint rhythm booming from inside the house. The house was smaller than Ezra's had been, and every room on the first floor was packed full of people.

The main activity was happening in the living room. There was a game of spin the bottle happening in one corner, and a dance battle happening in the other. The centre of the room was full of people grinding and dancing on each other to the music, and Ezra was amongst them. That was the last thing Colby wanted to see. Ezra wasn't really dancing. He drunkenly swayed from side to side, and Sophie and a few other girls rubbed themselves against every inch of his body. It was hard to say whether Ezra even noticed them doing it all as he kept downing beer, and then when he'd finished his, he'd swipe another bottle from anyone walking near him. How much had he drunk already? He was wearing a white button-up that clung to his toned chest and black jeans that made his ass look unbelievably tempting. Was Finley right about the jeans?

Colby watched Ezra and smiled at his silly state. To think the guy had told Colby that he was an irresponsible drinker. Oh, how the tables had turned. He had to look away from Ezra when some girl flung herself at him and tried to eat his face off. Did they know each other? When he turned back to Finley, he found he was doing the same thing to Brent. When did everyone become so horny? Not Colby though. He was a good boy.

Colby cleared his throat to get the boys to stop. Even with the strobe lighting that bounced around the room, it was obvious Brent was blushing.

"H-hey, Colby, glad you could come," Brent spluttered as Finley kept kissing his neck and whispering naughty suggestions into his ear.

"Yeah, thanks for inviting me. Hey, are the rooms upstairs free?"

Brent took a minute to think about it before answering. "Yes, but if you *do something* up there, please clean up after. I don't want my parents banning parties forever because they found out someone did it in their bed."

"Don't worry, I wasn't planning on it." Colby gave Brent a pat on the shoulder and a wink at Finley before heading upstairs to wait till the party was over.

Yes, he knew he was being a really bad party guest by hiding in a bedroom and watching stuff on his phone instead of joining in on the party, but he just couldn't find it in himself to be lively and happy, especially after seeing Ezra making out with some random girl. He was such a dick, not that there was anything he could do about it. Ezra made it clear that they were meant to be friends now. Nothing more, nothing less.

The bedroom he went into was probably either Brent's parents or a guest room. It had that sophisticated modern style with white walls and a grey bed. Perfect place to chill.

He took off his shoes and hopped on the bed, then started his night of ignoring what was happening downstairs and pretending Ezra didn't exist.

That plan didn't last very long as the very guy he had been trying to avoid slammed into the door and drunkenly hobbled in. With all the grace of a bull in a china shop, Ezra flopped onto the bed face first and made a small umph sound as he did. More sounds

138

came from Ezra, but Colby couldn't make out a single word as all of it was muffled by the blanket. He was pretty sure Ezra was mumbling incoherent words to himself, but he did keep making out the word *spin*. Did he feel dizzy, and was about to throw up?

Colby couldn't allow that to happen. He'd promised Brent this room would remain tidy, and Colby never broke his promises. "Ezra," he asked tentatively, "are you okay?"

Ezra turned his head with a growl. "I don't care about your stu-stupid bottle!" His eyes widened and he pointed at Colby in disbelief. "Are, are you my s-seven minutes?" he slurred.

"What do you mean seven minutes? Come sit over here. You look like you're about to keel over." Colby patted the bed space near him, and Ezra tried his best to get there. His feet tripped over each other with each step, so he ended up sitting incredibly close to Colby. Colby could smell the stench of alcohol on his breath.

"I was, I was downstairs playing the bottle spinning game, and if the bottle pointed at you"—he tapped Colby on the nose—"then you have t-to, um, go upstairs and do seven minutes in heaven with whomever else gets it. Is it you? P-please say it's you." Ezra leant against Colby until Colby had to bear all of Ezra's weight just to keep him sitting up.

"Are you sure it wouldn't be seven minutes in hell if you had to do it with me?"

Ezra shook his head frantically. "Heaven . . . heaven . . . with you. Dad's not here . . ." he whispered repeatedly.

Ezra was so far gone, he couldn't even hold his own head up. Colby couldn't send him back out to the party like this. Whoever his real seven minutes was might take advantage of him in this state, or anybody else at the party for that matter. If Colby could make him stay here, get him some water, and keep an eye on him in case he threw up, he just needed to think of a way.

Colby couldn't blame alcohol or the party atmosphere for his decision. "Yeah, it's me, but—"

139

Ezra didn't waste a second after Colby had confirmed it was him that he had seven minutes in heaven with. He pushed Colby onto the bed and attacked his mouth. It was slightly clumsy—teeth bashing together a few times—and the taste wasn't great, but it was filled with such passion, and Colby was man enough to admit that he had missed kissing Ezra.

That wasn't the point of this though. Ezra had no idea what he was doing. He could barely talk or think. He would come to regret most things he did tonight, and he would especially regret what he was doing right now, that Colby was sure of. With enough strength to make a point, Colby pushed against Ezra's chest.

"Ezra, that's enough," he protested. He tried to imitate his dad's stern teacher voice, but it didn't have much of an effect. "Ezra, I'm serious. Stop."

The second time was the charm. Ezra flopped down next to him. He buried his face against Colby's neck. "I'm sorry," he mumbled. "I'm so sorry, Colby. Don't leave. I'm sorry."

It was an oddly endearing moment as Colby stared up at the ceiling. All he could feel was the weight of Ezra's body against his, and the warmth Ezra always seemed to bring with him. The golden hairs on Ezra's head tickled Colby's face. He could still feel Ezra's lips moving against his neck, not to kiss him or anything. He was still repeating his plea for Colby to stay with him over and over again.

"You must be so drunk right now to do something like this," Colby teased.

Ezra shook his head. "M'fine." He fumbled his words. "Barely had nothin'."

"I don't believe you. How much did you have? Be honest."

Ezra lifted his hand into the air and his fingers randomly shot up in no particular order. "Brent gave me something, then Jordan . . . shots . . . saw Joanna, more shots . . . girl gave me her drink, so nice, too touchy . . . Sophie gave me a drink . . ."

"Sophie gave you alcohol? She hardly drinks herself."

140

"She lied," Ezra yelled way too loudly into Colby's ear. "Said it's vodka. It was water. Can you believed?" Well, there goes Ezra's understanding of grammar.

"Yes, I can believe that. It's such her thing to do." Colby's mind wandered back to the photo she had sent. "She's always been a good person. I'll go get you some more water, or else you're going to really feel this in the morning."

Colby sat up from the bed and was about to head off when Ezra pulled him back down. He hardly had time to realise what had happened until Ezra was staring down at him.

"Don't leave," Ezra begged. "Don't leave. Stay with me. Please."

Why did he look so sad? There was always something so ethereally beautiful about Ezra. Even within the depths of his hatred for Ezra, he more than understood why people were so attracted to him. His face was so familiar in the way that every ancient master of art had tried to capture the angelic beauty of someone like him. The echoes of his form could always be found in the statues of Ancient Greece to the paintings of the Renaissance. He had a face that had haunted Colby in his dreams for years, such an untouchable perfection now weeping above him, pleading with him not to leave.

Colby reached up and ran his fingers so gently, so carefully, so tentatively across Ezra's face—those high cheekbones and sharp jawline, that strong nose and full lips, and eyes as blue as the Mediterranean Sea waiting for a response. Since when had Colby had such a hold over him? Must be the alcohol.

"I'll stay," Colby agreed. "But, you're not going to be very happy in the morning when you've got a terrible hangover."

Colby grunted as Ezra collapsed on top of him, his face finding its way back to the crook of Colby's neck. What a cry baby. Colby placed a hand on Ezra's back and drew random shapes and images.

The bedroom door slid open.

141

CHAPTER SEVENTEEN
Everybody's Changing

"What are you doing?"

Colby shot his head up at the voice, his body unable to go anywhere under Ezra's weight.

Sophie stood in the doorway, the light filtering in behind her as she stuck close to the door. Her auburn hair fell in loose curls around her face, and her black dress was the shortest item of clothing Colby had ever seen her wear. It clung to her shape, lifted her boobs, and accentuated the wideness of her hips. It was a great dress, and she looked amazing in it, but it wasn't a very Sophie-looking dress.

"Sophie?" Colby called. "It's, it's not what it looks like." It was an automatic response to lie to her. He had never done so before, but he wasn't sure whether he was looking at the Sophie he knew. It looked like Sophie and sounded like Sophie, so it must be Sophie. He couldn't stop thinking about the photo that she had sent him. It was her. He'd checked multiple times, cross-examining the number that sent him the photo and Sophie's number multiple times. He'd even checked to make sure Sophie hadn't accidentally given him the wrong new number. She'd only just got it, easy to get the new number muddled up. So, he got four of her friends from the cheerleading team to send him her new number. It was hers. No getting around it. But he didn't know a Sophie who would do that to him. "It's not what it looks like, Sophie. He fell on top of me," he lied again.

She looked panicked. Even in the dim light of the bedroom, Colby could make out the way her grip on the door tightened and her eyes widened in terror. "Get off of him, Colby!" Sophie cried.

Why was she demanding that Colby get off of Ezra? Unless she'd suddenly gone blind, she could clearly see Ezra was the one pinning Colby down. Speaking of Ezra, he didn't even acknowledge Sophie yelling from the door as he continued to cling to Colby's body.

Colby was mortified and pissed off. He hadn't expected anyone else to walk into the room, and he was annoyed that Sophie did and that she was yelling at him about it. He placed his hands on Ezra's shoulders and tried to push him off, but Ezra was unrelenting.

"Can you come back later?" Colby asked in frustration.

"No, I can't come back later!" Sophie insisted. "What if something happens?"

If something happens? Colby could feel—much more hear—Ezra snoring away. The guy was dead to the world and wasn't about to start doing Sophie's insinuated *something*. Ezra was also a huge deadweight on top of Colby, so it's not like he was about to get up and do *something*.

"He's sleeping, Soph," Colby explained without waking Ezra. "We're not doing anything."

She nodded but still looked rather distressed. "I'll help you get him off."

"It's fine. I don't want to wake him."

Colby's insistence of his own acceptance of the situation fell on deaf ears. Sophie wasted no time coming into the room. She grabbed onto Ezra's side and used all her strength to force him to move. The job wasn't easy. Ezra groaned and complained in his sleep, drowsily trying to slap Sophie's hands off of him and get back to Colby. She would not relent. The more she fought against Ezra, the more Colby failed to recognise her as the Sophie he was familiar with. There was something so frantic about her actions, a wild frenzy in her eyes. She wanted Ezra to move, and she wanted him to move now.

Colby decided to shuffle out from under Ezra himself if that was all it would take for Sophie to stop manhandling Ezra. Indeed, it was. Sophie now turned her attention to Colby.

"Are you okay?" she asked. She forcibly tilted Colby's head back so she could look at his neck. She even pulled back his collar and looked down his shirt.

"I am fine," said Colby. "What the fuck is your damage though?"

"Me?" she asked as if she hadn't just tried to fight a sleeping boy and check Colby's neck for something or other.

"Yeah, you."

She stood up from the bed and pulled down her dress, not without accidentally flashing Colby first.

"Since when did you have thongs?" he asked.

Her face turned red, and she spluttered out an answer, "Since . . . forever."

"No, not since forever. Or at least, not since I was last round your house before you went off to summer camp, remember? I helped you pack, and I tried on a few of your bras, and found out that we're the same cup size. Come on, you don't remember?"

"I remember. It's just been a while." She paused. "Joanna and Netra got me these thongs for tonight."

Colby knew he'd seen that dress before—Joanna had worn it a few times in the past. She must've lent it to Sophie. Strange, though. The two were friends, and Colby hadn't entirely minded them staying friends even after the collapse of his relationship with Joanna, but Joanna had always hated sharing things. She was the kind of girl that if you asked for a fry off her plate, she'd stab you

145

with her fork instead. She must really like Sophie to give her anything.

"Can we go somewhere else?" Sophie asked.

"I need to get some water."

Sophie dutifully followed Colby down the stairs. They didn't speak at all as they went, not that they would've been able to hear each other very well with the party music still blaring out of the speakers. They shuffled and bumped their way through the congregation of drunk teenagers in the living room. At one point, Colby spotted Finley finally meeting Brent's friends from outside of school. He didn't seem very engaged in the conversation, but he kept responding and politely nodding his head from time to time. It looked like it was going well. Colby would have to ask him later.

After a little searching and a few refusals to drinking games, they found the kitchen near the back of the house. It was of a more modest size compared to the living room and was thankfully left uninhabited by any of the partygoers. The music still thrummed through walls, but it was much more tolerable in there and didn't make Colby's ears ring.

He began his scavenger hunt for a cup as Sophie stood and watched.

"What were you doing with him?" she asked.

No cups in the bottom cupboards, only bowls and dinner plates. "I don't see how it's any of your business."

"I'm trying to help you here, Colby. You don't realise what a mistake you're making."

Maybe the top cupboards had something in them. "Listen, Soph, I know you sent me that picture of Ezra and me making out at that party, and I have no idea why you did it or why you did it anonymously instead of coming to me directly about it. How about you explain that, then I'll explain what I was doing with Ezra?"

"I didn't mean to send it to you anonymously. I forgot I hadn't given you my new number yet. I was wondering why you hadn't come to speak to me about it, so I was waiting for you to say something first."

"For me to say something? What did you want me to say?"

"That you weren't going to do it again. I was trying to warn you. You always go on about how much you hate Ezra and it's understandable. He's hurt you so much. You were drunk and sad and confused that night. I spent most of that night comforting you as you cried on my shoulder about how much you missed Jo and hated Ezra."

That was a little embarrassing.

"I left you alone for a few minutes, and when I came back, you were with him. It's not right, Colby. You're better than this."

"I-I don't really understand what you're talking about. I'm better than this? I think everyone kisses someone drunk at some point in their lives and then regrets it in the morning. It's not that big of a deal." He heard Sophie sigh behind him.

"No, you don't get what I'm trying to say. It's not that you kissed him drunk, but it's that he is a *him*."

"Of course, Ezra is a him. He's a boy and he goes by such. Duh."

"And you don't see a problem with that?"

"With Ezra being a boy? No? Don't think I do. Am I supposed to?"

"Yes!" Sophie's feet thumped around the room. Why was she pacing so much? "I don't know what to do, Colby. I'm trying so hard. This isn't easy, but I'm trying. What else can I do? I can't lose you."

In the top cupboard to the left of the refrigerator, Colby found a cup. He placed it on the counter. "Lose me? You're not losing me. If anything, I feel like I'm losing you."

Her pacing stopped. "What? No, please don't say that. Please."

"You're acting so differently these days. You said you wanted to tell me something really important before you disappeared for the summer, and then I didn't hear from you at all. What were you going to tell me?"

"It doesn't matter anymore. It didn't matter in the first place."

He didn't want to turn around. To do so was to be forced to look upon a Sophie he no longer understood. He couldn't avoid such a realisation forever though. Sophie was doing things Colby couldn't comprehend, but that was okay—he didn't comprehend much anyway. She was changing, and that was . . . okay. She couldn't remain the same Sophie he'd known since they were kids. Everyone would change eventually. It was just particularly sad to see when it came to her.

He turned around. "Sophie—"

She threw herself against his body. She leaned up on her tiptoes and kissed him. "I love you, Colby," she confessed. She stared up at him with a love in her eyes that he was familiar with, but it was not the kind that she claimed it to be. Such despair, such tragedy in one person. Had she always bore a face painted with melancholy? She had never been someone who looked at ease all the time, but since she hit puberty and especially since she came back from the summer, she always looked so tired, so sad.

"I love you too," said Colby, stroking the hair back from her face. "But, you don't love me like this. I know you don't."

Her head fell against his chest, and he held her there for a moment. "I wish I did," she whispered. "I wish we could do the cliche movie thing where we fall in love after we're all grown up. It would make everything so much easier."

"What's wrong, Sophie? What's happening to you? You can tell me. You can always tell me."

She shook her head. Her hands tightened into fists, clenching the fabric of Colby's shirt within her grasp. "I can't lose you, but if you keep doing these things with Ezra, I'm going to."

"No matter what happens with Ezra, you'll always have me. No one's going to take me away from you."

148

He was pretty sure he heard her laugh a little bit. "I've always loved how optimistic you are, but not all of us can afford to be like that." She took a step away from Colby. Her eyes were all teary, but she smiled despite that. "Please don't go back to him."

"I-I don't know if I can promise you that."

Sophie was about to say something else until the kitchen door burst open and some drunk girls stumbled in.

"Sophie," one of the girls whined, "where'd you go?"

"Did you get your seven minutes in heaven with Ezra?" another one teased.

"I'm so jealous," said another one.

So, that's what she was doing upstairs. Did she hate Ezra for taking Colby, or did she actually have a crush on Ezra?

"I'll leave you girls to it." Colby grabbed the cup, filled it with water, and waved the girls goodbye.

The drunk girls immediately surrounded Sophie and hounded her with questions about Ezra.

It was a good thing he swore nothing to Sophie as he would've broken his promise within one minute of making it. He snuck back upstairs and went to the bedroom of the sleeping Ezra.

He slumped on the bed and buried his face in his hands. Truthfully, he'd never thought that hard about the fact that Ezra was a boy. It was a matter of fact to him. Colby would've initiated Operation Revenge on Ezra whether he was a boy, girl, or neither. Revenge didn't discriminate. Not that Colby fussed himself with ideas of revenge anymore. No, Colby wouldn't hurt Ezra. He'd grown too fond of him. He really, really, *really* cared about Ezra. There was no denying it.

So, would Sophie no longer be friends with Colby because of how he felt? Wow, he never thought he'd say that. He'd never imagined Sophie would ever come to hate him. They'd been through so much together. He stared up at the ceiling, but his vision was blurred with tears.

Was there anything he could do to fix things that didn't involve not being true to his feelings? Would she hate him forever if he pursued them?

He couldn't stand the idea of it. They'd been friends for so long and yet she'd disregarded all of that recently because of a boy. Okay, that boy was Ezra, and even Colby thought Ezra was pretty special, but come on. What happened to bros before hoes? A small sob escaped his lips.

What was he supposed to do?

"Colby? Why are you crying?" Ezra whispered. He unfurled himself from the blankets that Colby had tucked around him and placed his hands on Colby's face. "Why are you upset?"

The action made Colby's heart flutter. Drunk Ezra was too cute. "It's nothing," Colby tried to say with confidence, but his voice cracked.

Ezra placed lots of small butterfly kisses all over Colby's face. Sometimes he'd miss Colby's face completely—obviously still drunk—but most of the time, he'd kiss some part of his face. Colby couldn't help, but giggle at the gesture, which made Ezra smile.

"Come, come sleep next to me." Ezra fell back against the bed and rested his head on the pillows. He patted the space next to him for Colby to come and lie down.

The rational part of Colby's brain told him to go home and end the night early, but fuck that. He'd had a rough couple days and he wanted compensation. There was nothing wrong with taking a quick catnap, then leaving in a few hours.

Colby got under the blankets with Ezra and was immediately engulfed in a tight hug from the guy. "Why were you sad?" Ezra asked again.

Colby leaned into the hug and rested his head against Ezra's chest. He could hear his heart and the sound soothed him. "It was nothing really. I had a talk with Sophie, and she just said some things that I would've never expected from her and"—he swatted Ezra's hand away and laughed—"stop trying to touch my

150

nipples. I thought you were being a gentleman who wanted to hear about my feelings."

"Oh yes. Yes, yes, yes. Very much, yes," Ezra rambled. "Can you tell me about your feelings . . . naked?" Ezra's hands slipped to Colby's sides and he began to tickle Colby. Colby erupted in fits of laughter.

"Ezra . . . stop . . ." he pleaded in between laughs.

Eventually, Ezra did stop, but not out of any kind of chivalry.

Colby looked up and saw Ezra had fallen asleep during his tickle attack. "Asshole," Colby muttered with a wide smile on his face. He completely forgot about how shitty things had become recently. He just enjoyed the moment.

Well, he tried to think until he heard a banging coming from the room next door. It was a constant and quick pounding against the wall, accompanied by a lot of moaning. It didn't take a genius to figure out that it was a bed frame that was banging against the wall and two horny teens on top of the bed that were doing the banging. Poor Brent, he was going to be so upset when he found out someone had broken his upstairs rule.

Damn, whoever it was had crazy stamina. It didn't stay a mystery for long as a deep voice cried out, "Ah, Finley!"

Colby smiled to himself and internally congratulated his friend for finally banging Brent and—from the sounds of it—doing a really good job at it too.

CHAPTER EIGHTEEN
Wanted

Ezra was sure he must've been dreaming.

After all, how else do you explain that he was lying in a bed with Colby sleeping in his arms? It had to be a dream, a really fantastic dream, but a dream nonetheless.

It was a very realistic dream. Ezra could feel the warmth of Colby's body pressed tightly against his own. He could smell the lingering scent of his body spray. He didn't know what fragrance it was, but it was nice. He could hear Colby's gentle breathing occasionally interrupted by a murmuring of something in his sleep. It was a very realistic dream that he hoped to never wake up from.

He buried his face in Colby's dark hair and squeezed him a little tighter, carefully though so as not to wake him from his sleep. There wasn't anything in the world Ezra wouldn't give right now to stay in this moment forever. Warm, comfortable, and happy.

Of course, he couldn't entirely focus on this perfect moment as he began to wonder what had happened for them to end up in this position.

Ezra had arrived at Brent's party last night with Sophie. He'd picked her up at her house and headed there together, and he went to Brent's with one plan in mind—get wasted. His week had been shit. If he wasn't avoiding Colby at school so Ezra would stop lusting after him, then he was avoiding his father at home—if his father ever was home—so that taunts about his mystery boy would stop coming up. He had shown up to the party, was welcomed by Brent, then immediately started drinking.

He took every drink someone would offer to him. He was pretty sure he'd taken the drinks whether somebody had offered them or not. Some unlucky party guest would walk by Ezra and he'd snatch their drink from them before they could even notice it was gone. He vaguely remembered a girl he didn't personally know trying to kiss him. Thankfully, Sophie came and stopped her. Then he had gone to dance with a group of school friends and the rest was a blur. He didn't feel ridiculously ill as he'd expected, but his body was dead. Every small movement felt tiresome. His limbs were too heavy for his body to move, and his eyes ached when he tried to focus on what he was looking at. If he wasn't so focused on keeping Colby asleep to cuddle for longer, he would be slumped over in agony by now.

He stayed perfectly still, trying to memorise the feel of Colby's body against his just in case this was the last time this ever happened. He didn't want it to be. In Ezra's wildest dreams, they were together every night, and Ezra wasn't sickened by himself and neither was his father. But he couldn't disillusion himself with farfetched fantasies.

There was a loud clattering outside of the bedroom they were in, and two voices were talking to each other. One was Brent who kept grumbling about being in pain and the other was Finley who sounded very pleased with himself.

"My butt hurts," Brent whined, his voice muffled by the door.

"Come on, baby, you have to admit it was pretty good though, right?" Finley replied suggestively.

"Yeah, it was really good," Brent said in a quieter voice, sounding almost embarrassed. "But you could've gone easier on me."

"I'm sorry, but I do recall you screaming for me to 'go harder,' so am I a bad boyfriend for not going easy on you, or am I a great boyfriend for doing exactly what you said?"

Ezra could tell Finley had a shit-eating grin on his face, even without being able to see him.

"Hey, didn't Colby stay the night? Where is he?"

"Ezra did too, according to Sophie. They're probably downstairs or in a bedroom."

Finley whistled at Brent's remark.

"What? Is there something weird about that?"

Panic erupted in Ezra's chest.

Finley knew about him and Colby. How? What if he tells Brent? Ezra wasn't ready to tell anyone. No one was supposed to know. *Please don't tell him,* Ezra chanted in his head. *Please, please don't tell him.* Instead of moving away from Colby in case Brent or Finley walked in, Ezra found himself pulling Colby even closer into his chest. The smart thing to do would be to let go and pretend nothing had happened, but he couldn't. He had Colby in his arms. How was he supposed to let go now?

"Nothing," Finley responded. "I'm just whistling, baby." He then carried on whistling as if to prove he did it normally.

Thank God Finley was one devious pain in the ass. The door handle rattled and attempted to twist. Once again, Ezra pulled Colby closer towards him.

Luckily, the door was locked. Finley pounded his fist against the door.

Well, it was actually a small tap, but with Ezra's hangover amplifying the sound, a swat team might as well have been trying to break down the door.

"Colby! Colby! You in there, man?" Finley asked from the other side of the door.

Colby began to stir in Ezra's arms. Ezra feigned being asleep to avoid any potential awkwardness. He didn't want Colby to wake up yet, couldn't they have had their moment for a few more

154

minutes? Damn you, Finley. Colby didn't seem too surprised to be in Ezra's embrace, which surprised Ezra. He stretched, then called back to Finley.

"Yeah, I'm in here. So is Ezra."

"So that's where he is," Brent commented. "Do you want breakfast?"

"Sounds good. Be down in a bit," Colby replied.

The sound of the floorboards creaking faded as Brent and Finley went downstairs.

Colby laid back down in the bed and began to stroke Ezra's hair. It was so carefully done that Ezra thought he was imagining the sensation of it.

Don't do that, he thought. *Don't give me hope.*

Colby laughed to himself before getting out of the bed and heading downstairs. Ezra peeked at Colby as he left the room and couldn't help but admire the way Colby still looked radiant first thing in the morning. It was times like this when Ezra regretted not developing some sort of artistic skill. Words never came naturally to him when he was tasked with wring a creative piece in English Literature, and he was useless at art. A semi-decent stickman was the best he could do. He'd always been scientifically and mathematically orientated, but he wished he wasn't, so he would have some way of capturing in words or paint what Colby looked like to him.

When Colby was gone and the sound of his footsteps had long since disappeared downstairs, Ezra decided to try and get up. It was painful, but he couldn't stay here all day. Actually, Brent would probably let him stay all day, but Ezra didn't want to impose on him and his family like that.

He tried to look at his phone to check the time, but the brightness blinded him as soon as he turned it on. His eyes adjusted eventually, but the light still stung. He had two text messages from Sophie.

"Just in case you need a little guidance in your life. It worked for me," Ezra read Sophie's text out loud. "What the hell is she on about?"

He clicked on the website she had attached to her text message. His heart stopped when it finally loaded. Conversion therapy. She had sent him the link for conversion therapy for homosexuals in the next state over.

She knew. How did she know? He understood Finley knowing—him and Colby were as thick as thieves—but Brent said Sophie was drifting away from them. Colby wouldn't tell her. Colby shouldn't be telling anyone. What if Sophie told someone? His life was over if his dad found out he was still acting . . . this way. He'd be out on the streets with nothing. His mother wouldn't help him because she had a new family, new life.

He didn't know what to do, so he decided to play it off. *"Not sure what you mean by this, is it a joke I'm not in on? :/"* He texted Sophie.

She replied quickly. *"Not a joke :) I just get what you're going through, and I did this when I felt that way. My dad's a pastor. You're welcome to come and talk to him anytime. It's pretty tough at first, but it cures you afterwards xx"*

Wait, Sophie had gone through conversion therapy? Did that mean she was . . . No way. But why was she even recommending conversion therapy to Ezra anyway? Did he do something gay? Did he look gay? Did everybody know he was gay? Had everybody always known?

He quickly got up from the bed and ran downstairs. The only thing stopping him from doubling over in pain was the adrenaline pumping through him from the possibility of people knowing about his sexuality. He ran downstairs and into the kitchen, nearly slipping on the tiled floor.

"Morning, Ezra," Brent greeted. He was smiling at him with a cup of coffee in his hands.

Finley came up behind Brent and wrapped his arms around his waist. "You look like shit," Finley commented.

156

Brent whacked him on the arm for being rude.

"Fuck off, Finley. Where's Colby?" Ezra asked.

A smirk formed on Finley's face. "Oh, and why should I tell you?"

He did not need this right now. Brent looked at Finley curiously, still not happy about Finley's teasing.

"Where. Is. He?" Ezra asked again. He could feel himself becoming more and more aggravated, but he kept it down. The last thing he needed was to lash out at somebody right now.

"He's in the living room watching TV," Finley finally answered.

It occurred to Ezra in that moment that Finley knew Sophie almost as well as Colby did. Surely, he would know about Sophie's sexual preference. "Has Sophie ever dated anyone?" Ezra asked, hoping Brent didn't put two and two together.

"Why is that any of your business?"

Brent swatted his arm again. "Just tell him, or else I'm not going to make you any pancakes."

Finley made a childish pout. "I'm not sure if she has. She's never mentioned anything to me anyway. The only person she's suspiciously close with is Joanna, but come on, if Joanna wouldn't commit to Colby, she's not going to for Sophie. I'm not even sure if Sophie's allowed to date. Her parents are super-duper religious, not that religion is bad. My parents are Christians, but her parents are the old-fashioned kind of religious if you catch my drift. You know the there's-only-one-right-way-to-live-and-it's-our-way kind of thing. They're pretty freaky, man. I think they wanted her to wait until marriage before she slept with anyone. Could you imagine that? I would rather die than . . ." Finley looked up at Brent. "On second thought, my parents feel the same way."

"About what?" Brent asked. Damn, he really didn't care about this conversation. He was too busy measuring out bowls of flour and sugar.

"I'm not supposed to have sex until I'm married," Finley explained. "You've deflowered me, Brent. You have to save my honour and marry me."

Brent flicked a handful of flour at Finley. "Shut up. You're not funny."

"Then why are you smiling?"

"Because I'm thinking of something funny."

"So, you're thinking about me."

Ezra didn't stay in the kitchen any longer. Good for Brent for getting a boyfriend. However, he undeniably had terrible taste for liking Finley. Any other time, he probably could've tolerated it, but right now? Get that cute relationship crap out of his face. He stormed into the living room and slammed the door behind him. He had planned on being angry at Colby, to yell at him for letting it slip to both Finley and, possibly, Sophie that he had . . . homosexual tendencies. However, that changed when he saw Colby lazily lounging on the leather sofa and staring back at Ezra with sleepy eyes. Colby smiled at Ezra, and he could've sworn Colby's face was like the sun, and he felt warmer just being in his presence.

"Good morning," Colby said. Colby was still wearing his clothes from last night, but his Hawaiian shirt was crinkled and the top three buttons were undone.

Some twisted God was testing Ezra by presenting such an irresistible sight to him just as he'd decided to stop finding Colby so beautiful. What kind of monster puts a banquet with a *Do Not Eat* sign in front of a starving man.

"Morning," Ezra muttered.

Colby patted the space next to him for Ezra to come and sit down. "Sleep well?"

"Yeah, slept really well. Thank you."

He couldn't stay focused on being with Colby right now. Things in his life were moving so quickly around him that he didn't have the time to speak leisurely with Colby. "Does Sophie know what we did together? Did you tell her?"

That got Colby's attention. "Listen, Ezra, at the party last night—"

"Oh my god, you did. You told her!"

"No! Would you let me finish?"

Ezra stayed quiet, but he was an overwhelmed mess on the inside.

"At the party last night, you got very drunk, like stupid drunk. And I was upstairs and then you came in and then . . . and then you kissed me a little, not for very long though because you fell asleep on me, then Sophie walked in and saw us."

"How much did she see? What were we doing?"

"No, we were only cuddling. Technically, you were cuddling me more than the other way round, but that's beside the point."

Oh, crap. How was he going to explain that? *Oh, you misunderstood, Sophie! Colby and I were just wrestling on the bed. Easy mistake to make and not to worry, I am indeed the straightest of men.* She wasn't going to buy that. No one would buy that.

"Does it matter that she saw us?" Colby asked.

Ezra knew Colby could be a bit dumb at times, but he was just being naive now. Was he not able to see what could happen if this got out? Did he not care what his parents would think of him if they knew what they were up to? What his neighbours would think? What his friends, people at school, and random strangers on the street would think of him? "Do you not think it matters?" Ezra asked.

"I don't know, not to me. Because . . . well . . . I . . . and you . . . ugh," he stumbled with his words for a bit, his face turning pink. "Well, um because, because don't you want me, Ezra?"

More than anything was subconsciously Ezra's immediate reply, but he didn't say anything. Sure, it wasn't a confession or an "I love you" but this had to be pretty close, right? He had waited so long for something like this to happen and yet he was in no position to act on it.

159

"Maybe I just imagined it or misunderstood what you were saying, but I think I know what I feel. Actually, that's not true. I don't understand my feelings at all, but I want you, Ezra. Don't you feel the same?"

Ezra felt an onslaught of emotions. On the one hand, his heart was doing somersaults that Colby Williams had said that to *him*. On the other hand, he thought of his father and realised he had corrupted Colby with the same feelings that he had, and he felt like shit for it. Colby had liked girls before Ezra had tried to convert him to his way of thinking. Colby didn't know what he was saying. He was confused. Ezra had confused him.

"Hey, what's wrong?" Colby's voice intercepted his spiralling guilt. He wrapped his arms around Ezra and hugged him. "Whatever it is you can tell me, Ezra. I'm here for you."

Ezra wanted to wrap his arms around Colby too. He wanted to let out all his feelings, to tell him since the moment they met that Ezra had longed for Colby in ways he couldn't understand before, to tell him how hopelessly and desperately Ezra loved him. Those words didn't come to him.

Ezra had done enough damage. He'd confused Colby into liking him and wanting him sexually. That was it. Colby only wanted him sexually. Ezra had corrupted him; that's what his father would say and he was right.

He pushed Colby away.

"I'm sorry, Colby. I'm sorry, I did this to you," Ezra whispered hoarsely.

"What do you mean? You haven't done anything," Colby replied. He sounded concerned.

Ezra stood up from the sofa and left the house. He could hear Colby calling out for him to come back, even Brent and Finley tried to shout out to him, but he needed to go. He needed to go before he ruined Colby more than he already had.

CHAPTER NINETEEN
The C in Colby Stands for Confused

Was that a rejection?
But he didn't say no.
He apologised . . . then left.
What does that mean?

Colby stood in Brent's doorway. The crisp morning air caressed his face and helped to stop his brain from overheating. He'd been standing there for who knows how long, just staring out into the street. He wasn't sure why. Maybe in case Ezra came back or maybe just because he needed some fresh air.

He thought he'd made a breakthrough with his feelings this morning. After Sophie interrogated him about his relationship with Ezra and how Colby could no longer deny that he wanted to be able to touch Ezra again, he realised he wanted Ezra to himself. No more pretending he liked the idea of Ezra dating Sophie. No more bromance when he wanted it without the *b*.

He was pretty proud of himself as well. Normally, it took him weeks to figure out he liked somebody. It took him six months to realise he liked Joanna—not the best decision in hindsight but, whatever, he moved on—and that was with the assistance of his mom explaining his feelings to him. Yep, he was a big boy now. A big boy that knew how he felt. A big boy that may have just gotten rejected by the bigger boy he liked.

But was he rejected? He honestly didn't know.

He asked Ezra, "Do you want me?" He cringed just thinking about how desperate he sounded saying that, to which Ezra replied by apologising to him and leaving. Ezra said he did something to Colby, and Colby had no idea what any of that meant. Everything they did together was consensual and fun. If he was talking about the Joanna Incident, then Ezra should work on making it up to Colby, not running away from him. What could he be apologising for?

At first, Colby thought Ezra was apologising because he was rejecting him, but surely then he would've said "I'm sorry I don't feel the same" instead of "I'm sorry for doing this to you." Was *this* Ezra rejecting him? But surely not. But maybe. But no. But yes. But no. But yes. But n—

"Colby? You alright, man?" Finley placed a gentle but firm hand on Colby's shoulder.

He'd been in such high spirits this morning after managing to bang Brent last night and Colby had heard every single moment of it. It was an experience like no other. Listening to your best friend lose their virginity, it was a life-changing experience. In a way, they'd lost their virginity together. Well, Colby had lost his when he was fifteen because he was cool like that, but he'd lost his spiritual virginity as Finley had lost his physical one. They were virginity brothers now! Wait, no. That was the opposite of what he meant.

Damn it, Colby was too down in the dumps to contemplate the epic scale of being virginity brothers—he'd workshop the name later—he felt kinda guilty for bringing the mood down with his problems.

Colby didn't turn to face Finley. He kept looking out into the street. A blond boy walked up on the sidewalk, but it wasn't Ezra, and it made Colby's heart sink. "Yeah, I'm okay." He stood in silence for a moment before he plucked up the courage to ask Finley. "How do you know if you've been rejected?"

162

"Is that what happened this morning?" Finley asked carefully.

Colby could hear Brent singing to the radio in the kitchen, oblivious to the tension. Brent was sure Ezra would come back. Ezra had left his car on Brent's driveway, so he didn't really have a choice. The question was how long would Colby wait for Ezra to return? Should Colby wait at all?

"I don't know," Colby murmured just loud enough for Finley to hear. "It wasn't some big romantic gesture or anything, but I thought it got my point across. Then he left. He *just* left." Even saying it out loud didn't make it make sense to Colby.

"Wait, what?" Great, Finley was confused too, and he was supposed to be the expert in gay things.

"Do you think I should try talking to him again?"

"Yes," Finley said it with such conviction that Colby snapped out of his daze to stare at him. "He didn't give you an answer, plus . . . he's seemed pretty freaked recently, so maybe you just caught him at a bad time. I think it's worth a civil talking to. Give him some time though, a few days maybe, then go in for the kill. Or don't kill him, that's your choice. Promise me you won't do anything stupid, okay?"

Colby agreed.

Finley's serious face morphed into a shit-eating grin. "So . . . Colby's got a crush."

"No, I don't." Colby punched Finley in the arm, his face turning bright red. "Only a little."

*   *   *

Okay. So, Colby agreed he should try and talk to Ezra again, which he was going to do! But now he was standing outside of Ezra's house at six o'clock in the evening, having second thoughts about whether this was a good idea or not.

He'd promised Finley he wouldn't do anything too stupid, but it seemed like a good idea at the time to come over now and get it over with. He was so screwed. However, his mother didn't raise a quitter, so he knocked on the door and nearly shat himself when somebody opened it.

It wasn't Ezra who opened the door, but he looked a lot like him. He was around Ezra's height and had black hair streaked with grey. He looked to be in his late forties. His face reminded Colby of those photographs of Victorian men, where they stared directly at the camera with an emotionless face as hard as stone and they looked super-duper creepy. That was the epitome of the guy at the door.

"Can I help you?" the man asked, his voice low and unwelcoming.

"Um . . . is Ezra home?" Colby asked. Who the hell was this guy?

"And you are?"

"Oh, my name's Colby. Colby Williams. I'm a friend from school." He probably should've led with that instead of standing on the porch and demanding Ezra like a freak.

Something flickered in the man's sky-blue eyes. "Have you been here before?" the man asked.

This guy is weird, Colby thought. Colby smiled politely and nodded. "I was here last weekend. Ezra let me stay over."

The strangest thing happened—or at least, an unexpected thing happened. The man smiled widely and ushered Colby inside. "Come in, come in. I've just finished making dinner if you would like some food."

Colby wasn't given a chance to accept or deny.

"Of course, you do. You're a growing boy after all, always hungry. Even when you shouldn't be." The man's voice was harsh at the end, but he was still smiling.

The man shut the door behind Colby and locked it. Was he about to get murdered? Because that's what this felt like to him.

"Ezra, look! Your friend has come for dinner."

Colby immediately looked away from the locked door, all thoughts of how to escape the probable murderer leaving him as he saw the boy that had been consuming his thoughts for weeks now. He was wearing a tight black shirt with a pair of denim jeans. He looked straight out of a Calvin Klein photo shoot. Ezra was wearing a bit too much clothing to be a model, but that was a temporary problem.

"He's come to see you. Isn't that nice?" The way the man said it sounded like a threat, and it must've been working because Ezra looked terrified.

Did Colby seem like a stalker right now? It hadn't really occurred to him earlier, but it was weird to show up uninvited. Damn it! Why couldn't he ever think things through before he did them?

"Hey, Ezra," Colby greeted timidly. This was such a bad idea. Why hadn't Finley tried to stop him?

"Hey . . . ," Ezra muttered. He was still frozen in place on the stairs. ". . . I didn't know you were coming over."

"Surprise?" Colby awkwardly laughed. The atmosphere was thick. He could cut it with a knife, sprinkle his own dead brain cells on top for a little flavour, and eat that for dinner. Finley was so going to kill him if the man at the door didn't do it first.

Ezra managed to compose himself and come down the rest of the stairs. "What's for dinner, Dad?" he asked.

This guy is Ezra's dad? That, that, that makes a lot of sense actually, now that he thought about it.

"Lasagna. You like meat, don't you, Colby?"

That was an odd way of phrasing it, but who was he to judge how someone spoke?

Free food was free food though.

"Yep, love meat." He smiled at Ezra's dad. He had to make a good impression on the parents. It was the start of serious dating 101.

They walked in silence into the dining room with Ezra's dad keeping a firm hand on Colby's shoulder. He shoved Colby down in a chair and gave Ezra a weird look before he left the room.

Ezra sat in the chair next to Colby, but seemed to be keeping a distance from him as he shuffled his chair away. Ezra didn't look at Colby. He kept his eyes trained on the silverware that was already set out on the table but only for two.

"So—" Colby tried to break the ice.

"Why are you here?" Ezra's voice was quiet but aggressive.

Colby was really beginning to hate his choice in coming here. "I, um, I wanted to see you."

"Why?"

That struck a nerve with Colby. "What do you mean 'why'? You know why! You just stormed off without . . . without answering my question."

"What question is this?" asked Ezra's dad as he walked back into the room carrying a tray of lasagna.

Colby hadn't heard him walk in. The guy was as silent as a ninja. Ezra didn't answer him, and Colby was too confused by how quiet he was to answer him either.

"Well?"

"Colby was asking me . . ." Ezra began, ". . . to help him with his biology project. It's not his strong suit and our teacher recommended we work together."

"He came all the way here at six o'clock at night to ask you for help? I thought kids these days preferred to text or call each other. Almost sounds unbelievable."

Since when is six o'clock considered night? Colby thought.

Ezra's dad was still smiling creepily, as if something about this situation was almost entertaining for him. Ezra's dad cut each of them a slice and gave Colby a plate and cutlery.

"So, Colby," said Ezra's dad, "do you have a girlfriend?"

"No, I don't, Mr Dickinson," Colby responded. The question caused Ezra to visibly tense.

166

"A boyfriend then? And please call me Steven."

"Nope, I don't have a boyfriend either." He mentally added a hopeful *yet* to his sentence and glanced bashfully at Ezra, who looked like he was about to puke.

"But you would consider having one? A boyfriend, I mean." The smile on Steven's face dropped back into a solemn look.

Colby tried not to judge people too harshly based on first impressions, but there was something so fundamentally off about Steven that it made the entire house feel uncomfortable. When it had just been him and Ezra at the house, sure it felt empty, but there was nothing unpleasant about it. However, the house felt entirely different with Steven's presence. The house felt colder, more hostile, and extremely unwelcoming. Ezra had said his dad was almost never home. It was just Colby's luck to catch Steven when he was.

"I mean, yeah, I would consider getting a boyfriend." From Steven's sour face, it didn't look like Colby answered correctly. "Gender doesn't really matter to me."

Ezra looked shocked by his answer and glanced up at Colby.

"How very modern of you. If you don't mind me asking, what were you and my son up to when you slept round last weekend?" Steven asked.

He hadn't even touched his lasagna yet. It was going to get cold; Colby might have to eat it before that happens. Food waste was a terrible thing.

"What were we up to?" He thought back to when he was round. "Well, we watched a movie together. I think it was Paddington, and then"—*best keep up with the already established lie*— "we worked on my biology project, got some Chinese food, and then we got ready for bed, and went to football camp the next morning."

"You two shared a bed?" Steven asked

167

What an obvious question, Colby thought. Of course, they were in the same bed. How else could they have multiple rounds of excellent sex? "Yep. Top and tailed it." At one point in the night, they technically did, but they weren't sleeping when it happened.

"And you just slept? All the way through the night?"

They did fall asleep after they were properly worn out. Nothing like a bit of exercise before bed. "Yep, just slept until it was time to go to football. Ezra and I bunked together there too, with two other people, of course. That was a rough weekend. I was so sore by the end of it."

"I hope your body feels better. Do you know of a Reverend MacDonald?" Steven asked, primed and ready for another round of asking Colby weird questions. That was alright. Colby had weird answers. They were perfectly matched.

"Yeah, he's my friend Sophie's dad. I've met him a few times," Colby said. He glanced at Ezra.

Oh boy, if Ezra looked like he was going to puke before, he looked like he was about to drop dead now. Was he not enjoying the lasagne? Because Colby could take his too. There were starving children in the world, like Colby.

"He came up to me in the convenience store today, and was telling me about how close his daughter thought you and Ezra were at this party she went to. I didn't realise you two were such good friends. Even recommended an interesting summer camp for Ezra to go to," Steven said.

"Dad," Ezra suddenly spoke up. "It's not—"

"Hush, Ezra. I was talking to Colby."

Did Colby miss something? He had a really strong gut instinct right now telling him he'd missed something big, like really big, and Steven was being too fucking weird to tell him straight up.

"Yeah, Ezra and I were at the same party together. We're pretty close friends, I guess. Which summer camp did the reverend recommend? Was it the same one Sophie went to?" That was the best response he could think of as he tried to figure out what had gone over his head that Ezra and Steven were in on. Did Colby look weird or something? Did he have something stuck in his teeth? Was he on a prank show? He looked around, but there weren't any secret cameras, not any that he could spot anyway.

"I wasn't aware the reverend had sent his own daughter to the camp. Does she have a boyfriend at the moment?"

"Um, I think you're a bit old for her."

Steven put down his cutlery and stared at Colby. He waited for a moment, possibly waiting for Colby to say anything else. He shot Ezra a quizzical look. "I wasn't asking for myself."

"I mean, she might be into dilfs. I've never really asked her. She's only seventeen. I get that sixteen is the age of consent, but it's still a little odd. You know?"

Steven did not seem to know. He refused to talk to Colby for the rest of the meal. Colby didn't know why he was getting all quiet and pissy. He was the one being a pedo, not Colby. Only the sound of forks and knives scraping against plates was left.

After dinner, Steven kept mentioning how late it was and how worried Colby's mother must be. Colby wasn't the sharpest tool in the box, but he knew when someone was telling him to fuck off. Luckily, Ezra had volunteered to drive him home once Colby explained he didn't have his own license because he'd failed his driving test six times and his parents were sick of paying for him to resit it.

The ride began as quiet as the end of dinner had been, but Colby had a question to ask and an unrelenting drive to ask it.

"Will you go on a date with me!" Colby suddenly shouted.

The sudden noise caused Ezra's car to swerve wildly in the road before he regained control.

"What?" Ezra asked, frantically glancing between the road and Colby.

"Well, you know, do you wanna, like, hang out sometime? But not in a friendly way, but in a possibly romantic way." Colby applauded himself on what a smooth talker he was NOT.

169

Ezra pulled over to the side of the road, his hands gripping the wheel, turning his knuckles white. "Colby, I need you to properly listen to me for once. I know this is my fault for leading you into this—" Colby could feel a rejection coming. Had he really misread the situation that badly? It was pretty embarrassing "—but you don't know how you're feeling. I've confused you with my sexual advances."

"What?" That was not the rejection he was expecting. "I'm not confused."

"Yes, you are. I've confused you. I've influenced you into thinking you're into guys when you're not—"

"But I am into guys. I'm into you."

"You're attracted to girls. You always have been. You were obsessed with Joanna before I got involved, and you're going to grow up one day—"

"I'm not into Joanna. That's in the past. I'm into you."

"—going to have a wife and kids and . . . and you're going to be embarrassed that you ever acted this way, and . . ."

Colby reached in front of Ezra and hit the horn. *Honk!*

"What are you—" began Ezra.

Honk!

"What are—"

Honk!

"What—"

Honk! Honk! Honk!

"Stop talking nonsense," said Colby. "That's my job." He tore Ezra's hands off the steering wheel and held them in his own. "I am not confused. In fact, this is the least confused I've ever been. I know I'm not academically smart or street smart or emotionally smart or people smart or . . . I'm not that clever, but I know how I feel right now and I"—he took a deep breath—"I really like you, Ezra, and I don't want you to date Sophie or anyone else. I want you to go out . . . with me."

170

Colby tried to look sincere and brave on the outside, but on the inside, he was about ready to sprint away from the car, move to a different country, change his name, and pretend he wasn't about to get rejected by the first boy he'd ever had feelings for. He would become Fernando Santiago. He would move to Portugal and survive on the few Portuguese phrases his mom had been bothered to teach him, like *Hola* and *burro de merda*. Fernando's family had died in a skiing accident in the south of France, so he had to raise himself and had accidentally ended up in America due to a plane accident, which was why he had an American accident. It wasn't the perfect backstory, but Colby had a long flight to iron out the details.

"But . . . but . . . what about . . . really?" Ezra stuttered.

Oh, was this going well? Adios, Fernando. "Yes, really."

"But boys aren't supposed to date other boys."

Hola, Fernando. "What are you talking about? What about Finley and Brent?" asked Colby.

"They're different," Ezra replied simply.

"Different, how?"

"I don't know. They can do that."

"So, why can't you?"

Ezra didn't respond.

"Tomorrow? After school? We can go on a date, catch a movie, or something? Just say yes," Colby added with a cheeky grin.

Ezra didn't respond to that either, but he did nod slowly and unsurely, but that was enough for Colby.

He leant in and kissed Ezra on the cheek. "I'll see you tomorrow."

CHAPTER TWENTY
Help Not Wanted

"So, let me get this straight," Finley started with an exasperated sigh. "Even though I told you SIX TIMES not to do anything irrational or stupid, you decided it was a good idea to go to Ezra's house immediately after I told you that. You then had dinner with his dad, which was extremely awkward, which might be because he WASN'T EXPECTING GUESTS! And when you overstayed your welcome, you got Ezra to drive you home and then asked him out, even though he had possibly rejected you earlier that day, and he said . . ."

"And he said yes!" exclaimed Colby. "Well, I had to talk him round a bit, but he nodded his head, which is body language for yes!"

Finley stared at Colby the same way a teacher stares at a student that is in no way intelligent enough to be in the class. Colby was very familiar with the look.

"This is my fault. I should've known you'd do something stupid. Why did I even bother telling you to use your brain for once?" Finley shoved his face into his hands and let out a loud sigh.

"Are you angry?" Colby asked. He had come to terms that going to Ezra's house yesterday might have been a bad idea, but it worked out for the best. No need to dwell on the awkward past when Colby was pretty excited about the future.

Finley's shoulders began to shake as his face was still buried in his hands. At first, Colby thought he was crying until he could hear small laughs being muffled by Finley's hands. "No, man." Finley dropped his hands to reveal a broad smile that was erupting in laughter. "I'm not angry. I really should've known you'd do something like this. It's just so stupid and so *you*."

Colby didn't know how to feel about that. It had come to his attention recently that more often than not when people said the name *Colby* they related it to the word *stupid*, which seemed completely unfair to him. For example, he was smart at Literature and, um . . . and that other thing . . . and—"

"I am not stupid," Colby stated. "It was all part of my master plan. I'm five—no ten moves ahead of everyone else. If we were playing chess, then my queen would've done whatever the queen does and have won the game."

That only seemed to make Finley laugh harder. "Oh, for sure, man. I believe you." He took a few deep breaths and regained a bit of composure. "So, what kind of stuff did his dad ask you anyway?"

"He was kinda weird. The meal was really tense and awkward even though he kept smiling the entire time. At one point, he asked me if I liked meat and if I had a boyfriend. Maybe Ezra told him I'm a gay vegetarian."

"Bro, he was sussing you out!" Finley exclaimed.

"What does that mean?"

"It means he was trying to figure out if you were gay or not and if you were gunning for his son. Watch out, man. Sounds like he's got his eyes on you. That's kind of funny."

"How is that funny?" Colby asked. He hadn't realised he was being sussed out. Was that why Ezra was so tense the entire time? Fuck's sake, maybe he was stupid.

"It's funny because he's Ezra Dickinson," Finley said.

Colby wasn't following.

"His last name is Dickinson, and his dad is mad at you because you're trying to get your dick-in-his-son, you know, Dickinson."

Colby still didn't react to Finley.

"Whatever. My comedic genius is wasted on you people."

"That doesn't make any sense. I've never put my dick in his son. He's always put his dick in me. His last name should be DickinColby," Colby explained in all seriousness.

Finley erupted back into a laughing fit.

"What's so funny?"

Colby looked up to see Brent standing near their table. Brent sat next to Finley, who wrapped his arms around Brent's waist and kissed his neck in between his small giggles, and Brent smiled like a lovestruck fool at his actions. Colby couldn't help but imagine himself and Ezra acting like that towards each other, but that was probably jumping the gun considering they still hadn't gone on their first date . . . yet.

Now that he thought about it, he and Ezra were doing this whole relationship thing in a really weird order. First, they didn't like each other. Next, they had sex. Then, they broke up. And now, they were going on their first date. Not the typical order relationships go in. Although, a typical relationship probably wouldn't be with the guy your ex-girlfriend cheated on you with. Colby was special like that.

"Colby's going on a date today after he pretty much stalked the person into going out with him," Finley said, trying to stifle his own laugh.

"I'm not stalking him!" Colby exclaimed.

"Oh? Is this your date with Ezra?" Brent asked.

Huh? Since when did Brent know? It made sense that he knew. He was Ezra's best friend after all, but Ezra had never mentioned it before. In fact, he was adamant that Colby couldn't tell anyone so it was a bit ironic for him to go tell Brent.

"Who did you hear that from?" Colby genuinely had no idea whether Ezra had kept their relationship to himself or not.

"From Ezra," said Brent. "He was telling me all about it last night. He's got so many plans: a fancy dinner date, a bouquet, and a trip to the circus."

Two out of three of those things sounded nice, though Colby was more of a sunflower person himself, Ezra did not mention a circus. "A circus? With like, clowns and shit?"

"Aw, maybe he's taking you to meet his family," Finley joked.

"Yep." Brent nodded. "Ezra's family are circus performers on his mother's side. He's been training to become a strong man since he was ten."

Colby could believe that. Ezra was buff.

"He'll probably try and get you involved with something while you're there. You could become the lion tamer. They need a new one of those since the last one got eaten."

Oh god, Colby was pretty sure he was going to cry. He didn't have what it took to become a lion tamer. He hated cats, and they hated him. His own pet cat bit him all the time and pissed on his stuff whenever it got the chance. How far was he willing to go for love? He wasn't sure he could go that far. Colby, the Lion Tamer, didn't even have a ring to it. He was doomed!

"I can't," Colby whined. "I thought we were just going to do a movie and dinner or something. I can't run away with the circus. My mom would kill me." Great, he was going to lose Ezra forever all because he couldn't get along with cats.

"I was kidding," said Brent.

Colby wiped away his tears. What did Brent just say?

"You were kidding?" asked Finley, equally as confused as Colby. "You sounded very serious when you said it."

Brent looked quite embarrassed. "I thought we were making jokes about Colby and Ezra being together. I overheard your DickinColby joke and thought I'd join in. Wait, are you serious? Does Ezra have his—" Brent made a circle with one hand and attempted to put a finger through it with the other hand. He couldn't do it. He got too embarrassed and put his hands away.

"Pfft, no. Of course not. Me and Ezra? As if. No way José. Absolutely not. Gross."

"Oh my god, you're actually going on a date with him," exclaimed Brent. "He . . . he didn't tell me." Brent stared at Colby in silent disbelief. He didn't say anything.

Finley was the first to interrupt the heavy silence. He was looking at something behind Colby. "Why isn't Sophie sitting with us today?"

Colby turned around and sure enough, Sophie was sitting at a cafeteria table with Joanna and some other girls that Colby didn't really know. He recognised a few of them as girls from the cheerleading squad. Some were in the same classes as Colby, and the rest were friends of Joanna's that he'd met while they were dating. He remembered Joanna's friends always used to make weird comments about Joanna's love for Colby and laugh at him behind his back. He never thought much of it before, but after what Ezra and Finley had told him, he now knew why they acted that way.

"By the way, is everything good between you and Sophie, man?" Finley asked.

"We had a fight at Brent's party, but that's about it. Why do you ask?"

"Because she came up to me this morning and asked what time you got home from the party last night." Finley loosened his grip around Brent's waist without actually letting go, so he could look at Colby better.

"She's worried about me. She thinks I'm messing things up for myself and that somebody is going to stop us from being friends. I don't really get it, but it's stressing her out." Colby hadn't thought much about their fight. Yeah, she said some weird and pretty mean things but they were still friends in the end, or at least

176

he thought so. There had to be a reasonable explanation for whatever was going on with her.

"Maybe she's afraid you're pushing your gay agenda onto Ezra." Finley laughed.

Gay agenda? What did that mean? Was he supposed to have a gay agenda to be bisexual? Did he not qualify to be bisexual without a gay agenda? Did you need qualifications to be bisexual? "Agenda" implied some of a plan. Colby didn't have a plan. He never did. He hadn't realised sexuality was so complicated. Colby nodded his head in agreement at Finley.

"So," Finley began trying to lighten the mood as Brent still wasn't talking and Colby was considering the requirements he might need to be considered bisexual, "what are you actually going to do on your date?"

"Are you sure it's a date?" Brent interjected. "Not just two guys hanging out."

"I think so. Is the circus real?"

"No, of course not."

"Thank goodness. I don't want to get eaten by lions. Tigers maybe, but definitely not lions." That was one less thing to worry about. "Do you think that he thinks it's just a casual thing? Should I go talk to him to clarify?"

"I'll go ask him." Brent stood up from the table and removed himself from Finley's grasp. He walked out of the cafeteria with the urgent pace of a man on a mission.

Once Brent was gone and Finley had nothing left to distract him, he turned back to Colby and with all seriousness asked him, "Did you think the circus thing was real?"

"Yes. I didn't know Brent knew how to lie."

"Exactly. At first, I was like, this is way too ridiculous to be real, but I also thought Brent was way too pure to lie."

"He's really nice. You're really lucky, Fin."

"Thanks. Ezra's going to kill us."

"Oh yeah. We are so dead."

"So, what are you planning for this date?"

"The classic," Colby said. "Movie at the theatres, then dinner. Works every time." He added with a smug smile. Truthfully, he'd only ever gone on dates with Joanna, but it'd worked on her.

"Dude, the movie theatre was shut down on Friday."

"What? Why?"

"Bug infestation and health violations. Apparently, some kid got some nasty disease from eating the popcorn. If you still want to do a movie, why not do it at your house? You know, the old *Netflix and chill.*" Finley winked at him. "Now, *that* works every time."

"Geez, who died and made you the king of dates?" said Colby, playfully kicking Finley's leg under the table.

"What's this about dates?" The soft voice startled Colby, and from Finley's sour expression, it could only be one person.

"I'm going on a date today, Soph," Colby replied calmly, looking up at Sophie. Her hair was tied up in that super tight ponytail that all the cheerleaders wore, and she was wearing her cheerleading uniform with it.

"Oh." Sophie's smile faltered a bit. "With whom?"

"Maybe we should go find Brent," Finley interrupted.

"You're very close to him these days," Sophie said sweetly. "You should be careful. Don't want people getting the wrong idea."

"And what wrong idea is that exactly?" Finley scowled.

"Well, that you two are dating, of course. It would completely put off any girls who'd want to date you, and then how would you live a fulfilling and happy high school life then?"

"You should get a girlfriend then, if they are the key to a happy high school career."

Sophie blushed at his comment. "I'm only trying to help you. This phase you're going through won't make you happy. My parents told me so, and Ezra knows it too." Sophie glanced at Colby. "You're wasting your time and possibly affecting your entire life with these ideas." She looked nervously behind her at the table she had been sitting at. "Maybe, um, maybe you should try talking to Joanna again, Colby. She's single and she says she kinda misses you . . . only if you want to though."

Colby started laughing. "I don't know what you're on right now, Soph, but give me some because you are making no sense." Joanna? Miss Colby? Get back together with her? That was the most ridiculous thing he'd heard all day—even more ridiculous than Finley's Dick-in-son joke.

Sophie kept looking back at her table. Joanna was glaring at her, and the girls surrounding her all watched Sophie.

He lowered his voice to a whisper. "Are they putting you up to this?"

"Don't be silly. They're my friends."

"I'm your friend too."

She smiled at him. "I'll talk to you later." She turned and went back to the table. The gaggle of girls waiting for her instantly swarmed her. They would all ask Sophie a question, then glance at Finley and Colby.

"What the fuck was that?" Colby muttered.

"Don't know, don't care," said Finley.

CHAPTER TWENTY-ONE
Netflix and Chill

"I didn't realise you were serious," Ezra said. His face matched the surprise in his words.

"Of course, I was serious. Did you think I was joking?" Colby grabbed Ezra's hands and kept them in a strong grip in case he tried to wiggle free. It's not that he was forcing him to stay there, but Colby was very ready to chase Ezra across the car park, tackle him to the ground, and force him to enjoy a great day with Colby.

Finley and Colby had managed to find Brent before the lunch period had ended, but not Ezra. So, Colby had patiently—and kinda stalkishly—waited by Ezra's car for him to come out of school. Ezra had looked shocked to see Colby waiting for him as if he'd completely forgotten about their agreed date for today. It wounded Colby a little that Ezra wasn't into it as much as he was, but he was sure that was something he could make up for tonight.

"Yeah, kind of," Ezra replied. "I mean, after the last time I thought you genuinely wanted to spend time with me . . ." Ezra averted his gaze to the tarmac.

Was he about to run? Don't try it, Ezra. Colby had his running shoes on today.

"Well, I *was* being serious." Colby stepped closer to Ezra. "Do you still want to go?" He internally scolded himself for being so timid when he asked that. Surely, now was the time to show confidence, not reservation. He should've put his foot down, demanded Ezra come with him, and let Stockholm syndrome do the rest.

Ezra glanced around at his surroundings, then let out a heavy sigh. "This isn't some stupid revenge plot, is it?"

"Absolutely not."

"Promise?"

"Promise."

"Okay then."

Colby hadn't realised how wide he was smiling until his cheeks began to physically ache.

"What's the plan?" Ezra asked.

Colby stopped smiling. It would be a stretch to say he had a plan. Never in his life, no matter what he was doing or how important the thing he was doing, he never had the brainpower to come up with a coherent and functional plan. So, he suggested what Finley said. Finley was much more put together than Colby and had a good relationship with Brent. Therefore, he must know what he's doing.

"Well, I was going to take you to the movie theatre, but apparently that's being fumigated so wanna just come round to mine and eat a shit tonne of candy on my couch?"

Ezra chuckled at him, so Colby assumed he must've been doing something right. "Sounds good to me."

"What kind of movies do you like?" Colby asked.

Ezra thought for a second. "I like horror movies."

"No."

"I thought this date was for me?"

"It is, but the whole thing is cancelled if you choose horror."

"I love Western movies."

Colby could've guessed the horror bit, considering the amount of horror DVDs Ezra had at his house. Colby had never watched a Western movie before. He never really went through a cowboy phase, but the idea of Ezra in a cowboy hat with no shirt on and some denim trousers with big leather boots on was very appealing.

Ezra drove the two of them to the convenience store to grab some popcorn, slushies, and any other sugary treats they wanted. On the way, Colby explained the embarrassing stories that came from each of his failed driving tests—some stories ranging from nearly hitting an old lady crossing the road to driving away from the police when they tried to pull him over for driving too fast. For some reason, he thought the police were legally not allowed to intervene with learner drivers so he just kept on driving. Each story made Ezra laugh more and more, so he didn't really mind reliving the embarrassing memories.

The two boys were deciding what flavour of popcorn to get when a pair of girls came up to them. They couldn't have been older than twenty and both of them were very pretty. One had brown hair and the other blonde. They approached the two boys, and they all made small talk until the brunette asked them a question.

"We were on our way to the lake to have a few drinks with some friends. Wanna come?" She bit her bottom lip and looked up at Ezra in particular through her long lashes.

"Sorry, we've already got plans," Colby replied.

"Oh? What are you up to?" the brunette asked.

"We're on a date," Ezra said and laced his fingers with Colby's and pulled him closer.

The girls looked shocked, but not nearly as shocked as Colby.

"Oh my god, really sorry," the blonde started to apologise. "We didn't realise you two were together. Sorry for interrupting. Have fun!" The girls turned around and left in a hurry, looking slightly embarrassed.

"What's wrong?" Ezra asked.

"Oh, nothing," Colby muttered, his cheeks heating up. "We're on a date, that I asked you on and you said yes." Colby internally patted himself on the back for doing something right. Screw Finley, he knew it was a good idea to go round to Ezra's house and ask him out. Now, who was the real idiot?

"Yeah," said Ezra. He squeezed Colby's hand a little. "I'm really looking forward to this."

Colby was going to agree with him, but then he spotted a very strange old woman peeking at them from behind a large shelf of cereals and chips. She looked to be an elderly woman with her grey hair cut short, and she was wearing a blue cardigan that fell to her knees. She also had a pair of red horned glasses on. All in all, she was a very strange-looking old lady. What was even stranger was how intensely she was observing Colby and Ezra. Her eyes glanced up from Colby and Ezra's entangled hands and met Colby's eyes. She darted away when she realised she'd been caught.

"It's not even dark yet and the freaks are already out," Colby mumbled to himself as he watched the old lady hide behind a different shelf.

"What'd you say?" asked Ezra as he picked out a bag of salted popcorn.

"Nothing. Don't worry about it."

Ezra looked at him strangely, but didn't press him for answers whilst Colby kept an eye on the old lady. He didn't like the way she constantly watched them. He wanted to get Ezra out of her sight quickly in case she had some sort of meat cleaver hidden under that blue cardigan of hers.

Colby paid for all the stuff. Ezra kept on trying to pay for it, but Colby was a gentleman no matter who he was taking on a date. He did crack some of the sweets open on the drive home and refused to give any to Ezra since he didn't pay for them. When they got home, Ezra grabbed the bags of popcorn and candy and sprinted inside with them. Colby knew he'd put on his running shoes for a reason.

After they'd messed around for a bit, Colby looked for a movie to watch on the TV in his living room whilst Ezra heated up the popcorn.

He looked through the Western movies collection and saw some he knew, like "The Good, The Bad and The Ugly" and some he'd never heard of. He settled on one called "Brokeback Mountain" because it looked like the stereotypical cowboy movie Ezra might like.

Colby set up his sofa with blankets and pillows and arranged all their diabetes-inducing snack collection on a nearby coffee table. He dimmed the lights a bit and tried to look natural but sexy at the same time.

It wasn't really working, but the effort was put in.

Ezra came and sat down next to Colby and then the movie began.

Fuck, Colby didn't remember being remotely this nervous when they'd watched a movie at Ezra's house. Ezra had actually sat close to him this time. Colby didn't need to make up some weird excuse to get closer. Could he hold Ezra's hand? Was it really that simple?

His palms were sweaty, and his heart was about to leap out of his chest. He kept trying to think of ways to get some physical contact. However, it was like his body didn't even know how to do basic movements anymore. It all seemed too hard. Ezra was right next to him and yet, to hold his hand felt like reaching over an impossible distance.

Just seeing Ezra's handsome face glowing from the light of the TV made his heart beat faster and his brain turn to mush.

"I think I recognise this movie," Ezra mumbled while squinting at the TV.

Colby hadn't been paying any attention to the movie as he was too distracted. Why couldn't he remember how to be slick enough to hold someone's hand? It's not that difficult!

Just need to do it in one swift movement, Colby thought.

184

He was about to hold Ezra's hand when loud and deep moans erupted from the TV. He looked up to find the two male leads of the movie going at it like a pair of bunny rabbits. Had he accidentally put on a gay cowboy porno? Surely, even Colby couldn't make that mistake.

"I do recognise the movie," said Ezra, laughing. "It was a bit of a, um . . . sexual awakening of mine when I was younger. I only remember this scene though. I remember watching this scene on my computer, then smashing my computer because I was so scared my dad would find it, and I didn't know how to delete my internet history."

Colby's face felt like it was on fire. Of course, he would accidentally put on a cowboy movie with an intense gay sex scene. His luck really was the worst.

Ezra leaned in and kissed him.

Or maybe he had the best luck in the world.

The kiss surprised Colby for a second, but he swiftly began to kiss Ezra back. Like hell he was about to miss this chance.

Colby hadn't realised how much he missed kissing Ezra. His lips were always surprisingly soft which contrasted with his tough demeanour and moody little bitch attitude. He was only sort of kidding.

After the way Ezra had been avoiding him, Colby did not waste his opportunity to enjoy him whilst Ezra still liked him. He'd been thinking of what he'd do with Ezra if they were alone together again. He'd fantasised of possible locations, possible positions, dream scenarios, and dream dialogue. His family couch wasn't the first place his fantasies had gone to, but beggars couldn't be choosers, and Colby was ready to beg for some action.

He positioned himself onto Ezra's lap and took Ezra's shirt off. He decided to go the extra mile by swinging it around for a second, then letting it fly off in a random direction.

"Down in front. I'm trying to watch the movie," Ezra joked.

"Screw the movie." He was not in the mood for a joke. Netflix and chill was not to be taken seriously. It meant one thing, and Colby was going to get that one thing.

He enjoyed being so close to Ezra's face again. He ran his fingers across his sharp jawline and felt the small stubble scratch him.

"You need to shave," he commented.

"I was thinking of growing a beard. I want to look like one of those lumberjacks."

He knew Ezra was joking. He couldn't imagine Ezra with a beard. He didn't really want to. All he could imagine was a blond Santa Claus, even though Santa and Ezra looked absolutely nothing alike.

"No" was all Colby said. Even if they didn't go on another date after this, there was no way Ezra was getting a beard on his watch.

"Now, I definitely want one."

Colby was about to abandon his whole Netflix and chill plan to give Ezra a lecture on why he wasn't allowed a beard, but he didn't get the chance to speak. Ezra leaned forward and captured Colby's lips with his own. He moaned at the sensation of Ezra's domineering kiss and the way his hands squeezed his ass. They fooled around for a while, kissing and touching until Colby's lips were sore. Even then, they didn't stop.

"What time is it?" Ezra asked.

Colby reached for his phone and looked. "Six forty-five."

Huh. That time kind of rang a bell with him, like it was important or something. His brain was too fogged with pleasure to remember what. He leaned in and kissed Ezra again, who did not hesitate to kiss him back.

He soon realised why that time was so important when his dad swung open the living room door and yelled, "I'm home."

It took Colby's dad a moment to register that his only son was sitting half naked on the sofa with his favourite student wrapped in his arms as two gay cowboys made out on the TV.

CHAPTER TWENTY-TWO
Meeting the In-Laws

Colby's brain stopped functioning the moment he made eye contact with his dad.

He remembered the time his dad had found his porn history before Colby had learnt how to clear his search history, and that he probably shouldn't be doing stuff like that on the family computer. He wasn't looking at anything crazy. As a young teen, he'd simply typed "boobz"—yes, with a z—into Google and enjoyed the results. It had been humiliating, and one of the most embarrassing moments of his life that his mom insisted on bringing up every year or so. He remembered that at the time, his dad had been just as awkward about it as he tried to give Colby the good ol' birds-and-the-bees talk, which neither party enjoyed speaking about or listening to. That reminded him of what was happening right now.

Except now, it was a thousand times worse.

"What . . . ," his dad said quietly, "what are you boys up to?" His dad still looked beyond shocked, but he also looked like he was trying to process the situation now. "Hello, Ezra," his dad greeted.

"Hi, Mr Williams," Ezra replied carefully.

"We were just . . ." Shit, how was Colby supposed to explain this? Maybe he could convince his dad that Ezra was wearing a sheer shirt that made it look like he was shirtless when he actually wasn't. Then how would he explain the way they were sitting together? He could say he and Ezra were doing some very heterosexual, very friendly non-competitive wrestling and then it got too hot, so Ezra *had* to take off his clothes to cool down. No, that was stupid. "Ezra's got hot sauce in his eyes," Colby said with confidence.

"Alright." His dad nodded along.

"I'm trying to get it out."

"Why doesn't Ezra have a shirt on?"

"He got hot sauce on the shirt."

Colby looked back down to Ezra who was staring up at him. It wasn't quite the look of pure adoration like before, more of a what-the-fuck-are-you-talking-about kind of look. Well, unless Mr Smarty-Pants could think of a different excuse, they were going with Colby's plan. Colby brushed some imaginary hot sauce off of Ezra's chest and poked him in the eye. Predictably, Ezra flinched.

"I think he's still got some sauce in there," Colby told his dad.

"Okey dokey, hot sauce, yeah. Get dressed so we can, um . . . talk about this." With that, his father left the room to no doubt prepare some sort of speech on safe sex or gay relationships or something else that Colby would rather die than talk to his dad about.

He felt Ezra's body get even tenser—if that was physically possible—and his breathing became rushed and uneven.

"Oh god," he panted. "He's going to kill us."

"Nah. He's just going to give us a lecture." Colby put his hands over his face and groaned loudly. "This is so embarrassing! He's going to tell Mom too, and she's never going to let this go. She'll tell everybody."

Ezra's body shot up like a rocket, and he pinned Colby's wrists down next to his head. If Colby wasn't aware that his dad was in the other room, he would've totally been into this. Except,

189

maybe not due to the panic that had engulfed Ezra's face. Ezra's hands even trembled a little as he kept Colby pinned down.

"Ezra, what's wrong?" Colby asked softly, genuinely concerned for him.

"What's wrong? We were just caught by your dad in a very compromising position, and now you're saying your mom is going to tell *everybody*. Who's *everybody*? Because I don't want *everybody* to know."

"It'll be fine," Colby tried to reassure, but Ezra still looked panicked and very frustrated.

"No, it's not fine!" Ezra released Colby. He gripped his own hair in his hands and looked around frantically. "If my dad hears about this . . . hell, I don't even know what he'll do."

Colby sat up and grabbed the sides of Ezra's face so he was forced to look Colby directly in the eyes. "*It will be fine.* My parents are not assholes. My dad will lecture us for a bit. My mom will tease us, but if you tell them not to tell anyone, then it will not leave this house. I promise."

Ezra calmed down slightly, but not a lot. "Okay. Let's get this over with then." Ezra took a deep breath before getting off the sofa.

"Ezra, you're not wearing a shirt."

Ezra shyly covered his indecency until Colby found his shirt and he slipped it back on. Ezra's face was pale, and he appeared as though he was going to vomit at any second. Colby leaned forward and kissed him sweetly on the cheek.

"It'll be fine," Colby reassured him. He silently hoped Ezra would refrain from throwing up though.

They left the room and found Colby's dad sitting at the kitchen table. His dad looked like he was deep in thought with his brows furrowed and his face resting in his hands, propped up by his elbows on the table. His dad looked nothing like Colby with his fair skin and light brown hair, and their personalities greatly differed as well. His dad was a patient man who thought things through before

190

he did anything and was extremely intelligent both academically and emotionally. It was his kind nature that made him one of the most popular teachers in the school. Often being a trusted confidant of students who needed to talk about their problems. Colby did not share his dad's calm mindset. No, not at all. He took after his mom in all the best and worst ways.

His dad looked up at them as they entered, and he gestured to the dining room chairs on the opposite side of the table. "Please sit down, boys," his dad said.

Colby and Ezra did just that. Ezra looked even paler than before, now that he was sitting in front of Colby's dad. Colby subtly brushed his hand against Ezra's then interlocked their fingers, so they were secretly holding hands under the table. Ezra gave him a small smile for that.

"Now," said Colby's dad, "protection is *very* important when it comes to . . . sexual intercourse, no matter what gender the pair are. So, I want you boys to keep that in mind if you ever decide to take things further." His dad paused and his expression became uncomfortable. "I just think . . . that maybe . . . you could've told me or your mom that you two were engaged in a relationship before you . . . tried to do the devil's tango in the family living room."

"Devil's tango? Really, Dad? Just say sex. You're making this much more awkward than it needs to be." Colby grimaced.

"I am trying to maintain a levity by using euphemistic terms such as knocking boots—" his dad explained.

"Having sex," Colby interrupted.

"Or bumping uglies—"

"Sex."

"Or two-person push-ups—"

"Sex."

"Or Netflix and chill, which I was informed today by my sophomore English class is actually a euphemistic term that is meant to imply to the other person beforehand that you wish to, um . . . do the dance with no pants."

Oof, that was what Finley had called it, but he was too much on a roll to stop annoying his dad. "Sex, sex, sex, sex, sex, sex, sex—"

"Alright!" his dad yelled. "You two were doing improper things in the *family* living room, a *communal* space for *all* of us. It's not very appropriate." He kind of had a good point there.

Colby hadn't really considered moving to a different room once Ezra started kissing him. His mind turned to mush, and all he could think about was being with Ezra. He was a horny hormonal teenage boy. Could you really blame him?

"Not only that, you didn't even tell me or your mom that you were attracted to men, which there is nothing wrong with. I've always been a firm supporter of the LGBTQ+ community. In fact, just last year, I was personally invited to a drag performance by a former student of mine, but I didn't go, not because I don't approve of it but because I'm a married man. And the only nights he was performing were nights your mom couldn't do, and I didn't want to go to a bar alone, that's—" his dad rambled.

"Okay, we get it, Dad. Gay is okay. We know," Colby replied snarkily, just wanting this conversation to be over.

"Yes. Gay is okay, so why didn't you tell us, Colby? I don't care if you have a boyfriend as long as you are happy and they treat you well."

Boyfriend? That got Ezra out of his weird state by that. "We, um, your son and I—we are—we're not, um . . ." Ezra turned to Colby for help on the boyfriend subject, but Colby didn't interject. He didn't know what to say or what to call the two of them. Ezra being Colby's boyfriend, it didn't sound too bad.

"We only had our first date today," Colby said quietly, his face heating up. Ugh, why did his dad always make things so awkward and complicated?

"You were getting down and dirty on your first date?" Colby's dad removed his glasses and polished them on his formal button-up shirt. "Not leaving much to the imagination, huh, Colby," he teased.

"Are you calling me a slut?" Colby asked, appalled and insulted by his dad's accusation.

His dad only shrugged. "I'm not saying you're not one."

"You've got no room to talk, Dad. You got mom pregnant in a janitor's closet without even getting her a drink first."

His dad ignored Colby and continued to talk. Sore loser couldn't take the heat. "I have to admit though." He turned to look at Ezra. "Out of all the boys in the school, I wasn't expecting you two to get together. What, all those months of bitter rivalry just wear off?"

"We talked it out and came to the realisation that we get along better than we thought." Colby tried to sound mature as he explained things. He didn't want to go into the details of how immature he had been due to his anger over Joanna cheating on him, then directing all that rage onto Ezra, and then making up an elaborate revenge scheme that included Colby seducing Ezra, then breaking his heart, and then failing at that plan by liking Ezra so much he couldn't bear to be apart from him. It sounded really stupid and immature in hindsight.

His parents knew nothing about the Joanna incident to his knowledge. They knew what Colby told them. Joanna had ended things with Colby, and it had been incredibly messy. No extra details or names were spilled. He kept the uncomfortable business of catching Ezra and Joanna together to himself.

"Still, it's unexpected. Your mother thought you and Finley were secretly knocking boots with each other, but now she owes me twenty bucks, so I guess I need to thank you two after all."

"Ew, me and Finley? As if. He's got his own boyfriend now anyway. Brent, the really tall guy on the football team," Colby explained, his face twisted in disgust at the idea of him and Finley.

Gross. They were more like brothers than best friends. The idea of those two being together was practically incest.

"Oh, I know about Brent," said his dad. "Finley won't shut up about him. Every talk we have after class is about 5% talking about his grade and 95% about Brent. At least, he finally found the courage to ask him out. I was very much rooting for him."

"Finley told you about Brent before he told me?"

"He said last year that he tried to tell you, but he was pretty sure he'd been too subtle in his coming out to you and that you thought he was just passionate for muscular men."

"He is passionate about them. I was right."

His dad put his arms up in surrender. "Agree to disagree."

"Why are you interested in my son, Ezra?" his dad asked.

Ezra hadn't said anything during the entire conversation. He'd mostly hung his head in shame and listened in. He looked caught off guard by the attention shifting to him. "Well, um, Colby is, um . . ." He calmed himself, then dropped the stammering as he met Mr William's eyes. "I've liked Colby for quite a while, sir."

Was that true? Colby wondered.

"However, I was confused by these feelings which fuelled the rivalry that you noticed between your son and me. I may still be coming to terms with myself, but I know how I feel about Colby. I think he's handsome and kindhearted and dumb in a very endearing way."

Colby felt insulted by that last part, but his dad nodded in agreement. *Fuck you, guys, too,* Colby thought.

"I care for him very much."

Colby couldn't contain the blush that blossomed across his cheeks.

"Alright." His father smiled. "As long as you treat my son like the little prince that he is, then I don't think we'll have any problems." His dad stood from the table and placed a firm hand on Ezra's shoulder. "I'm here if you need to talk about what you're going through, as either your teacher or your boyfriend's father."

194

For the first time in a while, Ezra finally relaxed and smiled up at Colby's dad. "Thank you."

"And you," his dad began, patting Colby roughly on the head. "I don't care if you're having sex, as long as you do it safely and *not* in a public space. Come on, son, your mom and I use that room too. A little consideration, please."

"Whatever," Colby mumbled. His cheeks were still burning as the word *boyfriend* circled in his head.

CHAPTER TWENTY-THREE
End of the Line

Ezra couldn't really remember many moments when his parents had peacefully coincided in the same room with each other, so to see Colby's parents joking around together so lovingly was a brand-new experience for him. He didn't mean to seem bitter when he thought this, but he'd almost forgotten that people could genuinely love each other and not all marriages ended in painful divorces. It was most heartwarming to watch the way Mr Williams would look at his wife like she was the centre of the entire world. The moon, the stars, and the planets all moving around her to get a glimpse of what Mr Williams adored most, and she looked at him the same way. Ezra's parents—for as long as he could remember—had never held such an affection for each other.

His father had once described his marriage to his mother as one of *convenience* rather than love.

Seeing the Williams was refreshing, to say the least.

Ezra had been terrified when Mr Williams had walked in on them seconds after Ezra had, as he put it, *bumped uglies* with his only son. No, terrified does not even sum up how he had felt. He'd been afraid, nauseated, horrified, frightened . . . you get the picture. Then, when Mr Williams wanted to *talk* to the two of them. Ezra was already thinking of escape routes.

He was waiting for Mr Williams to start shunning them or to start yelling about how the prospects of their future would all disappear if they didn't stop now, but Mr Williams never did. Of course, Ezra was familiar with the kindhearted Mr Williams from school, but how people presented themselves in public could contrast with how they were in private. Ezra's own dad had a reputation for being a great single father around his law firm. None of that was true, but no one needed to know that. It was surprising and the complete opposite of how Ezra's father would've reacted if he had been the one to catch the two of them together. Not to speak ill of his own father, but that had been what Ezra was expecting Mr Williams to be like. When the talk was finished, Mr Williams had remained kind to him. He even asked Ezra to call him Trevor. Trevor was so kind.

Even Mrs Williams—who insisted that Ezra call her Jemma—didn't condemn Ezra and Colby for what they'd been doing. In fact, she'd found it hilarious that her husband had walked in on them. She kept teasing Colby by making sexual innuendos at him.

"Hey, Ezra," Jemma called to him. She was sitting in the living room—obviously avoiding the abused couch—with her legs resting on a bean bag. "Why don't you stay the night? I feel like we've interrupted your date night."

Ezra wasn't sure how to respond, but he didn't need to as Colby beat him to it.

"You can sleep in my room," he said happily.

His mother wiggled her eyebrows suggestively at him and caused Colby to start blushing.

"On the floor, of course. I don't like you that much," he grumbled.

"Sounds good," Ezra replied.

He and Colby decided to face the consequences of their actions and sat on the *sex couch*, as Jemma called it.

"Is Trevor okay with that though?"

"Trevor!" Jemma screeched.

Mr Williams popped his head into the living room doorway, wearing a white apron that had *Too hot to handle* written across the chest with two love hearts over the nipples.

He had the sneaking suspicion that Jemma had bought him that.

"Yes, my love?"

"Ezra's staying the night," Jemma announced.

"As long as there is no hanky panky—"

"What the hell is hanky panky?" Jemma laughed. "Just say sex, darling. You're making this weirder than it needs to be."

"That's what I told him!" Colby yelled. "He kept using all these weird terms like *knocking boots* and *bumping uglies*. It was super embarrassing."

"I think it's more embarrassing that you got caught *bumping uglies* with your secret boyfriend." Jemma's laughing kept getting louder. She sounded almost like a witch cackling at this point. She reminded Ezra a lot of Colby. Colby was pure Jemma. They were both loud and kind of abrasive, but something about them really was charming and cute. "Can't believe you got caught, and I call you my son. Back in my day, I was banging half the kids at my high school into oblivion and I didn't get caught once." She looked very proud of herself.

"Ew gross, Mom. I don't want to hear about that." Colby made fake puking and gagging sounds.

"Why not? Your dad was one of those people. He was this scrawny nerd in my class, but I thought he was kind of cute so I gave him a chance. That and he agreed to do my homework for me. The very next day, he told me he'd fallen madly in love with me."

Mr Williams swiftly left the room, looking a little embarrassed at the story.

"What a simp," Colby remarked. "I would never fall in love with somebody just 'cos we had sex once." Colby looked up to Ezra, then frowned. "I think I wouldn't anyway."

198

"Haha, you are your father's son alright." Jemma cackled again. "Nicely done, Ezra." She winked at him.

Ezra agreed to stay the night, which he didn't mind at all since it was better than staying home alone for another night. It was also rather sweet how Colby kept hiding how happy he was for Ezra to stay round by calling him an asshole and claiming his mother was the one who wanted Ezra to stay round, not him. He decided it would probably be best to grab some clothes for both tonight and school tomorrow and a toothbrush from home before he settled in for the night.

"You are coming back, right? Not that I care! Just making sure in case my parents ask where you've gone." Colby was leaning against Ezra's car door.

"Of course, I'm coming back. My favourite person is here." Ezra walked up to Colby and caressed his face and leaned in for a kiss. "I love spending time with Jemma."

"You're such a dick." Colby slapped him and walked off in a huff, but before he left, he gave Ezra a peck on the cheek. "Be back soon," he said quickly before scampering back into the house.

Ezra parked his car outside his father's house and walked inside, a goofy smile on his face just from thinking about Colby's passive-aggressive way of showing affection the entire drive. He heard the voice of his father talking to someone in the kitchen. He wasn't expecting him to be home.

"Dad, I'm home," Ezra announced. He was tempted to eavesdrop on the conversation, but after the last time his father had caught him doing that, he'd rather not risk it again just to please his own curiosity.

He heard the person his father was talking to scramble around the kitchen before they came walking out in a hurry. He shouldn't have been surprised to see her. An old woman walked out of the kitchen and into the foyer. She nodded in greeting at Ezra. She was a strange old woman and frankly very annoying as well. She was wearing a blue cardigan that fell to her knees with red horned glasses resting on the bridge of her nose, and her grey hair was cut close to her scalp. It was his neighbour, Miss Herson—a.k.a the self-elected neighbourhood watch, a.k.a the local gossip that constantly snitched on her neighbours to her other neighbours, and a.k.a the woman that couldn't keep her mouth shut and had some sort of grudge against Ezra as she loved to rat out all of his activities to his father.

He couldn't stand her. He almost pitied her, for it seemed her only source of entertainment in her old age was sticking her nose where it didn't belong. It was sad, but she was still a huge pain in the ass, so he didn't feel that bad about hating her.

"Hello, Ezra dear," she greeted politely. No doubt she'd just been telling his father the local gossip. His father was equally as curious about his neighbours as Miss Herson, but he was more subtle about it by getting Miss Herson to do the dirty work of investigating for him. "Did you have a good day today? No need to answer, because I already know." She giggled to herself.

Fuck off, he thought. He smiled at her. "Yes, I did have a nice day. Thank you for asking."

Miss Herson left the house, muttering things about the youth of today and how all good-looking boys were into that sort of thing and how it was such a pity. Old bat was going senile.

"Ezra, come here." His father's commanding voice came from the kitchen once the front door was shut.

Ezra suddenly felt uneasy. Well, being around his father in general made him uneasy. But something was off. His father never really wanted to talk. His father was no Trevor who would ask his son how his day was because he was genuinely interested. No, his father only wanted to talk if he needed something or wanted to scold Ezra for not meeting his expectations. Either way, this wasn't going to be good.

Ezra walked into the kitchen. His father was leaning against the marble countertops, his expression cold and calculating as it always was. Nothing new there.

"Yes, Dad?" Ezra asked.

"Should you really be calling me that right now? After all, "dad" implies that you have some kind of respect for me, which you clearly do not if your recent actions prove anything." His father gave nothing away to what he was referring to. He was scowling now, but he wasn't yelling. He was in "lawyer mode" as Ezra liked to call it, where his father seemed to interrogate him and make Ezra squirm before he got the truth out of him.

What had that nosey old woman told him? "Is something wrong?" Ezra asked, hoping to get more information on what he would have to apologise for once this conversation was done. The sooner this was done, the sooner he could go back to Colby. Now, that was a thought that was getting him through.

"Is something the matter?" his father mimicked. "I'm not sure, Ezra. How about you tell me where you were after school today? Then, we'll decide if something is the matter."

"I went out with a friend after school and had dinner round their house. I'm sorry I didn't text you where I was going to be. I didn't know whether you'd be home today." Ezra was getting frustrated at this guessing game. Why did he get berated by his father for not coming home when he was the one who was gone most nights with whatever woman he was seeing at the time? Last month, his father had gone on a romantic getaway with some random woman in Hawaii. Ezra had no idea his father had left the state until he suddenly came back with a tan.

"Don't catch an attitude with me," his father scoffed, crossing his arms across his chest and glaring at Ezra. "Which friend were you with?"

"Brent."

"You're lying. Miss Herson just told me that you were out with the same boy that came to stay the night a few weeks ago—the one that you made the error of sleeping with and the one that Miss Herson overheard you mentioning to some girls in a convenience store that you two were on a date."

201

Ezra's blood ran cold.

"I thought I told you to stop all this nonsense."

"She must've misheard," Ezra rebuttaled, but his voice wasn't as strong and certain as he had tried to make it.

"No, she seemed pretty certain she heard correctly, and frankly, I believe her."

The pair just stared at each other. Ezra stared at his father and internally begged any god that there was to make his father forget what he'd heard from that nosey old cow, and his father stared back at him like he was looking at the scum of the earth.

"Where did I go wrong, Ezra?" His father's face changed into one of sorrow, but Ezra had seen this trick too many times to believe it. "Have I not given you a strong male figure to look up to? Have I not given you everything you've ever asked for? Is it not enough? Am I not enough? Have you become so selfish and wrapped up in your own needs that you are now pretending to be gay and flinging yourself into the arms of another man, for what . . . attention, is that it?"

Ezra knew this trick. He'd seen his father play and act the betrayed perfect dad time and time again in order to guilt Ezra into doing whatever he wanted. Fine, whatever, now he knew how this was going to play out.

"I'm sorry, Dad," Ezra began, trying his best to sound sincere. "You've been a great parent to me and I don't deserve it—"

"You're right. You don't."

What? This wasn't how it normally went.

"That's why I've decided that enough is enough."

Wait a second.

"I've given you all that I have to offer: a roof over your head, warm food on the table, and a bed to sleep in, but clearly, that's not enough for you."

This wasn't right. This wasn't how it normally went.

202

"I want you out of the house. See if this boy that you so desperately want can give you all that I have."

No. No, this wasn't right. This wasn't how this went. It always went that his father would guilt him into submission. Ezra would apologise and agree to never do whatever misdeed he had done ever again, then they'd go back to their two separate worlds.

"But, I'm your son," Ezra said. Wasn't that enough? Wasn't that what was supposed to keep the bond between the two of them? The fact that they were father and son.

"An ungrateful son," his father replied. He pulled out a chair from the dining table and sat in it. "Hopefully, this experience will show you how much I provide for you, show you what a real man acts like. When you realise your mistake and properly swear to no longer even *think* about boys in a provocative manner and cut things off with this boy you're already seeing, then you're welcome back." His father gestured to the front door. "Until then, get out."

Ezra could only stand there. This was his father—the man who'd raised him and the man who looked after him after his mother refused. His childhood hero. Didn't that mean anything to him? Sure, they were never that close, especially once the divorce died down, but didn't that mean anything to him? Didn't Ezra mean *anything* to him?

"You can grab some things first, but I expect you out within the next hour. Do I make myself clear?"

Ezra could only nod solemnly.

"This is for the best, Ezra. You'll see. You can leave now." His father turned back to the kitchen table and began to scroll through his phone.

Ezra left the room and walked upstairs to his room. He grabbed a duffle bag from his wardrobe and stuffed as much clothes in it as he could. He also packed his football gear, toothbrush, toothpaste, shampoo, and conditioner.

It didn't feel real that he was leaving, that his own father had been the one to kick him out.

He packed any school supplies he had lying around, his phone charger, and a water bottle. He also grabbed a pillow from his bed and a thin blanket.

Where was he going to stay? He could go to his mother, but he couldn't even remember the last time they had spoken.

He zipped up his duffle bag and put his school bag on his shoulder. He headed for the door. He stood at the front door, staring at the kitchen door in hopeful expectation that his father would come out and change his mind. Ezra even opened the door quite loudly to see if that would draw the man to action, but his father did nothing and Ezra was forced to leave.

CHAPTER TWENTY-FOUR
Bold

Colby had been impatiently waiting for Ezra to return for a stupidly long time. Using his phone and google maps, he'd calculated that it would take twenty minutes for Ezra to get to his house, five to ten minutes to pack some clothes and other things for an overnight stay, then take twenty minutes to drive back; in total, around fifty minutes.

It had been over an hour!

His mind spiralled with what-ifs. What if Ezra got into a car crash during his drive? What if Ezra had gotten lost somewhere? What if Ezra didn't actually want to come back to Colby's house, and the entire thing was also revenge to get back at Colby for his elaborate revenge scheme? He'd never been so paranoid in his life, and all he could do was wait by the window for any sign of him.

"You're still waiting for your husband to return from the war?" his mom teased.

"He's not my husband!" Colby replied bashfully. He almost wished he'd never introduced Ezra to his mom because she was having a field day with all the jokes about it.

Just then, Ezra's car pulled into the driveway and Colby sprang from his seat and rushed to the front door. He fixed his hair in the hallway mirror and tried to make it look like he hadn't been waiting like a loyal dog for Ezra to get back.

"Took you long enough," Colby said as he opened the front door and walked up to Ezra's car.

Ezra was standing by his car, looking up at the night sky. The cold breeze of the evening ruffled his fair hair and was turning his nose pink. Something about Ezra was . . . off. He looked dazed and his eyes were slightly red and puffy, but it was hard to tell in this light.

"Hey, Ezra? Are you okay?" Colby walked forward and took Ezra's hands and cupped them with his own. He brought their hands to his mouth where he blew gently on them to get Ezra's to warm up a little bit.

Ezra gazed at Colby with a wistful expression. "Yeah, fine. Are you cold?" Ezra asked.

"I was about to ask you the same thing," Colby replied.

Ezra immediately took off the black jacket he was wearing and put it over Colby instead. It was a kind of cheesy thing to do, but Colby couldn't help but be flustered by the act. He kept the jumper on as Ezra grabbed a bag from his car. It smelled like Ezra, and what a wonderful smell that was.

Ezra went to grab his bag from his car whilst Colby looked through the front windshield to see if he could spot it. The car was much tidier than Colby's mom's car, but he had a lot of stuff in it. He had a duffle bag that looked near to bursting, his school bag, his football kit, a blanket, and a pillow.

"You didn't need to bring so much stuff. I would've given you a blanket," said Colby.

Ezra looked caught off guard by Colby noticing the stuff in his car as he quickly shoved some of it under the seats to hide it from sight. He laughed at Colby. "Yeah, I guess I just like to come prepared."

"Talk about overkill."

Ezra slung the over-stuffed duffle bag onto his shoulder and let Colby take his hand and lead him upstairs. They went to Colby's room, and Colby instantly regretted not cleaning it. He had dirty clothes piled up on his desk chair and random pieces of paper with scribbles covering his desk. At least his bed was—kind of—made.

He rushed over to the desk and tried to tidy it as best he could as Ezra laughed at him from behind.

"To think you'd take me straight to your bedroom," said Ezra. "You really are quite bold tonight, Colby."

Colby blushed at the statement and turned around to berate Ezra for being a dick and probably say something along the lines of "I didn't even want you here," which would've been a lie. Before some embarrassed remark could come out though, Colby examined Ezra's face in the light. Colby was right. Ezra's eyes were slightly red and puffy, and he looked exhausted, but at the same time not. It was strange.

"Are you sure you're okay?" Colby asked again.

Ezra didn't answer the question. Instead, he placed his bag on the floor and came right up to Colby's face. He held the sides of Colby's face as if they were precious, made of something so fine and delicate that Ezra was afraid to hold him any tighter.

"Everything right now feels so surreal," Ezra whispered. "Things keep happening so quickly and it's like I can't keep up. Everything around me keeps changing, but I like this. I like you. This is my favourite change that I don't want to change." He leaned in and kissed Colby so tenderly.

Colby didn't know what to say. He hadn't been expecting . . . whatever this was, but it was amazing to hear. At that moment, it felt like the world closed in around the two of them to give them their own private space where the outside world didn't exist.

"I like you too," Colby whispered back before leaning in to kiss Ezra again.

The two stayed in each other's embrace for a few moments longer, completely enraptured in the small gentle touches they could give each other. Colby wrapped his arms around Ezra's waist and let his hands carefully massage his muscular back. Ezra kept his hands on Colby's face. He ran his thumbs along Colby's cheekbones as if to ensure that what he was doing was even real.

However, they couldn't stand there all night. They reluctantly separated when they heard Colby's dad come up the stairs. His dad peeked around Colby's door and asked where Ezra would be sleeping. Colby said Ezra would sleep on the floor and Colby would make a bed for him. That seemed to placate his dad.

"I don't want you boys thinking there's anything wrong with the horizontal tango—" his dad began.

"Oh my god," Colby groaned. "Just say sex!"

"But!" Colby's dad said pointedly. "I want you boys to get a good night's sleep, so you're ready for school tomorrow. Night, boys."

Once they heard the door shut to Colby's parents' bedroom, Ezra turned to him and asked, "I'm sleeping on the floor?"

Colby's cheeks grew warm, and he replied bashfully, "Only if you want to . . . I wasn't planning on it."

Ezra smiled at him, and God, the things he would do to get Ezra to smile like that all the time. Colby kissed Ezra before they got ready for bed because he still looked beyond exhausted. Part of Colby wanted to ask for a third time if something was wrong, but he could take the hint that Ezra didn't want to talk about it.

They went to bed together and this time, Colby didn't mind being the little spoon for Ezra. He swallowed his ego and simply enjoyed being held. Ezra really must've been exhausted, just like Colby thought as he passed out as soon as his head hit the pillow.

The next morning, Colby's dad was a little disgruntled to find them sleeping in the same bed together, so as revenge took pictures of the pair that he now used as blackmail against Colby.

"Delete it!" Colby yelled.

"But I think they're cute," his dad whined whilst sending the pictures to his wife. "Do you two need a lift to school?"

"I can drive us, so we can head straight to football," said Ezra.

"Heading to football this early?" his dad asked. Colby felt his palms go sweaty. He tried to silently communicate to Ezra not to say anything, but Ezra completely missed the message.

"It starts in about"—Ezra checked his phone—"ten minutes."

"Colby Belmiro Williams," his dad said slowly. The dreaded full name. Colby's blood ran cold. "Have you been lying to me about what time football starts, so that you could sleep in longer?"

Colby grabbed Ezra's hand and dragged him out to the car. "Sorry, Dad. Gotta get going. Can never be too early."

"I can't believe you lied to me!" his dad yelled at the door, dressed only in his plaid pyjama pants and bunny slippers.

Ezra got in the car and started it as Colby yelled back, "I mean you work at the school, so you could've checked."

"I trusted you to tell me the truth." His dad sighed. "First, a secret boyfriend, now this. What's next? You secretly do know how to clean your room?"

He heard Ezra snort at that.

"Maybe I do." Colby got into the car and slammed the door dramatically.

Ezra was still trying to stifle a laugh.

"Shut up and drive, asshole."

They arrived on time for football practice. Everybody—Coach Clain, the teammates, and even the janitor—was surprised to see Colby on time for once. He didn't like it. He was sleepy and tired and not ready to be screamed at by Coach. Finley wasn't even here yet, which made it worse. Like Colby, he would sleep in for as long as possible before dragging his ass to school.

The entire team—minus Finley and some other late stragglers—was getting changed when one of them started to ask Ezra about Brent's party.

"I didn't see you all night, dude. Where'd you disappear to?"

"Probably went off with some chick," said another boy.

Others nodded and agreed with him.

"Who's the girl, Ezra? Haven't seen you with anyone in particular," another teammate remarked.

"Girl?" Ezra questioned. "I spent the night with Colby." It was so nonchalant the way he said it

The room went quiet as they all turned to look at Colby, his face red and burning. He couldn't believe Ezra would say that. Brent, who had been talking to another player when Colby came in, looked surprised as well.

"Funny joke, dude." The first guy slapped Ezra's back. "Because we all know how much Colby *loves* Ezra." The guy laughed and so did the others; though a few quietly asked whether that was a joke or not.

Now that Colby actually remembered his name, he realised it was one of the guys Ezra had mentioned that had also slept with Joanna when she was dating Colby. What did Ezra call him . . . Jordan Park? She fucked him in the back seat of his car. Yeah, that was him.

"Seriously though, dude, where were you?"

"With Colby," Ezra told him again.

Jordan shook his head and gave Colby a playful look when he noticed him looking over. "Don't look so horrified, dude. He's just joking."

Jordan was a handsome guy. He was Korean and had mono-lid eyes that just made his stare that much more intense. No wonder Joanna had cheated on Colby with him.

Now that he thought about it and looked around the changing room, all the guys here were handsome, especially the ones Joanna had cheated on him with. Jordan Park? Handsome. Roland Marin? Handsome. Jerry Winship? Handsome. Ezra Dickinson? The most handsome of the handsome bunch. Colby

Williams? Well . . . he definitely wasn't as handsome as those other boys, or at least he didn't see himself that way. Did Ezra think he was handsome? Did Ezra deserve someone better-looking than Colby?

Probably.

"Hey," Ezra whispered into his ear.

Colby awoke from his degrading thoughts and realised all the boys had gone out onto the field and left him alone in the changing room with Ezra. Ezra was smiling. He'd been smiling all morning. It was great to see, but at the same time, there was something off about it. "How about after we finish football, you, me, shower? Just like old times."

"O-okay," Colby stuttered out. Since when was Ezra so bold about doing these things in public? Not that Colby was objecting.

CHAPTER TWENTY-FIVE
Talk to Me

It was too hot in that shower cubicle.

From the heat of the water pouring down onto Colby's face, to the collective steam of all the other showers being on as well, to Ezra being on his knees and giving Colby the best blowjob he'd ever have. It was getting quite toasty in there.

Ezra had told Colby before football started that he wanted to go to the showers together, but Colby thought he was either joking or just going to kiss him a little bit. Something about Ezra was different today. He was unpredictable, more confident, and experimental with the things he wanted to do to Colby. It was an unexpected change, but not an unwelcome one. Colby couldn't help but wonder what had changed in such a short period of time to change his attitude.

Although, he didn't get much of a chance to think about it with Ezra going down on him.

Colby had gotten into the shower first after practice. It had been a meandering drag of a morning. He wasn't used to coming in this early, and he would never be this early again. He'd walked into the shower with nothing but a towel around his waist and as he'd gone to close the door behind him, a hand shot out and grabbed it. Ezra pulled open the door and slipped inside. He'd looked so giddy, the mischievous smile of a child about to do something so dangerously naughty.

Without thinking of why Ezra would smile in such a way, Colby opened his mouth to ask what Ezra thought he was doing. Ezra swiftly pinned him to the wall with a searing kiss. His hands had disappeared below Colby's waistline to remove his towel and chuck it on top of the wall.

"It's a reverse of what happened the first time," Ezra whispered in his ear.

Colby's brain could hardly process information in a regular situation. Add a surprise ambush by Ezra, and there was no way he was going to understand what was going on. He simply nodded and hoped that was the answer that would keep Ezra slowly working his way down Colby's body. He trailed his tongue down Colby's stomach, sinking lower and lower until he was on his knees. The lust Colby felt was indescribable. He didn't know if anyone had managed to put into words what it felt like to have a masterpiece on their knees. Although, even that description could imply that the power of the situation rested with Colby. It was possible for it too. Colby could bury his hand in Ezra's hair and force him to stop tormenting him. He could easily do that.

He placed his hand on Ezra's fair hair and began to twist it around his fingers until he had a tight grip. Ezra looked up at him and withdrew from his actions. It was a challenge, one that Colby was more than happy to concede.

Colby had to cover his mouth with both his hands to muffle the abundance of moans that wanted to escape. The shower was fun, but Colby couldn't forget that their teammates were in the next few cubicles. He wondered whether anyone had spotted Ezra coming into Colby's shower and not coming back out again.

Colby was so wrapped up in his ecstasy of having Ezra give him the best head of his life that he didn't even hear the showers turning off one by one.

"Yo, where's Ezra?"

Colby only just managed to hear someone say over the noise of the shower running.

213

"I don't know, but Coach wants to talk to him," someone else said.

In Colby's euphoric state of mind, their voices all sounded the same. All sound around twisted into an indistinguishable mass of white noise.

Ezra became more aggressive. He worked harder, taking Colby even deeper into his mouth so his dick was hitting the back of his throat. Colby's knees were weak and his legs were shaking. He wasn't sure how much longer he'd be able to stand. Ezra's hands were gripping his thighs in a possessive hold. They shackled Colby in place to keep him prisoner to Ezra's every whim—not that Colby was planning on going anywhere.

Colby couldn't take it any longer. It was too hot. His whole body was burning. He came down Ezra's throat. How he managed to not let out an incredibly loud moan, he didn't even know. He'd had to bite into his hand to stop himself.

Colby was panting and trying not to topple over by the time Ezra got up off his knees. He held Colby in his arms for a little bit, letting his head rest on Ezra's shoulder, which helped Colby stabilise himself. Could you get heatstroke from a hot shower and a blowjob?

"I have to go see Coach," Ezra quietly told him. He pecked Colby on the cheek. "I'll see you at lunch."

Colby could make some dumb noise to show he understood. He was still so dazed by the experience.

Ezra wrapped a towel around his waist and headed out. Colby heard him talk to some other guys before presumably getting changed and going to see Coach. All the other showers were off, and there wasn't a sound apart from a pair of feet slapping against the tiled floor towards the shower.

"Colby?" Finley called.

"In here." Colby grabbed his towel from up high on the stall door and put it around his waist.

"You decent?" Finley asked.

Colby hummed in response.

Finley peeped his head around the door and laughed at Colby's lazy and lustful expression. "What the hell, man? You look like someone just sucked your soul out."

Colby gave a wonky smile at that. "Someone just did."

Finley's eyes lit up at the realisation. "Damn, no way. I gotta try that on Brent." He shook his head. "Nah, that wouldn't work. He's way too loud."

Colby supposed that was his fun fact about Brent for the day. He wobbled out of the shower with bones made of rubber and a brain far far away.

"By the way," Finley tried to wake him up, "apparently, Ezra made some odd remark today about who he spent the party with. But you wouldn't know anything about that, would you, Colby?" Finley teased.

"He told everyone it was me, but they took it as a joke." He was unsure of how that made him feel.

"I know. They all think it's hilarious. The only joke they told during the whole practice. You can tell that none of them have been through trauma because none of them are funny."

"Finley. Your hamster dying of diabetes because you used to give it marshmallows is not traumatic."

"I was six years old, man. It was traumatic for me. Now look at me, hilarious because his fat ass couldn't take the heat."

Colby had gotten changed by the time Finley stopped explaining his "trauma." Colby had never seen the hamster in real life, but he had seen pictures. The poor thing looked like a tennis ball being held up by toothpicks.

Colby's phone buzzed and he looked to check on the notification.

It was from Sophie: *"Can we talk?"*

A part of Colby really missed her. They'd been friends since forever, and he thought he knew her inside and out. Sure, he'd known she was religious, but he didn't assume that also meant she was homophobic. Finley was Christian, and he was gay. His parents were supportive of it too.

"Sure." Colby responded.

"Meet me in room 18 at lunch x"

She sent a kiss. Maybe that meant she was being friendly now?

The rest of Colby's day was pretty mundane, the same run-of-the-mill school day.

At lunch, he told Finley that Sophie wanted to talk to him.

"Are you sure you wanna go, man?" Finley asked. "I get she's a longtime friend, but you've got to look out for yourself first. If she's making you feel bad about yourself, why keep her around?" His expression soured.

"I'll just talk to her. See what she wants. Maybe she'll apologise."

"Whatever," Finley grumbled.

Colby knew Finley was very anti-Sophie after the comments she'd made about his relationship with Brent. Colby couldn't understand why she didn't like them together. They were so cute.

"I'm sorry." Colby patted Finley's back. "I'll be back as soon as possible."

He went to the classroom that Sophie wanted to meet in. It was an English classroom, so there were pictures of Shakespeare and Edgar Allan Poe on the wall along with poems written by students. Some were good; most were terrible. Sophie was standing by the display of poems, reading a few to waste time. She looked more Sophie today, with her baggy high-waisted jeans that had small paint stains here and there, and a green halter top. Her hair fell down her right shoulder in a loose braid that was tied at the end with a length of green ribbon. She looked nervous, even more so when she saw Colby at the door.

"I was worried you wouldn't come." She laughed awkwardly.

216

"I'd always come to see you," Colby reassured. His posture was stiff as he lingered by the door. He was unsure if he wanted to do this. Part of him wanted to fix things, to hear Sophie out, but another part of him had an uneasy feeling that talking would only make things worse. "Did you want to talk about something?" He closed the door behind him for a bit of privacy.

"Yeah, yeah, I did." She took in a deep breath before exhaling. "Listen, I'm not as stupid as you or Finley may think I—"

"I don't think you're stupid," Colby replied instantly, cutting her sentence off.

She smiled sweetly at him. "Thanks . . . I see the way you look at Ezra. I have for a while. Even before the Joanna incident, you had a strange obsession with him where you'd constantly go on about how cool you thought he was and how you wished the two of you were friends."

Colby cringed at the memory of his younger self. It was true though. Before he'd dated Joanna, Ezra had joined the school late into freshman year, and Colby had immediately taken a liking to him, as did most of the school. He had admired Ezra for his popularity and general coolness. But then, he dated Joanna in the same year. They were together for most of high school and during that time, Colby put no thought into other people or why he liked Ezra so much. He'd caught Joanna cheating on him with Ezra during the summer before senior year. It had broken his heart in more ways than one.

"I just didn't think you'd do anything with the way you felt about him, especially after you started to hate him," Sophie continued. "You've been my friend since forever, Colby. I don't want you to throw your life away because of this fleeting want for him. My parents and personal advisor have shown me that these *types* of relationships never last. They can't make you happy, and they'll only cause more pain than happiness." She slowly walked closer to Colby.

He didn't like this. He didn't like having his feelings for Ezra questioned. He didn't like the way Sophie looked at him like she was genuinely worried. He didn't like the way she didn't seem to fully believe the words herself. There was something mechanical about the way she spoke. A practiced speech she'd heard enough times to memorise.

"I want to help you, Colby. Help you and Ezra like I've been helped." Her fingers brushed the silver crucifix that hung from her neck. She seemed to sag under its lightness like her entire body was struggling to hold her up with the weight of it around her neck.

"I don't need help, Sophie. I like my relationship with Ezra. It makes me happy. Plus, the 'help' that you're describing makes me . . . uncomfortable."

She looked frustrated. "Ugh, I'm not describing this very well, but it works, okay? I've done it myself, and now I don't feel those things anymore!"

"What type of things?" Colby asked. He took a step back as Sophie continued to advance towards him.

"You know . . . ," her voice lowered to a whisper, "attraction to those of the same sex."

"You're gay? What's wrong with that?" Colby asked, not whispering. "Is this the secret you wanted to tell me before you went to summer camp? That you are gay?"

She put a hand over his mouth to keep him quiet. "Was," she insisted. "But not anymore. I'm fine now. I want you to be fine too. I don't want you to have a hard life, Colby. You're too good for that, but people aren't going to care if they see you with Ezra. They won't care that you're a good person. They'll only see what they want to see, and they'll hurt you for it." Her thin shoulders trembled, and she wrapped her arms around herself.

He touched her arm. "Are you okay, Soph?"

"Yes!" she all but yelled. "Yes, I'm okay and I'm trying to make you okay too because I care about you, Colby. Why can't you see that you won't be happy with Ezra?"

"I don't think it matters what gender the person I'm in a relationship is. It can go well or bad either way. Joanna is a girl and what we had was a huge fucking disaster. Ezra is a guy and I'm really happy with him at the moment. It's about the person themselves, not anything else."

"I used to think that too, but it's not true." She frowned at him. "So, you think Ezra's not going to cheat on you?"

"Of course not! I mean, we're not even anything official yet, so technically he can't until he's my . . . boyfriend."

"But he slept with Joanna even when he knew the two of you were going out. Didn't that show where his loyalty lay? It's because of the nature of your relationship. It's doomed before it's even started."

Colby didn't respond to that.

"We all make bad decisions, Colby. Let me help prevent you from making this one."

"Are you saying all this because you liked him?"

"I don't know if I liked him," she admitted. "I wanted to. I could see it from the way he acted around you. We're similar, him and I. It was silly, but I thought if we met on the common ground of our similarities, then we could be happy together."

"I don't think that would've worked. Ezra's pretty sure of what he wants, especially today."

"Yeah, I guess I wanted to not be the only black sheep in the flock anymore. Actually, we're both the black sheep now."

"Don't think I'm a sheep. I think I'd be like a dumb dog or something."

She giggled a little at that. "You get my point."

She embraced him in a tight hug, and the scent of her sweet perfume engulfed him. "I care about you so much, Colby. I just want to see you live the best life you can. And right now, I'm

219

worried you're going to get hurt and have your heart broken." She sounded so sincere that Colby actually considered her words.

"Sophie."

She lifted her head off his chest to look up at him.

"Finley doesn't need help and neither do I," began Colby. "Maybe you do though. Maybe you need to talk to someone who isn't a part of your church and realise it's okay to like girls. I think girls are pretty cool, so it's nice that we think the same."

"I don't think that!" she shouted at him. "When you've realised that *you* need help, you can come find me." With that, she sidestepped Colby and left the room.

He didn't know how to feel. He was annoyed that Sophie insisted he and Finley needed help, but at least they were talking again. He left the classroom a lot more downtrodden than he was hoping he'd be. At the very least, there was a sliver of hope that he and Sophie could be friends again.

He walked into the cafeteria and sat with Finley, who was quite obviously whispering naughty things into Brent's ear. Brent's face was red and he had his bag covering his lap.

He looked around for Ezra, and that's when he saw him smiling and laughing with Joanna and her friends at their table. He was standing by them as one girl groped his arm, and the rest all looked at him with big doe eyes.

What were Ezra's loyalties?

CHAPTER TWENTY-SIX
Cheesy

"Yo, man! What are you staring at?" Finley rested his head on Brent's peck as he was not tall enough to reach his shoulder.

Colby couldn't even make a joke about that though as he was too distracted by a group of girls laughing and touching Ezra, not even just any girls but his cheating ex and all her friends with their grubby little hands. All her pretty friends could have their pick of almost any guy in the school, but *no,* these girls were only interested in Ezra.

Which made sense. Ezra was a modern-day Adonis.

Even when Ezra had first joined the school, Colby and many others were mesmerised by him. From his looks, to his grades, to the way he walked with such confidence—everything about him was amazing. Colby had been his number-one fan back in the day before the Joanna incident.

In a way, Joanna and Ezra suited each other. Both of them were the beauties of the school with their own little groupies following them around. If Joanna didn't have major commitment issues and if Ezra wasn't into guys, they could've been an incredible power couple. But so could've Sophie and Ezra . . . or any of the girls or guys with Ezra. How did someone like Colby get such a perfect guy to be interested in him? It didn't make sense.

Ugh. Why was he having all these self-deprecating thoughts today? His brain was off every other day, but today it decided to switch on and talk shit about him?

Sophie's question of whether Ezra would cheat on him kept repeating over and over and over again like a broken record stuck on a loop. He had gone to Sophie in hopes of fixing their relationship, but now he just felt confused and their relationship was still rocky—not forgetting that the answer to her question was "no" because you can't cheat on someone you're not even in an official relationship with.

"Colby?" Finley asked again, picking up a fry from his plate and throwing it at Colby's head. "You good?"

"Hmm?" The fry hit him on the forehead. "I'm fine. I was just . . . thinking."

"That's new," said Finley.

"About what?" asked Brent. He finally moved his school bag off his lap now that Finley wasn't teasing him anymore and he'd had a chance to cool down.

"Things," Colby replied, unable to think of something believable quickly.

"What kind of things?" Brent pushed.

Colby looked back over at Ezra to see him coming over. He really did seem different today. He always walked confidently, but now he was walking like the ground under his feet was gold. The table that Ezra normally sat at—a mix of the football team and people he had classes with—stared at him curiously when Ezra didn't come to their table.

The football team . . . Joanna and the football team . . . none of the football team telling him . . . he hated playing football in general. Why the fuck did he even play football?

"I'm thinking of quitting the football team," Colby replied to Brent.

"You're what?" Finley sneered.

"Jesus, Finley. Where's the fire?" came Ezra's voice. He sat right next to Colby so their thighs were touching under the table.

"If you're quitting the football team, then I'm quitting the football team!" Finley yelled.

Brent placed a hand on his shoulder to indicate that he should chill out a little bit.

"I only joined because you did and you only joined because you were worried about your body at the time. If you're out, I'm out. Ain't no way around it." He leaned back into Brent's chest.

It was true. Colby had considered himself quite chubby back in the day with terrible acne, and his dad was worried he was spending too much time inside, so he encouraged him to take up football. Colby agreed and had then dragged poor Finley down with him. Admittedly, the sport had been fun to try at first, but now he didn't like anything about it. He didn't like the people there. He didn't like the weekend practices. He didn't like watching the game in his spare time. What was the point anymore?

"Why would you ever worry about your appearance?" Ezra asked.

"I'm not—I wasn't exactly good-looking back when I was fourteen," Colby replied, suddenly feeling there were too many people looking directly at his face now.

"Well, I definitely don't remember a time when you were ever ugly." Ezra leaned in towards Colby's ear and lowered his voice to a whisper. "It'd be a shame if you quit football though. We'd have to shower together somewhere else."

Colby punched him lightly in the arm whilst blushing. "Don't be such a pervert, pervert."

Ezra smiled at him.

"How was the date?" asked Brent.

"It was good. We watched a movie and I met his parents and even got to stay the night," Ezra responded.

Finley whistled. "I hope you two were sleeping in separate rooms at least. Wouldn't want any naughty activities going on. Told you, you were a bottom." Finley kicked Colby's leg under the table.

"You still remember that?" Colby had long figured out whether he was a bottom or not, but it didn't bother him anymore. Only the toughest, roughest, manliest of men bottomed. He wasn't one of those pathetic tops who couldn't take a bit of rough and tumble. He was built different.

"What? You two have a bet or something?" asked Ezra, looking suspiciously between the two.

"Something like that," Colby mumbled. "When you think about it, the bottom is the most important role. Do you know how much work goes into being bottom? No! Because you two"—he glared at Finley and Ezra—"just want to shove your dicks into something, and Brent and I have to make that work somehow. Appreciate us more or we'll go on strike!"

"That's so stupid." Finley giggled.

"Yeah! We'll go on strike!" Brent genuinely looked pretty riled up over Colby's speech. He was scowling and looked buzzed to go on strike.

"Woah, woah, woah, woah, babe. Let's not get any funny ideas," Finley tried to convince Brent out of it. "You don't want to listen to Colby. He's a himbo. Himbos don't know what they're talking about. They're just here to look pretty. Ain't nothing going on between them ears. So, let's forget about all this silly strike business, okay?"

"Strike!" Brent said again. He pounded his fists on the table, and all the cutlery leapt in the air. "Sorry," he quickly apologised, reaching forward to reorganise it all.

The pair quarrelled for some time about the strike that probably wasn't going to happen.

"Do I not appreciate you enough, Colby?" Ezra smiled dopily at Colby, his hand holding up his head as he leaned on the cafeteria table.

"Well, you've always been a dickhead, so a lack of appreciation is to be expected," Colby quipped.

The response just made Ezra smile more. "Wow, I'm still a dickhead. I guess I'm the worst boyfriend ever."

Boyfriend? Boyfriend. Boyfriend!

"You are my boyfriend?"

"Well, duh. Who's else would I be?"

Colby said nothing. Ezra was sucking all the words right out of him today.

"Am I going too fast?" Ezra asked cautiously. "I only assumed since your parents kept calling us that, and you confessed that you liked me in that way. Too soon?"

"No," Colby said quickly. "I just . . . are you sure? You're handsome and nice and smart and good at sport and everybody likes you and you're really attractive and you have a huge—"

"Are you trying to stroke my ego?" Ezra teased.

"My point is . . ." *You could have anyone.* He didn't say it. It sounded stupid, and it was stupid. He knew that. But he felt that if he pointed out how out of Colby's league Ezra really was, Ezra would awaken from the daze that made him believe that Colby was attractive and go date someone who actually was.

"Your point is . . ." Ezra prompted.

Colby thought for a second. "What would your dad think? Yeah. What would your dad say about us in . . . in a relationship."

Ezra's smile fell away, and he scowled at the table instead. He shrugged. "I don't care what he thinks," said Ezra. "His opinion is worthless, always has been."

"Are you okay?" asked Colby.

Finley and Brent were still arguing in the background.

Ezra looked back at Colby. "I am now" was all he said.

School went on as usual after that. If Colby passed Sophie in the halls, she would smile at him, which was a welcome change from when they would blank each other. Colby noticed Sophie didn't smile at Finley though, not that Finley seemed to give a shit as he gave her the cold shoulder too.

Colby missed their old trio. It was fun and perfect. Now, it was gone. He missed just talking with the two of them together and going out after school to hang out. The three amigos. Now it was up to him to try and bring them back together.

But how?

Finley wanted an apology from Sophie for all the homophobic shit she'd been saying, and Sophie wanted to "help" Finley and Colby. They were the antithesis of each other.

How bad could this "help" be? Colby didn't understand Sophie's point of view. He'd never tried to. He didn't agree with her at all, but the least he could do was try to see it her way so he could tell her how wrong she was after understanding her. That could work.

He texted her when the school day was over. *"Willing to talk about help, but let's start slow."*

Sophie replied immediately. *"Great! Then you can come to church with me on Sunday. It'll be good! xx"*

Colby had a gut feeling it wouldn't be, but she needed him and he needed his friend back.

*   *   *

Colby and his mom were making dinner by the time his dad got home.

"I'm back," he called out into the house.

"In the kitchen," his mom yelled back. She was cutting a wide array of vegetables. "Should've invited Ezra round for dinner. Got too much food and not enough mouths," his mom told Colby.

"I'll text him now and see if he's free."

"What are my two favourite people in the world talking about?" His dad walked into the kitchen and poured himself a glass of water. He was always happy when he got home, a true family man.

"I've got too much food, so I was saying to Colby that he should invite Ezra round for dinner," his mom explained.

"Maybe you shouldn't have made so much food." His dad chuckled.

"I'm committed now," his mom said. "Plus, it's not your turn to cook tonight, so you can't tell me what to do."

"Yes, chef." His dad saluted. "Speaking of Ezra, has he started doing some sort of after-school club?"

"I don't think so. Why?" Colby stopped looking at his phone and turned to his dad.

"I thought I saw his car still in the parking lot when I was leaving. The white Volkswagen is his, right?"

Colby nodded.

"I just thought it was strange that he was staying after school so late."

"Tell you what," his mom interrupted. "I'll put the leftovers in a box, and you and Ezra can also have whatever's left for lunch as well."

"Okay, will do," Colby agreed.

His mom looked at her reflection in the knife she was holding. "We had a man staying for the weekend in room 104. The housekeepers went in it today, and he had puked all up the walls. It was so bad. I had to come help with it. Now look at me. I look like such a state," she whined.

"A state of beauty," his dad cut in.

His mom just turned to his dad, amused by his cheesy lines. He held her hands in his.

"You're such a sap," his mom teased.

"For you? Definitely." His dad kissed his mom's hands, causing her to giggle. "May I compare thee to a summer's day, m'lady?"

Colby made fake gagging sounds at his dad's corniness.

227

"Hush, Colby. Don't act like you don't say cheesy lines to your boyfriend."

Colby went back to his phone. Ezra agreed to come round for dinner and would be there soon.

My boyfriend. Ezra had called himself that. Ezra was his boyfriend.

CHAPTER TWENTY-SEVEN
Enlightenment

"It's not even that early, so stop whining," Colby's mom scolded him for complaining again.

They had been driving in the car for about ten minutes now after Colby had told her he was going to a church on Sunday. His mom's car wasn't exactly clean. There were wrappers on the floor and random junk in random compartments. Every few years, she would clean it if his dad nagged her enough.

"It's ludicrously early for a Sunday!" Colby argued back.

"You're the one who randomly wanted to go to church! I could be in bed too right now, so shut up before I turn us back around. Why are you going anyway?"

Colby stayed silent.

"Why aren't you answering?" his mom asked.

"You told me to shut up," Colby replied with stereotypical teenage snark.

His mom slapped his thigh. "So rude to your own mother. When I was a teenager, I always respected my elders."

"That's not what dad said."

"Your dad was a nerd, and I was the cool rebel sticking it to the man." She pumped her fist in the air.

"So, basically, you didn't respect your elders at all?"

"This conversation is over."

Colby laughed at his mom's childishness. He definitely wasn't just like her. No, no, no, he was *way* more mature. All the people who said that he was his mother's son were dead wrong.

They eventually pulled up outside a rather traditional-looking church. The building and the steeple were made of large stones painted white and the windows were all stained glass, depicting most of the tragic events that happened in the bible: the crucifixion of Jesus, the death of Abel, and the mourning of Mary. Not the most welcoming images to see.

Sophie was waiting outside in a pretty baby-blue dress that reached down to her ankles. Her auburn hair was tied back with a similarly blue ribbon. She looked lovely and made Colby feel slightly underdressed. He'd just chucked on a pair of black trousers and a white button-up shirt. However, Ezra had come round for dinner on Saturday and told him he looked very sexy in it, so he couldn't have looked too bad.

Thinking about Ezra made him feel a bit guilty. Ezra had been in pain the entire week, constantly rubbing his neck and popping his back. Colby had given him multiple massages throughout the week to try and help. Colby had asked him whether he was sleeping well and all that to which Ezra had insisted he just had a lumpy mattress, which seemed strange as Colby had been railed on that mattress and he remembered it being really soft.

Basically, Ezra wasn't having the best week physically, despite his improved mood. However, Colby felt like he'd ruined that mood as well by mentioning that he was going to Sophie's church on Sunday.

"Why are you going there? Is she forcing you? You don't have to go. There's nothing wrong with you!" Ezra had suddenly blurted out at the time, holding Colby's hands in a death grip.

"What? No. She just—I think she just needs a friend right now, and we've been friends since we were kids, so I thought if I went to her church for the day, understood her point of view, then I could talk to her for real. Hopefully, she'll realise she's wrong and we can all be best friends again." In hindsight, he knew he sounded naive at that moment, but it was essentially his entire plan that he was desperately counting on to work.

Ezra had loosened his grip and said, "That's sweet of you, but it's not going to be easy. She's been conditioned to think that way, and she might keep thinking that way until she actually leaves that environment." Ezra slumped his head and rested it on Colby's shoulder. "Just be careful. And for fuck's sake, Colby, if they ask you if you're gay, tell them you're not. Don't say yes to any help or treatment or therapy, promise?"

"Promise," Colby agreed for the sake of calming Ezra to a degree.

Sophie skipped to the car when she spotted it. She smiled at them as they both got out of the car.

"Hi, Colby! Hi, Jemma!"

"Hello, Sophie." His mom hugged her tightly when she approached. "It's been ages since I've seen you. Don't you look lovely?"

"Aww, thank you."

An older woman and her husband walked past the car. They looked about fifteen or so years older than his mom and were dressed quite formally like Sophie. The woman glanced at the three of them before doing a double take.

"Jemma?" the woman questioned. "Jemma Alvez?"

"Hi, Mrs Powers," his mom greeted unenthusiastically. "Still kicking, that's a surprise," she mumbled under her breath.

"It is you! Gosh, I haven't seen you since I taught you in high school. What do you do now?"

"I'm a hotel manager."

"Wow. That is a much better profession than I had expected. How did that little accident go by the way?"

"You're looking at him." His mom slapped Colby on the back. Accident? "Well, I better go. I got a cat . . . to water. Alright, see you. Call me when you want a pick-up, Colby."

231

His mom hurried into the car and sped away.

"So, you're Colby Alvez then?" Mrs Powers asked.

"Um, kind of, I'm Colby Williams."

"Williams? As in Trevor Williams?"

Colby nodded.

"Now that's an odd couple."

Odd couple? His parents weren't an odd couple. They were perfect for each other. What would some musty dusty old high school teacher know?

Colby's annoyance must have seeped onto his face as Sophie quickly grabbed his arm and ushered him inside, giving a courteous goodbye to Mr and Mrs Powers.

They went into the church and ended up greeting a bunch of people, a majority of them of a much older generation.

They sat down on a hard wooden pew near the front of the church as Sophie's parents set up at the front.

"Hey, Soph," a girl their age said as walked past. She was seriously pretty, with straight dark hair and skin like polished bronze. She was wearing a modest pink dress that complimented *everything* about her.

"H-hi," Sophie stuttered, her cheeks tinted with blush.

"Who's that?" Colby asked her.

"Avni Singh," Sophie said wistfully. "Her family are new to the area. They're Sikh, but they want to make friends with people in the community, so they're coming for a few Sundays to meet the locals."

"She's beautiful," Colby remarked, watching Sophie's face more than Avni's.

"Yeah . . . I mean, anyone could notice that. I'm just trying to be friendly because she's new. She's beautiful—gorgeous even—but in an objective way, you know."

"It's fine to like her."

"I don't! Well, I do. We're friends. I like her, just not in *that* way."

232

"Whatever you say," Colby hummed.

The church was not the cult Ezra had made it out to be. Cult could possibly suggest something exciting, which definitely was not a word that could be associated with this church.

Everything was so dull. Sophie's dad spoke in the same monotone voice the entire time. The longer you sat on the pews, the more you felt like your ass was being stabbed with a thousand needles. Even the songs were boring! How did they make the songs boring?

Colby had been to church with Finley before, and his church was the pinnacle of cool churches. They had cushions on the pews. The people would clap and yell excitedly at things that riled them up. They also sang the best songs. All the classics like Shine Jesus Shine—which was Colby's personal favourite—and had posters supporting all groups of people, including those of the LGBT+ community.

Sophie's church was the complete opposite of Finley's church. Ugh, he could be with Finley in the cool church right now or—even better—he could have had Ezra stay the night if he wasn't coming to this stupid thing. They could've been all cozied up in bed together right now. That sounded like bliss.

After two hours of Colby nearly dozing off and the old lady behind him kicking him awake and complaining about the kids of today, the church service was finally over.

"What did you think?" Sophie asked tentatively.

Colby rubbed his eyes and yawned. "Oh yeah, it was something else."

"Colby, it's been too long," Sophie's dad said as he came up to the pair. He was wearing a white robe with a purple collar on top of a black suit. He had dyed brown hair, which was obvious due to his grey stubble. Why not dye both or dye neither? What was this half-assed effort?

"Colby's mom's coming soon, so we're going to go wait for her," said Sophie.

233

"Then there's time for Colby and I to have a little chat then, isn't there?"

"But I—I'll give you two a minute," Sophie said. She surprisingly didn't look eager to leave Colby alone with her dad, but one stern look from him and she was off.

"Joanna and Sophie have told me a few things that have been happening to you, Colby."

Since when did Joanna care about the word of God?

"Temptation is a constant foe that we must combat throughout our lives and, especially, during these important teenage years of growth. The temptation to indulge in inappropriate sexual behaviour is compelling, I understand. You can confide in me what is compelling you to act this way. Do you understand what I'm getting at?"

No, he thought. But, "Yes," he replied.

"I'm glad. Homosexuality is a serious issue in today's society, but know that there are ways that I and my colleagues can help you." He patted Colby on the shoulder.

"Thank you, but I'm alright," Colby replied. He'd always thought Sophie's dad was a little weird, but now, from the way he scowled at Colby's refusal just confirmed that he was disgusting.

"You're not alright though, are you? There's something wrong with you."

"Nope."

"Yes, there is."

"Don't think so."

"There is."

"I think a doctor would know if there was something wrong with me."

"Doctors know nothing."

"You know nothing."

"No," the reverend spluttered. "*You* know nothing."

234

"And Socrates said that's what makes a man wise." Colby cringed at himself. He sounded like his dad when he referred to old people quotes like that.

"Do you think you're clever?" Sophie's dad grumbled.

"Not particularly."

"At least we can agree on something then. All I am doing is offering help that you so desperately need but are too blind to see it. I'm not sure I want my daughter associating herself with someone like yourself."

"Hold on," interrupted Colby. "You can't stop Sophie from seeing me."

"I can. This is the consequence of your own ignorance. Sophie's doing incredibly well for herself these days, and I won't let a delinquent like you ruin her future. If you truly care for her, then you'll respect my wishes and stay away." He paused and allowed the tragic idea of not speaking to Sophie again to sink in. "Or, you can accept the generous help I am offering and you and Sophie can stay friends for as long as you wish. Which will it be?"

There was no snarky remark or quick quip Colby could think of to respond to that. One or the other. Sophie or Ezra. "I . . . give me some time to think about it."

That was enough to placate the reverend. "Take all the time you need, though the choice is obvious."

An elderly couple called out to the reverend, and he went over to them, his arms spread open in a welcoming embrace.

As her dad left, Sophie shuffled back over. "Did, did you agree to anything?" she asked softly.

"No, but I was offered help. I refused it."

Sophie nodded, then wrapped her arms around his chest and hugged him.

He was confused by her actions until he felt her shoulders shake gently and his shirt become slightly wet.

"I'm sorry," she whispered. "I don't even know why I offered help to you and Ezra and Finley in the first place. I tried to convince myself that it helped, but it didn't. It's awful—worse than awful. I'm so sorry, Colby."

"Hey, it's okay." He placed his fingers under her chin and lifted her head to face him, his thumb wiping away her tears. "You thought you were helping, but there's nothing wrong, Soph. You're perfect the way you are."

That just seemed to make her cry harder. He held her until she managed to calm down. They moved towards the sidewalk and sat down on the curb.

"Your dad says I can't see you anymore."

She wiped her eyes and sniffled. "I had a feeling he was going to say that."

"I don't ever want to stop being your friend, but I don't want to get you in trouble."

His mom pulled up the car next to them.

As Colby was about to get into the car, Sophie stood up. "I'll see you on Monday," she said with conviction, standing there on the sidewalk with her shoulders back and head held high.

"Yep!" Colby agreed.

He got into the car with his mom again. He told her the church was boring, but it was wonderful seeing Sophie.

They were driving home and Colby was watching the world roll by his window, daydreaming of going back to bed when he finally got home. They passed the school that was entirely deserted, except for one lone car in the parking lot. It was a white Volkswagen.

He turned in his chair, trying to see whether it really was the car he thought it was. "Mom, can you turn back to the school, please?" Colby asked, straining his neck trying to see the school parking lot again.

"Is something there?" she asked.

"Maybe."

She pulled onto the parking lot that was still bathed in the orange light of the morning sun.

"Whose car is that?" his mom asked.

"I think . . ." He quickly got out of the car and walked over to it.

Clearly from the number plate, it was Ezra's car. Maybe Ezra had forgotten it here or was somewhere nearby and just needed somewhere to park. God, he hoped that was the reason. Colby's heart was hammering against his chest. The back pain, the bags in the car, and the lack of sleep. It was so obvious now.

He looked into the slightly tinted car windows. The car was packed full of unfolded clothes and a duffle bag. The front seat was leaning all the way back—and there was Ezra, curled up under a thin blanket, sleeping.

CHAPTER TWENTY-EIGHT
Mother Knows Best

Simultaneously, it had been the worst and best week of Ezra's life.

The best parts had been an indescribable feeling of liberation. The freedom of acting upon his own volition, doing what he wants, giving Colby a blowjob. Isolated, those aspects were fantastic, especially when he was at school and surrounded by people who genuinely cared about him.

However, once school ended and those people all returned to their homes, reality would strike Ezra to remind him that he no longer had that privilege. He hadn't thought going home to be much of a privilege when he could do it, as it would often lead to him either being yelled at by his father or simply returning to a house too cold and too big for one person alone.

As soon as the school day was over, he was forced to—once again—obsess over the fact that his own father kicked him out and his own mother was ignoring his calls.

He'd been sleeping in his car at the school car park for the past week. Nobody really questioned it as, in the past, he tended to stay late after school anyway to avoid going home. He still had access to his bank account, so he wasn't starving, and he used the showers in the gym and the school bathroom for other hygiene matters.

Maybe his father was right. Maybe he should've been more grateful for the roof over his head and for having his own bed. But, then again, aren't those just the bare necessities you're supposed to give your child? If so, somebody should tell his parents about this radical idea.

On Saturday evening, he ate a warm meal with Colby's family and lounged on Colby's bed. It was a welcome distraction.

Ezra was lying face down on Colby's chest with his arms wrapped around his torso as Colby gave him a shoulder massage. Sleeping in a car wasn't exactly good for your back.

"I just don't believe salmonella is real. I mean, how can you get sick from an egg? You're just eating a chicken's period. How can that make you ill? I've never gotten salmonella. I don't know. Maybe I'm built different," Colby rambled nonsensically.

Ezra laughed. "Something about the way you're built is definitely different. A brain malfunction, perhaps?"

Colby dug his elbow into Ezra's shoulder, causing him to yelp in pain. "Oi! I'm giving you a back massage. The least you can do is listen to my thoughts and try to catch up with my progressive way of thinking."

"Progressive? That's a big word for you, Colby," Ezra teased, turning his head up to give Colby a boyish smile.

Colby dug both his elbows into Ezra's back.

"Ow, ow, ow, ow, ow," Ezra whined. He didn't move away from Colby, but instead just hugged him even harder. Eventually, Colby let up his attack once Ezra had pleaded for mercy enough.

"You staying the night?" Colby asked. "I have to go to Sophie's church thing at six thirty in the morning, but I should be back by around eight. Can you stay here till I get back?"

"Can't," Ezra replied. He was thoroughly disappointed that he couldn't stay. Although Colby's new habit of inviting Ezra to stay over as often as he could was very endearing. "I'm meeting with someone tonight."

"Who?"

"My mom."

*　　　*　　　*

How long had it been since Ezra had last seen his mom in person? Four years? Three? They would talk on the phone when his birthday rolled around, but other than that . . .

He was sitting in a small coffee shop that was known for staying open late at night. It had the typical hipster aesthetic. The walls were painted red with the words "Live, Laugh, Love Coffee" written in white on top, and the floors were covered in laminated wood. The shop unsurprisingly stank of the bitter smell of coffee, and there was an indie song playing in the background that Ezra could hardly understand the lyrics of.

He felt unsettled. He couldn't stop fiddling with anything within his reach, from the paper straws on the table to the fabric of his own shirt. He tapped his foot to a fast-paced rhythm that he couldn't hear, and he kept scanning the street outside for signs of his mother.

She arrived twenty minutes later than agreed. She walked into the shop wearing a long fur coat. She looked much healthier and much happier than the last time he'd seen her. That must've been over four years ago when the divorce was still raging on. Did that make them estranged?

Ezra had looked like her once. She'd dyed her blonde hair black and it looked like she'd finally got that nose job she'd always wanted.

She smiled at him when she spotted him and came to take the seat opposite him. "You've gotten so big since the last time I saw you," his mother said sweetly. "It's been so long, darling." She placed her hand very gently on top of Ezra's that rested on the table.

He hadn't seen her in so long. It's not that he hadn't wanted to, but after what had happened in court, she made it clear that the feeling wasn't reciprocated.

"Yeah, it's been a while. You look good" was the best response he could muster.

She giggled. "Thank you. I'm sorry I couldn't get back to you sooner. my phone's been bugging out recently. I didn't even know you called me until I got it fixed yesterday."

How convenient.

"I have listened to all your voicemails and read all your texts about your current situation. Are you sure your dad won't let you back in?"

If you're asking me that, then you clearly haven't read my texts, Ezra thought. "He won't unless—"

Was this his coming out to her? He'd written in the texts about why his father had kicked him out, so technically she already knew, but saying it in person was a lot scarier than he had anticipated.

"Unless I stop seeing my boyfriend."

"I see," his mother replied. "Well, can't you just do that?"

"No."

"Why not?"

"Because I am tired of having to do everything he wants, not being who I am. I am exhausted from having to please him every second of the day just so he doesn't kick me out for not listening to him."

How could *she*, of all people, ask him why he couldn't continue to live under the tyrannical rule of his father when she had been the one to leave first?

"I understand, Ezra. I do. But this doesn't seem like too hard of a request. High school relationships don't tend to last and maybe it is all a phase. Don't throw away your relationship with your dad because of feelings that you have right now," she responded calmly, but he knew what she was doing.

241

"There is another option though, isn't there? I could come live with you so that I—a seventeen-year-old—could have a place to sleep, and I could live freely. Just like you."

His mother removed her hand from his, and the smile fell from her face. "I know what it is you're asking of me, Ezra, but this was already sorted out by the court. Your dad has full custody of you because I—"

Don't want you, Ezra thought. *Admit it. Say it.*

". . . don't have the capabilities and resources to look after you."

He looked at her luxurious long coat and remodelled face. They must've been cheap if she didn't have the resources. "All I'm asking for is a place to sleep. Nothing else. You don't have to pay for anything for me. Just give me a bed like mothers are supposed to." It was a low blow, but he was so fucking tired of this stupid game between his parents. Could he even call them his parents? He didn't think they deserved the title.

"The court said I have no custody of you. Do you want me to break the law? Plus, I've gotten remarried, and I don't know how he would feel about this whole arrangement. I want things to work this time around, Ezra. Don't you want me to be happy?"

He was furious. How dare she come here and use the court as her excuse. How dare she come and try and guilt trip him into going back to his father, so she didn't have to look after him. How dare she use all these excuses when it simply boiled down to the fact that she didn't want her old life interfering with her new one?

"I am sorry, darling. I can give you money to help with finances though. Maybe you could buy your own place. You're old enough to be independent."

"I'm only seventeen."

"Exactly, nearly old enough to be living alone while you go to university. Consider this practice for the future." She smiled at him as if she was offering genuine advice.

242

"I get it. I don't know how you and dad's marriage failed when you two and your fucking self-centred egos were practically made for each other. I'll take your money and I won't contact you again." He stood up from the table and stormed out.

His mother didn't try to stop him. After all, she'd gotten what she wanted.

He got back into his car and drove to the school's empty parking lot and tried to will himself to go to sleep so he didn't have to obsess about what he had done to deserve parents like his.

He awoke to a pounding sound. He tried to ignore it as his brain hadn't woken up enough to remember where he was. Once he'd woken up, however, he shot up from his lying down position nearly hitting his head on the car roof. His heart nearly stopped when he saw Colby standing outside his car.

He collected himself and put a brave face on before getting out of the car.

"What's up with you, Colby?" He tried to play off. "Can't a guy take a nap around here?"

Colby looked like he was about to cry but also like he was about to beat the shit out of Ezra. "You've been sleeping in your car for the past week, haven't you?" he all but yelled. Thank God nobody else was around.

"What? No. I was just out late last night and didn't want to be told off by my dad, so I decided to sleep here for the night. I'll tell him I stayed the night at Brent's and it'll all be fine. Don't worry about it."

"I'm not that stupid, Ezra! I'm sorry I didn't notice before, but I see it now, you dummy. Why didn't you tell me? I would do anything to help you."

Ezra still wasn't sure whether he was going to get cried on or punched by Colby, so he tensed a bit when Colby ran towards him.

Colby wrapped his arms and squeezed Ezra against him as hard as he could. "You're such an idiot. You're so stupid. You're the stupidest person in the world."

Ezra hugged Colby back and felt like he was about to collapse. There was something so draining about finally being caught, but not in a bad way. In this case, it felt like he finally had some of the weight taken off of him for a second. He was able to breathe properly, if only for a minute.

Colby took Ezra's hand and dragged him to a nearby car. That's when he saw Jemma looking at him with a worried expression as well.

She didn't ask him what was wrong or what was happening. She simply asked, "Should we take you home, dear?"

He didn't even have to answer as the mother-son duo forced him in. He locked his car and agreed that he'd get it on Monday.

Colby clung to his hand the whole ride home and Ezra refused to let go as well.

They arrived at the Williams household, and Trevor was in the kitchen cooking something that smelled divine.

"That took longer than expected," he called to them as they entered. He peeped his head around the corner to look at them. "Morning, Ezra. Fancy some breakfast?"

"He'd love some," Jemma answered for him. "Colby, why don't you go get some clean clothes and other things for Ezra," she gently ordered Colby.

"But—" Colby tried to argue and squeezed Ezra's hand tighter.

Jemma smiled at the action. "I'm just going to have a quick word with him, okay?"

Colby nodded and reluctantly let go of Ezra's hand.

She led Ezra out into the backyard, then sat down on some sun chairs and closed the glass door that cut it off from the house. "Do you want to tell me what happened?" she asked.

Compared to seeing his own mother last night, something about Jemma's genuine concern for Ezra made him tell her everything that had happened between him and his father that had led to him being kicked out. He even told her about seeing his mother last night and went as far as describing the divorce from years ago.

Jemma didn't interrupt and she listened intently to every word that Ezra poured out. He'd never told anyone so much detail about his life before. Even Brent only knew certain details. He didn't like burdening people with his personal issues, but he was so tired.

When he finally finished, Jemma began to talk, "Oh, my dear." She held his hand and—like her concern—there was something genuine about it. "When I was your age, I was kicked out of my house too, you know."

"Why?" he couldn't help but ask.

"When I was in high school . . . let's just say I got around. I didn't have the greatest childhood growing up and for some reason, there was something about sex that would just make me feel better for a brief amount of time. When I turned eighteen, I banged this nerd so he would do my science homework for me, and the very next day he said he was madly in love with me. Anyways, that scrawny nerd was called Trevor Williams, and I thought he was the cutest thing ever after he said that. Issue is, he had the weakest pull-out game in existence, and I didn't like the way condoms felt. It was a recipe for disaster.

Naturally, I got pregnant after a few hookups with Trevor from that killer combo we had going on, and my parents found out. They said, and I'll always remember this, *'My daughter isn't a whore. You are a whore, and therefore you're not my daughter.'* They said that in Portuguese though, so translate that in your head."

Ezra didn't know any Portuguese.

"And just like that, I was out on my own. Trevor had gone off to uni, and I just remembered so vividly how helpless and alone I felt. It was undoubtedly the worst time in my entire life.

After a few weeks of roughing it, I managed to get back in touch with Trevor when he came to visit his family and I decided I would tell him that I was pregnant with his kid. I was expecting him to give me some abortion money or tell me to get fucked. Instead, he promised me then and there that he'll do anything to look after the baby and me, and then he gave this big speech about how I was his first and only love. He's such a sap. People always say Colby is my little double, but I think he is so much more like Trevor." She laughed to herself as she looked through the glass door to see Colby throwing mushrooms at his dad who was batting them away with his spatula.

"I know what you're going through, Ezra. It seems like hell right now, but I promise you it gets better. The universe has got a plan, and that included getting you out of that horrid place. Now you can live for yourself, and that's what I want you to do." She leaned towards him and placed her hands on his shoulders. "Sometimes you gotta be a little bit selfish, Ezra. It's nice to think of others, but what do you want? Who is Ezra Dickinson, and what does he want out of *his* life? You can stay here for as long as you need. You're going to be okay."

His entire body gave in on itself, and he collapsed onto Jemma. She cradled his head and stroked his hair. She kept whispering to him as he wept, "You are going to be okay."

CHAPTER TWENTY-NINE
Thick Thighs Save Lives

"You've really fucked up this time, Colby. I swear to God there is nothing going on in that thick head of yours. You have clearly not thought about my feelings. You only ever consider yourself when you open your big mouth, and I've had it. We're done. We're over. This relationship is over before it even began."

Colby could only listen. He didn't know what to say.

"You've ruined my life. We are through."

"Please," Colby begged, "just tell me what I did wrong before you go. I can change. I can fix this. I swear to you."

"Alright, you get one last chance to fix this." Finley took a sharp breath in before he screamed at Colby over the phone. "GET BRENT BACK ON MY DICK! He thinks your stupid bottom strike is real, and he's avoiding me! I did not stay in the closet for over sixteen years and have a crush on somebody way out of my league, just for you to fuck it up by spewing some shit about a bottom strike. I've got blue balls, Colby! They're so big and heavy and—"

"Gross, I get the picture. What do you want me to do about it?" Colby asked. "I want to go back to bed."

"Just tell him the strike is over or something. I bet you haven't even been sticking to the stupid strike that *you* created."

Colby thought for a second before responding with absolute confidence. "Actually, for your information, I haven't had sex since I began the strike either, so joke's on you."

"Who are you talking to?" Ezra asked in a groggy voice.

Colby had given him some clothes to sleep in, and after Ezra had taken a shower, he had collapsed onto Colby's bed and immediately fallen asleep. When Colby awoke to his phone ringing, he found Ezra had managed to wrap both his arms around Colby's waist in an iron grip.

"Finley," Colby told him, "go back to sleep." Colby still felt sick at the fact that Ezra had been forced to sleep in his car for the past week. Even if it meant they were late for school, Colby wanted him to get some rest.

Ezra hummed in response and pulled Colby closer to him. It was quite amusing seeing the big, tough Ezra cling to Colby like a teddy bear.

"Is that Ezra?" Finley screeched across the phone. "You try and convince me that you haven't had your back blown out since the strike started while he is in your bed. You're a filthy liar, man. I have to suffer while you live the good life. I see how much I mean to you now." Finley made fake crying sounds that kind of sounded like a balloon deflating.

"Oh, shut up. Blue balls aren't even real."

"You'll see how real they are when I choke you to death with mine!"

"Ew." Colby cringed. "Have you tried seducing Brent?"

"I've been around him."

"Yeah, but have you tried seducing him?"

"Yes. I have been around him. My general presence and the suggestion that I might whip out my massive horse cock is how I seduce people, and it's not working," Finley spoke as if Colby was the idiot.

Granted, in most cases, he was. But at this moment, he was pretty sure he was giving smart advice.

"Do something romantic for him. Show that you care. People love that lovey-dovey crap."

"And what kind of *lovey-dovey crap* would you suggest I do, O wise Colby," Finley sarcastically asked.

"I don't know! Buy him flowers or something like that. You're the one with the brains, so you figure out!"

"No! You created this mess with your bottoms strike bullshit, so you figure it out before I make you allergic to nuts by shoving mine so far down your throat that they fuck up your immune system!"

"Bro," Colby began, "I'm not a biologist or anything, but I'm pretty sure that's not how allergies work."

"Why can't you just go with it? You know I'm failing biology. Anyway, tell him the strike is off, and my long schlong dong is waiting for him. Okay?"

Colby laughed at Finley's ridiculous names for his dick. "Okay, I'll talk to him. Bye, love you."

"Love you too, man."

Colby hung up the phone and settled back into bed.

"You tell Finley you love him?" Ezra asked.

Colby had thought he'd gone back to sleep. "Yeah. He's my best friend. I do love him. You don't tell Brent you love him?"

"No, not really."

Colby glanced down at Ezra, who in turn was peering up at him. There was something oddly unfinished about the way Ezra questioned Colby and Finley's affection for each other. Ezra closed his eyes again, and Colby left him so he could have a few more minutes of sleep.

He went downstairs to find his mom going on a rant about something, and his dad already dressed for school with his favourite bunny slippers on. His dad always tried to look professional by wearing dark trousers with a formal shirt, but he also wore a tie with some sort of dad joke or pun on it so his students didn't take him too seriously. His dad's silly ties were famous around the school with multiple students coming to talk to his dad just to see what tie he was wearing that day.

249

"Morning, Colby," his dad greeted. He was wearing a tie that said, "*Now that I've had my coffee, it's time to go Wilde!*" It had a picture of Oscar Wilde on it. No one loved English quite like his dad did. "Did Ezra sleep alright?"

"Yeah, he passed out as soon as he hit the hay." Colby began to rummage through the cupboards in the kitchen for food that Ezra might like for breakfast.

"Bless him," his mom said. "I'll never understand how you can do that to a child. Some adults need to grow the fuck up."

Mr Dickinson better pray he wouldn't cross paths with Jemma Williams. His mom had a temper like no other, and she was already very fond of Ezra.

"You'll never guess who I saw yesterday."

"Who?" his dad asked.

"Mrs Powers."

"The old science teacher? She retired years ago. Where did you see her?" His dad put down the cup of coffee he was holding to focus solely on his wife.

"At the church service Colby went to. You know what was the first thing she asked me? 'How did that little accident go?' " She pointed at her little accident for added effect. "How does she still remember that? I haven't seen her in over eighteen years!"

"In the words of my senior English class, you are living in her mind *rent-free* even after all these years. Apparently, Mrs Powers saw Stacey Longshore and started asking her intruding questions too."

"What did Stacey do?" Colby asked. "We got any eggs?"

"Eggs are in the fridge behind the lettuce. Stacey had a habit of committing arson in high school, and Mrs Powers kept asking her whether she still did it in front of a bunch of people at a crowded mall."

"She didn't mean any harm by it. She was a nice girl with a strange addiction. We've all committed arson at some point or another," said his mom.

250

"I haven't," said Colby.

"Nor have I," said his dad.

"Oh." His mom paused for a second before shooing Colby out of the kitchen. "You go wake Ezra up. I'll make breakfast. Go, go, go."

Colby went back upstairs to his room. Ezra had gotten up and was putting on clothes. He was currently shirtless, and Colby couldn't help but let his eyes indulge in watching his back muscles roll and flex with every movement. He was tempted to walk up behind him and place his hands—

NO! Bad Colby! He scolded himself. Ezra had just been kicked out of his house, and Colby's parents were downstairs. Now was not the time to mess around with his sexy boyfriend.

"Breakfast is ready," Colby said to stop his perverted thoughts.

Ezra turned and smiled at him. They walked downstairs together, and Ezra was immediately hugged by Colby's mom, who asked him if he slept well.

"Colby snores pretty loud, but other than that, it was the best sleep I've had all week," Ezra teased.

"Go sleep on the sofa then, asshole." Colby punched his arm.

"No, I'm fine. Thanks."

"Then stop complaining."

It had been agreed last night that Ezra was more than welcome to stay at the Williams house for as long as he liked.

*   *   *

The first order of Colby's school day: Get Brent to end the strike.

Finley had made sure to reiterate to him when he arrived at school that he would shove his ready-to-pop blue balls down Colby's throat if he didn't get Brent to end the strike. Colby had also found out that Finley had bought Brent flowers and an array of chocolates. Clearly, Finley hadn't thought Colby was being a complete idiot on the phone this morning.

"Where would Brent be right now?" he asked Ezra as they walked down the hall together.

"Probably out on the football field. He practices more than anyone." Ezra put his arm around Colby's waist and pulled him closer

"No wonder he's built like a juggernaut," Colby remarked.

Colby had always admired the way Brent looked. He was so tall, and whilst his muscles weren't defined, you could tell he could snap you in half like a twig, like a young Mountain from Game of Thrones. It's what made him so perfect for football. Finley would constantly gush about everything about Brent. At the time, Finley had insisted he just wanted to look like Brent, but in retrospect, it was super obvious Finley was crushing on him even back then.

"Yo, Ezra, Colby!" Jordan Park walked towards them in the hallway. He was smiling until he looked confused. "You guys are taking that joke about you two dating pretty seriously, huh?" He stared at Ezra's arm on Colby's waist.

Colby was about to pull away and laugh it off, but Ezra kept his arm firmly in place.

Ezra was also smiling, but not in a particularly friendly way. "Who said it was a joke?" Ezra questioned.

"No fucking way," Jordan mumbled under his breath, "but you both, uh . . . with Joanna . . . I thought . . . what?"

Ezra pulled Colby forward and slapped Jordan's back. "See you later, Park."

"You don't mind people knowing?" Colby asked Ezra.

"What are they going to do? Tell my dad? I've lost all that I could lose, may as well start living now." Ezra grinned at him. Ezra led him to the football field and sure enough, Brent was practicing his tackles on a dummy with some of the other guys.

"Hey, Brent!" Ezra called out.

Brent took off his helmet and turned to look at them, his curly brown hair sticking up in all directions. "Colby wants to talk!"

"Coming!" Brent called back. He jogged over and waved goodbye to the guys he was playing with.

"I need to go tell Coach why I wasn't at practice this morning," said Ezra.

"What are you going to tell her?" asked Colby.

"The truth. She knows I've been having problems at home. It isn't the first time it has interrupted my performance. She'll understand." Ezra made Coach Clain sound much nicer than she really was.

"What's up, Colby?" Brent was slightly out of breath by the time he reached Colby.

Ezra had already disappeared in search of Coach.

"I was just going to let you know that the bottom strike is over. Finley caved in. We won," Colby said charismatically, giving a little fist pump in the air.

"The what strike?" Brent asked.

"You know, the bottom strike."

Brent's face showed no recollection.

"I made it up on Monday, and you agreed to it. Isn't that the reason you're not around Finley? You two aren't fucking anymore?"

Brent's eyes shot open and he gasped at Colby. "You—you're very blunt with your words." He paused and looked down at his feet. "Can I tell you the truth, Colby?"

Colby nodded.

"It's kind of humiliating, but the first time Finley and I . . . you know, I was so embarrassed by the way I looked. Finley is so handsome and lean and really pretty, but I'm massive. I had to take some liquid courage before I had the guts to take my clothes off in front of him, and then when we . . . did the do."

Had Brent been getting sex ed classes from Colby's dad? Were they sharing euphemisms?

253

"It looked like I was about to crush him with my thighs. I didn't even dare go on top in case I flattened him."

Colby nodded again in understanding, but he was also confused about how big Brent thought he was. "I get it. I was embarrassed being naked in front of Ezra when we did it for the first time. He's so perfect, and I felt ugly next to him."

"Exactly!" Brent yelled excitedly. He cleared his throat and calmed down a bit. "It just seems pointless to try and explain it to him because I know it is silly, but I can't help thinking these things. Both his thighs are the same as one of mine. That's not self-deprecating. That's a fact."

Colby sneakily glanced down at Brent's thighs. They were massive and damn, were they nice. "I get it. However, I can 100% guarantee that you are unbelievably handsome, and no one knows that more than Finley."

Brent sighed and looked back at the guys he'd been playing with. "I've never really been flirted with before."

"I find that impossible to believe."

"Thanks. I mostly get friendzoned, or the people I like use me to get to Ezra. I hadn't even imagined being with a guy, and then Finley started flirting with me—which was completely unexpected—when we were at that football camp and one thing just kind of led to another." Brent covered his face with his huge hands. "I like him so much. I just don't look good enough for him."

Colby grabbed those big hands and ripped them away, forcing Brent to look at him. "Now, listen here. I've known Finley for years now, and I can guarantee you are good enough for him. You're his dream guy and for years, you were all he would talk about. You are tall and you're built like a bear, but that's what makes you look so amazing. You have the biggest best-looking thighs I have ever seen. They look so soft yet firm at the same time. Do you mind if I?" Colby squeezed the magnificent thigh. "Wow. My point is that you don't have to be small to be hot. Now, go to

254

Finley. Seduce him with that awesome body of yours and accept the flowers and chocolates he got you because I am going to be bullying him for months for being such a fucking sap."

"Thanks, Colby." Brent pulled Colby in for a bear hug.

Colby could feel his bones grinding against each other. It was worth it though because he got a face full of Brent's bountiful bosom. They were incredible. Finley's infatuation made so much sense.

"No problemo," Colby assured when Brent let go of him.

Brent went straight back to training, and Colby shot Finley a text that the mission was complete. He also told Finley he was going to quit the football team whilst he was hanging about. He went to Coach's office and sat outside. He didn't want to interrupt the talk Coach and Ezra were having.

A few minutes passed and Colby was getting a little bored of the games on his phone.

"Have you done it yet?" Finley came walking down the hallway towards him.

"No, not yet. Why?"

"I told you, man. If you're quitting, I'm quitting." Finley sat in the chair next to Colby.

"I didn't realise you loved me so much."

"Don't make this gay. I'm not into that shit."

"Took you a while to get here," Colby pointed out.

"Okay?"

"Did you give Brent the flowers and chocolates?"

Finley suddenly became very interested in what was in his bag. "Yes," he said quietly.

"Sounds pretty gay to me. Have you got the biology textbook in your bag?"

"Depends who's asking."

"Give it to me. I need to study." Colby held out his hands in waiting.

"Since when did you study?"

"Since Ezra promised I can top if I score well in the upcoming biology test. I forgot why I started this whole thing with Ezra. It all began because I tried to prove myself as the top *physically*. However, I have grown as a person since then, and now I'm going to show I'm a top, not through physical dominance but through my superior intelligence instead!"

Finley gave him that look. "Sounds like Ezra is just bribing you to revise stuff. I bet your dad's thrilled."

"My dad thinks Ezra is a godsend and a good influence on me."

Finley laughed at that. "He's got you so whipped."

"No!" Colby protested. "It is definitely the other way round." He opened the biology textbook and began to revise. He'd never done it before, so he was basically just reading the big fancy words and looking at the pictures. The book stated that "the mitochondria is the powerhouse of the cell." Colby scratched his chin thoughtfully. "Absolutely, it is," he whispered to himself. Whatever this mitoconshit was, Colby was very impressed by its description. Ezra would have to describe Colby like that after he aced this biology test.

Had the door to Coach Clain's office always been this intimidating? It appeared as a giant barrier separating the threshold between school and Coach's office. The final line of protection.

"You don't have to do this," Colby said to Finley. "You can go back to the team, play football, and give Brent a blowjob in the shower just like you wanted to. You can live."

Finley gave him a reassuring smile and shook his head. "Nah. If you're going to get murdered by Coach, then so am I. Maybe she'll let us share the same shallow grave. That and Brent isn't an exhibitionist like you and Ezra."

"What? I'm not really that into museum exhibitions," said Colby.

"That's not what exhibitionist means."

256

The door to Coach's office slowly squeaked open—Colby had seen a lot of horror movies that started this way. He wasn't sure what happened after that though. Usually, he would've chickened out and turned off the movie by then.

"You sure you want to do this, man?" asked Finley. The fear had penetrated the very bones of his being.

"Yes," Colby replied.

Ezra came out the door first and waved at the soon-to-be-dead boys sitting outside. Next came Coach Clain, so scary, so short. She smiled at Ezra and patted him on the back as he walked off. Was she in a good mood today? Maybe this was going to go a lot smoother than Colby thought.

Once Ezra had disappeared, she turned to the two boys with a face as hard as nails. "What do you two want?" Or maybe it would go as terribly as imagined.

Finley and Colby glanced at each other, then answered in unison, "We're quitting the team."

"No," Coach replied. She turned and went inside her office.

The boys tepidly followed her in, lambs willingly entering the slaughterhouse.

"Um, all due respect, Coach, but you can't refuse to let us leave the club," Finley explained carefully.

"Sure, I can."

"But we want to quit," said Colby.

"Yes, and I'm saying no." Coach sat at her very organised desk. "Close the door and make sure you slam it," she ordered.

Finley was confused, but Colby didn't even hesitate to nearly break the door in half when he closed it. Why would he actually close it? Now she was going to kill them where no one could see, and no one would dare to come and look for them.

Coach opened a drawer on her desk and pulled out a Swiss army knife and began to polish the blade with a small piece of cloth. "Now, boys. Explain to me again why you want to quit my wonderful team."

Finley was hesitant to answer. The boys would have to word their response carefully with the utmost politeness to get out of the office alive.

"I just don't like football anymore," Colby replied immediately.

'I'm going to die," Finley muttered under his breath.

Coach set the knife down and sighed. That was good. At least, she was kind of unarmed now. "That's it? You just don't like the game anymore?"

Finley nodded.

"Ugh, fine. You can quit and be pathetic losers. It's none of my business," Coach groaned, clearly annoyed. "You were a pleasure to have on the team, and we'll all miss you very much, yada yada yada."

It seemed fitting to Colby that Coach was a dick to him before he left, made him think of all the good times they'd had together, and she was a dick then too.

"Thank you for looking after Ezra. He's told me what you and your family are doing for him, and I'm very grateful."

Colby blinked in disbelief. He wasn't ready for Coach to say something sweet.

She stood from her desk and picked up the knife. "Now. You two aren't going to tell anyone that I've shown human compassion here today, are you?"

The boys shook their heads vigorously.

"Good. You're going to tell people that I gave you the beating of your life and I kicked you off the team. I can't have the rest of the boys knowing that you can just get up and quit. As far as they know, my football team is a lifelong agreement. If you see me walking past you in the corridor, I want you to flinch when I get close to you. Got it?"

They nodded their heads.

258

"Very good. Now get out!"

Finley didn't hesitate to get out of that room as fast as his legs could carry him.

"See you around, Coach." Colby waved goodbye as he left.

She shook her head at him and went back to the computer on her desk.

"That went really well," Colby said to Finley once they were nowhere near Coach's office anymore.

"It was a lot less bloody than I was expecting."

They kept walking down the hallway to their next class until they passed Sophie. She was absentmindedly walking towards them with her books in hand. She was speaking to Avni, who was walking beside her. She looked forward at just the right time to see Colby.

"Good morning, Colby!" It was in Colby's most biased opinion that Sophie had the prettiest smile in the whole wide world.

CHAPTER THIRTY
Alcoholics Anonymous

It could most certainly be argued that last week had been pretty rough. Ezra had been sleeping in his car, Sophie was struggling to come to grips with her identity, Brent had been much more insecure about his body than anyone really realised, and Finley had gone a whole week with blue balls. Despite all this, Colby had a good feeling about this week. With drive and determination, he could brighten the lives of those nearest and dearest to him.

First mission of the day: Reunite the three amigos! Finley, Sophie, and Colby would be best friends again before the day was up, or at least that was Colby's optimistic thinking getting the best of him.

Colby had managed to wrangle the pair of them to be in the same area without trying to kill each other. A big step in the right direction!

The three of them were sitting on a wooden picnic table that was situated on the field outside the school. Finley and Sophie sat opposite of each other—clearly not happy about the situation—and Colby sat in the middle of them as an adjudicator of sorts.

"Thanks for coming, guys," Colby began. He smiled at them both.

Finley looked pissed and Sophie looked nervous.

"What's going on, man?" Finley sighed with exasperation. "I already know it's something dumb, but I want to see if I can make even a little sense out of this."

Colby kept his smile on. In his mind, he was relieving the tension by smiling but in reality, he just looked insane. "Well, I think it's about time that we all sat down together and had a deep discussion about everything. We're all just going to speak honestly to get everything out in the open."

Colby was pretty proud of his plan. Last night, he had been watching a TV show with Ezra. In one of the scenes, a character was in an Alcoholics Anonymous meeting, and the person in charge of the meeting spoke calmly and got the characters to open up about their problems. He was going for the same vibe with his friends. Ezra had expressed he didn't have much faith in Colby's plan, but Ezra was definitely wrong.

"Who wants to go first?" Colby asked.

"I will," Finley interjected, still scowling. "I think Sophie is a homophobic bitch and a terrible friend."

"Okay," said Colby. Slightly dejected they were off to a bad start, but it wasn't over yet. "That was definitely honest. Sophie, your thoughts?"

Sophie stared down into her lap and clenched her fists into the white dress she was wearing, her auburn hair falling haphazardly around her face. "I know I haven't exactly been good to you guys lately—"

"That's a fucking understatement," Finley mumbled.

Sophie looked up and glared at him. "BUT, I really did think I was helping you two. It's what I've been taught. It's what I've been told. Everything I have done is because I care. I promise."

Finley slammed his hand on the table. "Bullshit! I'm not going to pretend like I know what you've been through or whatever, but you've done some inexcusable things that have nothing to do with trying to save our gay souls or whatever. First things first: you tried to blackmail your so-called best friend with a picture of him making out with another boy."

"I wasn't trying to blackmail him!" Sophie retorted. "I was trying to warn him about what he'd done with Ezra at the party."

"Which leads me to my second point," Finley took over once again. "What the fuck was your obsession with Ezra? Because at the time, none of us really knew him as anything other than the asshole who had slept with Joanna behind Colby's back. You knew as well as I did how hurt he was after that and yet you not only went and crush on him, but you became super close with Joanna again. How do you explain that?"

How could she explain that? Colby hadn't even thought about that. He'd purposefully pushed those thoughts to the back of his mind in fear of an answer. Sophie cared about Colby. He knew she did . . . didn't she?

Sophie seemed lost for words as her eyes looked around frantically for an answer. Her mouth would gape open like a fish out of water, but she didn't say anything. Eventually, she stuttered out, "I-I don't know. All the girls I know were in love with Ezra. They'd constantly go on about how nice and handsome he was and that he was totally boyfriend material. At the time, all my girl friends kept questioning me why I didn't have a boyfriend, and then Joanna said that it was because I was a . . . lesbian." Her expression became distressed.

Finley sighed. "So your plan was to use Ezra as your beard?"

Sophie nodded.

"What's a beard?" Colby asked.

"A beard is when a gay person dates someone of the opposite sex to hide the fact that they're gay. I'm not sure what the lesbian equivalent is." Finley rubbed his face in his hands. He'd redone his hair recently into cornrows, and it brought out his high cheekbones. "I'm guessing you didn't realise Ezra was gay."

Sophie shook her head. "I knew. It's not like he was very good at hiding it. I thought we could help each other. He'd-scratch-my-back-and-I'd--scratch-his kind of thing. I realised it wouldn't work though when a majority of what we'd talk about was Colby."

"What?" Colby's face felt warm at the suggestion that Ezra was into him back then.

"Yep." Sophie giggled at his reaction. "I used to think it was so weird that the guy who had slept with Joanna behind your back was obsessed with you. It was only at the party when I saw the two of you kissing round the back that I realised how he felt about you. So, I thought it was perfect. He could cover for me, and I could cover for him. I even thought I could convince myself to be genuinely into him, and I think I was for a little bit. I didn't expect you two to actually get together though. How did that happen?"

Sophie waited expectantly for Colby to answer, but it was a much more complicated question than she realised.

"Um . . . well, you see, when you sent me that picture of us making out, I was like '*I'm definitely not gay, and I'm not a bottom*', so to prove it I—" Colby curled his hand into a fist and pumped it up and down. "You know."

Sophie still looked confused.

"I gave him a handjob."

"You gave him a handjob to prove you were straight and a top?" Sophie turned to Finley to see if he could make it make sense.

Finley shrugged at her with a Colby-will-be-Colby expression.

"It made sense at the time," Colby defended.

"No, it didn't," Finley said. "In Colbyland, it makes sense, but in the real world, you were just giving Ezra severe whiplash with your constant change in attitudes towards him. He could sue you for bodily harm," he joked.

"He already got compensation when we fucked, and he nearly crippled me."

"You two have already had sex? Like . . . penetrative sex? When did this happen?"

"The Friday before the training weekend," replied Colby.

Sophie's eyes were wide, and her mouth hung open.

Finley looked kind of smug at her shock. "Afraid so, Sophie dear. Whilst you were trying your hardest to flirt with darling Ezra, he had already got a slice of the Colby cake." Finley leaned over and smacked Colby's ass, causing him to release a loud squeal. "But let's not get distracted here. Being closeted is hard, but you didn't have to be such a bitch about it." Finley was back on track.

Sophie snapped out of her little daze. "I know."

"It's fine, Finley." Colby placed his hand on Finley's shoulder. "She's apologised and she's growing. That's what matters. We should forgive her."

"I guess," Finley groaned. "You better not pull any shit like this again! And, don't you ever question my relationship with Brent! Okay?"

"Okay," Sophie agreed.

"Then, I guess we're cool or whatever, but there won't be any second chances. You mess up once more after this, and I'll never speak to you again."

Her eyes were brimming with tears, about to spill down her cheeks. "I won't let you down," she promised. "Thank you." That's when the tears could no longer be restrained, and they stained her soft pink cheeks.

Colby pulled the sleeve of his long-sleeved black shirt—technically it was Ezra's shirt, but Colby had stolen it for the day—and wiped away the tears with it. He hoped Ezra wouldn't mind the damp sleeves when he gave it back to him.

"Don't be such a crybaby, Sophie," teased Finley. He reached forward and placed his hand on hers.

"Shut up," her voice came out quiet and croaked. "Heard you were crying over blue balls. That's way more pathetic than this."

"Blue balls is a serious affliction. I'll have you know." Finley took his hand off of hers and stood up. "I've got to go have a meeting with my biology teacher about my grade." He patted Colby's shoulder. "Don't go and have sex in a public place again, okay, man?"

Colby spluttered, "I don't have sex in public places!"

"You kind of do. You and Ezra are freaky like that."

"Name one time!"

"The handjob in the team showers, making out in a hallway, giving Ezra a blowjob in his living room, fucking in the boys' bathroom, making out at Brent's house, getting a blowjob in the team showers, fucking in your living room—"

"*Okay*, I get the picture. But for your information, it's Ezra who wants to do those things, not me."

"Sure, man. Sure." He walked off back into the school building.

"I am sorry," Sophie whispered, her head leaning against Colby's arm. "I wasn't thinking for myself. I was just doing what I'd been told."

"I know," Colby replied and stroked her hair.

"Hiya!"

Colby and Sophie jumped at the sudden and loud greeting.

Avni was walking towards them. She was wearing a yellow crop top and bell-bottom jeans that he knew his mom would love. Her dark hair was in a long braid down her back and she had a gold nose ring in.

She came closer to the picnic table, then stopped when she saw that Sophie was crying.

"Oh my god, what's wrong?" She immediately went to Sophie's side and comforted her. However, Sophie wasn't crying anymore. She only looked flustered and embarrassed.

265

"She's just upset because . . ." *Come on Colby, Ezra and Finley have told you that you are bad at lying so think of something good this time.* ". . . she thinks she failed her biology exam."

Avni looked confused. "But the biology exam isn't till next week?"

Fuck!

Avni lifted Sophie's face and pinched her nose. "You can't have a failed test you haven't taken yet, you worry wart. How about we revise together if you're that worried about it?"

FUCK YES!

"Alright," Sophie agreed, her cheeks ablaze.

Colby decided he should leave them alone for any lesbian activities to occur. He had heard lesbians moved very quickly in relationships, so he thought it best to remove himself so the process could begin.

"I've got to go. See you two later." He ran off before Sophie could call him back.

He triumphantly skipped into the school, assured in the thought that he may be the best wingman on the planet after what he just pulled. Without even thinking about it, he skipped all around the school until he stumbled across Ezra, excited to tell him all about how great a wingman he was.

Ezra was talking to some girls from the hockey club, one of whom Colby was friends with and had been the one to tell him about what friends-with-benefits relationships were like.

"Hey, Parker." He fist-bumped his friend from the hockey club, a tall and wild girl with her hair dyed pink.

"'Sup, Williams."

"You look happy," Ezra remarked.

"I am over the moon and let me tell you why." Colby was smiling like the Cheshire cat. "Not only did my Alcoholics Anonymous trick work like a charm, but it also turns out I am a good liar, and I am an excellent wingman."

266

"I doubt all three of those things." Ezra wrapped one arm around his waist and pulled him closer, a move Ezra did so often that Colby was becoming very used to it due to the number of times he had done it.

The two other hockey girls whispered to each other about the rumours being true, but it was only Lola Parker that spoke up from the three of them.

"No way. Williams, you're actually banging little miss golden boy over here." She shoved her thumb in Ezra's direction.

"Little miss golden boy?" Ezra questioned under his breath.

"Yeah. I'm disappointed in myself too," said Colby, earning a tight squeeze from Ezra.

"Lol, that's hilarious." Parker giggled. "Come on." She kicked the other two girls to start walking away.

"Go on then," said Ezra, "how did Operation Alcoholics Anonymous go?"

"Good! Actually, we're all friends again and Finley is failing biology. It's great!" he explained. "The exciting part is when Finley left, Avni came over and I was the best wingman ever. Avni saw Sophie was crying and asked what was wrong, and I came up with the perfect lie," Colby explained the rest of the situation to him from his amazing lie to his wingman skills.

Ezra was trying to smother his laughter by the end of Colby's ramble. "So, basically, you didn't come up with the perfect lie. In fact, you really messed up the lie, but luckily Avni misinterpreted what you said and comforted Sophie without you really doing anything."

"What do you mean without me doing anything? I was highly involved."

"Okay, babe."

Colby's stomach fluttered a little bit at that. For some reason, Ezra had been trying out pet names on Colby. Colby

267

already had a pet name for Ezra and that was "asshole," or, when things were getting a little spicy, "dickhead."

"Sophie said that when she was flirting with you, all you would ask about was me. That's embarrassing," Colby tried to tease Ezra, but he was unbothered.

"Not really. I've had a crush on you since the moment we met."

"No, you haven't!"

"Yes, I have. I just wasn't very good at showing it."

"Are you saying this so I'll have sex with you in a public space?"

"What?"

"You're such a pervert, pervert."

CHAPTER THIRTY-ONE
Top of the Class

"If you do really well in the upcoming biology test, you can top."

That promise. It had consumed Colby. Every waking moment he could hear that promise ringing through his mind.

No. Promise didn't capture the meaning of what Ezra said. It was more than a promise.

An oath.

A pledge.

A sworn vow of the utmost importance held between two lovers.

That was the true meaning behind Ezra's words.

Colby had previously lost sight of his original goal. He was distracted by his hatred of Ezra, then blinded by his love for him. He nearly forgot the reason he kissed Ezra for the first time in that shower, was to prove he was a *top*.

Granted, he had arguably failed at proving he was a top since then as he had repeatedly bottomed for Ezra every time they had sex. Not that he was complaining about being in that position, it was not the best sex he ever had. Okay, it was great, but everything with Ezra was. Regardless, the point was Colby needed to achieve his original goal of topping, and he was ready to do anything for it, even study.

He sat at his family's dining room table and shoved his face into his biology textbook. He hated science, but for Ezra's ass, he would come to love it.

His mom had been staring at him in disbelief ever since Colby sat down at the table and started revising. His dad and Ezra were talking in the kitchen and Colby could hear them.

"I really think I should start paying rent. I insist on it."

Ezra's voice was so nice and deep. Maybe he could read the textbook to Colby, then he might actually have a chance of remembering it. No, that wouldn't work. If Colby's track record showed anything, it was that Colby couldn't help but try to get into Ezra's pants whenever it was just the two of them. He had to focus, god damn it.

"Don't be silly. You are part of the household now. You do chores, you go out to do the shopping when I'm busy, and you've managed to get my son to study. Trust me, you've done more than enough for us," his dad calmly replied.

The mitochondria is the powerhouse of the cell. He knew that one-off by heart now.

"But you're doing so much for me, and I'm just freeloading here. At least, let me pay for something around here, like the groceries."

Red blood cells carry oxygen around the body.

"Ezra, we didn't invite you into our house because we see you as some charity case or a way to get some money. We care about you, and we want to look after you. I'd no sooner be asking for rent from Colby than I would from you."

There are three main types of neurones: sensory, relay, and motor.

"He's right, dear. We're not taking you in for your money. We're taking you in so you can get Colby to do shit. It's incredible. What did you say to him to make him do this?" his mom asked.

An example of a single-cell organism is yeast.

Colby heard Ezra's feet patting against the tiled floor as he walked into the dining room and took a seat next to Colby.

270

"I, um . . . I offered him . . ." Ezra looked to Colby for help, but he was focused on revision.

"Say no more." His mom stood from the table and patted Ezra's head. "I catch your drift. I used to do the same thing to Trev to make him do my homework." She laughed evilly, then went to the kitchen to go harass her husband.

Ezra chuckled and rested his head on Colby's shoulder. He placed his hand on Colby's thigh and rubbed his thumb across the fabric of his jeans. "How much longer are you going to study for?"

"Don't you try to distract me, pervert. You know what you promised, and you can't distract me from it with your"—Colby gestured to Ezra's hand with disgust—"sexual advances."

"So you don't want me to give you a lift to school? Fine, walk."

Shit. Colby put down the textbook and lifted Ezra's hand to hold it to his cheek. "Can I have a lift to school please, best boyfriend in the world. I don't want to walk. Pwetty pwease." He batted his eyelashes at him.

"Since you asked so nicely."

Colby revised in the car. He revised in the first period and every period after that. He revised during break. He revised during lunch. Then time was up, end of the line.

Okay. He had to stay calm. It was time.

Within the next hour, Colby was about to prove whether he was worthy of being the top through this biology test. All he had to do was not to get distracted and keep his eyes on the prize.

Ezra was sitting in the row in front of him, talking to some of his friends. His back was curved which accentuated his ass. Eyes on the prize.

A delicate hand touched Colby's shoulder.

"You look a little nervous, Colbs." Joanna giggled. She still was the perfect embodiment of femininity with her strawberry blonde hair and freckled cheeks. She leaned over him more, so her cleavage could be spotted if he looked down her white blouse.

271

"I want to do well in this test."

"Oh?" She stroked a lock of his hair behind his ear and giggled again. "For any particular reason?"

"To be top!" He slammed his fist down on the desk, frightening the poor girl sitting next to him.

"I never took you to be someone who wanted to be top of the class, Colbs. Although, I guess you have changed a lot recently." She ran a soft finger across his jaw.

"Top of the class? That's not what I—oh yeah, definitely. To be top of the class. That's what *I* want to do!" He winked at her.

She grimaced a little bit. "Yeah, that's what I just said."

"Because *I* want to be top of the class." He snapped his fingers and pointed a finger gun at her. God, he was so good at lying recently. Just wait until he told Ezra about this one.

"Still a bit odd," Joanna mumbled quietly. "Anyway, Colbs, I heard the funniest rumour the other day. You're not going to believe this, but people have been saying you and Ezra are dating now. Isn't that crazy?"

"Not really. He's my boyfriend." Colby smiled to himself as he once again relapsed into his fantasy of topping Ezra. Eyes on the prize.

Joanna's soft touch lost its delicacy as she grabbed Colby's face and forced him to look at her. "So, it's true then?"

Colby's cheeks were now mushed together, and his lips were forced to pucker like a fish. "Yesh."

"Fuck off. No, it's not." Her face came closer to his. "You love me. You always have, and Ezra loves me too. That's just how it works."

Why was she so angry? Colby was pretty sure he hadn't even said anything stupid enough to compare to Joanna's bold claims.

"Ezra doesn't love you, and you don't love him."

She was crazy. "I don't like you anymore," said Colby. "I like Ezhra now. He treatsh me much nisher than you did. My parentsh like Ezhra too."

"Your parents loved me."

"Not really. My mom would alwaysh call you mean thingsh in Portugueshe when you would come round."

"What would she say?"

"I don't want to transhlate them. Shome are really bad."

Joanna looked shaken by the revelation. Her high horse was getting shorter by the second. "Ezra and I slept together when we were dating. He'll do it again even if you two are the ones dating this time."

Colby shook his head, although it was difficult with Joanna still holding his face in a vice grip. "He shlept with you 'cosh he had conflicted feelingsh about me. It wash never really about you."

She froze, still staring at Colby.

His cheeks hurt from talking. "Go ashk him."

"Jo!" Unbeknownst to Colby—as his vision had been limited by Joanna—Sophie had rushed over and gently taken Joanna's hand off of him. "Let's go sit down," Sophie said calmly. "We can still squeeze in some revision before the test starts."

Joanna made a noise of indignation. "One sec." She walked over to Ezra and began to harass him.

"Studying going good?" asked Sophie.

"I think so, I guess. We'll see. To be honest, I'm pretty nervous."

"You'll do great. You've worked really hard, and you're much smarter than you give yourself credit for. Once you apply yourself to something, you always do good at it. You're a hidden genius."

He didn't believe all that she was saying, but it made him feel more confident. He looked over at Joanna and Ezra. She'd asked him something, and Ezra had nodded his head. That did not appear to be the right answer as Joanna stormed her way back to Sophie and pulled her away.

"Go fuck yourself, Colbs."

"Jo, don't say that to him!" said Sophie. Joanna seemed surprised to be stood up against.

"Yeah, Jo," said Colby. "Don't get all pissy 'cos you found out you're not the centre of the universe. Also, Colbs is a terrible nickname. It doesn't even shorten Colby. It's the same number of letters either way."

Sophie was shoving Joanna back to her desk before she had the chance to open her mouth again.

"Good luck," Sophie said to him before she left.

"You too," he replied

The test papers were laid out in front of everyone.

"Is everyone ready?" the teacher asked.

Ezra turned to look at Colby over his shoulder. "*You can do it,*" he mouthed.

Eyes on the prize. Eyes on the prize.

"Start."

Colby turned over his paper. Name. That was easy. Colby Williams, duh. Date. Shit, what day was it? Thursday? Was it Thursday or Wednesday? Crap. It felt like a Thursday, so he wrote down Thursday in the blank spot.

He opened to the first page of questions about biology and couldn't answer question one. That was okay. Go to question two and start from there. He couldn't answer question two. That was fine. Go to question three and start from there. He couldn't answer question three.

This was going to be tough.

*   *   *

"Has it updated yet?"

"Nope."

Colby didn't know how much more of this agonising waiting game he could take. He was laying on his back with a pillow held over his face. Ezra sat at Colby's desk doing some homework and would periodically refresh the laptop that was next to him.

Their biology teacher had become ill in the following days after the test but had agreed to send everyone their grades via email. Colby hated waiting! Things were just better to get done in the present, not days later.

"I'll be proud of you no matter how well you do," Ezra assured.

"Yeah, but you won't let me fuck you no matter how well I do." Colby prayed to whatever god was listening that he got a good grade on this test. He had actually revised for it, which was way more than he usually did. He'd also convinced Ezra to douche just in case he'd done well. Although, even without the sex, that experience was hilarious. Listening to Ezra yell in horror and shout about how weird it felt to Colby was the highlight of his day. He had been such a big baby about it, complaining it was gross. Even if Colby didn't end up topping Ezra, at least now Ezra would appreciate the work Colby had to put into being a good bottom.

He wasn't sure whether it was a sign that Ezra didn't think Colby had done well. When a person said they would be proud of you either way, that was often because they were predicting failure. Perhaps, he didn't think Colby could do well, but Colby would prove him wrong. Hopefully.

"It's updated."

Colby shot up off the bed and raced to Ezra's side. "How'd I do? How'd I do? No, wait! Don't tell me. No, do. No, don't!"

"Boys! We're going out now!" his mom called from downstairs. His dad was taking his mom out for a dinner date, so it was Colby and Ezra alone in the house for a few hours. "Ezra! Make sure Colby doesn't burn the house down!"

"Will do!" Ezra called back. "You got 72%. Well done! You also got a teacher's note attached asking *Why did you only write*

275

Thursday in the date box when that is neither the way you write dates nor was it a Thursday?' What the hell, Colby?"

"I got 72%! That's crazy!"

"What did you get in your last test?"

"Eleven percent."

"Oh. Wow. That's a definite improvement."

"You bet it is." Colby straddled Ezra's lap and kissed him like crazy. He had no idea doing well in school could give you such an adrenaline rush. He was so happy. He was so excited. He was so horny.

His hands fumbled over Ezra's black basketball shorts as he tried to pull them down to get to his prize. He finally got a grasp on Ezra's dick and stroked it to hardness. He bit and kissed the left side of Ezra's face as he did so. He was about to pull his own shorts down and get to business as usual when Ezra interrupted.

"I thought you wanted to top?"

Oh shit. Yeah. He pulled his shorts back over his ass and nodded aggressively. He wrapped his hand around Ezra's throat and stared him in the eyes, giddy with excitement. "I'm the top."

Ezra smiled at him. "You're the top." Ezra took Colby's hand from around his throat and sucked on his index finger.

Colby could feel the softness of Ezra's tongue caress him and the wet heat of his mouth. Fuck.

"Get on the bed," Ezra demanded, removing Colby's finger from his mouth. Colby didn't really contemplate the fact that—as the top—he probably should have been the one making the demands. However, he was painfully hard and couldn't focus on much apart from the fact that he was about to fuck Ezra.

Colby got off Ezra's lap in a lust-filled daze. He took off his clothes and sat on his bed. That 72% must've really impressed Ezra as he gave Colby a show as he took off his own clothes. He allowed Colby an illusion of control as he was permitted to slide his hands under Ezra's shirt and unveil him. It was a pleasurable torture of sorts doing it so slowly, an endurance test, how slowly

276

could Colby enjoy the small details of Ezra before his impatient desire took hold and he longed to see the whole work of art. It reminded Colby of those times when he'd watch a TV show and the camera would pan ever so slowly towards the one thing he wanted to see. He hated when shows would do that. He was impatient by nature and yet, here he was inflicting that enjoyable slow-burn of revelation upon himself.

He was about to go down on the masterpiece, the slow reveal of Ezra's body was a treat to his eyes. No matter how many times Colby grabbed Ezra's hips, ran his tongue up his stomach, and placed kisses across his chest. He would never get bored at the sight of him. When Colby finally reached the summit of Ezra's chest, he slid Ezra's shirt off and let it fall to the floor. He was about to repeat the process again on Ezra's lower half until Ezra threaded his fingers through Colby's hair and pulled him back.

Colby was slightly surprised by the aggression. Ezra took off his own shorts and they became a puddle around his feet as he pushed Colby back on the bed and leaned over him. It was almost like Ezra was still dominant even without being the top . . . nah, no way. Colby was the top today, which meant he was the dominant one. That's just the way it worked. When Colby came out of his reassurance of top-hood, he was watching Ezra stretch himself out.

"You better be paying attention," he huskily groaned into Colby's ear.

Colby leaned up to kiss him and stroked Ezra's dick. Ezra moaned into Colby's mouth.

Ezra decided he was ready. Colby thought they were doing an easy starting position like missionary. However, Ezra seemed to have other ideas as he lubed up Colby's dick and began to lower himself onto it.

"Are you sure?" Colby tried to hold in the moan as he felt Ezra's large hands stroke him.

"You did good work. You deserve to be rewarded."

Something about the way Ezra said *rewarded* made him even hornier, but it was also kind of funny.

"You sound like a parent," he joked. "Thank you, Daddy."

All movement stopped.

"What did you just call me?"

"Daddy?"

Ezra nodded. "Let's keep that in mind for next time."

Colby had no idea what he meant by that. He had no brainpower to consider it. He'd only ever fantasised about Ezra being the bottom. Sure, he'd said he wanted that to happen lots of times, but he didn't actually think Ezra would agree to it. When did the room become so hot? His hands grabbed onto the sheets, taking as much fabric into his hands, and held on for dear life. He felt as though there was a coil inside of him and Ezra kept winding it tighter and tighter then tighter still. He tried to think of anything else than what was happening at that moment. He couldn't endure much more and they'd hardly even started.

Pleads for mercy rested on the tip of his tongue, but all that came out was moans of Ezra's name. It was a miscommunication of encouragement and Ezra aligned himself with Colby's dick and Colby watched helplessly as his dream of topping crumbled before his eyes.

He came.

Colby had managed to get Ezra to agree to be topped, after ages of insisting that Colby could handle it, that he was meant to top, born to top. All of that conviction gone in a moment of weakness.

Ezra froze for a second. He moved off of Colby's lap, then looked down as if to check that he hadn't imagined it. "Did you just—"

Colby released the sheets he'd been clutching and grabbed a nearby pillow, then tried to smother himself with it. The situation was so ridiculously embarrassing that there was only one way to escape with some semblance of dignity: he was going to kill himself.

"Colby, it's fine," said Ezra.

Colby said something back, but it sounded like garbled nonsense because he was speaking into a pillow.

"Sorry, what?"

Colby moved the pillow. "I said I'm trying to kill myself. You can have my room when I'm dead. Give my books to my dad and give my mom all my savings. Tell her to get herself something nice. Give nothing to my cat. I hate him." He began to smother himself with the pillow again. It was not a very effective way to off himself.

"You're not going to kill yourself." Ezra threw the pillow onto the floor. "It's fine. These things happen."

"Doesn't happen when you're the top," Colby groaned into his hands. "Ugh, I wanna die."

Ezra lay down next to him and stroked his head. "There, there. It's not that embarrassing. Only you and I know that you . . . couldn't hold it."

"Stop laughing! That's not even true. Finley and Sophie are going to know about it."

"How would they know?"

"Because I'm going to tell them, obviously."

"You don't have to."

"Yeah, but I'm going to," Colby groaned in embarrassment louder and hugged Ezra. "Can we try again?"

"Of course, we can. If you get over 80% in the upcoming math test."

"What? I've never passed a math test. It's my worst subject."

Ezra gave him a kiss on the forehead. "Best start revising then, shouldn't you?"

"You're cruel!" Colby shifted. Using the remaining strength he had, he managed to lift his face and rest it against Ezra's chest. "Did I do good before I came too fast?" Tops were supposed to be dominant and in charge, right? Colby wasn't sure if he had been in charge of anything that had happened.

"You were fantastic. You were a great top."

"Really?" Colby tilted his head up and goofily smiled at Ezra. "I was a good top?"

Ezra kissed his nose. "The best."

CHAPTER THIRTY-TWO
Daddy Issues

"Good morning, Daddy." His voice was soft and sweet, almost teasing. His hands toyed with a loose strand of Ezra's blond hair.

Ezra sighed and swatted his hand away. "Quit it, Finley."

"Oh. What's with the sour tone? I heard from Colby that you like being called daddy. Do I not do it for you?" Finley tried to hold in his laughter, but it kept slipping out in between words.

"You're just jealous I got Colby to call me daddy before you got Brent to do it."

"I don't have daddy issues. Be jealous."

"I'm over six-foot. Be jealous."

"How could I be jealous of somebody whose last name is Dickinson."

"Imagine having to moan out Finley during sex."

"Stop it!" Colby interrupted. "You guys are so mean to each other."

"I'm only teasing my little dicky-son." Finley pulled Ezra down into a headlock. "He knows I'm joking, and he better be fucking joking too."

"Did I hurt your feelings, Finny?" Ezra's phone buzzed on the table but he didn't check it.

"Not as much as you hurt my man Colby's feelings. You really pulled a fast one on him, huh? Told him he could top, and then went all power bottom on his ass. My boy didn't stand a chance."

"He still got to top. Didn't you, babe?" Ezra broke out of Finley's headlock and looked to Colby, who had a smug grin on his face.

"I'm the top. Ezra even called me the best at it."

"That's just cruel," Finley scolded Ezra.

Ezra's phone buzzed again, then again and again and again until it started to ring.

"I think somebody is calling you."

"Leave it."

"Who is it?" Colby reached forward to look at the phone, but Ezra snatched his wrist.

He tried to play it off by then holding Colby's hand, a way to try and convince him that the action hadn't been as brash as it was. However, the damage was already done.

"Are you okay, Ezra?" Colby asked.

"Fine, yeah." He picked up his phone and shoved it into the bottom of his school bag. It was still ringing and that was blatantly obvious to both Colby and Finley, but Ezra made no mention of it. He didn't even check the phone screen to see who was calling, because he already knew.

He was saved by the bell, literally. He threw his bag over his shoulder, gave Colby a quick kiss goodbye, and headed off. He briefly heard Colby try to call him back for a second and Finley asking what was wrong with him. Ezra did not want to talk about it right now.

For the rest of the day, he tried to act as casually as possible. He tried to pay attention in his classes—even with his phone periodically ringing—and he tried to act as normal as possible. He had lunch with Colby who tried to bring up his strange behaviour once more, but he would successfully change the topic of conversation every time Colby tried. Luckily for Ezra, Colby had the attention span of a squirrel with ADHD so was easily distracted by other things. Ezra even had a personal theory Colby could have ADHD, but he was still testing that hypothesis out.

At one point when Colby attempted to bring up Ezra's strange behaviour again, Ezra just pulled out his car keys, dangled them in front of Colby's face so they shimmered in the light and let him play with them and Colby did for a solid ten minutes. He was the cutest and Ezra would do anything for him, except involve him in his own messy business. Colby didn't deserve that. Colby stopped asking after that; instead, he went on his own phone for a little while, then did his regular thing of leaning against Ezra and telling him every random thought that came into his head.

Ezra's favourite Colby-thought of the day was "If unicorns did exist, they would probably be used by the military as a weapon. They would spear the enemy with their horns and the pre-established love for unicorns in children would be used as military propaganda."

Throughout the time, Ezra had spent listening to Colby—and he did listen very carefully to every word—Ezra still couldn't decide if Colby was a random idiot or a genius that just hadn't applied himself to the right thing yet. His personal belief was the latter. Either way, to listen to Colby's insane ramblings was to be soothed.

The final lesson of Ezra's day was English Literature with Mr Williams, a.k.a his boyfriend's dad, a.k.a the man who was currently letting Ezra live at his house. Needless to say, Ezra tried very hard in English Literature to impress him.

Mr Williams was the man Ezra aspired to be in the future. He loved his family. He loved his job. He loved living life. Today, he was wearing a tie that had a very crude drawing of a stick man holding hands with a stick lady and a smaller stick man. It had been drawn by a child; specifically, it had been drawn by Colby when he was five—as Ezra had found out this morning—and Mr Williams still wore it to this day.

They were analysing a poem by Carol Ann Duffy.

"Ezra," Mr Williams called on him, "what do you think Duffy was trying to say about the power balance between Mrs Midas and her husband?"

"I believe—" Ezra's phone started ringing, again. "I'm sorry, I'm just going to turn that off."

"That's alright, Ezra. Trisha, you answer the question, and then we can come back to Ezra."

Ezra searched through his bag, Trisha's high-pitched voice becoming background noise to him now. Why did he keep calling? There was no reason to. He thought things were clear between them now. Why was he trying to ruin what Ezra had now? Ezra became more and more furious the longer he contemplated that man's motives for harassing him.

Finally, he found his phone and powered it off. He was tempted to smash the damn thing. That would, of course, cause problems as then Colby wouldn't be able to contact him and he'd have to get a new phone.

He sighed and sat back in his chair. Mr Williams didn't come back to him to finish answering the question. He left Ezra alone for the rest of the lesson, for which Ezra was quite thankful for. It was also humiliating that Trevor thought he was so distracted that he couldn't answer the question.

It had come out of nowhere, but his father had decided that after weeks of Ezra being kicked out the house, he would try and get back in contact with him. It was ridiculous and selfish, and Ezra had no idea what to do about it.

It had started last night with a simple text from his father asking how Ezra was. What was Ezra supposed to reply to that? If it hadn't been for Colby and his family's generosity, he would still have been living out of his car. His father didn't stop at that though. Now, Ezra received frequent texts from him saying things like, "*I hope you've learnt your lesson* and *I'm willing to forgive you.*"

If Ezra was to theorise what had happened to change his father's attitude, it would be that he, too, had realised just how big and empty the house they lived in was. There was no welcoming energy or warmth in that house. The neighbours were rich assholes who bitched about you behind your back, and when there was no one else in the house, it almost felt like the wide space of the house was swallowing you whole. It wouldn't surprise Ezra if his father had come to understand how isolating that place was.

Despite all that, Ezra contemplated going back. Not because he had suddenly forgiven his father or that he missed his old room. No, nothing of the sort. It was the fact that the Williams family had let him stay in the house due to Ezra not being able to go home.

Technically, since Ezra now had a house to go back to—until his father's next temper tantrum—then he should return to it. Ezra was literally freeloading at this point and forcing an unnecessary burden onto Colby's family. He was now imposing himself onto them for nothing as he now was allowed back in with his father.

He didn't want to go back. The very idea of it made him feel physically sick.

If his closeted younger self could see that he now lived with his crush, he would probably—well, Ezra wasn't sure what he would do. He was quite the angsty teen when he was younger so he probably would've punched a hole in a wall somewhere. Yikes. He was glad he was over that.

Time had passed without Ezra realising it. Everyone began to pack up their things and go, so he did the same.

"Ezra, stay behind for a moment, please," said Mr Williams.

A few boys whistled at Ezra. "Somebody's in trouble," they joked, slapping him on the back as they left.

"He is not in trouble, I assure you. Don't you boys have other lessons to be in? Shoo, go." Mr Williams ushered them out of the room until it was only himself and Ezra left. "You seem a little distracted today, Ezra. Is everything alright?"

"Yes, I'm fine." Perhaps it was the gentle look from Mr Williams or the fact that Ezra was literally exhausted today, but he couldn't be bothered to put up a front anymore. He'd tried to do it when he was closeted and that backfired on him. He tried to do it when he was kicked out of his house and that didn't work at all. There was no reason to keep pretending. "No, actually. I'm a bit . . . fuck, I don't even know. My dad has been trying to get back in contact with me."

"I see. So, that's him who has been trying to call you all day?"

"Yeah. For some reason, he's being pretty relentless about it. I think he's finally had the epiphany that he's really just some sad, lonely old man."

"What has he been saying to you, if you don't mind my asking?"

"Basically, that he's willing to forgive me. I haven't even done anything wrong. I never did anything wrong to begin with. He kicked me out for liking guys—for liking Colby."

"Has he ever met Colby?"

"Yes, he has. Colby decided it would be a good idea to randomly come round one evening and accidentally got himself invited to dinner. It didn't go well." It felt like ages ago since that had happened, only a few months in reality. It was funny in hindsight, but it had been terrifying in the moment. He couldn't help but laugh when he remembered Colby's bold statement that *he loved meat*. How Colby had managed to ignore his father's interrogation techniques, Ezra had no idea.

"That boy, I swear. He is his mother's son, inherited her carelessness and lack of forethought. Can't help it. I still love them, though."

Ezra nodded in agreement, watching Mr Williams having a contented smile on his face after he spoke about his family. His eyes wandered to Mr Williams's tie again. He wanted a family like that. He wanted to have that with Colby. He couldn't go back to his father because there was no family there. He couldn't go back. "I know this is selfish of me and I hate being a burden to you and Jemma, but I don't want to go back to living with my dad. I can't."

"You are such a serious boy, Ezra. Got the weight of the world on your shoulders and yet you refuse to ever give yourself a break. Jemma and I have never considered you a burden. You're like a second son to me, and Colby adores you. You do not have to move out, nor would I let you return to a poor excuse of a father who would even contemplate kicking out his own son in the first place. Do you know what Jemma would do to me if I did? It would not be pretty."

"Thank you." It was all Ezra could manage to choke out, too overwhelmed with emotions to risk anything more.

Mr Williams placed his hand on Ezra's shoulder. "I'm glad you could talk to me, Ezra. However, I do believe you should tell Colby this as well. He told me earlier about how he was concerned about you. You very much have won over my son's heart, you know."

"I'll take good care of it."

"Yes, I believe you will."

Later in the day, Colby and Ezra lay on top of each other on the sofa in the living room. Jemma had made quite the dramatic show of washing the pillows and covers of the sofa in front of the boys to really hammer in her point of no sex on family furniture.

Ezra's head rested on Colby's chest as Colby ran his fingers through his hair absentmindedly. They were watching a film called "Borat" that Colby kept laughing at, but Ezra hadn't been paying too much attention to it. It was a warm and comfortable moment that Ezra was afraid to break. Mr Williams was right, though.

"It was my dad that kept calling today."

Colby paused the movie but kept stroking Ezra's hair. "What's he been saying?"

Ezra explained all that his father had done in the last twenty-four hours to Colby, who was very pissed off by the end of Ezra's explanation.

"What the fuck!" Colby raged. "Who does he think he is? What an asshole! Wait till I tell my mom about this. She's going to kill him."

Ezra could imagine Jemma reacting with the exact same exclamations and lack of chill as her son. It made Ezra smile. "I don't deserve you."

"What do you mean you don't deserve me?"

"I mean, you are far too good and beautiful and all around one of the most wonderful human beings, for a dickhead like me."

Colby pouted. "I don't actually mean it when I call you dickhead. It's just a joke."

"I know."

"And I am not too . . . everything you just said, apply it to yourself. Don't let that stroke your ego too much. You're really intelligent and everybody likes you and everybody thinks you're super handsome, especially me. So, you're the one out of my league." Colby pressed his index finger and thumb together. "Only by a little bit though. I am pretty cool."

Ezra stared up at him. "I love you."

Colby's face instantly flushed red, and he covered his face with his hands to hide it.

Ezra couldn't help but tease him. "What? Am I embarrassing you, Colby?" He leaned in close to Colby's ears, which were flushed red right to the tip. "Because it's true. I love you. I love you *so much*."

A muffled sound came from behind Colby's hands.

"What was that?"

Colby peeked through his fingers. "I said, I love you too. Dickhead."

288

Ezra removed Colby's hands and kissed all over his crimson-coloured face. He pulled Colby tight to himself and hugged him as if he was never going to let him go.

They finished watching the movie and went through to the kitchen for some snacks before dinner.

"We don't have anything," Colby complained. He didn't give Ezra a chance to look through the cupboards to check for anything. He closed the cupboard, then turned to Ezra with his big puppy dog eyes. "Can we go out and get some?"

The only answer was yes.

They went to the store, and it was weird. Ezra had expected a short trip like that to take about fifteen minutes top. All he had to do was take Colby to buy him some junk to eat and whilst he was out, he decided he might as well get more of the coffee that Trevor liked to drink because he was running short and he got a pack of gum for Jemma as well. It was not supposed to be a big trip.

However, Colby had different ideas. He took half an hour in the store to pick between the usual chocolate bar he always got and another one he'd never shown interest in before.

"Get your usual," Ezra told him. "The other one's got raisins in. You hate raisins."

"Yeah," Colby agreed, but not really.

It took Ezra two minutes to get the stuff he wanted to get for Trevor and Jemma. He even had time to pick up some extra bits and pieces. The rest of the time was filled with Colby staring at the two chocolate bars. Half an hour. Thirty straight minutes of watching Colby do that, only for him to repeat what Ezra had said to him oh so long ago.

"I'm going to get my usual," Colby told him. "The other one's got raisins in it. I hate raisins."

Ezra didn't say anything. He didn't dare. He kept repeating in his head the mantra of patience is a virtue. He dragged Colby to the front of the store, paid for everything, then swiftly got out.

Trevor would insist on repaying Ezra for everything when he got home, but Ezra would refuse. He wasn't using his money to pay for things. He was using his mother's *never-speak-to-me-again* money. He hadn't told her that he had found a place to live. She'd stop sending money otherwise. He was going to use every penny on the Williams until he felt his debt repaid. He doubted he ever would feel that way.

They were about to get in the car and go home when Colby suddenly told him to wait.

"Do you mind if we go pick up Sophie?" asked Colby. "She's stranded in the middle of the town and doesn't have a lift. Do you mind giving her a ride home?"

Ezra checked the time. It wasn't close to dinner time yet, so he supposed they had the time. He wouldn't leave Sophie alone in town. "Sure, we can pick her up."

The entire ride, Colby kept texting on his phone.

"Who you talking to?"

Colby put his phone away. "Oh, nobody. Just Finley. Talking to Finley about some things he's gotta do."

"What kind of things?"

"Um, hair things. Yeah, he's getting his hair redone."

"Didn't he get his hair redone quite recently?"

Colby laughed nervously. "He doesn't like it very much."

"Really?" asked Ezra. "I saw him yesterday, and he said it was his favourite hairstyle ever. His mom did it for him."

"He did say that, didn't he?" Colby looked back at his phone. "Sophie's just around the corner . . . there!" He pointed to her waiting by the road.

She hopped in. "Thanks for coming to get me, guys. I didn't want my parents to know where I was going. They would've slaughtered me."

"Your parents don't like the friends you were out with today?" asked Ezra.

"What? No, they like my friends who I was with just now. I mean they're not big fans of you two."

"How would they know you were with us? Also, we're about to drop you off in front of your house. They're going to see us."

Sophie glanced at Colby who shook his head. What the hell?

"Change of plans," Colby announced. "Sophie is coming round to ours and then a different friend can take her home."

"Why didn't a different friend take her home straight away instead of this weird relay thing we got going? No offense, Sophie. I don't mind driving you at all. I'm just a bit confused."

"No offense taken," Sophie assured, smiling for good measure.

"Why are you asking so many questions today?" nagged Colby. "I forgot her parents don't like me, alright? You gonna be a dick or you gonna take her to our house."

Ezra was getting far too fed up to keep asking questions. It'd been a long day. He didn't speak the whole drive home. He only listened in on the small talk between Sophie and Colby. Colby must've realised that he'd been a bit harsh earlier because he reached across and placed a hand on Ezra's thigh.

He wasn't angry at Colby. He didn't know what the hell he was up to, but he wasn't angry at him. The texts and calls from his father kept swarming in his mind like buzzing wasps using his brain as a nest. Why now? Why today especially?

He was fine before his father started calling. He was happy and more than content with his life. There were some nights when Ezra would stay awake much longer than Colby and think about his father. He hated himself for not being able to completely move on, for sometimes being moved to tears when he had moments of weakness and missed his dad. Jemma said it was completely natural and that she, too, missed her parents from time to time even after

291

all the time that had passed for her. It brought him some comfort, but not much.

When they arrived back home, Sophie immediately went inside and Colby asked him if he wanted to sit outside for a few minutes.

"I thought you were allergic to being outside?" Ezra japed.

"I love being outside, asshole. It is getting chilly though."

"You go in," said Ezra. "I need to make a call, so I'll be in a few minutes."

"Try to make it exactly four minutes."

Oddly specific, but alright. Once Colby had disappeared inside, Ezra turned his phone back on. Twelve missed calls, ten voice mails, and twenty-six text notifications. The phone rang and his father's number showed up on screen. Ezra answered.

"What do you want?" He wasted no time with pointless formalities or insincere niceties.

"I've been calling you all day," his father complained. "I thought you'd be happy to hear from me."

"I'm not."

It was silent on his father's end for a moment. "How have you been?" he eventually asked.

"Why do you care?"

"I'm your dad, Ezra. Of course, I care. That's my job."

"Well, you're pretty shit at it. I'm not sure if you've somehow forgotten, but you kicked me out. I wouldn't be in this situation if it wasn't for you."

"I know, I know. I'm sorry, Ezra."

He wasn't expecting an apology. He'd never gotten one before. He didn't validate it by saying Ezra had somehow managed to forgive him. If that's what his father wanted, he'd have to try a lot harder than that.

"I'm so sorry, Ezra. I was wrong, okay? I admit. I thought you'd come crawling back after one night, and everything would go back to normal. Where are you staying now?"

292

"I'm not telling you."

"Is it somewhere safe? At least, tell me that."

"Yes, it's safe."

"Okay then. I miss you, Ezra. This house wasn't made for one man alone. Don't you want to come home? You must be desperate to come back. Your mother said you even tried to move in with her. You must've been pretty desperate, huh? Could you imagine living with her? She'd probably make you apply her Botox and rub her feet at night."

That actually made Ezra laugh a bit. "She probably would've made me her personal pool boy."

"Yeah." His dad laughed. "She missed a trick there."

"When I saw her, she looked completely different. You remember that nose job she kept going on about?"

"Yeah."

"Well, she got it. She looks like Voldemort's ugly twin sister now, except she was all decked out in some stupid fur coat."

"Jesus. How many puppies do you think she skinned for that thing?"

Ezra laughed. He hated himself for enjoying the conversation. He had to keep reminding himself that this was his father in one of his good moments and if he went back home, those moments would be few and far between. "Why are you calling?" He forced himself to ask.

"Because I want my son back. I made the mistake of kicking you out. I know that now. You can't be happier wherever you are than you were at home with your own stuff. I'll tell you what, I've made some dinner reservations at that fancy restaurant on fourth street that you like. You swing by there, and we can have a big meal to celebrate your birthday."

It was his birthday? He'd completely forgotten. No one had said happy birthday to him, so it's not like he had any reminders. Even his mother didn't bother calling this year. She must be terrified that if they spoke again, he'd ask her to let him live with her again. As if.

"No, I'm okay," said Ezra.

"Oh, come on. Don't be like that. The dinner is completely on me."

"I'm not very hungry."

"You can even bring that boy you like!" his father bargained frantically. "You can bring Cody or whatever his name is. Please, Ezra."

"You'd be okay with me bringing Colby?"

"Yes! Colby, that was his name. Sure, you can bring him. God, wasn't he hilarious that time he came round to dinner? I really liked him. He was such a riot."

That's not how Ezra remembered that dinner at all.

"What happened to your precious reputation? You want to ruin it by having a gay son?"

"Well, none of the people I know need to know you're gay. Who knows what they might say? But I accept you, Ezra. You're my boy."

There it was. The character growth was all a façade, and he wasn't even trying to hide it. "You can cancel the reservation, I'm not coming. Goodbye—"

"Ezra, please."

He had never heard his father sound so desperate before.

"I'm begging here. We don't have to go to dinner. It can be whatever you want."

"I don't know if I'm ready to talk to you after what you did. If one day I do feel ready, then I'll call you. That could be soon or it might be never. Don't try to call me again because I won't pick up."

"But, you might call me one day?"

"Yeah, maybe one day. Is that alright with you? Because that's the only deal I'm offering."

"Yes. I'm okay with that. Happy Birthday, Ezra."

"Thanks, Dad." He hung up the phone and looked up at the sky for a moment. Colby was right; it was getting chilly.

Did he make the wrong decision by not accepting his father's peace offering? The power rested with him now on how he wanted to handle things with him. He'd meant what he said. Maybe someday in the future, Ezra would reach out to his father and get back in contact with him. Maybe someday, they could have a functional relationship, but that could never happen if his father held all the power. His father had always lofted his financial power and age superiority over Ezra's head. Until Ezra has no reason to rely on his father for support, they could not have a relationship like Trevor and Colby did. A sad fact, but nonetheless true.

Colby poked his head out from the front door. "Phone call done?" he asked.

"Yep, all done."

He smiled and came pattering down the driveway. He took Ezra's hand and dragged him inside. Ezra was unsure what he'd done to get escorted inside.

"Close your eyes," Colby instructed.

"Why?"

"Just do it."

Ezra did as asked and Colby put his hands over Ezra's eyes as well for good measure. Colby attempted to lead Ezra to the living room. By the number of walls and furniture he bumped Ezra into, you would've thought Colby hadn't lived there a day in his life.

"We're almost there," Colby announced.

"Ow!" Ezra's knee collided with some sort of wall.

"Sorry." Colby's hands moved away. "Okay, open your eyes."

"SURPRISE!"

In the living room, Trevor, Jemma, Finley, Brent, and Sophie all stood around the central coffee table that had a huge cake on it. They were all decked out with party hats, streamers, party poppers, and balloons that had "18" printed on them. The

295

cake was the most delicious-looking chocolate cake Ezra had ever seen, and it had "Happy Birthday, Ezra!" written on top with white frosting.

"What—" Ezra had no words. He barely noticed when Colby put a party hat on him. He was woken up when the elastic band slapped his chin.

"Happy Birthday!" congratulated Colby. "Did we surprise you?"

Ezra could only nod. He'd thought they'd forgotten. If he couldn't remember his birthday, why should all of them? But they did. They all remembered.

"Go sit, go sit." Colby ushered him to the sofa and sat next to him.

It was a surreal experience. Brent came up to him first and wished him a happy birthday and gave him a present. It was beautifully wrapped with a big bow on top, as expected from a gift given by Brent. It was a new video game that they'd been talking about recently. Ezra was desperate to play it. Other presents followed after. Sophie gave him two PlayStation remote controls, Jemma and Trevor gave him a PlayStation, Colby gave him a bunch of other games for his console, and—last but not least—Finley gave him a pair of white gym socks with the Gucci brand label drawn on with a black marker that had bled through the fabric.

"I didn't know about the PlayStation shit," Finley explained.

"I told him multiple times, but he just doesn't listen," Brent said to Ezra.

They all talked and laughed together. Finley was nice to him for the very first time. He said it was only because it was Ezra's birthday though, and that nice Finley would be gone when the clock hit midnight. Colby stuck to his side the entire time and Trevor kept taking photos of things on his phone whilst Jemma complained at him for constantly getting his thumb in the photo. Brent and Ezra gushed about how the new game was multiplayer, and that they would always be down to play it with each other. Ezra even had a nice chat with Sophie, who apologised for the seven millionth time about her behaviour earlier in the year. He assured her all was well. Then, they talked about anything they could think of.

"Make a wish," Trevor told him when it was time to blow out the candles. "How do I get this thing to record? Oh, Jemma, I've done something."

Jemma took the phone off of him. "You've done three panoramic shots. Just press the record button!"

"And which button is that?"

Jemma was put in charge of the camera after that.

Ezra looked at all the friends he had around him. They all smiled at him and sat with anticipation, waiting for Ezra to make a wish. He closed his eyes and blew all the candles out at once. Everyone clapped and began to sing "Happy Birthday."

"What did you wish for?" Colby asked once the song was over.

"For a better boyfriend."

Colby whacked his arm. "You've already got the best of the best."

Ezra kissed him. "I know." He was so happy.

He wished to always be happy. With the people he had around him at that moment, the wish, in Ezra's opinion, could easily be granted.

The End

Do you like lgbt stories?
Here are samples of other stories
you might enjoy!

PLAYING WITH THE

KING

E. K. MUZIC

CHAPTER ONE
Lavender Sweatshirts

All I can focus on is his hot breath hitting my face. That and his clearly muscled body pressed against mine. I can hear my heartbeat in my ears. A rhythmic thump-thump that makes my anxiety flare up even more. We are only centimeters away. If I move even in the slightest, our lips will touch. The bell has already rung, meaning I am more than just a little late for my first day of classes. The only reason I am trapped now is me being incredibly late.

"Let's play a game."

My eyes flicker up to his dark ones. God, that voice just oozes sex appeal. This man has just uttered the four words that start every cliche online romance novel you can imagine.

"Why would you want to play a game you know you'll lose?" I quip back. I don't know if this game is poker or chutes and ladders, but I'm confident I'd lose. The quiver in my voice gives that away.

"Come to my party, new kid. Let me show you the game," he whispers directly into my ear, his lips brushing it as he does. He puts a hand on the back of my neck, pulling away to look me in the eyes.

"Why?" My face flushes red at the intense eye contact. I'm not a party person. If I show up to this, I am undoubtedly getting pig's blood dropped on me.

"Because I want to have some fun with you. Once I get what I want from you, which is purely your total embarrassment and confusion of what you want, I'll leave you be." He pauses for a moment, looking me up and down. "Because right now, your body wants me to never leave, and your mind wants me as far away as possible." His hand grabs my shoulder to press me harder into the wall.

"N-no, it doesn't." I stumble over my words. Who the heck does he think he is? If I weren't so paralyzed with fear, I'd be giving this punk a piece of my mind.

"So you're telling me if I kissed you right now, you'd feel no attraction whatsoever?" He pulls back, allowing me a view of all of him. The boy's uniform pants are khakis. There is a dark blue sweater over his white long-sleeved button-up. The white shirt is rolled up to his elbow, showing off a magnificent tattoo sleeve. A beautiful mosaic of tattoos also creeps up from the collar of his shirt.

"None," I breathe out. I don't know if it's my hormones, but being pushed against this locker and kissed sounds heavenly.

He leans in and I close my eyes in blissful anticipation of his lips on mine. Then the bell rings, making him pull away as the hallways begin to flood with people.

"Guess it's your lucky day then. I'll get someone to give you my address so you can come to the party tonight." And, with that, he disappears into the sea of boys.

I feel the beginnings of heart palpitations. The thought of escorting myself to the nurse crosses my mind. Maybe if I faked being sick, they would let me leave. I'm paying to be here after all. What does it matter if I just bail?

But, for now, I am standing here, looking dumbfounded. Who is that guy? And what gives him the right to act that way? I know I will probably not be able to find these answers standing in the hallway.

I push my way through the hall, making my way to the office. I might or might not be on the verge of a panic attack. As I open the office door, a lovely woman looks my way. Her smile is soft and appears to be genuine. Her hair is in braids, and her lips are painted red. The red that tints her lips is the same shade that appears on her glasses.

"Do you need help?" she asks, looking me over. I am not in the uniform everyone else is wearing, and she has noticed immediately. On her desk is a nameplate that says *Mrs. Katherine Howard* in cursive letters.

"H-hi, Mrs. Howard. I'm Finn Green. I, um . . . Its, uh . . . Today's my first day." I hate talking to people. I trip over the words I try to say every time I speak to someone older than me.

The smile never leaves her face as she replies, "I wondered why you weren't in uniform. Glad I don't have to give out a dress code violation." She laughs to punctuate her sentence.

I chuckle softly as well. I'm sure it isn't every day a 5-foot-6 kid walks into her office in a lavender-colored sweatshirt, black jeans, and worn-out vans.

"Well, we can get you fitted for a uniform on Monday. We have some extras in the back. You can pay the sizing fee and uniform cost today if you'd like," Mrs. Howard sweetly explains. She stands up from the chair she has been sitting at behind her desk. She opens the door behind her, disappearing into what I assume is the storage for the uniforms.

I feel my heart clench at the mention of extra expenses. I will eat nothing but ramen once a week for a month to afford them after emptying out my bank account to pay the year's-worth of tuition. "A-and how-how um . . . How much would that be?" I ask, hoping she can't hear the poorness in my voice.

"Oh, not that much. It's $200.00 for the uniform sets and an additional $50.00 for the sizing," Mrs. Howard answers as she emerges from the room with a box of old uniforms in her arms.

She sets them on the table in the middle of the room. "Seems like the smallest we have is a large."

I am not a large. I am a small poor kid who is freaking out over the $250.00 fee that had just been mentioned to me as though it was only $3.00. "Okay, can I write you the check tomorrow?" I ask.

I honestly need the extra time to scrape together that money. I don't need the bank charging me an overdraft fee when the school cashes the check and finds only $150.00 in the account. Thank god it's pay day today.

"Sure! Or if you'd rather put it on a card, we have the swipey thing," she offers.

But I can't use a credit card.

"Check is f-fine." Just don't cash it for a month, I say silently in my head.

Mrs. Howard pulls out a neatly folded stack of clothes. It's a blue Polo with the school crest on the left side. She hands me a pair of khakis to go along with it. "Here you go. We have some paperwork for you. Simple things: the handbook, medical forms, that stuff."

I hold the uniform against my chest as she goes to fetch me a stack of papers.

Mrs. Howard comes back and hands them to me. I set the uniform down on the table with the box of uniforms. I open the bag to pull out one of the folders I brought. I carefully place the documents inside, leaving out my class schedule.

"The bathroom is across the hall. You can change and then head to your first period. Luckily, you've only missed Homeroom." Mrs. Howard smiles as she settles back into her desk chair.

"T-thank you," I say. Being treated kindly after being practically assaulted is a nice change of pace.

I grab my schedule before I make my way to the restroom. I lock myself in one of the stalls to change. The shirt is so big that I have to roll the sleeves up twice to get them to sit at my wrists. The pants, as I expected, are too big and needs to have a belt. I sigh and shove my clothes into my bag.

I check my schedule to find out about the next class. It's AP Government in room 222. A lovely way to start the day. I search the halls for room number 222.

I knock on the door to be greeted by a teacher in his late twenties. He is wearing a green and grey sweater vest over a dark gray shirt. His overly styled hair is a dark shade of auburn.

"S-sorry. Sorry I'm late," I tell him.

The teacher responds by saying, "Well, you're new, so I guess I'll give you a pass." He laughs as though he is telling some hilarious joke. "Welcome to AP Government. I'm Mr. Martin." As Mr. Martin introduces himself, he opens the door wider for me.

I look out at the sea of spoiled brats. Unattentive, uninterested faces look back at me. My eyes fall on one guy in the back row. It's the same face that not even fifteen minutes ago had my heart racing. The guy just smirks back at my stunned expression.

"How lucky I am to have something that makes saying goodbye so hard." -Winnie The Pooh

If you enjoyed this sample, look for
Playing with the King
on Amazon.

My
CELLMATE

S. GLASSSVIAL

CHAPTER ONE

The day after my eighteenth birthday, I was no longer able to stay in the juvenile detention center, and I was whisked off to another prison facility. But this time, it was a facility for adult criminals.

"Look at that tight little ass!" some guy yelled as I followed a female guard down the long austere hallway that led to my cell. The shackes clanked with every step I took.

"Come here, boy. I got a nice meal for you. We call it a cockmeat sandwich in here, and I have one with your name written all over it!"

The inmates banged against the bars and made all kinds of sexual comments, taunting me with jeers and catcalls. When I looked at them, they squeezed and rubbed their dicks while smiling at me. Some even mimicked blowjob movements. I had barely stepped foot in this place, and it was already shaping into a horrible experience.

"Now, that is some fine-looking piece of new hot meat for me right there! Wait till I come for you. Gonna make you my little cockslut!" a large, broad man yelled in my direction.

"Shut up, Leroy!" the guard shouted. She slammed her baton against his hands, making him cry out in pain.

"You fucking cunt!"

"Keep going on like that and you'll find yourself in isolation again." She banged the baton against the metal bars a few times, making a lot of noise. "Stupid prick." She shook her head and walked on.

The inmates scared me, but honestly, she did too. I guess she had to be tough to work in a place like this.

Where the fuck am I? In hell?

"That hot ass is mine."

"You will suck my fat dick till you gag, pretty boy!"

After a few more similar comments, it was the next one that made me even more scared.

"Oh, is that little fairy Skull Crusher's new cellmate?"

The guy who said it started laughing. "Oh, boy. You're gonna be in trouble!"

"Skull Crusher?" I asked out loud.

The lady guard stopped in front of the next cell.

"Hmm, yes. He's in isolation now, but he will be your cellmate." She then sighed. "Just a word of advice. Be on his friendly side as much as you can." She unlocked the door and nodded her head in the direction she wanted me to go—inside my cell. "This is it. Try to behave, will you? You look like a sweet boy. The better you behave, the sooner you might come out of this place." She looked at me with sympathetic eyes. "And really, try to become friends instead of enemies with your cellmate. He has gained a lot of respect from the other inmates. He pretty much stands on top of the pile."

Inside the cell, she uncuffed my wrists and ankles. "He will be back this afternoon."

She then slammed the door shut, leaving me alone inside.

This was the place where I would have to survive for the next two years. I'd just turned eighteen, and I was convicted of murder two years ago.

I took a deep breath before I walked further inside. It definitely looked different compared to juvenile prison.

There wasn't much to see: A metal bunk bed with thin mattresses stood bleakly against one wall. In the corner of the cell stood a small table with two chairs, and one little cabinet filled with . . . books?

At the back of the cell was a stainless steel toilet with a sink. I could just die thinking I had to shit in front of someone else, but I guess it was either that, or just not shit at all. I shook my head, trying to not think about that right now.

So, which bed should I take? In the movies, they always wanted the top bed, right? Something to do with not wanting to have the other person's farts in their face or . . . I didn't really know if that was true, so I just went with my gut and laid down on the bottom bed.

I thought about Skull Crusher. What did that guy do to earn that kind of name? My stomach twisted at the thought he would come back to this very cell this afternoon, and I would unavoidably meet him. What if he hurt me?

I then thought back to the words of the prison guard. She said I should befriend him. It made me feel that I needed to do that in order to survive.

The way I saw it, I had two options to protect myself from these wolves. Option one: I would beat up the most feared man in here to gain respect. But if I needed to fight a man named Skull Crusher, I knew I would have a ridiculously small chance of succeeding in that. This option wasn't very attractive, and frankly, I preferred my skull to remain just the way it was. Option two: I would cut a deal with my new cellmate. I could convince him to become my personal protector. It wasn't hard to guess what this feared man would want in return, though . . . but at least with this option, I would only have to endure the horrendous, revolting torture of sleeping with only one man instead of getting violated by all the other monsters in here.

"Get the fuck off my bed!"

"What?" I gasped as I woke up with a startle at the loud noise that made my eardrums tremble.

I got goosebumps all over when I was forcefully yanked off the bed.

Skull Crusher was here.

He pulled me off the floor and shoved me against the wall, pressing his body against mine. I almost pissed myself when he brought his hands against my head and pressed at my forehead. Was he going to crush my skull now? Do his name honor?

"Oh, Uh . . . I . . . my name is—"

"I don't care what your fucking name is," he said, and he sniffed at my neck. I didn't dare speak again.

"In here, you don't use your old name. You become a Unicorn, a Four Eyes, a Spiderleg, or"—he pointed at his chest while staring at my soul—"a Skull Crusher."

I swallowed. "Oh . . . okay."

"Now, you . . . hmm, what shall I name you . . ." He looked at me from head to toes and back again. "Your name will be . . ." He then leaned in and whispered in my ear.

"Twink."

If you enjoyed this sample, look for
My Cellmate
on Amazon.

THE
Bartender

BETHIE SIMONE

CHAPTER ONE

AIDEN

"Bye, Mom," I said as I kissed her on the cheek. It is another beautiful day to go to school. I really couldn't wait to arrive there, since I had been absent all week. I had missed a lot.

Days ago, my best friend Kyle had moved back to St. Lawrence, but I hadn't had the chance to meet him yet. It had been quite a while, so I couldn't wait to see him.

Aside from my best friend moving back to town, I also missed my other friends at school, especially Andrew. He had helped me a lot since Kyle moved away, and I wanted to introduce them to each other, especially since Kyle was the new kid.

I knew what it was like to be one. There were a lot of bullies in school who made fun of new and unpopular kids, and I knew this because I was one of the bullies. I didn't bully for the fun of it. I have a good reason why I did it; at least, according to me. It was the only way I knew to ensure that I wouldn't become a victim anymore. I honestly just wanted the person I bullied to change. I knew it was wrong, but what had I ever done to Jimmy in fifth grade? He still punched me in the face with my fist.

There was just this one particular kid that I worried about all the time. He was a year younger than me. I didn't do it to make him feel bad—okay, maybe a bit—but that was because he was a terrible kid. He was gay, and I hated those perverts.

I drove my car—a birthday gift I had received from Mom—to school. I lived with her. She was a successful businesswoman who worked from home. My dad, however, was always away on business trips, so I didn't see him as much as I wanted. In the past, he had stayed home one weekend every month, but his visits had started to get less and less by the time I turned ten years old. We were quite rich. In fact, the car I drove was a BMW convertible, but I always kept the hood up because showing off had once gotten me into trouble.

I arrived at school in time before the bell rang. I didn't see any of my friends, so I just walked straight to my locker. After checking my schedule, I picked up the books I needed and placed them in my bag.

I wasn't the brightest kid, but I wasn't dumb either. I'd say I was an average student. I was fine with Cs and Bs; I didn't try so hard. I didn't really like school, but I wanted to go to university or at least get some higher education, so I decided to work up my grades. This was my final year, and the least I could do was put in some effort to finish with a small bang.

I closed my locker and leaned on it, waiting for my friends. I stared at some of the girls who passed by and smiled at me. I smiled back, not wanting to seem rude. Many of them were friends with my girlfriend or at least acquainted with her, and I didn't want to get on their bad side. Sometimes the attention I got was annoying, but other times it boosted my ego. I wouldn't say I was the hottest guy in school—the jocks had that position—but I was good-looking.

"Hey, babe," my girlfriend Gabrielle greeted as she hooked her arm around mine.

I bent down and placed a soft kiss on her lips. I wasn't tall, just 5'8", three inches taller than her. "I missed you, love," I said as I put a strand of her long brown locks behind her ear.

"Try taking it to the janitor's." Andrew gagged. He was much taller than me, standing at six feet. He had short black hair that was always trimmed on the sides and light brown eyes that complimented his dark skin. I chuckled before turning away from them.

Fuck! I hate that kid, I thought as I turned to see Niall walking towards his locker. Unfortunately for him, it was next to mine.

"Well, if it isn't the fag." I grinned wickedly, or so I thought.

Hey, I can't see my face.

I grabbed his arm forcefully, making him wince in pain.

"Please don't hurt me, Aiden," Niall mumbled.

"I'm not gonna hurt you," I whispered on his earlobe, "but you like the pain, don't you?" I wasn't sure why I said that, but it was a running joke between Gabrielle and I. She had once mentioned she didn't like me bullying Niall because he could fall in love with me. Thinking about the way she described it alone made me grimace. As if that would happen. I wasn't gay.

Seeing Niall wince in pain always left me conflicted, mostly because I knew I didn't have to do this, but what if he turned on me at some point? Besides, seeing the kind of effect I had on him made me feel a little good about myself. It meant I had become the strong one; I was no longer weak. Yeah, I was insecure, sue me.

"Don't you wanna know how a pussy feels, fag?" I hissed as I kneed him in the balls, wincing inwardly at what I did. However, that would teach him not to be a pervert.

I watched as Niall whimpered on the floor. Sometimes I regretted what I did to him, but he was gay and he deserved it. So, with a satisfying smirk, I turned back to my friends. Andrew just looked bored as he tapped away on his phone while Gabrielle smirked at me.

"The fag has a boyfriend." Gabrielle laughed, making me turn to look at who the supposed boyfriend was. I felt my jaw drop as I saw my best friend helping Niall up.

"Get away from him, Kyle. He's a freak."

"You know him?" Andrew asked, finally paying attention to me.

"Yeah, that's my best friend. I told you about him," I answered. I had texted Andrew a few times about Kyle moving here before, as well as last night. Smiling, I walked over to Kyle.

I watched on as Kyle looked at Niall, who was close to tears. Why was he even helping him? He shook his head and handed Niall a tissue. "I'll see you at lunch," he said to the boy and I frowned.

"Okay," Niall whispered before rushing off to class.

Kyle turned to me with a frown. "What was that all about?"

I was shocked to see my best friend glaring at me with so much anger. This was not how we were supposed to be meeting after two years. We were supposed to be smiling and hugging, showing how much we had missed each other. I knew I had missed him, so why was he scowling at me?

"What do you mean?" I asked.

"Why were you hurting the poor kid?"

"Kyle, come on. He's a fag and a pervert. Someone's gotta teach him a lesson," I stated and tried hugging him, only to get pushed away.

"What the fuck?"

Kyle was still frowning at me, looking pissed. "This is not the Aiden I know. You never hurt anyone."

"Well, I didn't ask him to be gay. He chose to be gay."

The bell rang and everyone rushed off to class, leaving Kyle and me in the hallway. We both had English as our next class, so we went to the same direction.

"Come on, Aiden," Kyle whispered. "Is that what this is about? Because he's gay?"

I raised an eyebrow as if to say, "duh!" Was that even a question?

"I can't be your friend if you go about hurting people because of who they are."

His tone was resolute and unwavering. I froze in my steps as I watched him walk off. My best friend would stop talking to me because of that gay kid? Really?

I was brought out of my trance when someone rushed past me. That's just great. Now, I was late for class. I threw my hands up in the air with a groan and went ahead. I noticed Kyle was sitting at the far end of the room, away from me. When our eyes locked, he frowned and looked sideways.

What's his problem?

I shook my head and sat down. I couldn't concentrate. I knew being gay was bad, so why was Kyle defending Niall? That was just wrong. Maybe he defended him because he was a caring person? I sighed.

None of my classes went well as I kept asking myself the same question over and over again. Okay, maybe bullying was bad. If I really wanted Niall to change, I should just talk to him.

This made me grimace as I remembered the time I had been bullied in middle school. It had been awful, and I hadn't done anything wrong. They had thought it was fun because my parents were rich.

The bell for lunch rang and I quickly packed my books. I met up with Gabrielle and we went to the cafeteria. I didn't like what the school served, so Mom always had lunch packed for me. I had a chicken sandwich with apple juice today.

When I sat down, I looked around to find Kyle, and got a little bothered when I saw him sitting with Niall. What the heck was going on? Where did he even know him from? Kyle had just moved back, so there was no way he had known Niall. Besides, Niall was a year younger than us. I couldn't put my finger on it.

I whined as Gabrielle tried to kiss me. I loved her kisses, but I wasn't up for it today. I had Kyle on my mind. I needed my best friend back and away from that boy. I looked over at Kyle, and he was laughing at something Niall said. I couldn't help but feel jealous, only slightly though.

"It's probably not funny," I mumbled.

"What, mate?" Andrew asked.

So that came out loud enough. I sighed and shook my head. "Nothing."

I couldn't wait to go home and tell Mom what happened, but I knew she would back him up anyway. She didn't know I bullied people at school. If she did, she would lock me up in my room, for sure.

When the final bell rang, I hurriedly picked up my bag and tried to meet up with Kyle before leaving. I saw him at the car park talking to Niall, and walked over to them.

"Kyle!" I exclaimed, finally getting his attention. I noticed Niall looking down at his shoes as if he was scared of me. Well, he should be. He's just a good for nothing gay asshole.

"Aiden," Kyle said and he wasn't smiling. He pulled me aside to talk to me. "I think you should apologize to him."

"Why would I do that?" I asked. What Kyle was asking was simply outrageous. I would never stoop so low to apologize to a fag. Never.

"Because you hurt him. I mean, you should have seen him when he was crying. You and I both know what happens to people when they get bullied."

"So you want to lecture me about my past now?"

Kyle glared at me. "No. I'm trying to tell you that you could make him go through what you went through. You think he chose to be gay?"

"Well, he wasn't born that way," I grumbled.

Kyle sighed. "Don't be like this. You can't make someone be what they are not."

I didn't reply. Instead, I bit my lip as I remembered what I had gone through when I was in middle school.

"I can't be your friend if you continue to do this."

I watched as Kyle left with Niall, and rolled my eyes. Now, the fag just stole my best friend from me. Great. That's just great.

If you enjoyed this sample, look for
The Bartender
on Amazon.

AUTHOR'S NOTE

Thank you so much for reading *Enemies with Benefits*! I can't express how grateful I am for reading something that was once just a thought inside my head.

I'd love to hear your thoughts on the book. Please leave a review on Amazon or Goodreads because I just love reading your comments and getting to know you!

Can't wait to hear from you!

Lavender Fields

ABOUT THE AUTHOR

Lavender Fields is a young author whose work gained a large audience after publishing her first book online. Her debut book, Enemies with Benefits, was created during the national lockdown in 2020, in an effort to bring herself and any possible readers a fun distraction from of the real world. Inspired by both her own experience as a queer teenager in high school and the longing for a heartfelt laugh in hard times, Lavender Fields aims to show a realistic but entertaining view on stupid gays in love.

Printed in Great Britain
by Amazon

41439537R00185